THE FIRE WENT WILD

A SLASHER ROMANCE

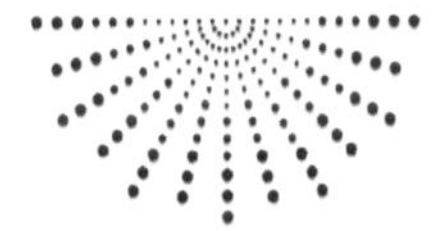

ROSE BITTERLY

A NOTE FROM THE AUTHOR

Thanks so much for picking up *The Fire Went Wild!* This is a dark horror romance featuring a morally black hero and potentially upsetting material, including graphic depictions of sex and violence (often intertwined together).

Because a certain online bookseller has a history of removing books with comprehensive content warnings, I have opted to put the full, detailed list of content notes on my website, which you can access at rosebitterly.com/content-notes or via the QR code below:

Once you're on the site, just click or tap on the book's title to expand the full list of warnings.

In addition to the graphic sex and violence mentioned above, this book does deal somewhat with religious trauma and homophobia, including familial homophobia. It's only a small part of the story, but I wanted to mention it here.

If you have any questions or would like further clarification, don't hesitate to contact me via the form on my website.

-Rose Bitterly

PROLOGUE

JAXON

This neighborhood stinks of wealth. The houses are monstrosities, boils of architecture growing out of the cleared wetland. I wonder if the owners know what this place was before the developers smoothed it over with their little gated community. I wonder if they know the whole place will be underwater after the next bad storm.

I hope it's a surprise for them.

I park my car in the shadows created by a blazing street-lamp, three houses down from the house I need to go to. It's not late, only 9 PM, but no one's out. The people who live in these houses are tucked away inside, faces illuminated by their blaring TVs or the little black boxes of their phones. I hate places like this, the way they subsume the marshland I love so much and spit it out as a glossy facsimile of—I don't know what. Some British aristocrat's manor? It's all so fucking ugly.

But it's also sterile. Empty. No one will see me coming and going.

I go now. Leave the car. My supplies are in my bag. No mask, of course, not until I'm inside. If anyone does happen to drive by or—unlikely—glance outside their window, they won't register me. I look normal. It's how we blend in, creatures like me. Monsters. Boogeymen. Hunters.

The house that contains my soon-to-be victim is understated compared to the others. It's a little smaller, without all the hideous architectural flourishes these houses have. The yard is landscaped with native plants—beds of milkweeds, sunflowers bobbing around a stone birdbath, a few bursts of Gulf Coast yucca. Of course, it has the same flat carpet grass as the other houses.

I go around the side, toward the garage set in the back. I've been here twice already: once as a surveyor, the orange vest rendering me invisible, and once as a landscaper, offering my services for cheap. That second time, I spoke to my victim. He squinted at me from the doorway, the top few buttons of his shirt open, a glass of gin in one hand. "I already got someone," he told me when I pressed my card on him. "Maybe try Frank Davila."

I didn't try Frank Davila; I'd gotten what I'd come for. I confirmed it was *this* man my Guardian wants, because as soon as he opened the door, all this light flooded my vision. He was haloed by it, my Guardian's touch streaming out from behind his head. My eyes burned. My heart raced. All the usual signs.

The garage is closed up tight, but it has a little door on its side, and I break the lock easily. Inside I find two Audis. Expensive but tasteful. One of them is a hybrid.

Here, I work quickly. I pull my mask out of the bag, its power thrumming between my hands. I made it myself, welding the metal in endless spirals to create its shape and then affixing the antlers on top, the white bleached bones of the first creature I ever killed.

When I slide it on, I feel my Guardian awaken inside me, a burning core of heat in my heart. I'm hungry, it says, and I'm hungry too.

I pull my knife out of my bag. And the pistol, just in case.

That I slide into a shoulder holster that I cover with a black suit jacket.

Then I go inside.

The door leading from the garage into the house is unlocked. It takes me into a dark and silent laundry room that opens into a dark and silent hallway. I follow the house's arteries, guided by my Guardian's urgent whispers as much as I am the smell of my victim: old cologne, chosen blood. Someone else is here too. A woman. My victim has an ex-wife. An adult daughter. It could be them. It could be someone else.

Whoever it is, both my victim and his companion are upstairs. I move slowly, listening through the hurricane of my Guardian's hunger. It whispers to me in an ancient language, barbed like roses. A language that gets my blood up.

I lick my lips behind the mask's metal cage, excitement urging me forward.

Light spills out of a room up ahead. So does the mindless buzz of a TV. Every part of my body is burning with electricity. My Guardian moves through me.

I push the door open so it swings inward, revealing the scene:

My victim, sitting in bed, shirtless, smoking, watching the enormous flatscreen TV on his wall.

A woman, naked, sleeping beside him. Neither his ex-wife nor his daughter. I don't recognize her from my research.

He laughs at something on the TV. I step into the room, fingers curled around the knife's handle. My victim drags on his cigarette. Laughs again. My Guardian sings.

I take another step closer, and that's what finally gets him to turn toward me. His reaction is immediate and very satisfying. He jolts, eyes going wide, and slams up against the headboard. The woman beside him mumbles something and rolls over.

"Fuck fuck fuck," he whispers. "Already?"

This brings me up short. It almost sounds like he's... expecting me.

This changes nothing, my Guardian whispers. I can feel its hunger as my own, a wide, cavernous chasm deep in my belly.

My victim dives toward his bedside table, hands flailing, arms trembling. He pulls out a black pistol not all that different from the one I carry for backup. I stare at it through the mask as he holds it up toward me, shaking.

I served five tours in two different Iraq wars. I've been shot hundreds of times. I barely notice anymore.

"Tell Tyloch to go fuck himself!" my victim roars—

Who's Tyloch?

—before firing off three shots. Two of them miss. The third one lodges in my belly, a starburst of bright pain that makes my Guardian roar with pleasure and my cock stiffen.

The woman gasps awake, sees me, and screams.

Too much noise. It's all too much fucking noise.

I lunge at her and draw the blade quickly across her throat. It's fast enough I doubt she realized what happened, but her blood is hot and thick and jeweled in the fancy track lighting, and my Guardian rasps with need. She isn't what it has a taste for, though.

"What the fu—" My victim fires again, too panicked to aim. Something shatters behind me. I grab his wrist and twist it so the gun falls onto the bed, thin white smoke curling up between us.

"She had nothing to do with it!" my victim babbles. "She doesn't even fucking know about the deal, do you hear me? I literally picked her up at the fucking club, okay? Why the fuck did you do that? Why the—"

I don't know what he's talking about, the deal and Tyloch, and I squeeze my fingers around his neck so I'll stop hearing about it. It makes me uncomfortable, the way he's talking to me like he thinks I'm someone else. As I grip his neck, I throw my whole weight on him so we topple hard against the floor. I'm still holding my knife with the other, my hand drenched in that woman's honeysweet blood. I wish I could take her home with me so we can play, but I'm not prepared for transport.

Besides, my Guardian needs to be fed.

My victim strangles and gasps against my grip, his body flopping beneath mine. I lean close, listening to his frantic rasps and the wet gurgling noises he makes as I dig my fingers into his trachea.

Blood, my Guardian says.

My Guardian loves blood. I love bodies. It works out, how creating one provides the other.

I shove the knife up through my victim's rib cage, pressing my weight against it until I feel the slight resistance of his heart. I release his neck as he makes a beautiful bony rattling sound and dies, and then I flutter my eyes closed, sighing into the release of penetration. His blood gushes between our bodies, hot and sticky, and I moan softly as my Guardian feeds, heat and energy coursing through my veins.

When it finishes, I peel myself away from the body, blinking and a little disoriented. That's not unusual, not when my Guardian is along for the ride, but it feels worse this time. This room is very bright. There were gunshots. Screams. In a neighborhood like this?

Someone's going to call the cops.

"Fuck," I whisper, stepping away from my victim's body. He stares up at the ceiling, jaw slack, eyes wide and glassy. I had big plans for him. I was going to slice him down the middle and split his ribcage open to display his heart, each chamber carefully cut open to reveal the emptiness inside. I was going to stuff his mouth with holly berries, scoop his eyes out and replace them with white camellias. Carve my gods' true names in delicate patterns across his skin.

But I don't have time for any of that now.

Still, I can't leave the scene like this. I hate leaving bodies where they fall, where they're just bodies and not works of art. So I shove my knife back into its holster and work as quickly as I can, rolling my victim onto his back, setting his arms carefully at his sides. He's heavy, but I'm strong, designed by my gods to move dead weight. It's not enough, though, arranging him on the floor. Do I have time to go back down to the garage and get my bag of supplies? The camellias and holly?

No, whisper my Guardian. ***No. Something's coming.***

I freeze, skin prickling, and listen. All I hear is the buzzing of the house's electricity and the thrum of its central A/C.

A storm is coming. Be prepared.

"Shit." I grab my knife and dig the tip into the skin of my victim's chest. His dead blood oozes up, forming the sigil I leave at every scene: the true name of The Being Who Can Not Be Known. The God Who Created Me. The Unnamed.

It's not much, but it's enough. I turn to the woman. She's exquisite in her death, already flat on her back, her arms draped gracefully across her belly, flaxen hair turning pink with her blood. I launch myself onto the bed and lean over her, smoothing a few loose strands of hair out of her shining eyes. She looks surprised more than frightened. The blood from the cut across her throat has already started to harden into a rusted breastplate, so perfect and uniform I refrain from squeezing her breasts the way I want to. Fucking her, of course, is out of the question. I only do *that* in the safety of my home, where I can dispose of the evidence.

Still, she's so lovely and she died so beautifully that I can't leave her unblessed. I don't cut her, though. Instead, I scrape the Unnamed's sigil into the dried blood right above her undamaged heart, using the dull side of my knife. Then I press my gloved hand over the design to swipe away the blood flakes. It creates a gorgeous contrast, the grey-white of her dead skin against the darkening crimson rust of the life I took from her.

Something's coming, my Guardian whispers, and the soft feathery hairs on the back of my neck stand up. I can't stay here.

With some regret, I drag myself away from the scene even though it's woefully incomplete. I try to tell myself it's minimalist, like a Donald Judd sculpture, but it still feels sloppy and amateurish. The kind of thing I did when I was a teenager.

Be prepared, by Guardian whispers, and an electric feeling races over my skin. This house feels tight and constricting. I bound down the stairs and into the garage. My bag is still there, undisturbed. I slide off my mask, breathing the clean air, and then I dart back out to the shadows, breath tight in my chest.

The street is dark and silent. No sign of the police.

Someone's coming, my Guardian whispers, although it sounds further away, slipping back into the Abyss where it lives. ***A storm you've never faced. Be prepared.***

I walk as quickly as I dare to my car, never letting it turn into a run. Running is suspicious in the middle of the night when you're dressed in black and carrying an oversized duffle bag. I climb inside; I turn the ignition. The engine roars to life.

The neighborhood is as empty as the apocalypse as I drive away.

CHAPTER ONE

CHARLOTTE

"Was Scott Hensner's death set up by the CIA?"

The middle-aged man asking this stupid-ass question goes by the name of AlphaWinner69 online, and he has filmed approximately 58,038 videos on this general theme. In every single one of them, he's sitting in his car.

Always with these guys. Always with the car.

"Here's the thing," he says, leaning so close to the camera that his forehead gets huge. I suck boba up through my straw, watching him on the very minuscule chance that he'll have something new. Something I haven't heard yet. "The three vets on the campsite. Why were they there? I *know* the 'official story'—" He makes quote marks with his fingers— "is that Hensner hired those men from Ironshield Security Solutions. But why? He was meeting his wife."

"Ex-wife," I mutter to the phone, then suck down another mouthful of boba and milk tea. It makes my skin crawl, how everyone—from the true crime podcasters to the social media stars to the nerds on the CrimeSolvers forum where I've been doing most of my research—keep calling my best friend Edie his "wife."

I realize it's not their fault. They don't *know* that Scott tried to kill her and that was why she was in Virginia in the first place. But I hate it. I hate that this is how people are remembering her.

As Scott Hensner's fucking wife.

"—so obviously it indicates CIA involvement," AlphaWinner69 is saying. "He didn't hire those men. They were there to assassinate him. But the CIA had to clear out the evidence, right? So—"

I swipe away from the video, rolling my eyes. I should have known better than to expect anything from someone named after a disproven theory about lupine social structures.

Defeated once again by short-form true crime videos, I toss my phone face down on my patio table and lean back in my chair, looking out at the swimming pool in the center of my apartment building's courtyard. They still have the Christmas decorations up even though New Year's was three days ago. Big silver-and-red bows in the palm trees. A couple of strategically-placed Santa Clauses.

Edie went missing on Halloween, the same night Scott Hensner and the three armed security personnel he hired met their apparently extremely gruesome ends—not that I give a shit about that. Just Edie.

It's been three months.

Nothing.

I try to suck down more boba tea, but I've exhausted my supply. Frustrated, I toss the cup aside, watch it roll across the balcony and bounce up against the pot of bougainvillea that I've managed to keep alive.

Unlike my best friend.

No, I tell myself. It's the same thing I've been telling myself since I got the phone call two days after Halloween from the Altarida sheriff's department. *You don't know she's dead.*

Because unlike Scott and his soldier boys, who left four mangled bodies behind, the Altarida sheriff hardly found a trace of Edie anywhere on the old campgrounds. They certainly didn't find her mutilated corpse. Just some blood splatter, fibers from her sweater, footprints in the snow. And all her stuff—her clothes, her car keys, all of it—in the cabin where she'd been staying. Including her cell phone, which was why they called me, since when they charged it they found my messages.

Except she had told me, a few days before Halloween, that she *wasn't* staying at the cabin. That she had been with a friend in Roanoke.

So why did Edie, my best friend in the whole world, lie to me?

I stand up, scraping my chair across the concrete balcony. It's starting to get chilly out here, and my oversized sweater isn't doing much to keep me warm. Although that might not have anything to do with the weather.

I always get cold, thinking about Edie. Cold and sick to my stomach.

Because when she fled Virginia to escape Scott, I promised to protect her. And I didn't do shit.

I grab my phone, shove open the sliding glass door, and go back into my cramped little apartment. Half-finished paintings are sprawled all over my living room, commissions for an art gallery that are going to be late in about two weeks. Since Edie's disappearance, my mind hasn't exactly been on art.

It's been on trying to find out what the hell happened to her.

That's why I watch videos by people like AlphaWinner69. It's why I spend the better part of my days reading through CrimeSolvers, this website where, ostensibly, people try to solve crimes. In reality, it's a lot of bloviating and bullshitting and no small amount of harassing victims' families.

Normally, I wouldn't want anything to do with a site like that, except Scott Hensner's death has been huge on there. It's not surprising given he's sort of famous among the kind of douchey techbros who think they're smarter than everyone else. The consensus on CrimeSolvers isn't that Scott was killed by the CIA—because that's dumb as fuck—but that he was murdered by a copycat emulating the infamous spree killer Sawyer Caldwell.

With whom Edie has a... *history*.

I plop down on my couch, flip open my laptop, and head over to CrimeSolvers. My breath gets all tight in my chest, the way it always does when I log on there. I know it's probably not healthy for me to read every idiotic word posted on this site, but I can't help myself. I grew up in one of those weirdo churches where suffering and aestheticism are supposed to purify you, and I think that's what I'm doing here. Purifying myself for letting Edie go back to that camp.

There's a megathread about the "Scott Hensner Case," as CrimeSolvers calls it, but nothing new has been posted. I still doomscroll through the old comments, though. It's a compulsion at this point, and one that I find almost possible to break.

EyesOnSasquatch: Scott Hensner was married to EDIE ASTOR? The survivor in the Fat Camp Killings? Why the fuck was she back at the camp? I thought they closed it down.

model187: They did but someone opened up one of the cabins as an Air B&B a few years ago. Me and my girlfriend stayed there.

EyesOnSasquatch: Fucking weird. And with a copycat around? Do you think she was the copycat?

redlipsticklove: Don't be a moron. The killer got her, too, just dragged her off. Sawyer Caldwell kept his victim's <u>bones</u>—

The word "bones" is highlighted with an annoyingly helpful link to Sawyer Caldwell's Wikipedia page

—so the copycat probably did that with her. Took her back to wherever he's hiding.

EyesOnSasquatch: Moron? Really? Why so aggressive?

redlipsticklove: Edie Astor is a victim and you're accusing her of killing her husband. She's likely dead. It's a copycat. I'd stay the fuck away from that AirB&B until they catch him.

repruler420: There's no evidence of a copycat.

redlipsticklove: No evidence? Are you insane? Read what happened to Sawyer Caldwell's victims. Now read what happened to Hensner and his hired soldiers. It's the same fucking shit. At the same fucking location. AND Caldwell's lone survivor was involved.

repruler420: But, like **EyesOnSasquatch** said, why was Edie Astor even there? Who goes back to the tourist version of the place where they were almost murdered? If you've seen pictures of her, it's bizarre Scott Hensner would even be married to someone like her. Have you seen a picture of her? Like, a recent picture? She let herself go.

My theory is he wanted a divorce and she

wasn't having it, so she lured him out there to kill him and collect the life insurance money. She made it look like Sawyer Caldwell for the obvious reason—

I click away from the thread in disgust. I've read that particular exchange dozens of times, and it always makes my skin crawl. Because it was the other way around. *She* wanted the divorce, and *he* wasn't having it. *He* tried to kill *her.*

And she didn't "let herself go." She went into recovery for fucking anorexia.

I don't know how Scott wound up dead. I won't say I'm sad about it. But there's no way Edie did it. Absolutely no way.

Even if she did tell you she was in Roanoke—

My face feels hot. My heart rate's up, pounding in my throat. I've got the beginnings of a migraine, something that used to happen when I was younger and only started again after Scott tried to kill Edie. After I swore to myself I was going to fucking protect her.

And here's the truth of things, what no one on the Crime-Solvers site is willing to admit: No one knows anything about what happened. Scott is rich enough and important enough that the cops are throwing their backs into it—big surprise—but they don't care about finding Edie. They care about finding Scott's murderer.

And currently, they have no leads.

I scroll through some of the other threads, massaging my temple. I don't know why I do this, why I think I might find some kind of connection between Edie's disappearance and Scott's death and the dozens of other strange, unsolved murders popping up across the country. But I keep looking. I keep reading.

I read about the disappearance of a couple of hikers up in the Rocky Mountains, vanished without a trace.

I read about three college students who went missing down

in Texas on the way back from a spring break along the Mexican border.

I read about a man who was found beheaded behind a fast food dumpster.

Thread after thread of death and misery and terror. And I wonder if that's what Edie's feeling right now, if she's chained up in some maniac's basement. Or if she's already dead.

Either way, I'm determined to find her.

I click on a new thread, one that was just posted an hour ago. It catches my eye because of the title: `Am I crazy for seeing a connection here?` Because that's what I want to find. A connection.

It's not about Scott Hensner's death at all. It's about a recent murder in Beaumont, Texas. Some drug dealer and his mistress slashed in their beds.

`RamblinMan1988:` So my cousin works for the Jefferson County sheriff's department in east Texas. He's cool with me, he knows I'm interested in this stuff, and he'll share case details with me that don't always get released to the public. He'd KILL me if I knew I was posting this on here, but we're behind a password and it's too good not to share. I have GOT to know what y'all think about this.

So there was a gangland-style murder a few weeks ago outside Beaumont. The Dennis Randall murder, for those of you who know about it. Open and shut case, right? He pissed off the wrong people and they came for him? That's what it looks like.

Except my cousin showed me a picture from the crime scene. There were markings left on both bodies—carved into Randall's skin and

left in Kayley Burton's blood. My cousin
said he didn't know what they could mean,
but I recognized them IMMEDIATELY. From the
Pellerin case. We had a whole thread about
it here.

I don't click on the link right away, just skim the rest of the
post and jump down to the comments. Which are wild.

emd89039: Holy shit, those are the exact
same. It has to be connected.

FlapsyMcGee: Did you tell your cousin?
What's the Jefferson County sheriff's
department doing about this? They're investigating it, right? Please tell me they're
investigating it.

WombatCombatSlombat: This is occult shit.
Those are Satanic symbols. Probably MS-13-
related or something.

My curiosity gets the better of me. I'm as susceptible as
anyone, I suppose. I scroll back up and click on the link to the
Pellerin case.

It's not a text post, like I'm expecting. It's a set of three
blurred pictures, a trigger warning for graphic content. I click
through without thinking.

A body.

A man's body, naked, spread out crucifixion style in a field of
soft, silvery grass. His eyes have been replaced with sunflowers.
His mouth is stuffed with morning glory vines. Animal bones
are arranged around him in an ornate, intricate design, almost
like sound waves rippling away from him. Antlers are attached
to his head somehow, the points decorated with more flowers.

And then I see it. Something's painted on his chest in careful, neat lines of black paint.

A symbol.

A symbol I've seen before.

For a moment, I just stare down at my laptop screen, my breath squeezing tight in my chest. I can hear my blood rushing through my ears like the ocean. The entire room seems to buzz.

The last time I spoke to Edie, I saw that symbol. We were on a video chat and she told me it was street art in Roanoke. I'd taken a screenshot of it because it reminded me a little of the series I was doing for the Moonrise Gallery, kind of primal and eerie.

She said it was *fucking street art*. And I believed her.

But if she was lying about being in Roanoke, what else could she have lied to me about?

I fumble for my phone. It's hard to breathe. It's hard to *think*. But somehow I scroll back through my phone's camera reel until I find it. Black paint, a white wall. A smudge of Edie's dark hair in the corner.

It's the exact same symbol.

Adrenaline surges through me, and I scan through the information about the pictures, hardly registering the words. The body was found in southwest Louisiana, down in the marshes there. The victim was a fisherman in the area. Well-liked. No criminal record. Police are baffled.

I click back to the first post, about the gang killing. My thoughts fill with static as I read through the responses. No one knows anything. The Jefferson County sheriff's department is looking into it.

I shove my laptop away and stare at the half-finished paintings leaning up against the far wall. The picture is still up on my phone, the sigil almost glowing. Almost buzzing, like it's pulsing with electricity.

I know what I should do is call the cops. But I don't trust them to actually give a shit about Edie. There's pressure to solve Scott Hensner's murder, not find his ex-wife. And she was estranged from her parents, more or less, so they haven't shown a ton of interest in finding her, either.

Which means I have to do it.

Which means—

I decide to do what I'm going to do in a span of seconds. I know I shouldn't. I know it's stupid and expensive and very likely dangerous. I'm doing it anyway. For Edie.

I'm going to Louisiana.

CHAPTER TWO

CHARLOTTE

My rental car sweeps down the highway, Louisiana unrolling out in front of me—golden-green grass and weepy-looking live oak trees trussed with Spanish moss. I flew into Houston and then rented a car and went east, leaving Houston's glittering glass-and-steel civilization behind for this. Swamp land. Old trees. An enormous pressing sky.

It's been almost twenty-four hours since I saw the symbol on CrimeSolvers. In that time, I paid an exorbitant amount of money for a plane ticket, shoved my stuff haphazardly in a suitcase, and came here, to this place, with one $25,000-limit credit card, a printout of my favorite photograph of Edie—currently taped to the rental car's dashboard—and no real plan.

I'm also starving. Food wasn't exactly on my mind in the whirlwind of getting to the airport, and all I've eaten today was an overpriced croissant from the terminal before I flew out of San Jose. There doesn't seem to be anything on the highway leading to Pellerin Parish, though. Just a few run-down gas stations that don't even look open.

So when I see a tattered billboard for some place called

Bandit's Diner, I'm thrilled. The sign says it's fifteen miles down the road, which should put me in Pellerin Parish. I press a little harder on the gas. I can get something to eat and maybe find out the best place to stay.

It takes about twenty minutes before I reach the diner, and I see it immediately: a big shiny chrome building glittering on the side of the road, a faded neon sign with a pink arrow pointing at the gravel parking lot, and another big white sign that reads, simply, HAMBURGERS.

I'd eat anything at this point. I certainly wouldn't say no to a hamburger.

Still, when I park, I don't get out right away. I catch sight of Edie's picture, and then I can't stop staring at it and thinking about her. Thinking about the picture itself. I took it about six months ago, so three months before Scott tried to kill her and she fled to her doom. We'd gone down to Twin Lakes to surf, and I brought my waterproof camera and snapped a bunch of shots while Edie and I were splashing around in the waves together. Edie didn't know what I was doing; she never liked having her picture taken. But I managed to catch her gazing out over the waves, smiling like she was happy, and the way the sun caught on her hair that day turned it kind of coppery. After the shit happened with Scott, I used the picture as a reference for a painting that I was going to give her as a divorce gift.

Needless to say, I haven't touched that painting in months.

"I'm going to find out what happened to you," I tell the smiling, glowing Edie in the picture. Then I step out of the car.

It's warm, like in California, but humid in a way California almost never is. I can feel the frizz forming in my wavy hair, currently dyed fire engine red over the bleach job I did right before Edie disappeared. My roots are showing, too, about a half-inch of dark brown. I like the contrast, though.

A bell rings over the door as I go into the diner. There aren't many people there: an older Black couple drinking coffee at one of the booths, a row of cowboy-looking guys sitting at the bar. The cute, twenty-something waitress smiles at me when I come in and chirps out a charming, "Welcome to Bandit's!" with the faintest hit of a Cajun accent. "Sit anywhere you like."

I go for one of the booths, choosing one that's near a guy about my age—maybe a little older. He's cute, too. Well, maybe *cute* is the wrong word. He's handsome in a severe kind of way. Long black hair pulled into a low ponytail, an aquiline nose, lips pursed in concentration. He's drawing, sketchbook pages scattered around his table.

He glances at me when I walk over to the booth behind him. His eyes are strikingly blue. Not pale and icy but almost cerulean. Ocean water blue.

He scowls at me, then turns back to his drawings. I slide into the booth while the waitress brings over a menu.

"Don't mind Jaxon," she tells me. "He's moody from being Pellerin's resident artist."

"You don't have to tell everyone that," Jaxon grumbles. I like his voice. It's deep and velvety, with the same faint Cajun accent as the waitress.

"Why not? I think it's cool." The waitress grins at me. "What'll you have to drink, hon?"

"Just water." I look at the back of Jaxon's head. "I'm an artist, too, actually. I'm visiting from California."

"Well, how 'bout that?" The waitress beams. "Jaxon, looks like you finally have someone to talk to."

Jaxon makes a kind of scoffing sound, but I see those eerie blue eyes glance at me from over the top of the booth seat, drinking me in. The way he looks at me makes me feel kind of pinned in place, like I'm in an entomologist's display.

I feel a brightness behind my right eye that means a migraine is on its way. Weird. And also annoying.

"What medium do you work in?" he asks.

This was not the conversation I expected to be having when

I came into this diner. "Gouache, mostly. Oil if I'm feeling spicy."

"You're a painter." He shifts in his seat, turning around to look at me head-on. "I do mixed media."

"Cool. I've dabbled in that a bit." I look down at my menu, although I don't read it. I can feel Jaxon staring at me. It's intense, bordering on creepy but never quite crossing the line. Which makes it hot.

This is not why you're here, Charlotte.

"What brings you to the marsh?"

"The marsh?" I look up at him again, thrown off by his question. He gestures toward the big windows, although all I can see are the tangle of oak trees and pale grasses. "The marsh. The swamp. Where we are. This isn't exactly on the road to New Orleans."

I narrow my eyes at him, irritated. "I'm not going to New Orleans."

He stares at me expectantly, but I just look down at my menu. Hamburgers, chicken finger baskets, fried shrimp. My stomach grumbles. My temple pulses.

And Jaxon's still staring at me. I can feel it. I look back up at him, and he doesn't even bother looking away. Although the way he's staring at me isn't bad, exactly. It's not the stereotypical judgmental stares I might expect from being in a red state. His expression is more—curious. Interested. A little hungry.

"You're making me uncomfortable," I tell him, which isn't *exactly* true but isn't exactly a lie either.

To my annoyance, he grins. I'm sad to report that it is devastatingly handsome. "I do that," he says. "Just ask Maggie." He tilts his head toward the waitress.

"Well, could you stop?"

"Not until you answer my question." His blue eyes bore into me. If we knew each other better, if he was a friend of a friend, or if this was some art gallery in California and not a redneck diner in Louisiana, I'd probably want to take him home with me. I've always had a taste for intense, socially maladjusted assholes of both the male and female variety.

"What question was that?" I look over at the waitress. Maggie. She's flirting with the cowboys at the bar while she refills their coffees.

"Why are you in the marsh?"

I sigh and settle back in my booth. Jaxon just keeps watching me, waiting for my answer. And I realize—I should just tell him the truth. I might as well start my investigation now.

"My friend disappeared three months ago," I tell him. "I'm trying to find her."

Jaxon's brow furrows. Then he turns around and drops back into his booth just as Maggie comes back over with my water.

"Really," she says. "Don't mind him. He's like this with everyone."

"Shut up, Maggie." His voice drifts up from his booth, but Maggie just laughs.

"We're all used to him," she says. "Now, what can I get you?"

I order a hamburger since that's what's on the sign outside, and I figure it's probably the best thing on the menu. Maggie talks me into some curly fries, too. As she leaves, she calls out to Jaxon, "You behave yourself."

He doesn't respond.

I slump down in my booth while I wait for my food. Jaxon doesn't bother me anymore, and I'm not sure if I'm grateful for it or not. He's strange. But I like strange.

I pull out my phone and go over to CrimeSolvers, skimming through the latest updates. There's nothing interesting. Nothing new. I force myself to stop doomscrolling, only to pull up the screenshot of the symbol that I took when I was talking to Edie. I've stared at this picture hundreds of times, trying to figure out where Edie was when we were talking. Not the campgrounds—if there had been a huge occult-esque symbol painted on the walls of any of the buildings, the nerds at CrimeSolvers would have known about it. So she was somewhere else. Maybe she was in Roanoke and just came back to the camp to meet Scott. Or maybe she was somewhere nearby.

Somewhere with a killer.

"Here you are." Maggie's voice drags me away from my phone. I look up at her as she sets down my plate: a big, greasy burger and a mountain of crispy, golden, perfectly seasoned curly fries. "Everything look okay?"

"Everything looks amazing." I move to set my phone down, but something stops me. Jaxon clearly wasn't a good place to start my investigation, but maybe Maggie is. "Actually, can I ask you a question?"

Maggie gives me a smile. "Depends on what it is."

I pull up the symbol again and show it to her. "Do you know what this means?"

Maggie frowns, then shakes her head. "No, I've never seen that before. You should ask Jaxon, though. He's into all that creepy stuff."

The top of Jaxon's dark head pops up over the edge of the booth seat. "Stop volunteering me for shit."

"Oh, you can't take five seconds to look at a picture? It's not like you've moved from that booth in about two hours." Maggie winks at me like we're in on some game together. That game being annoying the crap out of Pellerin Parish's apparently only artist.

Jaxon gives an exasperated sigh but does, to my surprise, slide out of the booth. It's my first time seeing him—*really* seeing him—and my dumbass pussy reacts in its usual dumbass way of wanting to jump his bones even though he's a weird, somewhat creepy asshole.

He's got that soft yet muscular body I've always liked, with strong artist's arms and thick thighs and the faintest hint of a belly. He said he works in mixed media, but he looks like might do welding or metalwork—those types always have a particular type of strength to them. His hair really is gorgeous: black and straight and silky, a stunning contrast against his golden-brown skin. And, of course, the blue eyes, currently scowling at me and Maggie.

"What?" he says.

Maggie shows him my phone, completely unfazed by his attitude. Unfortunately, I *am* fazed by his attitude in that the bitchiness just makes him hotter to me.

See, this right here is why I never judged Edie for being married to Scott Hensner, the king of the douchebags.

Jaxon stares down at the picture for long enough that excitement sparks in my chest, because I'm *certain* he recognizes it. His expression doesn't change, but he studies it like it's a stolen answer key and he's an eighth grader who's about to fail algebra.

So when he says, "Never seen it before," the disappointment feels like a gut punch.

"Really?" I ask before I can stop myself. Jaxon looks at me, his expression unreadable.

"Yeah," he says. "Really." Then, a beat later: "Sorry."

He doesn't sound like he means it.

Well, at least I tried. Maggie gives me an apologetic shrug and goes back to flirting with the cowboys. I drop my phone in my bag and dig into my burger, which is, in fact, fucking delicious. Or maybe I'm just hungry.

Halfway through my meal, Jaxon slides out of the booth again, this time with his stuff all stacked up against his chest. He's clearly leaving, but he stops by my booth and stares down at me until I look up at him. I swallow my curly fry. "Yes?"

"What was that thing?" His eyes are blue laser beams burrowing into me. The bright spot flares behind my eye again. "In the picture?"

"I don't know." I sip my water. "My friend, the one who disappeared—the last time I talked to her, she was standing in front of it."

It's the first time I've ever said that out loud to anyone. These past three months, I've kept everything with Edie close to my chest. My snotty artist friends never understood why I wanted to hang out with her, and, just like with the assholes on CrimeSolvers, Scott's disappearance is more interesting to them anyway, although for different reasons.

This is something I have to do by myself, finding Edie. But still, it feels nice to say it to someone, even if that someone is a weird redneck asshole.

"I see." He keeps staring at me in a way that feels like entrapment. I curl my fingers around my water cup. The hairs prickle on the back of my neck. A wave of vertigo washes over me, although it dissipates almost as fast as it comes on. "Well, I hope you find her."

And then he's gone.

CHAPTER THREE

JAXON

Fuck, fuck, fuck, *fuck*. This is bad.

This is really bad.

I pull out of the Bandit's lot and park my car on the little dirt road across the highway, hoping the fans of palm leaves hide me well enough that the red-haired woman won't notice me waiting for her. I need to know where she's going. I need to stop her.

Don't kill her.

The Unnamed's command is loud. It's *been* loud, blaring in my head from the moment she walked through the door and I looked up, my eyes drawn first by the bloody red of her hair and then by the lush curves of her body and the gauzy, vintage sundress wrapped around them. Every single atom in my system erupted at the sight of her, and my fingers twitched and I had an onslaught of images of all the ways I could pose her corpse after I was finished, turning her from one work of art into another.

But it all came crashing down with a single command.

Don't kill her.

Don't kill her, but why did everything feel like she was

marked by my gods? Why did the winter sunlight in the windows twinkle and flash around her as she strode across the diner like the gods were blessing her? Why did my skin thrum when she came and sat behind me? Why did she smell like dying roses and dark incense, my two favorite scents in the whole world?

It made no damn sense.

And then it got worse.

She had a picture of the sigil of the Unnamed, but it's not just any picture. It's the picture of the one I painted for Sawyer right after he revived, right before he blew up his whole damn life for that human girl, that survivor he fell in love with. Edie. The one I said might have been chosen for him by the gods.

And maybe she was, if her friend is striding into Bandit's glittering like a fucking angel from on high right when I happen to be there,

Still, I don't like this. I don't like any of it. The gods are telling me I can't kill her. Even if I didn't listen to them and did it anyway, Sawyer would dismember me if he found out I killed his girl's friend. Dismember me and spread me in six different states so it would take decades before I could pull myself back together.

But I can't just let her go. Not if she knows what the sigil looks like. Not if she's sniffing around and investigating Edie's disappearance, which was *supposed* to look like her death. Sawyer explained the whole thing to me and our friend Ambrose because he was clearly pleased with himself for pulling it off.

I tap my fingers against the steering wheel, staring through my windshield. The palm blocks most of my view, but it does let me watch Bandit's entrance. When that red-haired woman comes out, I can follow her to wherever she's going, and then—

Do something.

Unfortunately, she doesn't stay in there long. Probably fifteen minutes. I was hoping she'd take her time, maybe keep chatting with Maggie, because that would give me the space to think of a plan. The best I come up with is kidnapping her. It doesn't anger my gods, and I don't think it'll anger Sawyer, either. Much.

I'm still not fully convinced, though, not even when I catch the fiery flash of her hair through the spiny green palms. She steps through the door, the marsh wind blowing her dress up around her thighs, and then vanishes out of my view.

I turn my car on and ease down to the end of the road, catching her just as she climbs into her own car—a dark blue Honda. She pulls out to the driveway and then turns left. Heading toward Pellerin.

I count to five and follow her.

I've never liked tailing people, especially not on the narrow, two-lane highways that wrap around the marsh like old scars. There isn't enough traffic, and anyone with a healthy sense of safety—like a woman traveling alone, looking for her missing friend—will notice you pretty quick. Still, I do my best, hanging back, keeping my eyes focused on the glint of her silver bumper. I wonder where she's going. Pellerin? It's the closest thing to a town around here, even though it's small, the population only about 1,500 people. Everything else is the marsh, and people who live in the marsh like their space.

The highway stretches out, flat and straight, no curves or trees to hide me. She's almost certainly seen me by now, although she might not do anything about it until we reach Pellerin. Once we hit those first few signs of civilization, the little neighborhood roads and dusty old strip malls, though, she'll start wondering why I'm still behind her.

So what happens if she keeps going south, heading deeper into the swamp?

I curl my fingers around the steering wheel, heart pounding. My Guardian is nearby, watching me without saying anything. Holding me back from killing her.

"I can't let her go," I mutter.

My Guardian doesn't have a response.

She's speeding up, pushing 70 even though the limit here is 55. She's *definitely* noticed.

That's when a thought comes to me, sparking out of nothing like it was delivered by my Guardian itself. This stretch of highway is lonely. We're still at least twenty minutes out from the edge of Pellerin. If there was a car accident, it's unlikely anyone would drive by—

Don't kill her. This doesn't come from my Guardian but from the Unnamed, shouting in the thorny language of the Abyss.

I scowl and respond in kind. "***I know. Message received.***"

Then I press my foot on the gas.

My car's engine roars, and I jerk forward, my own speed picking up. The redhead's car glimmers up ahead. I glance at the speedometer. *70. 75. 80.*

Every nerve in my body sings, and I brace myself, pulling my muscles in tight. I've died five times. Let's just hope this won't be the sixth.

Her car gleams in front of me, glowing like a target.

I pull into the opposite lane like I'm going to pass her. I *am* going to pass her. I press harder on the gas. *90. 91. 92…*

But I swerve over too early, slamming my foot down on the brakes and jerking my steering wheel to the right. My entire car turns diagonally, slicing across the front of her bumper with a terrible metallic scream. Everything goes shaky, and my bones rattle around in my body and my Guardian howls at me and my car plows into the grassy ditch on the side of the highway. The airbag explodes in my face.

I'm alive. I'm not even hurt. Hunter's privileges. I just have to cross my fingers that she's okay, though. Okay-ish. Okay enough that my gods and Sawyer won't take turns dragging me into the ground.

I spill out of my car, leaving the engine running, my legs wobbling from the adrenaline. Her car's twisted sideways, the silver bumper laying in fragments on the asphalt, the hood smashed up like an accordion. Through the windshield, I see the balloon of her airbag. The driver's side door is still closed.

I stumble over to her, swiping my hair out of my face. The wind's blowing in from the north, and it's got a chill on it. Cold front's coming.

I see her hair before I see anything else, just like when she walked into Bandit's. It splays against the window like blood. For a minute, I think it *is* blood, and my pulse quickens. But no. The color's not quite right. Neither's the texture.

Also, she stirs inside the car.

I move quickly. The driver's door is crumpled, but I'm strong enough to wrench it open. The redhead leans sideways, catching herself on the steering wheel. Then she looks up at me.

"You," she says, dragging the word out. She's bleeding, a small line of crimson across her forehead. Nothing major. Her eyes are dazed, though. I'm about to make it worse.

I don't say anything, just tangle my fingers up in her long red hair. It's silky against my skin, and I like that, although I try not to think about how I like it. Her dazed eyes go wide, and she reaches up for my wrist. I'm too fast for her, though.

I slam her forehead against the dashboard. Just once. Just hard enough to knock her unconscious. I can still feel her heart beating.

She slumps forward, and I pull her out of the driver's seat. I'm a gentleman about it. I don't touch the places I want to touch, tempting though it is. I keep telling myself she's not dead, that she'll wake up in a few hours, maybe less, and look at me with those big brown eyes. I don't know how to deal with living girls. Especially pretty ones like her.

I set her down gently next to the car, propping her head up

against the tire. Then I crawl into it to grab her purse. Her ID. Anything else she might have that identifies her.

When I do, I see a picture on the dashboard. I recognize the woman immediately.

Edie. Sawyer's girl.

I swipe that too and slide it into the redhead's purse for safekeeping. I also pull her wallet out so I can look at her driver's license. I want to know her name.

Charlotte Careta.

I sit with that for a moment, her name buzzing a little in my thoughts. Then I slide her ID into place and check the back seat. Nothing there.

I pop the trunk and crawl out of the car. The redhead —*Charlotte*—is still slumped against the car. Still breathing. Blood still pumping. I can't stop myself from reaching over and touching her silky hair again, tucking it behind her ear. Then I go around to check the trunk.

There, I find a suitcase, which I pull out. Maybe she'll hate me less if I bring her things to her.

Then I load everything up in my car. Charlotte I lift in a fireman's carry, draping her over my shoulder so her hair falls down and tickles the top of my ass. I grip her by the waist, pressing my fingers into her flesh. She's so warm. So much warmer than what I'm used to. It's like I'm carrying an armful of fire.

My cock's been hard since I rammed her car, but it's only now that it becomes a distraction, straining against the inside of my pants. I'm surprised how much I like it, her soft heat. All the movement coursing through her body, like she's filled with a million butterflies.

Why the hell would she fuck a freak like you?

It's another of the gods, a cruel one I rarely traffic with. It's not wrong, though.

I lay Charlotte down in the back seat of my car, tugging the skirt of her dress down to her knees so she knows I didn't do anything while she was out. I do let my touch linger a little, though. On the bottom of her thigh, right above her knee, spreading my palm so I can feel her heat and her blood. My cock throbs, and I close my eyes and soak her in, imagining what it would be like if she did want to fuck me.

She doesn't.

I yank my hand away. Readjust her hem. Look at her for a moment, admiring the outer stillness that hides the riot of movement inside her.

Go. My Guardian's voice surges up, louder than the others. **Hurry.**

I slide into the driver's seat, throw the car into reverse, and slam backward out of the ditch with a squeal of tires and spray of mud and grass.

And then I drive me and Charlotte into the swamp.

CHAPTER FOUR

CHARLOTTE

I wake up with a hangover from hell, a pounding, rhythmic throbbing banging through my skull. For a moment, I just lay in my bed, trying to remember what the hell I did last night that I feel like I got run over by a truck.

And then it hits me.

I *did* get run over by a truck.

Well, not a truck. A car. Driven by that guy I spoke to at the diner—

The diner. I'm not in my bed. I'm not even in my *state*. I'm in fucking Louisiana.

I jerk up to sitting, and the room tilts sideways and then spins around, my head still throbbing. I squeeze my eyes shut, peel them open again. I'm in a bed, a silky patchwork quilt pulled over my legs. The room is dim. It's nighttime, I think, but there's a dull yellowish lamplight coming from the corner.

I whip the blanket off my body and roll off the side of the bed. Something jangles, a noise I don't place until I put my bare feet on the ground and realize there's a metal cuff around my left ankle that trails a long, heavy chain.

For a minute, all I can do is stare at that chain, barely visible in the room's sulfurous light. Then I pick it up, the metal cold against my palm, and run through it link by link, dropping it against the dusty hardwood floor with a steady, repetitive clanking until I confirm the other end is attached to the heavy wooden bed frame.

This can't be real. It doesn't *feel* real. It feels hazy, like a dream. I keep waiting to wake up and find that I'm hungover in some crappy Louisiana motel. Or even better, my apartment back in California.

It doesn't happen.

"Help!" I scream, the first thing I think even though I know it's dumb. The only person who's going to hear me is the one who did this. Surely.

Fragments of memory flash through my head. A pretty Southern waitress. *Don't mind Jaxon.* An enormous greasy hamburger. Bright blue eyes watching me over the top of a booth. And on the highway—

Staring at me right before he reached into my car.

I scream again and bang the chain against the floor like I'm a ghost in some Victorian penny dreadful. It feels like I'm in a penny dreadful, actually, with the decor in this room. Everything's dark and wooden and heavy. Thick velvet curtains. A huge, weird painting on the wall that I can't make out in the dim light. Some kind of mannequin in the corner.

"Let me out of here!" I scream, slamming the chain down as hard as I can. There's enough slack that I'm able to get out of the bed, dragging the chain with me, and I almost make it to the door. Almost, but not quite. I pound the chain against the floor some more, hoping I'm scraping the hell out of the wooden slats. "Let me the fuck out, *Jaxon.*"

If that's even his real name. If he's even the one that's keeping me here. He could have been some kind of honeypot or something.

I stop, breathing hard. The only answer I get is the heavy, creaking stillness of an old house.

"Fuck," I whisper, falling backward on the bed. There's a ceiling fan overhead, spinning in slow, lazy circles. Fear clenches in my stomach as I work backward from the moment of the crash. Everything's fragmented and my head's still pounding and I can't think straight.

Edie. This has to do with Edie, right? I show Jaxon the symbol, and the next thing I know, he's pulling open my car door after an accident on the highway and grabbing my hair and—

I scream again, swinging my leg around so the chain makes as much noise as possible.

And *this* time, I do get an answer. Footsteps.

My fear clarifies. It's one thing to be chained to a bed. It's another to have the psycho who did it let himself into your room.

I scramble backward over the bed until I half-jump and half-fall off the other side. A key rattles in the lock. The brassy, old-fashioned knob turns. I keep stumbling back until I press up against the cool slick wallpaper.

The door swings open, and there he is. Pellerin's resident artist.

"You don't have to make all that noise," he says coldly. "I know you're up here."

"Fuck you."

He steps into the room, his eyes fixed on me. I sweep my gaze over him, looking for a weapon. His hands are empty, though. And he's wearing dark, baggy sweatpants, an oversized black T-shirt. His hair's kind of mussed, too.

"Were you *sleeping*?" I spit out.

"Yes." He keeps staring at me. "Which is why I'm asking you to keep it down."

"Keep it *down?*" I laugh, shrill and hysterical. "You know what'll make me quiet? If you let me fucking go."

He sighs, shoulders hitching. "I'm afraid I can't do that."

I press against the wall, trembling, waiting for him to explain. He does not.

"Why?" Maybe a prompt will get him to talk.

He doesn't answer. But he also doesn't try to come closer to me. He stays in the doorway. Just out of range of the chain, I'll note.

And for a minute, we stare at each other. It's still hard for me to think, the way my head feels like it's splitting open. I'm not sure if it's a return of one of my migraines or some lingering symptom from the crash.

"Why did you kidnap me?" I ask.

His eyes gleam in the yellow light. "I can't kill you."

My terror erupts at the word *kill*, just for a second before I register what he actually said. I take a deep breath, steadying myself. "Why not?"

"I'm not allowed."

"Not allowed? Not *allowed?*" My voice is shrill enough to cut glass. "Not allowed by who?"

He answers in what is possibly the most irritating manner I could imagine.

"Whom."

"What?" I want to kill him. I want to wrap the chain around his throat and kill him.

"Not allowed by whom," he says.

I burst into disbelieving, hysterical laughter. He's dead serious. "Is that why you kidnapped me?" I asked. "Because you're a fucking grammar Nazi?"

Irritation flashes across his face. "I told you why I kidnapped you," he says. "I can't let you go, and I can't kill you, so you're going to stay here until I decide what to do with you."

"You didn't answer my question."

He glares at me.

"Not allowed by *whom?*" I can hear the mocking tone in my voice, and part of me knows is this so, so stupid, that I'm taunting what is apparently a psychotic killer. Who the hell knows what he's going to do to me?

Or maybe that's making me stupidly brave. The fact that I have nothing to lose.

"You wouldn't understand," he says flatly. "Now, please be quiet." He turns to leave, then stops and says over his shoulder, "There's a chamber pot under the bed if you need to use the bathroom."

"Are you fucking kidding me?" I can't stand it anymore. Adrenaline surges through me, and I launch myself at the bed, bouncing off the old creaking mattress and slamming toward him, only for my foot to be jerked backward by the chain. I topple forward, and the piece of shit steps up and catches me, sliding his arms under my arms before I can fall on my face.

"Careful," he says mockingly. "You're still chained up."

I kick at him, trying to squarely slam my shin up against his balls. It doesn't work; he catches my leg with his thighs, pinning me into place. As he leans over me, his silky black hair falls like a curtain and tickles my skin. His eyes bore down into mine, intense and heavy.

If this were literally any other situation, I'd feel like I was in the process of being seduced.

"There's no point in trying any of that," he says smoothly. "I'll win."

I try to wrench my leg away from where it's clamped between his distressingly strong thigh muscles, but he just squeezes it harder and jerks my torso up close to him. His lips are dangerously close to mine. His eyes blaze.

"Don't you fucking dare," I say.

"I wasn't going to do anything."

I swear his voice sounds ragged, though. A little desperate.

He eases me down so I'm lying on my back, my leg still clamped between his thighs. Then he jumps away from me, light and nimble. I kick at him, but it's pointless. He's already several paces away.

"Are you going to be quiet?" he asks me.

"No." I sit up, moving cautiously, never taking my eyes off him.

Jaxon frowns. "Why are you being so difficult?"

I laugh. He can't be this clueless, can he? To answer, I shake my left leg so the chain rattles and scrapes against the floor.

Jaxon sighs. "You don't have a choice."

"Well, you do."

His bright blue eyes narrow. "Actually," he says, "I don't."

When he says this, his expression is dark and dangerous and cold, and fear squirms through me again, quieting my urge to talk back to him. I'm fucking lucky, actually, that he's crazy and decided he can't kill me. I'd be luckier if he decided to let me go, but still. I should work with what I have.

We glare at each other.

"Be quiet tonight," he says. "And I'll bring you breakfast in the morning."

I don't want to think about what a guy like this eats for breakfast. Still, I don't say anything. Just push myself up to standing, bracing myself against the bed. He watches me warily, like he expects me to attack him again. Not that I'd reach him. He's still in the doorway, just outside of the range of the chain.

For a moment, we stay like that, sizing each other up. Then Jaxon steps backward to leave me alone. And I don't want to be alone. I'm scared and panicky, but I'm also angry. I want answers. I want to know why he's doing this.

And so before he can slam the door shut, I blurt out, "This is because I have a picture of that symbol, isn't it?"

He freezes with his hand on the doorknob. When he looks up at me, his eyes are storming.

"I knew you recognized it," I say, keeping my voice low. "I saw it on your face in the diner."

The darkness in his features deepens. He squeezes the doorknob, tightens the line of his jaw. "That's not something a human like you should have ever seen."

Human?

And then he slams the door shut so forcefully that the walls shake, and I don't know if my heart will ever stop racing.

CHAPTER FIVE

JAXON

I can't believe I got to touch her again—and while she was awake, no less, her blood coursing through her body, her eyes wild with fear and anger in equal measure. I've never had a woman's breath on my skin like that, our bodies all tangled together, and me with no intention of killing her.

It made my cock hard.

That surprises me, but everything about Charlotte has been a surprise, from the moment she pulled out the picture of my sigil to the way she tried to fight me even with a chain around her ankle and no hope of escape. I keep thinking about it as I go down the hall to my bedroom, one hand listlessly rubbing my dick over my sweatpants.

When she starts up her racket again, slamming her chain around and stomping against the floor, I'm not even irritated by it. It just reminds me of how she tried to grab me. How she tried to *touch* me.

What woman wants to touch me?

Charlotte's tantrum plays out in the background as I lay out on my bed, still distractedly touching myself. There are little reminders of her scattered around the room because I went through her purse earlier—not that she had much in there. Just her wallet, which I left alone, and her phone, which I took out and smashed with a hammer in my studio. The only other thing was a slim, vintage cigarette case filled with five neatly-rolled joints. Brave girl, driving that shit through Texas, which was where her rental car was from.

They're currently sitting on the bedside table.

I fiddle with the cigarette case, but it's too detached from her. The cold, smooth metal distracts from my memory of her hot, soft skin. So I swing myself off the bed and look over at her suitcase.

I set it in the corner of my room for safekeeping, and I study it now, my heart pounding up in my throat. Charlotte's still clanking around down the hallway, reminding me that I've got a living human in the house for the first time in... months. Over a year, I think.

Before I can stop myself, I roll the suitcase over to my bed and unzip it and let it fall open like a clamshell. It's full of hastily-packed clothes, with a Ziplock bag of toiletries and makeup lying on top. I set that aside. The clothes make my heart beat faster because they all smell like her, that sweet, sandlewoody scent that I breathed in when I had her pinned down a few minutes ago. My cock jumps at it, and I plunge my hand into the mess of fabrics, plowing through until I find the silky slip of one of her panties.

They're black, with little lace trimmings. I press them against my nose, breathing in her scent—faint, here. They're clean. I sit back on my heels, letting out a soft, shuddery sigh. I don't know why I'm doing this. Why I'm letting myself get obsessed with a girl I can't kill and therefore can't really *be* with.

I lay on the bed again, clutching her black panties in my fist as I pull my cock out. Then I wrap her panties around my shaft, shuddering at the soft, silky fabric. My eyes flutter closed as I stroke, listening to Charlotte clanking her chain around. The more noise she makes, the harder I abuse myself, squeezing my dick until it's painful. I like pain, though. Maybe I should have let her kick me in the balls the way she wanted. I stopped her because I didn't want her to know that catching her before she fell, feeling her soft flesh and her warm living breath, had given me such a huge erection.

Down the hall, Charlotte shrieks, her voice muffled. I imagine she's shrieking because I'm fucking her, or maybe cutting her. Putting something in her. I groan and jerk myself a little faster, strangling my cock with her satiny underwear. I realize I'm matching my strokes to the rhythm she's using to pound the chains. That makes it even easier to imagine that I've got her tied up, helpless, and I'm thrusting into her over and over while she spasms around my cock.

That does it. Pleasure tears through me, and my cum floods through her panties, soaking into the fabric. I slump back against the mattress and let the mess fall on the floor beside my bed and listen to Charlotte trying to—do something. I'm actually not sure what she hopes to accomplish with all that noise. Annoy me into killing her, maybe. Although she probably thinks she can annoy me into letting her go.

Neither option's possible, though. Fortunately, a Hunter like me doesn't really need that much sleep even though I had been enjoying a good rest before she woke up and started her futile little campaign.

Her tantrum plays out in the background while I lay on the bed and imagine fucking her again, although this time, I imagine her the way she looked after I knocked her out, slack and unmoving, her lips parted. Shame heats my cheeks. It's not that I *prefer* them when they're dead, it's just that it's *easier*. The closest I ever came to fucking a living woman, she gazed into my face before I could slide inside her, and she saw it. The void behind my eyes. The emptiness granted to me by the Unnamed. That blackness that makes me what I am.

And then she told me to stop and shoved me off her and fled the motel half-dressed. I didn't follow her; she didn't know my name and she hadn't been marked by my gods for killing. And I hadn't done anything she could take to the police.

But she saw it. She knew. She recoiled from me like the prey she was.

The dead ones don't do any of that.

I lean over and pick up Charlotte's soiled panties and then toss them in my laundry hamper. They're mine now. Then I dig around in the suitcase to pick out a new outfit for her to wear: a yellow '50s-looking sundress, clean underwear that I don't let myself dwell on, and the lone bra in the suitcase, which is nowhere near as sexy as her lacy black panties.

I'll take them to her in the morning, when the sun rises.

CHARLOTTE'S still going at it, but at least her racket is quieter when I'm downstairs. Just a dull, rhythmic thumping overhead. Easy to ignore.

I'm antsy. Agitated. My gods are quiet, not bothering to give me any direction except the occasional sharp reminder that I can't kill Charlotte. I pace around the downstairs rooms, weaving between the formal parlor and the dining room and the kitchen, watching the darkness outside. I just don't know what to do.

More than once, I consider calling Sawyer and telling him everything, but something stops me. If Sawyer finds out she's here, he's going to tell Edie. But Edie's human, just like Charlotte, and she's going to want to make sure her friend is okay. And that means explaining to Charlotte that Sawyer Caldwell isn't dead, that he's not even human. He's a Hunter, and I'm a Hunter: beings designed to kill for centuries at a time.

It's a whole can of worms, and I don't want to be the one to open it.

It would be easier to take care of this issue on my own. But I *don't* want to deal with it on my own.

I decide to call Ambrose.

Of the three of us, Ambrose is the oldest. He's been around, Hunting, since the 1800s. He found me in the '90s, a few years after I went MIA during my first tour of duty. Well, after I got shot in the desert and buried myself in the sand and revived eight months later and the war was over. A lifetime ago.

He's usually got decent advice, though.

When I call him, he answers on the second ring, barking out a harsh, "I'm busy," instead of a hello.

"I've got a problem," I tell him, figuring that will get him to listen.

I can practically hear him scowling on the other end of the line. "A real problem or a Jaxon problem?"

"Asshole."

"Seriously." It sounds like he's outside, the wind howling around him. "I've got my eye on a target. What's going on?"

"Why the hell did you answer, then?"

A pause. The wind sounds like static. "Bored," he finally says. "I'm just watching him. Is this a real problem?"

I take a deep breath. Charlotte's losing some of her steam. She's still thumping around, but the thumps are slower and quieter and more half-hearted. "Yeah," I say, and then I tell him everything. When I finish, he's quiet for a long time.

"Fuck," he finally says. "You're sure she's looking for Edie?"

"She had her picture on her car dashboard." And I have the picture tucked inside her cigarette case. I think she'd be mad if I destroyed it.

"You never should have painted that stupid fucking sigil."

Anger bristles through me. I'll paint my gods' sigils

anywhere I want. "*Sawyer* shouldn't have let a human girl wander around his place."

"On that, we can agree." Ambrose sighs. I can picture him in his dusty Oldsmobile, leaning back in the bucket seat. That fucking car is almost as old as I am. "But it's too late now."

"Think we should tell him?"

"No." Ambrose says it fast. "He's not thinking clearly about any of this shit." He pauses. "Are you sure you can't just—"

"No." The word explodes out of me, heat buzzing in the back of my head. "It'll piss off the gods. And Sawyer."

Ambrose is quiet. He's more willing to believe in the gods than Sawyer is, even if he doesn't pray to them the way I do. But he understands my devotion. "Sawyer wouldn't have to know," he finally says.

"I'm not doing it." I squeeze the phone, my heart thudding. "And I'm not letting you do it, either." The thought of Charlotte draws the gods out of the Abyss until they're squirming like snakes through my thoughts, making me sick to my stomach at the idea of her death.

Ambrose sighs. "Fine," he says. "Just—keep her there for now. Like you're doing. Is she secure?"

"Of course. This isn't my first time."

"It's your first time keeping someone around for longer than a few days before you kill them."

I scowl.

"Let me finish this mark," he says. "I should be done in a week or so. Then we'll figure something out."

He hangs up before I can respond. I throw the phone down on the sofa beside me and look up at the ceiling.

Charlotte's finally gone quiet. If I concentrate, I can sense all her bodily functions: her heart, her breath, her scent. All those signs that point me toward my prey. In a way, it's almost as distracting as the constant clanking.

Still, I told her I'd bring her breakfast if she stayed quiet tonight. And while she didn't *exactly* obey—it is still nighttime. Won't be morning for at least another few hours. Maybe if I bring her breakfast, she'll see the benefit of letting me have some peace.

Plus... it's an excuse to look at her.

And it gives me something to do with all this nervous energy. Something that isn't killing, which I can't do right now. Not with Charlotte in the house. I'm sure as hell not leaving her alone.

Breakfast it is, then.

CHAPTER SIX

CHARLOTTE

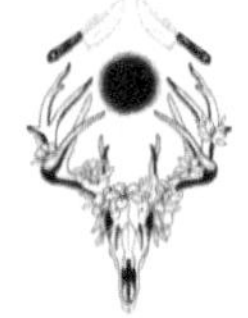

I’m startled when I open my eyes and the room’s not dark anymore. It means I fell asleep somehow. I’m chained to a bed in a madman’s house, and I still fell asleep.

I sit up, blinking the bleariness from my eyes. The thick velvet curtains block out most of the morning’s sunlight, but plenty of it streams around the edges, illuminating the motes of dust floating around like stars. The room looks less intimidating in the daylight, I will say that. Shabby and dusty and faded, rather than some gothic nightmare. I get a better look at that mannequin in the corner, too—it’s armless and headless and painted black, and someone’s glued bones around it like a cage. I can’t tell what kind of bones.

Animals, hopefully.

I do mixed media, Jaxon told me back when he was just a hot weird guy and not a psychopath. I shiver.

I have to pee, and I remember the other thing Jaxon told me, about the chamber pot under the bed. As much as I *really* don’t want to use it, I guess I don’t have a choice. I sit up, moving cautiously, and crawl off the bed. My head doesn’t hurt as bad as it did last night, although there’s a deep-rooted ache in my rib cage. From the car crash, I guess. The airbag exploding in my face.

I slide off the bed, and that's when I notice something new in the room: a little folding table with a plastic lawn chair beside it. There's a bowl on the table, too. I regard it with suspicion while I crouch down to see if Jaxon lied about the chamber pot.

He didn't.

It takes me a few minutes to get situated, but I manage to use the stupid thing. He even left a roll of toilet paper sitting beside it. How thoughtful.

I slide it back under the bed as carefully as possible, harboring thoughts of throwing its contents on him when he comes in here again. Throwing it on him, and then—the next steps don't materialize. I'd still be chained up, and he'd be pissed off. He'd also see what I was going to do from a mile away, given the way he reacted to me trying to kick him in the balls last night.

That's not something a human like you should have ever seen.

The last thing he said to me materializes unbidden in my thoughts. He's crazy. That's all it means. He's obviously fucking crazy.

He probably killed Edie.

That's a thought I've been worrying about since last night. She was near that sigil. He admitted to me he recognized it, albeit in that weird, creepy way. Now she's gone.

Granted, I'm currently a thousand miles away from where Edie disappeared. He must have gone there. She said she was staying with a friend, and I wonder, for the first time, if that friend was really Jaxon. She'd been willing to lie to me about leaving the cabin. Why not that this, too?

"Why'd you do it?" I whisper, sinking onto the mattress. Tears prick at my eyes. "Why didn't you just *tell* me what was going on?"

But Edie, wherever she is, doesn't answer.

I sit with my sadness for a little while, listening to the creaks and groans of the old house. Then I wipe my tears away and stand up. I'm not going to die here. Maybe I won't throw my piss on Jaxon, but I have to do *something*.

So I go investigate the table since it definitely wasn't here last night when Jaxon wrestled me to the ground with his surprising strength. I can't believe I slept through him setting it up, and the thought uncurls a dark discomfort in my chest. Because what else might I have slept through?

Not there's any evidence that he did anything like that. A small relief, I suppose.

As it turns out, the bowl on the table is filled with oatmeal, congealing in the cool air of the room. It actually looks kind of good; there are pecans and strawberries and mini chocolate chips sprinkled on top. A pitcher of water, an empty glass. I frown at the setting. Hadn't he said he'd bring me breakfast if I got quiet? Expect I hadn't got quiet.

Until you fell asleep.

That irritates me, that I gave him what he wanted. So even though I'm hungry and my throat is dry, I don't touch any of the food or water.

But then I see something else on the table that leaves me feeling cold and shivery. A yellow sundress.

My yellow sundress, the one I distinctly remember throwing in my luggage back in California. It's currently folded up as neat as a store display on the lawn chair. My bra sits on top of it.

The motherfucker went through my suitcase.

Went through my suitcase to, apparently, bring me a change of clothes, but still.

Something about the clothes makes me feel even more suspicious. Why the hell is he being nice? I'm his prisoner. He thinks he can't kill me for whatever fucking reasons, but I'm still chained up in here.

I won't touch anything on the table. No way. Absolutely not.

I move around the rest of the room instead, the chain dragging behind me. It has enough slack that I can touch every wall except the one with the door. I spent a few minutes studying the weird mannequin sculpture, just long enough to determine that the bones have been epoxied into place and I won't be able to pry one off to use as a weapon.

Long enough, too, to see how big they are. How familiar. Bones I've seen in high school science textbooks and doctor's offices.

I pull away from the mannequin, my skin crawling, trying not to think about why that thing is in here. A warning of what he's doing to do to me?

I can't kill you, he said, but what happens when he decides he can?

No. Nope. I will get out of this before then. I'll find out what he did to Edie, and I'll get the fuck out of here.

I investigate the curtains next. They're thick and dusty, and when I push them open, I'm disappointed by the sight of the thick metal bars caging in the windows. I peer through the glass, trying to get a sense of place. I'm on a second floor, that much is clear. Directly beneath me is an overgrown garden, thorny dead roses competing for space with wild shrubs. A few yards from the house is a metal shed, although it's hard to make out any details through the window's ancient glass, everything wavy and distorted.

Other than than that, the house is surrounded by the lush, verdant tangle of the Louisiana swamp.

I tug on the window. It won't budge.

"They're painted shut."

I shriek when I hear Jaxon's voice and jerk away from the window, chain rattling, to find him standing in the doorway. Neatly dressed, long hair pulled back in a low ponytail. Barefoot. Something about him reminds me of a jaguar or a panther—a big, sleek, dangerous cat.

"Okay." I hate that he caught me unaware.

"Even if you could open them," he continues, "nobody will hear you scream. This is the only house for ten miles. We're in the middle of the marsh. It's mostly wetlands."

"Thanks for the ecology lesson." Why the fuck am I doing this? Sassing him? It's like I can't stop myself the second I see him.

"If you want an ecology lesson," he says coolly, "I'm happy to give you one. I've lived here my whole life."

I have absolutely no idea how to respond to that. I can't tell if he's joking. Or if it's some kind of veiled threat.

And his handsome face doesn't give anything away, either.

"I don't want an ecology lesson," I snap. "I want to know what you did to Edie Hensner."

That *does* get a reaction. A coldness washes over his features, and his mouth draws tight and thin. "I didn't do anything to her."

"But you recognized her name."

His expression turns even colder. Cold enough that fear curls around in me, strangling out the bravery that's gotten me this far. I'm glad I'm on the other side of the room from him. And glad he stays put in the doorway.

"You didn't eat the breakfast I brought you," he says.

He's changing the subject away from Edie, which just makes skin prickle with icy fear. "If you killed Edie, why don't you just say so?" For the first time, my voice comes out shaky. I think it's because, for the first time, I've found a topic of conversation that feels genuinely dangerous.

Jaxon fixes his eyes on me, and it's like they're burning through my skin. I press against the wall, my feet tangling up in the curtain.

"You're asking the wrong questions about Edie Hensner," he finally says, and his voice is flat.

I don't really understand what he means.

Before I can respond, though, he points at the table. "Why didn't you eat the oatmeal?"

Because you're a psychotic killer and fuck knows what's in it. But with that sharp deadliness radiating off him, I bite my tongue and instead say, "I'm not hungry."

Jaxon narrows his eyes. "I made it for you."

All the more reason not to eat it, as far as I'm concerned. Still, I just repeat myself. "I'm not hungry."

"You didn't change, either."

I cross my arms over my chest. "Hard to change with my foot chained to the bed."

"That's why I brought you a dress."

Then he steps backward, slams the door, and leaves me alone in the room once again.

CHAPTER SEVEN

JAXON

I resolve to ignore her for the rest of the day.

She doesn't make it easy. She keeps thumping around her room, dragging her chain across the floor, just generally making noise. At one point, I hear a loud, splattery crash, like she's showing me what she thinks of my oatmeal.

Fine. If she won't eat in her room, then she'll eat downstairs, with me. After all, I'm the one with the upper hand here. She's in *my* house, wearing the chain that *I* welded around the bed three years ago. If it weren't for my gods, she would be in my studio now, a beautiful art piece preserved by frost and ice until I find the sculpture hidden in her flesh.

I'm the one with the upper hand, and yet I feel like she controls me every time she fixes me with those brown eyes.

So I go to my studio to try to find some solace in my work. Not that I have much to work with; I haven't brought anyone back to my studio in quite some time. At least two months. There are a few limbs in the deep freeze, the skin marred useless by freezer burn; I should be able to salvage the bones, though. A few jars of old blood that I could stretch with paint. Assorted ephemera—locks of hair, loose teeth, finger bones. I dump them out on my work table and rattle through them, looking for inspiration. Nothing.

My gods are silent, too, having retreated into the Abyss without any word of advice, as useless as Ambrose. I sweep the ephemera back into their box and pull down one of the jars of blood. Charlotte told me she was a painter. Perhaps I can paint her. I can't kill her, but I can still capture her essence in that way.

It would be better if I had her blood, though.

That idea perks me up, and perks up my Guardian, too, given its love of fresh hot blood. **Only a little,** it whispers to me. **Don't kill her.**

I know, I know.

But how the hell am I going to get her blood? If I get too close to her, she'll fight me; I can sense that intention radiating off her. Now, I would *win*, of course, but I don't want her fighting me when I'm trying to cut her with a knife. It's not like she's going to sit still while I bleed her out into a bowl.

A syringe? Do I even have a syringe? Probably not a clean one.

I give up that little fantasy for the time being and just use the old blood, pouring a few drops into my pallet and then mixing it around with gouache from some crusty old tubes I found shoved in the back of my paint drawer since Charlotte said she paints with gouache most of the time. It mixes better than I would have expected, the blood thickening up the gouache and giving it a kind of rusty undertone that I like. Dilutes pretty well in water, too.

I don't plan anything, just start painting her from memory, using the four colors I was able to find: a sickly yellow, a dark blue, some ancient white, and your basic Kelly green. All of them are streaked with rust from the blood. I'm not crazy how the colors look together, even when I try to blend them, but I like the way her eyes start to come out from the thick, smeary lines I slap on the watercolor paper I'm using. It's an ugly mess except for her eyes. They peer out at me, pinning me in place even as I'm trapping her in the gouache and blood.

I lose track of time. It's not until the light in the window starts to change that I realize how late it is. How hungry I am, too—I haven't eaten anything since breakfast. And I was going to bring Charlotte down for dinner.

I put the paint away and leave everything else and go back into the house, which feels warm after being out in my chilly studio. I keep that cold for obvious reasons. Charlotte's quiet. No thumping, no screaming. I can't help myself; I go upstairs to check on her before dinner.

She's stretched out on the bed, still wearing her dress from yesterday. I think she's asleep, but she lifts her head when I open the door and looks up at me the same way she looked out at me from the painting.

"My chamber pot's full," she says balefully.

I knew that already; I've got a Hunter's sense of smell. I wasn't going to say anything, though. "I'll change it out while you're downstairs for dinner."

She pushes up on her arms, fear flickering across her face. "Dinner?"

"You'll need to change." I really want to see her in that yellow sundress. "Be ready in an hour."

"Or what?"

Her eyes gleam, challenging me. This would be so much easier if I could kill her, but even thinking about it sends jolts of electricity running through my limbs. My gods storm around.

"I'll tie you down and do it myself."

The idea excites me. Makes my skin prickle. Charlotte just glares at me.

"An hour," I tell her.

Then I leave, my heart thumping.

Since it's cold out, I make crawfish étouffée, using the big bag of frozen crawfish I keep in my food freezer. I'm not like Ambrose. Animal meat only, thank you very much.

Once the étouffée is done, simmering quietly on the stove, I set everything up in the formal dining room, using my grand-mother's fancy porcelain china from the 1920s, two decades after she and my grandfather built this house. I light some candles. Dim the chandelier that hangs up above the table. Lay out cloth napkins. Open a bottle of expensive red wine and set it next to my place setting so it can breathe.

Then I go to my room and grab my carving knife from its place on my bedside table. My Guardian screeches a little. "I'm not going to kill her," I mutter. "But she might need some convincing."

Charlotte was quiet the whole time I was cooking. I don't know if she's resigned or she's worn out or if she's planning something. Maybe all three.

When I go to her room, I stand outside the closed door and listen for a few minutes. Listen, and try to calm down my racing heart. I hate how nervous I am about this. About entertaining a living girl.

She shuffles around inside, the chain clanking softly.

I push the door open.

Charlotte stops when I do, looking up at me, her expression unreadable. What stuns me, though, is that she actually did change. The yellow dress looks like she's wrapped in sunlight, and it has these off-the-shoulder sleeves that show off the top part of her chest, the bodice tight enough to squeeze her breasts upward. She stares at me, red hair falling around her bare shoulders, her smeared eye makeup suddenly more notice-able than it was earlier.

"Happy?" She stalks over to the chair and pulls up the

change of underwear I brought her. "I couldn't put these on, by the way." She shakes her chained leg to illustrate her point.

I swallow. Clutch my knife a little tighter, for strength. Her eyes flick down to it, noticing it for the first time. Fear wafts off her, the usual spicy scent that, on her, has a dark, bloody undercurrent that drives me wild.

"You can change your underwear after I unchain you," I tell her. "But wait here."

She opens her mouth like she wants to protest but I slam the door shut, breathing hard. She isn't like a typical victim. I *knew* that, of course—I knew that the second I saw her walk into that diner, glittering like a victim but marked with clear instructions from my gods not to destroy her. She has this defiance about her that would be infuriating in an ordinary victim, the sort of thing that would earn them a slower-than-usual death. But that defiance only adds to her allure. Even when she obeys me—putting on the yellow dress, say—it feels like defiance.

She planning something. And that just sparks my blood even more.

I dart back into my room to grab two things: her makeup bag from her suitcase and the cigarette case of weed, which I slip into my back pocket. Then it's back to her room, where she's still standing beside the bed, arms crossed over her chest, glaring at me.

"Redo your makeup." I toss the bag on the bed.

"Why?" She doesn't take her eyes off me.

"You're going to dinner." I answer her calmly, although I squeeze the knife, prepared to threaten her with it if she gets *too* defiant. I'm hoping she does. "You need to look nice."

Her mascara-smeared eyes narrow. "I need to look nice for you, you mean."

I shrug. She rolls her eyes but does sit on the bed and rummages around in her bag. Her fear perfumes the air. I bet she figures getting out of the room will be her chance to escape. But she thinks I'm a human man, some loathsome serial killer idiot, and not a being designed to do exactly what I'm doing to her.

I watch her clean the old makeup off her face with baby wipes and then apply it fresh. She doesn't put on as much as she was wearing yesterday, but that's fine. Honestly, it would be fine if she didn't wear any. I just didn't like that the smeared makeup reminds me that she's been crying.

"Happy?" she says when she finishes. She looks up at me, her eyes dark and smokey, her lips bare.

I gesture for her to stand up.

She does, sighing, putting the makeup bag aside. The chain snakes from her ankle to the bed.

"I'm going to take that off," I tell her. "And you can change your underwear." I hold up the knife, and her eyes settle on it with a fearful yet avaricious gleam. She thinks she can use a weapon against me.

"Then what?"

"Then you'll come downstairs."

Her eyes glitter. She wants to know if I'm going to chain her up. She's worked through the different possibilities, I think. What to do if I handcuff her. What to do if I lead her downstairs on a leash. What to do if I threaten her with a knife.

I smile a little. She has no idea what I am and what I can do. Even if I can't kill her.

I pick up the clean panties, relishing their silky fabric. Charlotte watches me, and, to her credit, keeps her expression blank. Although when I hand them to her, she snatches them away, curling them up in her fist.

I crouch down at her feet, my muscles tense because hers are tense. I can smell her adrenaline.

I wear the key to her lock around my neck, along with the key to the room, and I can feel her staring at me as I set down the knife on the ground and pull the keys out from under my shirt. She says nothing as I slide the key into the cuff, but I sense the shift in her heart rate.

As soon as the cuff springs free, Charlotte lunges sideways—going for the knife, no doubt. But I expect it, and I move faster than I've moved for her yet, grabbing her by the waist and throwing her onto the bed so quickly it's clear she doesn't understand what happened. Because her fear shifts. Sharpens. And it's clear on her face, now, too.

"How—" She stops herself.

"Don't do things like that," I say. "Just because I can't kill you doesn't mean I can't hurt you."

My Guardian and the Unnamed both hiss, but Charlotte doesn't need to know that.

"Let me go," she whispers. I'm still pinning her down by the waist, her knees spread on either side of my hips. It's what you might call a compromising position. My cock certainly notices.

"You need to change your underwear," I tell her.

She glares at me. "Why do you care?"

"Why do you not?" The truth is I want the dirty pair for my own use, but I don't want to see her look of disgust when I tell her that. "If you're good at dinner, I'll even let you have a bath."

We both know she's not going to be good at dinner.

"Fuck you," she says.

There it is. That delicious defiance. It floods me with a sudden surge of confidence.

"Give me the underwear." I feel suddenly very powerful, with her strong, thick body pinned by my strong, thick hands. Her eyes flash angrily, and she squeezes the underwear even tighter.

"Give me the underwear," I tell her again, hardly believing the words as they come out of my mouth. "So I can change them myself."

CHAPTER EIGHT

CHARLOTTE

I gape up at Jaxon, still not sure I heard him correctly. When I don't move, he releases my waist to curl his hand around mine, prying my fingers open one by one to get at the clean panties inside.

His strength is—startling. I try to resist, out of principle more than anything. Honestly, I would love to have clean underwear. And a bath. But I'd love not being a psychopath's prisoner a hell of a lot more, which is why I went along with his demands. Putting on the dress. Playing nice. I figure if I can get downstairs, I'll have a better chance of escaping.

It was just a lot easier to do when he wasn't here, smoldering at me. Because as soon as I see him, I want to defy him. I want to piss him off—

So he'll do exactly what he's doing right now.

No. I will absolutely not be thinking like that.

Jaxon's eyes burn into me as he snatches the panties out of my hand and tosses them over his shoulder. I wish I could squeeze my legs shut, but he's currently situated between them. I glare up at him, my face hot. With rage, I tell myself.

I know it's not just rage.

Don't be a fucking dumbass, Charlotte.

As if to prove to myself that I do not, in fact, enjoy having this monster bear down on me, I try to squirm away, hiking my dress up in the process. Jaxon keeps his gaze fixed on me as he grips my hips, pinning me to the bed.

"I won't look," he says.

"Fuck you."

Something like hunger flashes across his face, and I suddenly hear what I said. What it implies when he has me pinned beneath him.

Jaxon spreads one hand across my belly, pressing just enough weight to hold me down. I try to wriggle out anyway, kicking my legs up, but he grips my thigh with his other hand, his palm warm against my skin. I bite back the urge to gasp.

"Hold still," he growls. Then he reaches up under my dress, and I do, because I know if I keep moving he's going to touch something I'm not sure I want him to touch.

He hooks his fingers over the waistband of my panties, right at the joint of my hip, and pulls it down. I suck in my breath. Because this is happening. Edie's fucking murderer is undressing me.

He does, however, keep his gaze fixed on mine, his blue eyes burning. I'll give him that much.

"Is this so hard?" he murmurs, peeling the panties over my hips. He releases my belly, cautiously, and then slides his other hand up under my dress to pull the panties lower over my thighs.

I stare at him, my breath caught in my chest. A strand of his hair has worked out of his ponytail and hangs down to tickle my cheek. I resist the urge to bat it away.

"Good girl," he murmurs, and I really, really do not like how those two words send heat flooding between my legs. I just hope he doesn't notice.

He drags the panties over my knees. Only once they're free

of my skirt does he glance down to pull them off completely. I hardly dare to breathe. To move. I just watch him, half-terrified by what he's going to do next—

And half-aroused by what he just did.

Jaxon balls the dirty panties into a ball and shoves them in his pocket.

"What the hell?" I snap.

He gives me an expression that would almost look guilty if I didn't know better. "I'll wash them," he says. "With your other dress."

Then he grabs the clean panties from his shoulder and kneels in front of me. For a moment, I lay there like this is something I want. Then reality sinks in, how close he is to my foot, and my survival instinct activates with a sudden, pounding rush. I swing my foot up in a big, firm arc—or try to. Jaxon grabs my ankle without even looking.

"And you were behaving so well." His eyes lock with mine. "I told you, I won't look."

"You shouldn't be doing this at all," I snap. "I'm not a child. I can dress myself."

"And yet, when I gave you the opportunity, you didn't take it." He smiles darkly, and I hate that I like that smile, that I like the way his hand feels wrapped around my ankle, my leg propped up so the cool air of the room brushes against my bare pussy.

I hate it so much that I try to kick him with my other leg even though I know what's going to happen, and it does: he grabs that ankle too, then jumps to his feet so he can press himself between my legs again. He leans over me, the loose hair brushing my lips.

"You can't fight me," he says softly. "A human woman's no match for a monster like me."

Human. My thoughts snag on that word again, the way he wants to delineate between the two of us like we're different species. Something about that feels more dangerous than anything else.

Including the fact that he called himself a monster.

"Now let me finish this so we can have our dinner." He steps back and lifts my foot up. This time, I let him, because what choice do I have? He's a madman. He very likely killed my best friend, even if he claims he didn't. And I'm far more exposed and vulnerable than I've been since I first laid eyes on him in that greasy diner.

Jaxon slips my feet through the clean panties, pushes them up to my thighs. I stare at him the whole time, hardly breathing, trying to ignore the feathery touch of his fingers against my skin. When he reaches my hemline, he raises his eyes to mine and keeps pushing.

"Lift up your ass," he tells me, the panties bunched around my upper thighs. His eyes are daggers. When I don't make any attempt to do as he says, he digs his hands into my hips, his fingers long and sharp, and hoists me up with more of that surprising, hidden strength. He shoves the panties into place. Drops me.

His hands are still on my hips, still under my skirt, and he's kneeling in front of me almost like he's the one in supplication.

"L-let me go." I hate that there's a shiver in my voice. "The stupid things are on."

For a moment, I'm afraid he's not going to release me. But then he slides his hands out from under my skirt and stands up, looking at me expectantly. I don't move.

Jaxon sighs, crouches down, and grabs that cruel-looking knife he brandished against me. I want that knife. It almost feels like a hunger inside me, the desire to have a weapon and use it against my captor.

Pain sparks in my head, like a warning not to do anything stupid.

"You will come down and have dinner with me," he says calmly. "If you're good, you'll get a bath."

He steps closer, and I brace myself against the bed, my eyes on the knife, watching as he lifts it so that it catches the overhead light. When he lays it against the side of my throat, I whimper a little, even though it's just the flat side, and he doesn't actually cut me.

"We can also talk about what happened to your friend Edie." He gives a slow, curling smile. "Assuming you ask the right questions."

I stare at him, breath shuddery, the knife warming against my skin. He said just the right thing to snag my attention. To remind what I originally set out to do.

Behave.

Play along.

Find a way to escape.

I swallow against the knife and then nod, one short tiny motion. Jaxon doesn't move right away, though. Just stares at me, his eyes stormy. I hold my breath, curling my fingers against the blanket. The skin of my hips still tingles from where he touched me.

Then he steps back, taking the knife with him. "Come on," he barks, and I stand, my legs shaking. He comes around behind me, eyes never leaving mine, and loops his arm around my chest so the knife grazes my neck again. "Walk." He's close enough that his breath whispers across my ear, and my bitch of a pussy clenches with heat.

I do what he says.

He's surprisingly graceful, guiding me out of the room and into a dim hallway with his arm around me and the knife to my throat. I sweep my gaze around, taking stock of my surroundings. Everything out here looks old and dusty, too. Faded wallpaper. Strange paintings on the walls—some of them portraits, of people that sort of look like Jaxon, and some of them odd abstract art that makes me feel vaguely queasy.

The stairs are on the other end of the hallway from my room. Distressingly far. Jaxon nudges me downward, and I take slow, careful steps, pressing my fingers against the wall, running them over the photographs hanging there. All black and white. Old. Unfamiliar faces posed beneath sprawling oak trees.

"That your family?" I ask. I can't help myself.

"Some of them." He's dropped the knife a little so that it rests against my collarbone, but he still has his arm around me. I can feel his strength, even in that loose embrace, and I'd be lying if I said it didn't frighten me.

I'd also be lying if I said it didn't turn me on.

Don't be fucking stupid, Charlotte. I repeat that mantra to myself as we go down the stairs and step into a foyer illuminated by yellowish globe lights affixed to the walls.

The front door is only a few feet away. There are windows above it and beside it, dark from the night outside. My breath catches. My heart quickens.

And Jaxon notices, because he presses the knife a little more firmly against my neck.

"This way." He whispers the words into my ear like a lover, and his arm tightens across my chest as he veers me away from the door. I hate how firm he feels against my back. Hate the way he did that thing with my underwear by hand, too, his eyes never leaving my face. Hate that it makes me wonder what other things those hands could do if these weren't the circumstances we'd met in.

The thought evaporates when he guides me into a cramped, dusty living room, though.

Because there are two corpses in there, propped up on the tattered, threadbare furniture.

I shriek and then think better of it, my voice lodging in my throat. The corpses stare at me. They're preserved somehow, the skin leathery and discolored. A woman and a man. Hair combed and styled, their bodies dressed in old-fashioned clothes. They stare at me with strange, shining eyes. Glass, I realize after a moment. Glass reflecting the yellow lamps.

Did he *taxidermy* them?

"Don't mind them," Jaxon says gruffly, pushing me past the corpses, which stare at me. "They're for the Unnamed."

"The *what?*"

Jaxon doesn't answer, just guides me through another doorway. A dining room. There's an enormous walnut table with two formal place settings. Some covered silver platters. A chandelier turned low. More taxidermy on the walls, although animals this time. Alligators. A bear. Half a dozen deer heads. They all look ancient, cobwebbed and moth-eaten.

"Are those for the Unnamed, too?" I ask, immediately regretting it.

"Those are my grandfather's." Jaxon directs me to a chair and pushes me down to sitting, then slowly draws the knife away. I immediately look down at the place setting, but there's no knife to be found. Not even a butter knife.

I sit very still, my hands curled in my lap. Jaxon moves around the table, opening up the platters. White rice. Biscuits. A thick, rich stew with a salty briney scent that reminds me of the ocean. A salad, oddly bright compared to all the other dim colors in the room.

"I'll serve you," he says stiffly. "Keep your hands in your lap."

"If I don't?" I peer up at him, my hair falling into my eyes. It's already starting to turn greasy. *If you're good, I'll let you have a bath.*

Jaxon looks at me. His face is unreadable. A killer's mask. He doesn't answer.

And that frightens me more than anything.

CHAPTER NINE

CHARLOTTE

I watch him serve me dinner. I keep my hands in my lap. I pray he hasn't changed his mind about not being allowed to kill me.

"Crawfish étouffée," he says as he spoons the stew into the porcelain bowl at my place setting. "They probably don't have this in California."

I look up at him, squeezing my napkin in my fist. He's so close to me that his arm brushes against my shoulder as he serves my food. I've seen how fast he can move, and I can only imagine how quickly he'll hurt me if I say the wrong thing.

And yet, that compulsion to talk back to him rears up anyway. "How the hell do you know I'm from California?"

He smiles lightly at me. "You told me. At Bandit's."

Embarrassment flushes up through my cheeks. Oh. Right.

"Although I did look at your driver's license." He lays out a biscuit, scoops up some salad, and pours the wine glass half full. Then he moves to his own place setting, his movements careful and measured, like he doesn't want to mess up.

If this were literally any other circumstance, if he didn't have two mummified corpses in the next room and hadn't chained me to a bed for the last twenty-four hours, I'd be charmed.

I'm almost charmed anyway.

"Eat," he says, sliding down into his chair. "It's not poisoned or anything."

"Right," I say, not moving my hands out of my lap. "You can't kill me."

He just stares at me, eyes dark. The truth is I'm absolutely ravenous. I haven't eaten anything since yesterday, having rejected his admittedly delicious-looking oatmeal. He didn't bring me lunch, which shouldn't be a surprise. Making sure I'm good and hungry.

He sighs, irritation flickering across his face. "If you eat," he says, "we can talk about Edie Hensner."

"Astor," I say without thinking.

Jaxon smiles strangely. "What?" He picks up his spoon and stirs his étouffée around, which wafts the spicy, salty scent into the air. I can't fucking stand it. My stomach feels like a bottomless cavern, and I fucking love Cajun food. Contrary to what the psychotic redneck sitting across from me thinks, you can, in fact, get étouffée in California.

"Her name is Edie Astor," I say as I pick up my own spoon and drop it into my étouffée. I can feel Jaxon watching me as I lift it to take a bite.

Fuck, it's better than the étouffée I get at that little hole-in-the-wall place whenever I'm in Los Angeles. Creamy and rich and layered, the spices blended together perfectly.

"The papers say her name is Edie Hensner," Jaxon says. "How do you like it?"

I swallow the étouffée and lie. "It's fine."

His eyes turn black and flinty. But he's going to know I'm lying when he sees me shoveling it into my mouth, which I'm rapidly failing at *not* doing.

"Try the biscuits," he says.

"Stop fishing for compliments."

He scowls at me, but he also looks embarrassed, in his way. Busted. However, I do try a bit of biscuit, and I'm not particularly surprised when it's flaky and buttery and absolutely perfect.

How the hell did I get kidnapped by a psycho who's so good at cooking?

"Let's talk about Edie," I tell him firmly, reaching for my wine. That's good, too. I don't know much about wine, but even I can tell it's not the cheap vinegary shit I always pick up at Aldi. "I'm eating. You promised."

"Yes, but you have to ask the right questions." He eats slowly, watching me the entire time, like he's afraid I'm going to spring away and try to escape. Which is fair. The thought *has* occurred to me. But I need my energy if I'm going to escape, and besides...

I do want to find out about Edie. That's why I came to Louisiana.

"Fine." I have no idea what he means by the "right questions," but I figure I'll just throw things at him until I find something. "So you didn't kill her."

"No."

"Do you know who did?"

Jaxon tilts his head at that, and the loose lock of his hair brushes across the top of his shoulder. "Not the right question."

I stab a forkful of salad because I know I can't stab him without getting tackled to the dusty wooden floor. I try again. "Who killed Edie?"

"Not the right question."

"This isn't fair." I glare across the table. He just keeps eating. "You said you'd talk about her."

"I also said you need to ask the right questions about her." He lifts his gaze to meet mine. His eyes seem impossibly blue in the dim, hazy light of the chandelier.

I take another few bites of étouffée to hide my irritation. Drink some more wine, enough to drain the glass. Jaxon pushes the bottle toward me and I don't even think twice about it, I'm so focused on my food and on trying to get him to talk. I pour another glass. A much heavier glass than what he poured me.

"Fine." I take a deep breath. "What does that symbol I showed you have to do with anything?"

That one's *definitely* the wrong question. I can see it even before he answers, because storm clouds crowd across his expression, and he squeezes his spoon tight in his fist like it's a knife. "That's—"

"Not the right question. Yeah, I figured as much." I stir my étouffée around. What little of it is left. *Think, Charlotte. Think this through.*

Jaxon says he didn't kill Edie. Actually, he said he didn't do anything to her. I scrape my spoon against my bowl, the porcelain singing out. I look up at him, watching me, eyes guarded, and something catches in my throat. A possibility I haven't let myself even consider because I want it so badly to be true.

I take a deep breath. The words barely come out a whisper.

"Is Edie still alive?"

Jaxon's face cracks into a wide, devious smile. His teeth glean. "Now that," he says, "is the right question."

My body thrums. "Is she?"

"She is."

Suddenly I'm not hungry anymore. I don't care about food. I don't even care that Jaxon's keeping me a prisoner in his creepy old house. Everything tunnels in until it's just me and Jaxon and my pounding hope.

"Where is she?"

"Not for me to say."

"The fuck does that mean?"

Jaxon shrugs a little. Sips his wine. "It means what it means. I can't tell you."

"Well, why the fuck not?" I shout the question, and Jaxon's shoulders hitch a little. But his eyes gleam like he's enjoying himself, and I'm so irritated by that fact that I spit out, "Is it the same reason why you *can't* kill me?"

He sets the wine down and fiddles with his napkin. "Partially."

I want to strangle him. I know it's dumb. I know if I push away from this table he would be on me in seconds—I've seen how fast he moves. Uncomfortably fast. *Unnaturally* fast. I still want to strangle him, my fingers flexing against the table.

And pain flares in my temple. Fucking migraines. I haven't had them in years, and now I keep getting miniature versions of them, like they're trying to claw back into my life.

It must be the stress.

"Ask the right questions," Jaxon says calmly.

I take a deep breath and the pain retreats. I look down at my half-eaten bowl of étouffée. Then I stuff one of Jaxon's hatefully delicious biscuits in my mouth and wash it down with a big swig of wine.

Jaxon waits, watching me over his plate.

"Fine." I wipe my lips with my napkin and then look across the table at him. "Is Edie safe?"

Jaxon tilts his head like he's considering the question. "More or less."

My breath catches. "Could you explain that a little more, please?"

He grins. It almost feels like he's mocking me, but at the same time, it also feels like we're in on some kind of joke together—not that I can see what it is. "She isn't going to die anytime soon. She's not hurt. But the situation she's in—" He shrugs. "I'm not sure *you* would call it safe."

My skin prickles as I wait for him to continue, but he just takes a bite of salad. What he said actually makes me feel a little better, assuming he's telling the truth. She's not hurt. She's not in danger of dying. Even if she isn't *safe*, that gives me time to find her.

Assuming I can get away from Jaxon.

"This *situation* Edie's in," I say carefully. "Could she leave?"

Jaxon lifts his gaze to me and raises an eyebrow. I tense, waiting for him to say, *That's not the right question* in that smug way of his, but instead, he says, "Yes."

My breath gets all tight in my lungs. I stare at him, blood pounding in my ears. This doesn't make any sense. "You're lying," I tell him, anger surging up in my chest. "If she could leave, she would have called me."

Something flickers across Jaxon's face, so fast I can't name it. But I think it's pity.

"That's not a question," he says softly.

I screech and drain the rest of my wine. Pour some more. Is it stupid, to be drinking this wine? Almost certainly. Am I going to do it anyway?

Absolutely.

"Fine. You want a question?" I empty the bottle into my glass. "Why are you lying to me about Edie?"

He narrows his eyes. "I'm not."

"She would have called me. If she's safe—or mostly safe, whatever the hell that means—she would have called me." The words spill out, angry and desperate. I want Jaxon to laugh or snicker. I want the cruelty to flash in his eyes. I want *something* that tells me this whole time he's been fucking with me. Because otherwise it means Edie didn't bother to tell me where she is, and that hurts.

At least if she were dead, she'd have an excuse.

The thought flowers to life and then immediately withers on the vine. How could I think something so fucked up? Of course it's better for her to be alive. Of course I want her to be alive and mostly safe.

But *fuck* does the idea that she wouldn't even send me some kind of bullshit letter in code or something, anything—my heart gets all hard and black and shriveled at the thought.

I turn back to my étouffée and take a few bites, hardly tasting them.

"Are you okay?" Jaxon says.

I glare at him as I swallow my food "You just told me my best friend, whom I thought you *killed*, is not only alive but safe and didn't see fit to tell me that. How do you think I feel?"

His eyes get a little stricken. "Not the right question," he mutters.

"Shut the hell up." I scrape out the last of my étouffée, spear the last few bites of my salad. Eating is the only thing that makes sense to me right now. Well, eating and drinking the rest of my extremely-full glass of expensive red wine.

Jaxon watches me in silence. I can feel his eyes on me, hot and burning. I don't care. I finish my meal and then drink the wine, a little too fast. It's already starting to go to my head. The chandelier's pale glowing glass seems a little brighter. The dead animals on the wall seem to breathe.

And Jaxon is looking a little too handsome for a psychotic killer.

It's a good feeling, warm and dreamy. Better than anything I've felt in the last twenty-four hours. And especially the last five minutes.

Jaxon clears his throat. I snap my gaze over to him, daring him to say something annoying.

Instead, he says, "I'm sorry your friend didn't contact you."

It's weird, how sincere the words are. He stands up, his strong body unfolding from the heavy wooden chair.

"Why wouldn't she?" I say. "It doesn't make any sense."

He considers this for a long time. God, his eyes are so blue. As blue as the Pacific Ocean.

Then he says, "She's probably trying to keep you safe."

He sounds like he means it. And I wonder where she is. What she's doing.

I'm trapped in this nightmare house, and I'm not any closer to finding out what happened to my best friend.

I stand up, bringing my wine with me. Jaxon doesn't launch himself at me or tackle me to the floor, though. Instead, he clears the space between us with two easy steps, his arm circling around my waist. "Come on," he says softly. "I've got a surprise for you."

I laugh, my voice shrill. "Thought you can't kill me."

He doesn't say anything as he leads me out of the dining room.

CHAPTER TEN

JAXON

I'm pretty sure I told Charlotte too much about Edie.

It was a fun little game, though, and I want to keep playing it. The back and forth between us—it almost felt like a conversation.

I take her into the den in the back of the house, where I don't have any offerings to my gods set up. I saw how she looked at the offerings in the parlor, and I need her to stay focused on me.

"What are you going to do?" she mutters as we step into the room.

"Talk some more." I sit her down on the sofa. She slides back into the cushions, wine sloshing around in her glass. Maybe I shouldn't have let her drink so much. Or maybe it'll make her more likely to play the game.

"Talk?" She scoffs and takes a long sip of wine.

I stay standing, kind of towering over her. She peers up at me through her lashes, her lips stained red from the wine. I force myself to focus.

"Don't you want to find out more about Edie?"

"You're not going to tell me anything." She sounds annoyed,

but I know she's afraid of me. She puts on this mask that she's not, the way she talks back to me like she's trying to goad me into something. The wine just makes her even more bold. But I can smell her fear beneath her false courage, sweet and dark. I can see the way her eyes dart around like she's looking for an escape.

It doesn't matter. I move faster than her. I'm stronger than her. She's lucky I can't kill her.

You're lucky you can't kill her.

I push the thought aside.

"I told you," I say. "You just have to ask the right questions." I reach into my back pocket, fingers slipping past the silky tangle of her underwear until they wrap around her cigarette case, which I slide carefully out. Charlotte's eyes narrow as the box gleams in the lamplight.

"Is that—"

"You shouldn't have brought these into Texas." I pop the case open and pull out one of the joints. Charlotte watches me without saying anything. "It's not California. Or even Louisiana. They'll throw you in jail and—"

"This is what you wanted to show me?" she snaps. "That you're going to smoke my weed?"

I set the case aside and sit, somewhat cautiously, on the opposite side of the sofa from her. She watches me with baleful eyes, and I'm reminded why dead women are so much easier. They don't judge. You can't disappoint them.

They aren't *scared* of you.

"Ask me the right questions," I say to Charlotte. "And I'll let you have some."

She rolls her eyes. "It's my weed."

"It's mine now." I grab the lighter and ashtray from where they sit on the end table beside the sofa; as long as I can remember, there's been an ashtray there. My father used to chain smoke in the living room whenever he started getting the urge to kill. When I'd come downstairs as a boy and see the smoke curling up around the ceiling like storm clouds, I knew it was almost time to Hunt.

I don't smoke cigarettes like him, but I'll smoke weed occasionally. When I need to clear my head. Like tonight.

I light the joint and inhale. Charlotte shakes her head, drinks her wine. "Fine. You want me to ask a question? Stop fucking around and tell me where Edie is."

"That's not a question."

She glares at me, her pretty brown eyes full of poison. I take another hit, and then I let the joint burn.

"Fine." She smiles coldly. "Where is Edie?"

I consider her question. I know the answer, of course. Sawyer told me and Ambrose all about it, how they bought a house in Pensacola and he finally saw the ocean. And then Ambrose told him the Gulf of Mexico didn't count because he's an asshole.

"She's by the sea," I finally say.

Charlotte blinks. I know she expected me to refuse to answer. I should have. But I have something she wants, and I like it, that she wants something from me. It's—a strange feeling, from a living woman. From any woman.

"Where? Surely not California—"

"No, not California." I take another hit from the joint as Charlotte's eyes follow the ember through the air.

She drains her wine. She's not looking at me like she hates me anymore. She looks determined.

"She told me she met a friend from high school," Charlotte says. "That she was staying with him. Is that true?"

I smile a little. I can't kill her. Can't hurt her. But I can toy with her the way I do my victims sometimes. "In a sense."

She throws up her hands and tosses back her head, groaning in frustration—and giving me a view of her creamy throat. I imagine her wearing a necklace of blood, which stirs up the Unnamed.

Don't.

What if it wasn't her blood?

It's my question, and it still surprises me. But I like it, the idea of Charlotte covered in someone else's gore. My cock stirs. The Unnamed seems to like the idea, too.

I lean forward, the joint dangling from my lips. Charlotte watches me warily.

"So her friend wasn't from high school."

I'd almost forgotten what we were talking about. "Not high school."

"But there was a friend."

I nod, even though I'm crossing into dangerous territory. There's a reason Edie didn't contact Charlotte to tell her she's alive and safe. Probably to keep Charlotte out of this world. My world. The world of the Hunters.

And yet Charlotte came stumbling into it anyway. She's right in the middle of it, sitting on my sofa, with her tousled cherry hair and wine-stained lips.

"You want some weed?" I ask her.

"Tell me who the friend was."

I shake my head. Scoot a little closer to her. When she doesn't pull away, I keep going, moving across the cushions until my knees knock into hers. She looks down at them. Up at me.

I suck down a deep lungful of weed smoke.

Then I lean forward, press my lips against hers, and exhale.

It's not a kiss, but Charlotte reacts like it's one—and one she *wants*. Because she doesn't push me away. Doesn't shriek and call me a disgusting weirdo freak.

Instead, she parts her lips and accepts the white cloud of smoke as it passes from my lungs into hers.

I sit back, trying to mask the trembling in my hands. I can't believe I did that, although I can feel the Unnamed circling nearby, and I suspect that's where the bravery came from.

Charlotte breathes, the smoke curling out of her lips and nostrils and forming a halo over her head for just a second before dissipating into the lazy circulation of the ceiling fan.

"What the fuck?" she says.

I want to do it again, desperately. Her lips are so astonishingly *warm*. But this is a game, and there are rules.

"Ask another question," I say roughly. "The right one."

It doesn't matter what she says. I'm going to do it.

Charlotte's lips part. Her fingers tug down on her dress hem. Her eyes bore into mine.

"Have you spoken to Edie?"

The question brings me up short. Edie is the last thing I'm thinking about. But at least I can answer truthfully.

"Yes," I say. "Once." She had been in the room when I called Sawyer not long after he faked her death. He introduced us. I remember her voice, small and a little scared. The shy, whispered, *Hello*. Nothing like Charlotte, who puts on her mask, trying to hide that she's afraid of me. Edie didn't care that I knew.

And why should she? She knows I won't do anything to her. Not as long as she's Sawyer's girl.

Charlotte falters. Her eyes seem big and damp. "And she's okay?"

I suck down another lungful of weed smoke and lean forward. Charlotte doesn't lean forward to meet me, the way I want her to, but she doesn't pull away, either. Nor does she protest when I press my mouth to hers and exhale.

In fact, this time, she tilts her head, sealing our mouths together, her hot living breath mingling with mine as she draws the smoke away.

She exhales, her eyes never leaving mine. Waiting.

"Yes," I say. "Edie's okay. You really don't need to worry about her."

Something slumps in her shoulders. "I just have to worry about myself," she mutters. There's a slight slur to her words, from the wine and the weed. A faint lack of focus in her gaze.

I don't respond except to suck down the last of the weed to the joint's cardboard filter, lean forward, and shotgun her again.

She lets me. Parts her lips. Tilts her head. I press a little harder against her strangely hot mouth, trying to make it more of a kiss, and she lets me do that, too.

At least for a few seconds. Then she jerks back, exhaling the smoke between us. Through the pale haze, her eyes are wide with confusion.

Not disgust.

Not *disgust*, which was all I had gotten from the last living girl I tried to kiss. Five years ago. I don't even remember her name. But we had kissed in a motel room and she had seen what I was, even though I wasn't going to kill her. My gods didn't want her. The only one who wanted her was me.

It wasn't reciprocated. It never is, with living girls. They know I'm a predator—even more of a predator than a human man. And they react like prey.

It's strange how Charlotte is different. Maybe because I'm not trying to hide anything.

"You could have just passed me the joint," she says, jerking me out of my thoughts.

"Where's the fun in that?" My response startles me—how quickly I let it out. How my voice curves up like I'm flirting.

Charlotte's response startles me, too, the way she tamps down a smile. Like she doesn't want me to know she finds me charming.

Then she says, "You're not what I would expect from a serial killer."

I jolt, the words *serial killer* searing through my skin. "I'm not a serial killer," I say sharply.

She laughs coldly. "You have corpses in your living room."

"That's a parlor. And those are offerings."

"Are they or are they not corpses?"

I don't answer. A human woman like her won't understand.

"Did you not kill them?" she asks, arching up an eyebrow. Her fear has sharpened. She's terrified, asking me this, but she's doing it anyway, and that makes my chest feel kind of warm and tight, almost like something's hugging my heart.

I scowl. "What I did to them is beyond killing."

"Sounds like something a serial killer would say."

"I'm a Hunter," I snap.

"Sorry," she says. "A serial *hunter*, then." As strong as her fear scent is, there's a kind of dancing light in her eyes that belies it. I can't decide if that's her mask or not.

"No," I say darkly. "A serial killer is something a human becomes. I'm not human."

"Then what are you?" She doesn't believe me, that much is clear. She thinks I'm delusional, that I'm some human psychopath who thinks he's better than his equals. "Or is that not the right question?"

"The question is fine," I say stiffly. "And I've already answered it. I'm a Hunter." I stand up, moving more quickly than I really need to. Quickly enough that her fear spikes and I hear her fast, frantic pulse through the quiet of the den.

"What's a Hunter, then?" She looks up at me. Fearful. Expectant. I want to kiss her for real. I want to do so much more than that, too.

"We're the ones who stalk your nightmares," I tell her, which is the explanation my father gave me a long, long time ago when I was a little boy and hadn't yet killed anyone. I grab Charlotte by the wrist and yank her to her feet. She doesn't resist, but there's a slackness in her body, like a rag doll. She's stoned. A little drunk.

"That tells me nothing," she says, but I only shrug and drag her back upstairs.

CHAPTER ELEVEN

JAXON

I bury my nose in Charlotte's dirty underwear, breathing in her scent as I fist my cock, my grip strong enough to be painful, the way I want it sometimes. The way I want it when I need to remind myself that I'm too much of a monster to fuck a living woman.

I lean back in my bed, thrusting up into my hand, smothering myself in the soft, pungent silk of Charlotte's panties. She's quiet in her room, but I just keep picturing her at dinner, skin luminous in the soft chandelier light, her hair blazing like a fire, her plush body filling out that yellow dress in a way that revealed everything underneath the fabric.

My cock convulses in my palm, and I groan and squeeze it even harder, hard enough that I'm abusing it more than I'm actually jerking off. It fucking hurts, but it feels good too, that pain bursting behind my eyes like starlight. Charlotte's scent threatens to drown me—her sweat and her arousal, all those reminders that she's alive trapped in the silk.

I groan as I release, white ribbons of cum spurting across my fingers and beading across my lower belly. The pleasure lingers, though, pulsing in time with my heartbeat. Especially with her underwear still draped across my face.

I wonder what she's doing now.

I roll over, letting the panties drop onto my pillow, and stare at my door, which I left hanging open like an invitation. Not that Charlotte can accept it; I chained her to the bed again. But I still let myself indulge in the fantasy that she'd escape somehow and go wandering in the halls while I tortured my cock on her behalf.

There's no sign of her, though. She's not even making any noise.

I ease myself off the bed and clean up my spilled cum, then pull my jeans back on. I sit on the edge of the bed, elbows pressed into my knees, hair hanging into my face from having worked its way out of my ponytail.

She's so *supple*. So warm. There's a pink tint to her skin that drives me wild, and the lights in the dining room brought it out. All through dinner, throughout our conversation about Edie, I kept admiring it, the blood pumping just below her skin.

I want to see it again. Just a peek.

My breathing's ragged as I go out into the hall. Some of that's from coming, but some of it's from the anticipation of seeing her again. Of not knowing how she'll react when I step into her room. I know she's not exactly thrilled to be here, trapped in my house, but what choice do I have? I can't risk her going to the police and having them come out here and discovering my workshop and my offerings. I'd have to die again. I hate dying.

Worse would be if she led the cops to Sawyer and Edie. Or, gods forbid, Ambrose.

This is the best course of action, really. Keeping her locked up.

I stop outside her door and listen. It's quiet in there. I knock softly.

No answer.

She's either asleep or she's ignoring me. Either way, I'm the one with the key to the lock.

I pull out the chain with the keys and unlock the door, then put it back on, tucking it into my shirt so she can't see. Then I press the door open.

It's dark. The lights are all turned off. Of course, I'm a Hunter, and I can see in the dark, more or less, and I do see her, spread out on her back on the bed.

She's asleep—no wonder I didn't hear anything. I move closer to her, grateful that my bare feet barely make a whisper on the hardwood floor. I do switch on the little yellow-shaded lamp in the corner, just because I want to see her in the light. Her rosy skin. Her shining hair. The gentle rise and fall of her breasts.

My living girl.

No. I push the thought aside. She's not *mine*. I'm just keeping her here until I know what to do with her.

But gods—wouldn't that be something?

I stop at the foot of her bed and stare down at her. She hasn't stirred to my presence at all, and I think she must be knocked out from all that wine she drank and the weed smoke I blew into her lungs.

That memory snags on me, and I run my tongue over my lips as if I might be able to taste her. I can't, though. Which isn't so surprising, since I didn't taste her when we sort of kissed.

I could taste her now, though.

The idea flushes through my thoughts, and I curl my fingers up into fists. Although I just came, my cock stiffens a little.

Because I *could* taste her. She's knocked out, her legs spread across the top of the bedsheet, her dress hiked up to reveal her thick, tanned thighs. It would probably be my only chance to taste her, honestly. She only let me press my lips to hers because she wanted the weed. This way, I can have my taste without disappointing her with my fumbling.

I'm used to dead girls. To their stillness. And this is close. With the wine and the weed, I don't think she'll wake up—

I wonder if I can make her come, though. If she'll feel the pleasure of my mouth in her dreams.

I lick my lips again, a dull ache throbbing in the back of my jaw. A cigarette craving, except I'm not craving cigarettes.

Very slowly, very carefully, I ease myself onto the bed. When the mattress sinks beneath my weight, I freeze, eyes on Charlotte, waiting for her to wake up. She doesn't even move, just continues her slow, steady breathing, her eyes flickering behind her lids.

She's dreaming. Well, I'm going to make her dream about me.

I lean forward, running my hand up her smooth leg until I reach her dress. Then I push that up, too, my breath caught in my lungs as I reveal more of her thighs. Inch by inch. Centimeter by centimeter. An agonizing strip tease.

Charlotte mumbles something and squirms a little on the bed. I freeze, watching her. But she's not awake.

"Just stay like that," I whisper to her, flipping the dress up so I can see the view I had so studiously avoided when I was sliding on her underwear earlier.

It's fucking gorgeous.

Her panties cling to her pussy, the silken fabric just barely outlining the pattern of her folds. For a moment, all I can do is stare down at it, my heart pounding in my throat. It's the blood that makes it different from my usual encounters. The heat radiating off her skin.

"Don't let her wake up," I whisper to my Guardian. I can sense from it a vague, uneasy caution but no reprimands to stop. The Unnamed is nearby, too, watching from the black shadows in the corners. From it, I only sense approval. "Stay asleep," I whisper as I hook my fingers in the waistband of her panties for the second time tonight and drag them down over her wide, soft hips.

When I catch my first glimpse of dark pubic hair, I go still for a moment, listening to her heartbeat and her breath. They're both slow. She's still asleep.

I drag the panties lower. I feel like I'm unwrapping a present on Solstice morning. My father always wrapped the gifts in butcher paper and made me thank the gods when I got what wanted. Those early offerings were simple, just a prick of my own blood dropped on a candle flame to smoke and sputter.

I'm about to get what I've wanted since Charlotte breezed through the door of Bandit's diner.

"Thank you," I breathe as I pull her panties low enough to finally see her soft cleft. My tongue darts out.

Just a taste, whispers my Guardian.

Devour her, whispers the Unnamed.

Gods, do I want to devour her. I bow my head low and press a kiss against the dark triangle of her pubic hair, where I'm met with a wash of her scent like from the panties. I have to stifle my groan. Have to adjust my quickly-hardening cock so that it isn't squeezed up against my thigh.

I kiss her again, moving lower. Her legs shift on either side of my head, but I focus on the sounds of her body as it sleeps. Everything is a quiet, faint susurration.

Emboldened, I slide my tongue out to swipe it between her lips.

And I taste her.

For the first time, I taste her.

She tastes *alive*. She tastes like skin and blood, like the fiery march of a heartbeat. There's none of the underlying sweetness of rot I'm used to, only a richness like the wet marsh soil out in the front yard.

I can't hold myself back any longer. I kiss her cunt the way I wanted to kiss her mouth, plunging my tongue inside her to lap at the wetness there. Her heartbeat quickens, a rhythmic pulse I can practically taste on my tongue as I suck and lap at her pussy. She's still asleep—still, I think, dreaming—but her body reacts to my attention. The wetness deepens. Her living heat flares.

Cautiously, I push her thighs a little wider apart, moving carefully so I don't wake her. This gives me more access, and I explore her pussy with my tongue until I find the hard nub of her clit, which is hotter than the rest of her, pulsing with furious blood.

She whimpers.

My whole body goes still. I peer over the gentle mound of her stomach and the pile of her dress's yellow fabric. Her eyes are closed, and there's a quietness in her body that tells me she's still asleep even though her heart is beating faster. But her lips are parted. Her cheeks are flushed.

I kiss her again, striking my tongue against her clit like a match. Now that I've tasted her, sweet and musty all at once, I want to know what happens to her body when she comes. I've never made a woman come before. The few living ones I've been with never let me touch them long enough. And dead women don't orgasm.

But with Charlotte—with Charlotte, I think I can make it happen before she wakes up.

I focus my mouth on her clit like I'm trying to suck down her heat. But I also slide one finger along her slit, parting her soft, damp folds until I can slip inside her, where her pussy is so wet, so hot, I can hardly believe it.

She whimpers again, then moans. Mutters something that I can't quite decipher. Her legs widen for me, moving with the slow laziness of someone still asleep, or mostly asleep. Her muscles tremble, too, and I attack her with more fervor, burying my nose in her soaking pubic hair as I keep sucking and licking furiously at her clit. Her heart sounds like a jackhammer. Her breath is a hurricane, and I want to be swept away.

And then something amazing happens. Her entire body goes rigid, all her muscles tightening and contracting. Her heart races and her pussy walls flutter around my finger. She keens and bucks her hips up against my mouth. Once. Twice. Like she's trying to fuck me.

Did she just come?

I keep kissing her through it, eager to make it happen again. I push her legs further apart—a little too roughly, as it turns out.

Maybe it's because the orgasm masks it. Maybe it's because I'm too drunk on her pussy and her arousal.

But I don't notice that her system has woken up. That *she's* woken up.

I don't notice until I hear a shouted, "What the *fuck?*" and feel a cold length of chain wrap around my neck.

CHAPTER TWELVE

CHARLOTTE

I'm having a decent sex dream. My ex-girlfriend Maddie, the one who loved to eat pussy, has her head buried between my thighs. But it's not really Maddie, the way people are never themselves in dreams. She has long black hair instead of her trademark brown pixie cut. And we're in Jaxon's creepy-ass parlor, his taxidermied offerings or whatever the fuck they are watching as she eats me closer and closer to orgasm.

But then I slam awake—

And it's not a fucking dream.

I'm in that ancient, uncomfortable bed with a chain around my ankle and Jaxon's head between my legs, his glossy black hair peeking up between my thighs.

I'm also in the midst of the best orgasm I've had in months.

Waves of pleasure pulse through my body, and I arch up into Jaxon's shockingly eager mouth as he presses my thighs wide like he's trying to dive inside me. And for a split second, I just *let* him—let him swipe his thick tongue along my slit, let him make me come. It feels too damn good.

But then the reality of the situation slams through me:

I was asleep, I didn't give him permission, and he's a goddamn psychopath.

"What the fuck?" Suddenly, I'm acting on some deep-rooted instinct, like something snapped open inside me and is now telling me what to do. Without thinking, I kick my left leg up so I can grab the chain and loop it around Jaxon's neck, all in one movement like I've trained for this my whole life. I have no idea where this coordination came from. Maybe it's the adrenaline. Maybe it's the orgasm.

I can't *believe* Jaxon made me come like that.

Jaxon whips his head up as soon as the chain is around his neck, eyes wide and feverish, mouth wet with my desire. He stares at me for a second, stricken, and I can feel the same expression on my face.

Then the instinct flares up again, along with an annoyingly sharp pain behind my eye. I ignore the latter and lean into the former, yanking so hard on the chain that the metal digs into the skin of Jaxon's throat.

He makes a strangled, rasping noise and slides away from me, grabbing at the chain like he doesn't believe it's there. I roll out from under him and cling to the chain with every ounce of my strength—and I'm surprised by how much there is.

It helps, too, that Jaxon is thrown off-balance, too. He doesn't even really try to fight back, just watches at me, his skin turning an uncomfortable shade of red.

"What the fuck did you think you were doing?" I shout, pulling tighter on the chain. I fantasized about killing him like this more than once. Unlocking myself. Escaping. I can't believe it's actually going to happen. I also can't believe my head is pounding with the start of a migraine. What the fuck is in this house that's making me sick?

Jaxon keeps watching me, his eyes bulging and shiny with tears, his lips red and swollen.

Then he grins.

"You creepy asshole," I growl, my arm muscles straining. We're in a weird position, our legs tangled up on the bed together. Jaxon makes a noise like he's trying to say something, drool spilling out of the corner of his mouth. He still doesn't fight back, even though I keep expecting him to launch himself out at me or yank the chain away. It seems impossible that I'm stronger than him.

But he doesn't, and I don't question it. This is my one chance to escape and by god, I'm going to take it.

I wrap the chain around my wrist to get more leverage. Jaxon chokes and wheezes, his eyes bulging. The whites are turning pink. And he's turning a sickly blue color, like a bruise.

But he's still grinning. In fact, his grin widens.

That's when I realize that he has his hand down the front of his jeans.

The motherfucker's touching himself. I'm strangling him, the chain's metal links digging painfully into his skin, and he's using the last of his strength to stroke his cock. What's more, he keeps eye contact with me the whole time, his grin going wider and wider.

It should be gross.

It's not.

I act like it is, though. "You sick fuck!" I shriek, pulling harder, desperately ignoring the little quiver of heat between my thighs and the burst of pain behind my eye. Jaxon makes a sound that might very well be a moan and rolls his bloodshot eyes upward, thrusting into his hand. His pants have slid down enough that I can see the flash of his cockhead, swollen red like his lips.

My clit throbs, but I tell myself it didn't.

"Come on," I mutter, my muscles aching and my migraine a fire searing through my brain. But if this is what I need to do to escape, then I'm going to do it. "Come *on*."

Jaxon makes an absolutely horrible noise, a kind of wet,

thick choking. Then his head slumps back just as cum shoots out, splattering in pearly, gleaming ropes across the mussed-up bedsheets. I shout and jerk away, the chain slackening.

But Jaxon falls sideways across the bed, all the fight gone out of him. I assume he's passed out, but I pull on the chain with all my strength. Because I want to kill him. That's the only way I'm getting out of here.

What I don't do is dwell on the dark, terrifying thrill all of this has given me. Jaxon making me come while I sleep. Jaxon staring at me as he jerked himself off while I strangled him.

This woozy, dizzying rush of adrenaline pushing past the throb of my migraine.

"This is self-defense," I whisper, wrapping another loop of chain around my arm. "He's a murderer." The chain digs painfully into my skin, but that's nothing compared to what it's done to Jaxon's neck, where the links cut so deeply into his flesh that he's bleeding.

Jaxon gasps suddenly, wheezing, his eyes flying open. He looks right at me again, and his eyes are a nightmare—bloody and blazing. But there's something in his expression that turns me cold.

Recognition. Excitement.

Lust.

And then it's all gone. Blinked out. His empty eyes stare at me and his mouth falls open, slack.

The reality of what I've done hits me all at once. I scream and drop the chain, clawing at the place I have it wrapped around my forearm until it falls with a loud, thudding clank. Then I scramble backward off the bed, panting and terrified. Jaxon doesn't move, his eyes blank and flat.

I did it.

He's dead.

For a long time, I just stare at him, trying to comprehend what I'm looking at—

A dead body.

And trying to comprehend what I'm going to do next. Everything happened so fast that I hadn't even thought about what I was doing. Something whispered in my head to loop the chain around his neck and pull, and that's exactly what I did.

I close my eyes and take a deep breath, trying to calm down my frantically racing heart. At least my headache has vanished. Small favors.

When I open my eyes again, I half-expect Jaxon to be sitting up, grinning, like this was all a game.

He's not. He's still slumped sideways, tongue lolling out of his slack mouth, his hair clinging into damp strands to the side of his face. His cock flops out of the fly of his pants.

I should not be looking at his dick.

"Focus." The sound of my voice in the empty room grounds me, even though I still have a weird woozy feeling in my stomach. It's not exactly guilt but more a sense that something's off. Something's wrong.

Of course something's wrong you just killed a man.

I push past the feeling. Focus. I need to focus.

I'm still chained to the bed.

The weird, sick feeling in my stomach blooms: how the hell am I going to get out of this? But Jaxon did unchain me yesterday. He had the key on a necklace. I just hope to god he's still wearing it.

I slide off the bed and walk over to his body, my hands trembling. I keep expecting him to leap back to life, like the killer in a horror movie. Every time the ceiling fan blows dark strands of his hair across his face, my heart jumps. But his eyes are open and red with burst blood vessels. His face is a dark mottled purple color. He's dead.

I'm going to have to touch a dead body.

I swallow back a surge of bile and reach over to tug down on his shirt. His skin is still warm, which makes it easier, somehow. I can pretend he's alive.

When I see a glint of silver chain, I let out a loud, gasping sigh of relief. I hook the necklace with my finger and drag it out from under his shirt until I reveal the two keys. But I'm going to have to lift up his head to get the necklace off him.

I squeeze my eyes shut as I slide my hand under his temple, picking his head up just enough to pull the necklace away from his neck. When I let go of his head, it drops heavily against the bed like an inanimate object.

Don't think about it.

I scramble away from the body, my chain dragging over his akimbo limbs, and then crouch down to the cuff around my ankle. When I slide the key into the lock, I hold my breath until I'm able to turn it, until I hear the click of the lock falling out of place. The cuff snaps open.

And just like that, I'm free.

For a moment, all I can do is stare down at the open cuff. The weird feeling in my stomach intensifies, and I glance over at Jaxon. At his *corpse*. Because he's dead.

I tell myself that I killed him in self-defense. He's a murderer and a kidnapper. No one, not even in Louisiana, is going to fault me for that.

I jump to my feet and run.

I'm barefoot like I've been since I woke up in bed, but I have no idea where my shoes are. That's the first thought I have, that I'm going to need shoes if I want to get out of here. And a car. Jaxon has a car. That was how he kidnapped me in the first place. I need to find the car keys. Shoes and car keys.

A phone, too. If I can find a phone, I can call for help.

I ran down the hallway, slamming open each of the closed doors. The rooms are furnished but look abandoned, the furniture pale with layers of dust. I've almost let my guard down when I check the third room, which is full of old bones.

I scream at the sight of them: hundreds of bones lined up neatly on an old twin bed and dark mahogany roll-top desk, the lid pushed up. Without thinking, I pull the door shut so hard the walls shudder.

Don't worry about the bones. Shoes. Car keys. Phone.

The last door in the hallway is different from the others. It has the same heavy, old-fashioned furniture, but there's no dust, and it's immediately clear that this is where Jaxon sleeps. There's a stack of books on the bedside table, a pile of clothes in the corner. My suitcase in the middle of the floor.

Car keys. Shoes.

I fling it open grab the spare tennis shoes I'd packed and put them on without socks. My purse isn't there, though. Nor my cell phone or my ID.

I go over to the bedside table, fling open the drawers. Nothing useful.

"Car keys," I whisper. If I can find his car keys, if I can find his car, I can drive to civilization and get some help.

I don't see them in here, though, and it occurs to me they might be in his jeans pocket, a thought that makes the queasy, unsettling feeling in my stomach worse. No. I'll check downstairs first.

I don't want to look at his body again. At everything I did to it. Because seeing it—the red marks around his neck, the blood-shot, staring eyes, the purple skin—makes me feel weird.

Not bad, necessarily. Just... strange. And that's unsettling all on its own.

I race downstairs. In the foyer, I immediately fling the front door open—testing it, I think, to make sure it's not locked. It isn't. But there's also no sign of the keys by the door, either. Where else would you keep car keys? The kitchen, maybe?

I run through the creepy living room, refusing to look at the mummified corpses. The dining room is cleaned up, our dishes cleared away, the table wiped down. I shiver, seeing it all. Remembering how he claimed Edie is safe.

But that can't be true, can it? He's a murderer. A psychopath. He—assaulted me, technically, even if I'm not particularly bothered by it. Not after everything else he's done.

There's no reason to think he's telling the truth about Edie.

In the end, it's just another thought I push aside. Another thought that doesn't matter, because the only thing that does matter is getting away from this terrible place.

The kitchen shows more evidence of our dinner than the dining room does. Dirty dishes are stacked high in the sink, a big silver pot sitting on the counter full of soapy water, the empty wine bottle. I sweep my gaze around, taking in the old-fashioned wallpaper and ancient Formica counters. This place looks like it was last updated in the 1960s.

No car keys.

"Fuck!" I really don't want to be in the house another second longer, even though it's the middle of the night and I know I shouldn't go out into the Louisiana swamp by foot without even a flashlight. I swing around and check the kitchen drawers.

Well, now I have a flashlight.

I go out through the kitchen door, letting the screen slam behind me. A porch light kicks on when I step onto the little cement porch, flooding the overgrown yard with sallow, yellow light—but also throwing the surrounding swamp into black shadows.

This is probably stupid. But there have to be other people around here somewhere. Jaxon brought me here in his car, which means there's a road. I just have to follow it until I see another house.

I step into the tall grass, sweeping my flashlight around when I leave the sphere of light from the porch. It's surprisingly chilly, and I'm still only wearing that yellow sundress, my arm prickling with goosebumps. It's fine. I'm sure I'll warm up soon enough.

My flashlight beam glides across the metal shed I saw from my room, and that weird sick feeling in my stomach surges again. I feel like something's watching me in the darkness.

I keep going.

And then I hear a soft, low hum.

"Hello?" I call out stupidly, flashlight dancing on the grass ahead. Is it frogs or insects? But no, it sounds mechanical.

And then something catches in the flashlight. Thin, silver wires.

The sickness in my stomach plummets and all I feel now is a cold, overwhelming dread—

Because stretching out in front of me, dividing me from the swamp, is a towering fence humming with electricity.

CHAPTER THIRTEEN

JAXON

Well, that was stupid. But it seems I've found a way to enjoy dying.

Coming from Charlotte squeezing my trachea shut with the same chain I used to imprison her was transcendent. The grim, violent determination on her face as she wrapped the chain around her forearm and pulled—biceps bulging, lips parted with exertion? Gorgeous. Fucking gorgeous. The only way it would have been better is if she had been riding me while she did it, her cunt wet from my sloppy, eager kisses.

I'm dead, technically. Everything in my body is still. It always feels fucking odd, this part, to be floating in this technical death Hunters get before we revive. Six deaths and the stillness in my chest still unnerves me. Everything feels heavy, like I'm made of lead.

Strangulation is a fast recovery. With my experience, it'll probably take a couple of months, although I'll need to conjure up the will to drag myself downstairs and outside to burrow myself in the dirt, the way my dad taught me to do anytime we died. You heal faster underground. I also don't want the authorities finding my body and sending it to the coroner's office.

Because they will be out here, sooner or later. Charlotte will figure out some way to get through my electric fence and she'll go to the cops and tell them everything. I fucked up, no doubt about it. It just felt so damn good, her killing me while I stroked myself to completion. *Way* better than dying usually does.

But there was also another reason I let her keep going—I saw something while she was killing me. An electric shimmer in the air that I only get whenever I'm around one of my own kind.

Which is *impossible*. She's human. She smells like a human and acts like a human. Hunters can recognize Hunters, and I would have sensed her as such the second she walked into Bandit's. Earlier, even. I would have tasted the fire in her blood and the adrenaline of another killer moving into my space.

There was none of that. She walked in like prey.

Death delusion, I think, something I've heard other Hunters talk about but not something I've ever experienced myself. But that has to be it, doesn't it? The truth is I was so turned on that I let her kill me even though it was stupid as hell, and that weird electricity arcing between us was just wishful thinking on my part. Because it was *profoundly* stupid of me to die, even an easy death like strangulation.

Now she'll escape. She'll tell the cops that Edie is still alive, and fuck knows what Sawyer will do to protect his girl from getting found out.

Don't let him kill her before I revive, I think in the Abyss of my mind, speaking the language of the gods. I can feel them stirring nearby, the Unnamed and my Guardian both. Listening, even if they don't respond.

I don't feel like dragging myself downstairs. I want to sit with the memory of Charlotte murdering me. One last gift we gave each other. I gave her freedom; she gave me a fucked-up Hunter's sort of affection.

I do pull myself under the bed, though. Ambrose told me once that being covered can trick whatever magic it is that brings us back, make it think we're underground. Every little bit helps until I make the journey downstairs to finish out my revival.

The chain scrapes against the floorboards as I pull myself across the floor. Time doesn't mean much when you're dead. It expands and contracts all at once. So who knows how long it takes. A minute, an hour, a day. By the time I'm done, all I know is I'm in a cramped, dark place, and coolness seeps up through the floorboards. It's the only thing I can really feel right now, except for my own stillness.

Six deaths, and this was the best one even if Sawyer and Ambrose are both going to be furious with me. It'll probably stay the best one until I go to sleep for good, centuries from now. My first death was my initiation ritual, my father drawing his hunting blade across my throat when I was seventeen years old. I was in the ground for a little under a year, and when I came out, I was a full-fledged Hunter, a monster to haunt the dreams of humans.

My second death, though, was unexpected. It was in 1991, out in the endless Kuwaiti desert. I was nineteen, still an infant by Hunter standards, and had enlisted out of rebellion against my family—I decided I would let the American government exploit my nature to protect freedom or oil or whatever bullshit they were fighting for then. I didn't die in combat; almost no Americans died in combat in the First Gulf War. But I went Hunting in the desert town near the base, in a country where I didn't know the customs or the people, and I was, predictably, caught. Shot in self-defense. It wouldn't be the last time, although Charlotte's self-defense was certainly much more enjoyable.

I replay the memory for a little while, drifting in the haze of death. I can't see anything but darkness, can't smell anything but emptiness. Charlotte is a billion miles away. I can't smell her, can't hear her moving through the house or scrambling across my yard.

My worry for her lingers, though, a fragment of my living self. It'll take her some time to get through my electric fence, but she's smart and crafty, and I have no doubt she'll find a way. I doubt she found my car keys. I keep them well hidden, the way my daddy taught me. So she'll be on foot. It's ten miles before the road passes another house, and that's old man Eli's place. He might help her. More likely he won't answer the door.

So if I'm lucky, it'll be another five miles before she gets to that gas station on the highway. They'll help her. Then the cops'll find out everything she knows.

Fuck, I hope she doesn't talk her way into an actual death. A *human* death.

But there's nothing I can do now. Not in the realm of the gods. Not in the Abyss of annihilation.

I settle down into the darkness, nothing more than a soul with memories. For a little while, I sift through those memories, focusing on my now-favorite one—the squeezing and gasping, the slow deprivation of oxygen as I stroked myself closer to orgasm. I timed it just right because the explosion of pleasure tore through me right in the seconds before I passed out. Sublime.

But there's only so long I can think about my death, and I can feel my gods waiting for me in the dark. They're closest when you're in the ground, like my grandma always said. And that's true. I first met my Guardian after my father threw my corpse into a grave I dug for myself. The Unnamed I met ten years later after a drastic mistake in Dallas. It was what led me to Ambrose, and then to Sawyer. The closest things to friends I have.

Friends I betrayed by letting Charlotte kill me. I need to warn them somehow.

So I do what I was taught to do when I was very young, long before I died for the first time, which is to pray in the dark cathedral of my mind, in a language I learned before I ever learned English.

I call you, Guardian. I call, and I will listen.

But my Guardian still doesn't answer, even though I can feel its presence nearby. Something like dread tightens through my body, even though I shouldn't feel anything in this state.

The Unnamed wants to speak to me.

I call you, The One Who Cannot Be Named. I call, and I will listen.

The air shifts. I feel like I really am in a tomb, a dank place made of stone, and not stashed under my grandmother's old bed. There's a dampness on the air that makes me think of rot.

I wish I could breathe so I can take a deep breath. Wish I had a heartbeat so I can feel the blood rushing through my ears. It's always strange how much I miss anxiety when I can't feel it.

Look, the Unnamed says. ***Listen***. It sinks into me, that cold black rot, filling up my empty blood vessels with decay until I see what it sees.

Charlotte.

It sees Charlotte.

She's a blackened husk beside my fence, her yellow dress smoldering, wisps of white smoke floating up toward the starry sky.

No, I think before I can stop myself. I know the Unnamed is mocking me from the way the rot curdles in my veins.

Then I see her again. This time, she's trudging along the side of Guillmar Road, the sky that pearly grey of early dawn. I feel, briefly, all the aches of her body, her burning feet and sore muscles. But I also see what she doesn't: a rattlesnake coiled in the grass. Docile from the cold, yes, but she steps right on it and it reacts anyway, sinking its fangs into her ankle.

Charlotte screams and falls into the tall golden grass and time passes and she dies there, because Guillmar Road is always empty, especially this time of year.

Why are you showing me this? I ask the Unnamed in the dark caverns of my thoughts, the language of the gods reverberating through my skull. ***Are you going to kill her?***

It doesn't answer. Only shows me another image. My house, Charlotte dead. But not from the electrical fence. She's splayed across my porch and riddled with bullet holes, the blood blooming like roses across her chest.

This one bothers me the most of all. It makes no sense. Who could have shot her out here, on this side of the fence? On my property? MeeMaw and Papa are somewhere in South America. I have no idea where Dad is, but if he killed her, it wouldn't be with a gun.

Watch, says the Unnamed.

I see all three visions at once. All three futures, I think, all three ways Charlotte can die by some hand that's not my own.

Is this why you didn't want me to kill her? I ask, yearning for a heartbeat and breath so my body can react to all this discomfort. I don't like seeing her dead, a fact I'm only distantly aware of.

Watch, says the Unnamed.

I watch. It's not like I have much of a choice.

Charlotte charred and blackened.

Charlotte's ankle rotting away from a snakebite.

Charlotte bleeding into my feather grass.

And then, in all three visions, she gasps back to life, arching her back to sit up, all the death washing off her like black ink. My body vibrates strangely, almost like I have a heartbeat again. But it's much too soon.

I think of the electricity buzzing between us as she choked me to death.

How can she be a Hunter? I barely know how to ask this question of the Unnamed. ***She feels like prey.***

She is not prey. The Unnamed pulses through me, steady and rhythmic. The same oceanic push-pull as my heart. As my breath. ***She is ours. But suppressed. Dangerous, if she revives like this.***

The rhythm quickens. I can feel the machine of myself grinding back to life. I don't understand what's happening—not with me, not with Charlotte.

It's too soon for me to revive.

She needs a Guide before she's killed. The Unnamed's voice rasps through my thoughts and my body both. A lightning storm ignites in my head and sends white hot electricity sparking through my nerves until my limbs shake and convulse and flop against the floor. I shriek in agony, my vocal cords knitting back together so fast it's painful. It never hurts like this, reviving.

The pain is necessary if you are to revive in time. The Unnamed seems to enjoy my suffering, but I'd expect nothing less from it, the black seed that grows in the heart of all Hunters.

My heart. Sawyer's. Ambrose's.

And Charlotte's.

My neck twists, jerking my head violently sideways. The pain is blinding, worse than when I died. I feel it everywhere, a flooding surge as my blood rushes back into my veins and my lungs expand to contain my dust-choked breath. I scream and slam up against the underside of the bed. My skin feels brand new, tender and sensitive. I can smell everything in this fucking house. Mice that died in the walls. Bluberries that rolled behind the counter and rotted. The old blood out in my shed.

And my Hunter Charlotte, the sweet tangy scent of her

sweat. She's not in the house, but she hasn't made it past my fence.

She'll be there waiting, the Unnamed rasps, **when you've passed through the fire.**

And then the agony is too blazing for me to think of anything else.

CHAPTER FOURTEEN

CHARLOTTE

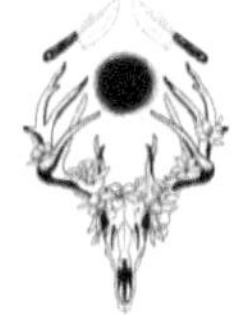

I sit in the damp, overgrown grass, my hands draped over my knees, staring at the fence as it crackles and hums in the dark. I've already walked around the perimeter and confirmed that it does, in fact, encircle the entire property, hemming me in with the house and with Jaxon's dead body.

I never found the car keys, but I did find Jaxon's car. My one consolation is that it's all scraped up from when he rammed into me on the highway. He clearly managed to drive it home, but it needs to be fixed. I hope he can't afford it.

Something tells me he can, though, if he can afford to build a fence like this. It looks like the sort of thing you'd find around a prison.

I stand up again, the hair on my arm tingling from the electricity pulsing through the air, and walk over to the garage for the third time tonight. My flashlight's in the grass from where I threw it thirty minutes ago in frustration.

The reason for that frustration is that the fence has a gate big enough for a car to pass through—but it's locked with a digital keypad. And I can't figure out the code.

I punch numbers in randomly like I've been doing for the

last hour. The keypad lights up a sickly green and buzzes every time I get the number wrong. Then a digital feminine voice chirps out, *"Incorrect key. Try again."*

Part of me hopes that if I try enough times the system will send some kind of message to the police, but I know how dumb that is. There's no way Jaxon would have this thing linked to law enforcement. I certainly wouldn't, if I was him.

When I hear, *"Incorrect key. Try again,"* for what feels like the billionth time, I screech and whirl away from the gate. The house looms up ahead, a dark silhouette against the star-smeared sky. A thin, weak light on the porch seems to create more shadows than it does anything else. There's a bug zapper, too, glowing pale blue.

Electricity, I think.

Maybe that's my way out of here. If I can cut the power, then the fence won't have electricity anymore, and maybe I can crawl over the thing.

I grab the flashlight and shine it over the fence, taking a good look at it again. It's tall, maybe seven feet, and topped with loops of barbed wire. If I climb over it, I'll probably cut myself. Assuming I can even get to the top. I'm not exactly the world's most athletic person.

But I really don't have much of a choice, do I?

For the first time since I looped that chain around Jaxon's neck, I feel like I have an actual plan and am not just reacting on some long-buried instinct. I'm still buzzing with old adrenaline and there's an ache in my arms and fingers that reminds me of what I did.

And Jaxon's face keeps flashing through my thoughts, too. The way he grinned at me when I realized what he was doing. The way he didn't even try to fight back.

That—that unsettles me more than anything.

I tell myself not to think about it, that there's no point. My only goal now is shutting off this absurd fence.

Fortunately, I find the electrical breakers fairly easily—there's a panel of them in the garage. I shut off everything, snapping the breakers to OFF one after another. But when I go back out to the fence, it's still humming and coursing with power.

"Motherfucker," I say.

It must be powered by a generator or something. Some outside source. I didn't see anything obvious when I walked the perimeter earlier, but I try again anyway, sweeping the flashlight around so that it illuminates the swamp in blurry patches: a rough glimpse of trees, a spray of palms, a burst of tall, rippling grasses. The fence keeps humming, mocking me.

But then I come up on the shed I could see from my window. It squats like a toad, the windows two black eyes that reflect my flashlight beam back into my face.

Something about it gives me a queasy feeling in my stomach, like what I felt after I attacked Jaxon.

After I *killed* Jaxon.

I peel away from the fence and approach the shed, light dancing over its side. The door has a huge padlock with another keypad. No surprise there.

But there's also a small, bare bulb shining with light. This shack still has power.

I stop and listen for a generator. All I can hear is the buzz of the fence, the howl of the wind—

A man screams.

I freeze, my skin prickling. Did I imagine that? It happened so quickly that I can't say where it came from. The swamp? The house?

No, it couldn't have come from the house.

My heart thuds furiously in my chest. I move cautiously away from the shed, swinging the light around, listening for a generator. Here, the fence disappears into the swamp, and I'm wary of going into the overgrowth in the dark.

"Shit," I whisper, turning back around. This is pointless. I can't do anything in the middle of the night. Even with the flashlight, I can barely see a few inches in front of me.

That's when I hear something.

Not another scream. A rustling. Almost like—

Footsteps?

Fear clenches in my chest, and I dive back over to the shed, pressing up against its cool, metal wall. Then I listen.

Definitely footsteps. Slow, quick, careful. But they're coming from the direction of the swamp.

I switch off my flashlight and edge carefully around the side of the shed, hardly daring to breathe. The darkness creates monsters out of everything, and the fence's constant, steady hum is the loudest sound in the world—

More rustling. And voices. Low. Soft. Male.

I freeze, squeezing my hand tight around the flashlight. Why the fuck did I assume Jaxon was acting alone? Why hadn't I realized he *must* have someone else working with him, someone who—

The humming stops.

It takes me a second to understand what I'm hearing. The fence's electrical hum had become such a constant that its absence suddenly sounds enormous. And then the implications rush through my head.

Someone turned it off.

The footsteps. The voices.

"Clear," a man says. "Cut it."

I take deep, shuddery breaths. Cops? Did the cops track me down somehow? Or did they know about Jaxon, and I just got lucky?

Are these even cops at all?

Who else would they be?

I peer around the corner of the shed, adrenaline pumping through my body. It's too dark for me to see much beyond flur-

ries of movement. But I can hear everything. The click of snapping wires. The rustle as two shadowed figures slide through
the fence that had me, five minutes ago, completely
confounded.

"Crazy motherfucker," one of them says.

"Stay alert," says the other.

Guns? Do they have guns? I'm delirious with confusion. But
at the same time, this looks like a rescue.

"Hello!" I shout, stepping around the side of the shed and
lifting my arms overhead.

The men jerk toward me. Two red dots dance across my
chest.

"Don't shoot!" I shriek, my voice ringing out into the chilly
night. "He kidnapped me! I—"

"Who the fuck are you?" one of the men says. Then, to this
partner. "Who the fuck is this?"

"He kidnapped me!" I say again, panic pounding in my head.
"Jaxon. He's a murderer. He—" I falter as the two men come
toward me, their guns still pointed at my chest.

They definitely aren't cops.

They're dressed all in black, wearing balaclavas and dark
gloves. Their guns gleam in the moonlight, the barrels dark and
gaping as they close in on me.

"Yeah," one of them says. "Yeah, we know he's a murderer."
His voice is icy. Dangerous.

"Are you here for him?" I keep my eyes fixed on the guns.
"Because I—I had to get away from him. I—"

"Who are you?" the man says. I can't tell the two of them
apart, not with their faces covered. They're the same height,
same build. They even have the same Texas drawl.

"You mean my name?" I still have my hands up. And they
still have their guns trained on my chest.

The man nods.

"Charlotte Careta." My voice wavers. "I told you, Jaxon—

the man in this house—he kidnapped me. I escaped. I don't know who you are—"

"We're here for *Jaxon*," the other man snarls. Then he says to his partner, "This is a problem, isn't it?"

Me. He's talking about me.

"Jaxon's dead!" I blurt out. "I killed him! That's how I escaped!"

Both men turn to me, their eyes pale behind the black shadows of the balaclavas.

"You killed him," the man on the left says flatly.

I feel dizzy, especially every time I glance down at those sleek dark guns. "Y-yes," I stammer out. "He's in the upstairs bedroom. You can go see."

The man on the left studies me for a long time. I don't move, even though my heart is racing furiously. Then he barks out, "Watch her."

"You can't be serious!" his partner hisses. "You believe her? That she killed that fucking psycho?"

"I don't know what I fucking think," the first man says. "But we came here to take care of Jaxon Doucet. And I'm not leaving her alone until I know for sure he's dead."

Then he stalks off, leaving me along with his partner, who tightens his grip on his gun and steps toward me. His eyes glitter from behind his balaclava, and I keep my hands up, my breath tight.

"You know what he did?" the man says.

I shake my head.

"How'd you end up here?" he asks. "Why are you still alive? Everything we heard, Jaxon Doucet doesn't leave people alive."

Who are you? I want to ask, but the man still has his gun pointed at my chest. Funny, how I could be so brave around Jaxon but absolutely terrified in this moment.

Of course, Jaxon straight-up told me he wasn't going to kill me.

And he didn't.

The man's still staring at me. Waiting for an answer. I swallow and glance over at the house. The porch light has come back on. The house must be connected to a backup generator.

"Well?" The man's voice is as sharp as a knife. "Better make it good. If I can convince my partner to feel sorry for you, maybe we'll let you live."

I jerk my gaze back to him, and he laughs, cold and cruel. Even in the dark, even though I can only see a faint gleam where his eyes should be, there's something leering about the way he looks at me.

And I realize the truth I had been avoiding—that I escaped one trap and walked into another.

"I-I don't know," I tell him, lowering my arms cautiously. He doesn't say anything about it. "He ran me off the road. Knocked me out. Brought me here."

"He's crazy," the man says. "Completely batshit fucking insane."

I think about the mummified corpses in his living room. *That's not something a human like you should have ever seen.*

The way he didn't even seem to care that I was choking him to death.

"I know," I finally say.

The man snorts. "You know what he did? Killed Dennis Randall in his own home. We figure he's working for someone. The Eclipse Brotherhood, maybe."

I have no idea what this man is talking about, and no idea why he's telling me any of it. "I don't know about any of that," I finally say. "But I know he's killed people. He has bodies in his liv—"

I don't get to finish speaking, though. Because gunfire explodes behind us.

And then the screaming starts.

CHAPTER FIFTEEN

CHARLOTTE

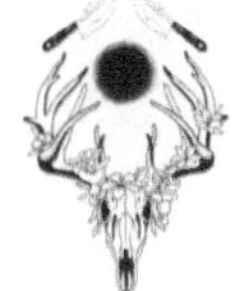

"What the fuck was that?" My babysitter whirls around, gun lifted—then seems to think better of it, because he jerks his gun back to point the barrel at my face. Immediately I shoot my hands over my head again.

"You said that motherfucker was dead," he barks. "Who else is here?"

"No one!"

I'm immediately answered by another scream. It's long, loud. Undeniably male.

"Then how do you explain that?" my captor snarls.

"I don't know!" The gun barrel leers at me. I feel dizzy. I killed my kidnapper with my bare hands only to get shot by some random asshole? How the hell is that fair? "I was kidnapped two days ago. I don't know what the fuck is going on—"

More gunfire. But worse—another long, agonized scream. Then: begging. I can't make out what he's saying, not exactly, but his desperation is more than clear.

Suddenly, lights flare on from the direction of the house,

white and blinding and throwing everything into harsh, jagged shadows. The metal shed. The man pointing a gun at me. The dead fence.

"What the *fuck?*" my babysitter spits out, his voice trembling. "You said—"

"Maybe I didn't kill him!" I shriek-whisper, panicking because the floodlights reveal a terrifying truth: his finger is on that gun's trigger. "Maybe he just—maybe he passed out and I didn't—" The man glares at me. "I was *kidnapped,*" I finish.

Screams echo across the yard.

He believes me. Or at least part of him does. That's why he's hesitating. But I'm not sure I believe myself. Because I saw Jaxon's face. His blank, empty eyes. He was dead. I'm certain of it.

"Go," my babysitter snarls, gesturing toward me with his gun. "Find out what the fuck is going on."

"No!" I shout it just as the screaming stops, so my answer is unimaginably loud.

My babysitter whispers a furious, "*Fuck,*" and then lunges at me, grabbing me around the waist and pressing the cold barrel of his gun against my temple. I choke out a sob and fight against him, but his grip is tight. Determined.

It occurs to me that I only won my fight with Jaxon because he let me.

"Come on," the man whispers in my ear, his breath hot even through the balaclava. "Let's see if you're telling the truth."

He kicks at the back of my legs, forcing me to stumble forward. I fight against him, digging my feet into the damp grass, but he's stronger and shoves me forward. The gun never breaks contact with my skin.

"I will shoot you in the head," he snarls.

He forces me around the side of the shed, and for a second, the light blinds me. All I can see is a blaze of white, like I'm staring at the sun.

Then a shape emerges. A silhouette. Tall. Strong shoulders. A sturdy build. Walking toward us in slow, lopsided steps.

"Let her go."

I scream because it's Jaxon's voice. After the last forty-eight hours, I'd recognize it anywhere.

"She said she killed you!"

The cold steel of the gun disappears from my temple, and for a second I think my babysitter's actually going to listen to him, that he's going to let me go. Escape a trap, fall into another, then get thrown right back into the first.

But no. He's pointing the gun at Jaxon now.

Jaxon keeps moving toward us. He's dragging something. A sack. A—

Body.

A headless body. He's dragging it by the arm, and I can see the bloody, ruined stump where the head should be.

My babysitter fires his gun. It's not pointed at my temple anymore, but the stupid thing is still right next to my head, and I feel the blast deep in my ear. Everything rings.

Jaxon says something and laughs, but it sounds like he's underwater, and I can't make out his words.

My babysitter fires again. Jaxon doesn't even react.

How is he not hitting him?

I sob again, and then Jaxon flings the body toward us, an assault of blood and bone and degradation. Something hot and wet splatters across my face. My babysitter roars in terror, but he does let me go, shoving me aside and firing his gun in rapid blasts. Blood bursts up. I don't think it's Jaxon's. I also don't care. I dive sideways and run as fast as I can, looping around the shed until I come to the place where the two men cut a hole in the fence.

Behind me come more terrible, protracted screams, then a wet, rhythmic thumping.

I duck through the gap in the fence without thinking—the

fucking power's back on, what if it's electrified again? But it's not. It must be connected to some source separate from the house. I don't dwell on it. I'm focused on one thing.

Getting the hell out of here.

I plunge into the thicket on the other side of the fence. Tree branches and vines and grasses and other unidentifiable plants—at least, I hope they're plants—claw at me, like they're trying to suck me deeper into the swamp. I splash into a shallow pool of stagnant water, the mud squelching into my shoes. But those screams keep echoing behind me, and that's enough to drive me forward into the thick, muggy darkness.

The screams cut off suddenly, just like they did before, and a cold, sick emptiness fills up my stomach. The silence is worse somehow, because it seems to amplify my footsteps as I splash deeper into the swamp. Every splash, every rustle. I hear things moving in the dark, and I'm not sure if they're me.

The road, I think. *There has to be a road nearby. Get to it.*

The fence gate, and therefore the driveway, had been to my right, so I veer in that direction, throwing my hands up to block the woody vines crisscrossing over my path. I can't believe how dense this swamp is, so close to Jaxon's property. His house feels a million miles away.

But it's not. *He's* not.

He's still alive.

I can't think about that right now. I was panicked; I must have imagined seeing his blank eyes. He probably only passed out just long enough for me to escape. Maybe he was stalking me this whole time and only got interrupted by those two men—

Whoever the hell they were. *Dennis Randall*, they said, which sounds familiar. A name I've heard before. I can't place it right now, though. I just need to get to the road.

And then I hear something. An echo of my footsteps.

I freeze, trying desperately to still my panicked breaths. They sound as loud as a hurricane.

Silence. Or at least as much silence as a swamp can muster, even in the middle of a winter.

I take one hesitant step backward, moving slow as molasses and still managing to step on something that snaps in the dark. I freeze, my body tense with anxiety.

"Charlotte."

It's him. Jaxon. He says my name like he's caught me doing something I shouldn't.

"Charlotte, you can't run through the marsh at night."

Footsteps echo between the trees. Every now and then, there's a rustle of leaves, a splash of watery mud. I back up, two quick steps, and slam against the wide, smooth trunk of a tree. I can barely see anything. Just shadows braiding through more shadows.

"You're just going to get lost out here." His voice rises and falls with the damp wind. "I know it a lot better than you do."

He's close. I can sense him crashing through the under-brush, not even trying to hide his approach.

Well, then I won't hide my escape.

I take off running, plunging into the darkness, my head ducked to avoid the attacks from all the plants that call this place home. Behind me, Jaxon curses.

Then he's running too.

"Fuck," I whisper, pumping my legs to go faster. It's not easy. I'm not much of a runner to begin with and running in a muddy marsh isn't exactly something you can train for in San Jose. I claw away the vines and palm leaves and splash through the thick, squelching mud. A branch slaps at my arms like a cypress tree is trying to catch me on Jaxon's behalf.

"Charlotte!" he shouts. He's close. I swear I him breathing. Or maybe it's my own panting breath. "You're going to fucking hurt yourself."

"What do you care?"

He laughs, cold and cruel. A killer's laugh.

I veer sideways and run straight into some kind of tangled bramble, shrieking as the thorns slash through my bare skin and stick like Velcro to my dress's fabric. I flail my way through, tiger stripes of pain all over my arms and legs, only to step into a black puddle of water—

And fall.

I hit the puddle with a splash, and filthy, muddy water soaks my hair and dress. Jaxon's footsteps loom closer. The motherfucker doesn't even sound like he's running.

"You okay?" he calls out.

"Fuck you!" I try to stand up, but the bottom of the puddle is slick with mud and loose rocks, and I lose purchase and fall sideways—

Right into Jaxon's arms.

"Got you," he whispers into my ear, and it doesn't sound like a threat.

Not exactly.

"Let me go!" I squirm against him, but he just tightens his grip around my waist, his big arms impossibly strong. And covered in something wet and warm and sticky that's definitely *not* mud.

"I don't think so." He hauls me out of the water and presses me up against a nearby tree, close enough that I can see him even in the dark. His hair is loose, hanging in sweat-damp strands around his face, which is splattered with gore. He reaches up and brushes my wet hair out of my eyes, and his hands are black with blood. It streaks across my cheek.

"Don't touch me!" I jerk away from him and choke back a surge of nausea, then try to rub the blood from my skin.

"Don't do that," he says softly, smoothing more of my hair away from my face. "It looks good on you."

I slap his hand away and glare up at him, trying to mask the terror surging through my system. He matches my glare with an intensity of his own. Hot. Burning. Not angry, though.

In fact, it reminds me of the expression he gave me right before he died, and my pussy reacts in a way it absolutely, positively shouldn't.

"What did you do?" I whisper, flattening my back against the tree like I might sink through it and disappear out the other side.

Jaxon tilts his head a little, his eyes never leaving mine. He smooths my hair again, then keeps running his blood-sticky hand down the side of my neck, over my shoulder, along my bare arm. His touch sends electricity jolting through my body, but I still jerk away.

"Why is there so much blood?" I add.

Jaxon grins. Leans a little closer to me. "I killed two men with my bare hands."

My stomach twists, and the scene from earlier flashes through my memories. "That's not possible," I spit out, even though I saw the evidence. "You—that—" I swallow, and Jaxon just keeps watching me. Keeps grinning. "There was—*You threw a corpse at me.*"

Saying it out loud is even more absurd.

"I know. Sorry about that, by the way. I wasn't aiming *at* you."

I shake my head wildly. Jaxon's so close to me, his body hemming me up against the tree, and I'm reacting to it in a way I shouldn't, the same way I reacted when I woke up coming with his head between my legs.

The way I reacted when I killed him.

You clearly didn't kill him.

"You did not decapitate that man with your bare hands." My voice shudders. Even though he's clearly strong enough to fling a grown man's corpse through the air.

Jaxon cups one blood-sticky hand around my neck, sliding

his thumb softly over the tender flesh of my throat. I stiffen, drop my eyes to his neck.

Are those bruises ringing where the chain had been? No, it's blood. It's too dark to see anything else.

"You're not asking the question I expected," he says softly.

I immediately jerk my eyes up to meet his. They're black. Soulless. He keeps thumbing my neck, the touch gentle enough that it feels like a lover's caress, not a murder threat.

Even if he is smearing more cooling blood across my skin.

"Let me go," I whisper.

Jaxon stares at me. "I can't," he says. "Especially not now."

He presses into me, still pinning me up against the tree by my throat. His thigh slides between my legs. His breath is warm on my skin. Warm. Hot. *Alive*.

"Please," I whisper, even as I sink down on his knee, sighing a little when his rough, blood-soaked jeans make contact with my clit.

You do not like this. You do not like him.

But to my horror, Jaxon notices, because he makes a surprised little noise in the back of his throat. And then he smiles again and presses his mouth to my ear.

"You killed me so sweet, Charlotte Careta," he says softly. "And now I want to return the favor."

CHAPTER SIXTEEN

JAXON

The adrenaline from killing two men so soon after my revival is still surging through my system. I feel stronger than I have in years. More powerful. Hell, I ripped that one guy's head from his shoulders, unabashedly moaning as his blood soaked over me. The other's head I bashed to a pulp against the side of my shed.

But neither of them compares to having Charlotte pinned up against the tree, her hot, wet cunt pressing down on my leg.

Claim her, whispers the Unnamed. It wants me to fuck her. I *want* to fuck her, desperately. I just don't think she wants to fuck me.

Especially since my dumb ass implied I want to kill her.

"Y-you said you can't." Charlotte stares up at me with glassy, terrified eyes and tries to jerk away, the scent of her fear an absolutely devastating aphrodisiac. I grip her thick right hip with my free hand, pinning her down in three places at once: throat, hip, cunt.

"Yeah, that came out wrong." I cringe, hearing myself say it, but something flickers across Charlotte's face. I massage her throat, rubbing my thumb over her frantic, fluttering pulse. She stiffens again, the sweet honeysuckle scent of her fear nearly overwhelming me.

I want to kiss her so badly. I know what her pussy tastes like, and now I want to taste her mouth. But I also want her to kiss me back, to lick the blood off my neck and run her tongue over the faint, sensitive scar where she killed me, the chain digging deep into my flesh.

"I'm not going to literally kill you." I brush my lips against her cheeks as I talk, breathing in more of her scent. "Although even if I did—you'd be fine."

"What?" She pulls away from me again, more forcefully this time. I let her neck go. Not the rest of her. I can't help but notice that the movement has her grinding her pussy down on my leg, and I return that favor with delight, pressing my thigh up against her until she gasps and bites her bottom lip.

"It's complicated." I knead the flesh at her hip the way I did when I was eating her out earlier, and the memory makes my cock strain against my pants. I didn't think I could get any harder after dispatching those two interlopers, whoever the fuck they were. I'll worry about them later. Charlotte, my Hunter who is not a Hunter, feels much more important right now.

Much more *warm*.

Much more *alive*.

Charlotte searches my face, her pupils blown out. Is it to see me in the dark? Is it because I'm still grinding my knee up against her pussy, and she's rolling her hips in return, ever so slightly? I think it might be both.

"You were dead."

She says it suddenly and very, very softly, like she didn't intend for me to hear it. I do, though. All my senses are on high alert.

"Yeah," I say. "That's why I said you killed me."

And then, before she can react and before I can talk myself out of it, I kiss her.

For a moment, neither of us move. I don't try to deepen the kiss, but she doesn't pull away, either.

And then she tilts her head and parts her lips and kisses me back, the tip of her tongue pressing into my mouth. I'm so stunned I almost forget to react. But then my body takes over, and I slide my tongue over hers, licking her and tasting her. Devouring her in a brand new way. I force myself to go slow so I don't seem too eager, and it seems like the right move because Charlottes makes a soft whimpering noise and draws her hand around my neck, holding my head as she deepens the kiss and ruts against my leg.

Then she breaks it, gasping. All her living blood and heat rise to the surface of her skin, and she stares up at me, eyes wide with shock. Confusion.

"I killed you," she says breathlessly.

"And you did it so fucking beautifully."

I capture her in another kiss. I don't want to talk. I don't want to explain what it means to be a Hunter or try to figure out how she got to be twenty-nine years old without knowing what she is. I don't want to deal with the headless corpses in my yard.

I want to fuck a living woman for the first time in my life.

"How—?" She pulls away from me just long enough to start to ask the question, and I kiss her again to keep her from finishing it. The question melts into a low, satisfied moan as she rides my thigh, her hands clenching at my blood-soaked shirt.

But Charlotte's persistent. After a few seconds, she stops the kiss and jerks away from me, her hand on my chest to hold me in place. She doesn't have a Hunter's strength; I could overpower her easily, just as I could have when she was killing me. But the gods never lie, and I saw the shimmer in those moments before my death. I felt the connection of seeing another one of my kind.

It doesn't make any sense, but I recognized her as I died. It was the last thought I had as I slipped into oblivion, before my gods woke me back up.

"Stop it," she says. "Stop distracting me. I *can't*—Not with *you*—"

"Why not?" Because she's still humping my leg, smearing her arousal with my latest victims' blood and the muddy water from the creek.

"You *kidnapped* me. You—" Her eyes flash. "You assaulted me."

Embarrassed heat flushes into my cheeks. "I didn't want to disappoint you," I mutter.

She goes still, something softening in her expression. I push her hair back again, not sure what that softening means.

"I'm so confused," she whispers. "You—" She pulls her hands away from me and looks down at them, dark with blood. "Why do I like this?"

I hesitate. I know why. She's a Hunter. But I really, really don't want to explain it right now. I need to put my cock in her pussy. I need to feel the inside of her.

"That's complicated, too," I finally say, pushing up the skirt of her dress so I can access her panties for the third time tonight. She gasps a little and settles back against the tree.

She also doesn't stop me as I slide my fingers into her panties and then between her folds.

"Tell me to stop," I order, my cock throbbing at how wet she is. How slippery. How *warm*.

She's going to feel so fucking good.

Her lips part. I almost think she's going to say it. But instead, she just stares at me defiantly.

I pull out my soaked finger and rub it over her clit. *That*, at least, I know how to find after years of exploring with the dead.

Even if they never react the way she does right now, keening and bucking against my hand.

"Take your panties off," I tell her, still working her clit.

"W-why?" Her question is jagged. Sharp. She rolls her hips in time with my touch.

"Because I just killed two men without a weapon and I'm covered in blood and I need to fuck you right now."

The words come out before I can stop them. I fully expect Charlotte to pull away.

Instead, her clit pulses hot against my fingers. I'm uncovering all the strange delights of living women this evening, aren't I?

"If you want them off," she says darkly, still fucking my hand, "then you can take them off."

That's the only invitation I need. I grab the silky fabric with both hands and pull. My revival has me strong enough to rip a man apart; Charlotte's panties shred like tissue.

"Fuck," she groans, slumping back against the tree.

I toss the tattered fabric away and palm my cock over my jeans, adjusting it before I drag down the zipper. Charlotte watches me with hooded eyes, her hips rolling a little against the air, her skin and dress both streaked with dark smears of blood. I know that once I'm inside her, I'm not going to last long.

"Touch yourself," I tell her as I pull out my cock.

She gives me another one of those defiant looks and I nearly come in my hand. But then her gaze drops down to where I'm gripping myself, fingers tight around my erection.

She licks her lips. Slides her hand between her legs. Looks back up to meet my eyes.

"I shouldn't do this," she says even as she runs her fingers in fast, frantic circles over her clit, widening her legs and bracing her back up against the tree.

"Why not?" I step closer to her, willing myself not to stroke my cock. I'm afraid that if I do, I'll come.

Charlotte just stares at me, her chest rising and falling as she works her clit. "You know why not."

I grin at that. And then I throw out what little restraint I've been clinging to because none of it matters. The only important thing is fucking her hot, living cunt.

I move like I'm Hunting prey: clearing the space between us in a blink, grabbing both her wrists and pinning them over her head with one hand. She stares up at me, lust burning through her gaze. Then I hook her knee with my free arm and jerk her wide. Charlotte groans, arching up toward me.

"Keep your hands right there," I growl into her ear.

She smiles. "Or what?"

I squeeze her wrists more tightly, making her moan. "I won't let you come."

Her eyes flash, and I let her go, keeping our gazes locked as I reach down to grip the base of my cock. Charlotte curls her hands into fists, but she doesn't drop them.

"I see you want to come," I say, praying to my gods that I'll be able to make her do it again.

She doesn't say anything, just tilts her hips a little toward me.

An invitation.

I press my swollen, sensitive cockhead against her pussy. She's drenched, and I slide in too easy—so easy I have to brace my thigh muscles to stop myself from plunging my full length inside her. I want to tease her. Torture her. Even if it means torturing myself.

"Good girl," I mutter, dropping my hand away from my cock so I can run it over her hip, the side of her waist, then over her tits, feeling her nipples through the fabric of her dress.

"I thought you were going to fuck me," she gasps.

"Is that what you want?" I keep massaging her tits. Looking her straight in the eyes. I want to hear her say it.

Charlotte glares at me. I give her another inch, and I can't believe I'm pulling off this self-control, because her fiery, soaking-wet cunt is like nothing I've ever felt. It's almost as good as killing.

"I'll end this right now," I tell her, releasing her tits so I can reach up to wrap my hand around her throat again. Charlotte moans softly, fear flickering across her features.

And somehow, her pussy gets even wetter.

"Tell me," I rasp into her ear, hooking her leg around my hip. "I want to hear you say it."

"Say... what?" she gasps.

I tighten my grip on her throat. I've got no intention of choking her anywhere as tight as she choked me. But I like reminding her that I could.

And given the frantic, fluttering pulses in her pussy, she does too.

"You know what." I speak softly into her ear. "Tell me you want me to fuck you."

She whimpers. I nibble at her earlobe, then kiss along her jawline, licking away the blood I smeared there earlier. "Say it," I whisper into her skin. "Say it, and I'll make you come so hard you won't give a shit that I'm a murderer."

I think it was the Unnamed that compelled me to say that, because it's like I stumbled across the magic words. Charlotte jerks her hips, lifts her chin in defiance, and says what I've been waiting to hear.

"I want—" She spits the words out like she's fighting them. "I want you to fuck me."

And then I do.

CHAPTER SEVENTEEN

CHARLOTTE

Jaxon has the biggest cock I've ever seen in real life, and it's currently buried so deep in my pussy it hurts.

It hurts, but in a way that feels good, too. Like being whipped by a flogger or spanked hard on my ass. The pain heightens the pleasure somehow.

The blood smearing between us heightens the pleasure, too. So does the knowledge of what Jaxon did to those two men.

And I don't care.

I don't fucking care.

Jaxon pulls his cock halfway out and then slams into me again, eyes rolling back in his head, his groan deep and throaty. I shriek at the starburst of pain and then, because there's clearly something deeply wrong with me, I gasp out, "Again."

He chuckles and looks at me, his gaze unfocused with pleasure. He still has his fingers curled around my throat, and I'm still holding my hands overhead. Doing as he asked. Part of me is afraid if I drop them, he won't just stop me from coming—he'll kill me.

Another part of me, hungry and gasping, wants to try it and see.

"You like that?" he mutters as he pulls his length almost entirely out of my cunt. I nod and brace myself.

He bottoms out again, and I scream in pain and pleasure, my voice echoing up into the trees.

"So do I," he whispers into my ear.

And then he starts to fuck me for real, his thrusts firm and fast, one hand around my throat and the other spreading my leg wide so there's room for him between my thighs.

And I love it. I love every second of it. I fuck him back as best I can, rolling my hips in time with each of his sharp thrusts. I can't think about what any of this means, that I'm letting this murderer and kidnapper fuck me. That he's about to make me come again—and this time, I can't even claim that I didn't want it.

"You're so wet for me," he rasps, and there's a kind of wonderment in his voice, his breath warm on my ear.

I don't respond, just arch my back like I can pull him deeper into my body. My arms ache from holding them overhead. His hand around my throat is almost uncomfortably firm. His cock is splitting me in two.

And I don't want any of it to end.

"Say something," he orders, plowing into me. "Tell me why you're so wet."

I groan, legs trembling. He tightens his fingers and I lift my gaze to him, daring him to keep going.

"Is this why?" he whispers, squeezing my throat a little tighter. Tight enough that it's hard to breathe. Tight enough that the pleasure consuming me from the inside out burns that much hotter.

"No," I spit out, which isn't exactly true.

He grunts and thrusts into me harder, slamming my spine up against the tree. The smooth, damp bark rubs against my bare ass. The quickly-drying blood seems to glue our bodies together. And I slide closer and closer to coming.

"Well?" Jaxon pants, each word punctuated by the searing heat of his cock. "Why are you so wet for me?"

I hook my leg around him and drag him up against my belly. He groans and kisses me, his tongue plunging into my mouth, his teeth snagging on my bottom lip. His other hand joins the first, his long artist's fingers wrapping around my neck and squeezing until my vision goes black at the edges and stars dance across the night.

"Thought you—" I choke out, trembling and shaking and rolling my hips so my clit rubs against the base of his big cock. "Thought you—can't kill me—"

"I'm not going to kill you." His eyes flash. "I'm going to make you come."

I whimper, although the noise strangles in my constricted throat.

He is going to make me come. I can feel it, the pressure building around my neck and in my clit, and I jerk my hips against him, as desperate for release as I am for air. All I can see is Jaxon's blood-spattered face; his wild, fiery eyes; his twisted, grinning mouth.

"Come for me," he snarls, tightening his hands around my throat. "Come on, cher. I want to feel this pussy co—"

It hits me all at once, an onslaught of deliciously painful pleasure. My entire body convulses, and Jaxon loosens his grip around my throat. As soon as the air fills my lungs I proclaim my ecstasy with a scream that would be indistinguishable if he were killing me.

I'm barely aware of what's happening. There's only pleasure and breath and Jaxon's thick cock still slamming up into my pussy. Then, suddenly, there's not even that, because Jaxon's wrenched himself out of me. I start to protest—my pussy's still contracting wildly from my orgasm—but Jaxon puts his hand on the top of my head and shoves me down so I'm kneeling on the soft, wet ground.

I'm eye-level with his cock, swollen and wet and gleaming.

"Open," he orders, jerking my head back by my hair, and I'm so drunk and delirious from that monster of an orgasm that I do exactly as he says. He groans as his cum erupts out in thick spurts, coating my tongue and lips with a thick, pungent saltiness. Then, as roughly as he pushed me down, he drags me back up, using my hair as a handle, and kisses me, swirling his tongue over mine. Tasting himself. Tasting me.

It's the hottest fucking thing I've ever done.

Then, abruptly, he pulls away, wiping his mouth with the back of his hand. For all his searing eye contact while he was inside me, now he seems—almost embarrassed. He ducks his head, his hair falling across his face, and he looks out at the dark, shivery swamp. He's a shadow in the darkness.

I swallow what's left of his cum and wipe my lips, still feeling breathless and lightheaded. But I also feel cautious. On guard.

Jaxon mutters something.

"What's that?" The question comes out smaller than I intended.

He looks over at me like a startled deer. "Nothing."

I fuss with my dress, rearranging the skirt around my sticky, blood-streaked thighs. Jaxon's watching me, something I feel more than I actually see. "You said something," I tell him. "It wasn't nothing."

A pause. The weight of the swamp bears down on us. Then he says, "It was a prayer."

This is the last thing I expect. I blink out my surprise. Jaxon shifts, rustling the plants. "We should go back."

"You *pray?*"

Jaxon's stare is heavy in the dark. "Not to the god you're thinking of, no. But yes. I pray."

"Then what god—"

"Don't worry about it." His voice is sharp-edged. A warning. "We need to go back to the house."

Suddenly, I'm plunged back into reality. I can't go back there. I'm *free*.

"No."

Jaxon moves so fast that it's like he doesn't move at all. One minute he's in the shadows. The next he has me pinned up against the tree by the wrists, my hands pressed flat against the trunk. He glares at me, his expression twisted and terrifying.

"We need," he says in a slow, even voice, "to go back to the house."

I try to twist away from him, but it's no use. He presses his forehead against mine, squeezes my wrists a little tighter.

"I'll drag you back there if I have to," he mutters.

I lash out with my leg and knee him in the balls. He grunts, grins, twists me around so my belly presses against the trunk instead of my back.

"Stop fighting me," he says, low and terrifying. A reminder that he's a killer. No amount of orgasms is going to change that. "I'm not letting you go."

"Why not?" I try to look at him over my shoulder, my cheek pressed against the tree. He looks like the monster he is—hair wild, eyes burning, blood smeared across his skin.

I try not to think about the blood smeared across my skin, too.

"I can't," he says darkly. "Now, you can come willingly and behave yourself, and I won't chain you to the bed again."

I consider spitting in his face, but I suspect he'd enjoy it.

"And if I don't come willingly?"

He rolls his eyes. "No matter where you go in this swamp, I'll find you. I know it better than you can possibly imagine." His lips curl back, and he shows me his white, shiny teeth, like he's a predator. He *is* a predator. "And then we'll be right back to where we are now. So you might as well make it easy on yourself."

I want to fight back. I really, really do. But I've already seen what he's capable of. Stalking me in the pitch-black wilderness. Tearing men's heads from their bodies.

Coming back from the fucking dead.

"If I go with you," I say. "Will you tell me what the fuck is going on?"

His fingers loosen around my wrists, and he steps back. I hate myself for it, but I miss the dangerous press of his body against mine. "I'll explain why I'm not dead," he says.

Which is fair enough, but there's more that I want to know, too.

"Tell me where Edie is." I turn around to face him. His shoulders hitch, and he looks out at the swamp again. Brushes his hair out of his eyes.

"I can't do that just yet," he says, after a beat. "I'll tell you what I can. She really is safe, by the way."

"More or less?" It's mocking, the way it comes out.

"She's safe," he says, more firmly. "The person she's with—he won't let anything bad happen to her. Okay? Happy?"

"Who's she with?" I'm getting more and more irritated by his constant games.

But Jaxon just gives an exasperated sigh and shoves his hands through his hair. There's none of that flirtatious coyness from dinner earlier. "I can't tell you that," he says. "Really. I can't. Frankly, I've told you more than I should. Now come on, before I throw you over my shoulders and carry you back."

I just scoff at that, gesture down at my plus-size body. Jaxon, though, flashes me an annoyingly handsome grin and says, "Don't make me try it."

"I'm absolutely going to make you try it." I cross my arms over my chest and challenge him. He's certainly strong enough to lift me for a few minutes, but there's no way he can carry me through the woods. "You can't think I'd just go *willingly*—"

And then my feet are off the ground. For one stupid second, I think I'm flying. Then I think he's hit me. Then I realize he's tossed me over his shoulder like a sack of grain.

"If you fight me," he says, stomping into the swamp. "I'll drag you behind me. And that won't be much fun for either of us."

"Put me down!" I shriek, kicking at his chest as the tree where he fucked me disappears into the shadows. He has one arm around my waist, which he tightens against my wriggling. The other he presses brazenly against my ass.

"Stop squirming." He ducks a little as he marches into the overgrowth, and I realize when I feel a tree branch graze across the top of my ass that he did that for my benefit. In fact, he takes a strange, meandering path, like he's trying to avoid all the branches that scraped and clawed at me when I ran into the swamp in the first place.

"How are you lifting me?" I gasp out.

"You're not that heavy."

"I'm heavier than you think."

He chuckles, a sound that I feel in my belly when his shoulders shake. "Charlotte. I'm carrying you. I know exactly how heavy you are."

I slump against his back. I feel defeated. Not just because I'm getting carried back to my prison. But because—

Honestly?

I really don't mind that much.

CHAPTER EIGHTEEN

CHARLOTTE

Jaxon carries me all the way back to his house. He doesn't even sound out of breath.

"How are you doing this?" I twist my head to try and look at him but can't see much. Just the swamp plants, clearer in the lightening sky. We've been out all night.

"I'm a Hunter," he says, like that answers anything.

"So what?" I try to lift myself up, but he smacks my ass, hard enough to feel good, and I slump back down. "Lots of people are hunters," I continue. "And they couldn't carry a—"

"We're here." He stops abruptly. "I'm gonna let you down now. If you run—"

His grip tightens suggestively around my waist.

"I'll catch you."

Heat flushes to my cheeks. And elsewhere. "You made your point."

"Did I?" He crouches down and gently slides me off his shoulder. When my feet touch the ground, I straighten up and find myself looking him right in the eye. He's close enough to kiss.

"I'm not running, am I?" I am thinking about it. The sun's

coming up. I'll be able to see. If I could just get to the road, I wouldn't have to worry about getting lost in the swamp.

But he has a car. And he's fast even on foot. Faster than me.

"Not yet." His eyes glitter, and I both hate and love the way he looks at me like he's going to devour me whole.

Then he pushes past me, heading back toward the house. I turn and watch him, hesitating. We're at the same place in the fence where I escaped, the hole in the wires big and jagged. I doubt he'll be able to fix that anytime soon. Maybe I can wait a day. Get his guard down. Then I could—

"Don't make me pick you up again!" Jaxon shouts as he ducks through the fence. He glances over at me, grinning a little, and my clit throbs with a sudden, unexpected need. Well, maybe not totally unexpected.

His tossing me over his shoulder like that *was* pretty hot.

"I'm coming," I mutter, following him through the fence. The yard looks strange in the grayish dawn light. Unfamiliar, like I wasn't just here an hour ago, cowering in the dark with a gun in my face.

The gun in question is still here though, glinting in the grass.

Its owner is here, too, a dark misshapen lump. Jaxon walks over to the body and crouches beside it, studying it thoughtfully. He nudges it and rolls it over, the arms flopping like a rag doll.

I expect to feel something, seeing that. Disgust. Horror. I want to retch and vomit into the grass. But I just stand there, the cool morning wind blowing my skirt around my knees like I'm not covered in that man's blood.

Jaxon stands back up and tilts his head toward the shed. "I need to get him in there."

"And you expect me to help you?"

Jaxon looks over at me, his hair blowing in his eyes. "No," he says. "I'm just telling you."

Why the hell would he tell me something like that? I cross my arms over my chest, trying to ignore the grimy, sticky feeling of the blood on my skin. "Who was he?" I finally say, my mouth dry.

Jaxon steps over the body and walks through the overgrown grass. I think he's ignoring me at first, but then he leans down and picks something up off the ground.

A balaclava-covered head.

"Not sure." He peels the balaclava away and throws it on top of the body. I feel myself drifting closer to him, pulled forward by—curiosity, I think. I don't know.

I feel so strange.

Jaxon holds the head up, frowning at it the way he did the body. All I can see is a thatch of messy brown hair and the jagged, red cut where the neck was. "Don't recognize him," he says, turning the head around to show me the face, like he thinks I might.

It's horrifying, the way the man's mouth is twisted up in fear, his stiff tongue lolling out. His wide, unseeing eyes—so much like Jaxon's when I left him upstairs.

I look away, heart racing. "I don't, either."

Jaxon chuckles. "Yeah, I didn't think you would." He throws the head like it's a soccer ball and it lands beside the body with a heavy, vaguely wet thump. "Did they say anything to you?"

I jerk my head up, startled, as he ambles back over to me, his hand shoved in the pockets of his jeans. The wind blows his hair around.

I hate that I notice his hair.

"Why would they say anything to me?" I ask darkly.

Jaxon shrugs. "When I came out here, they were pointing their guns at you. Which means they weren't here to rescue you."

I don't say anything.

"I have some suspicions about who they might be," he continues. "So I'm curious what they said."

Why should I help you? The question hangs right on the tip of my tongue. But Jaxon's staring at me with this sweet, puppy-dog hopefulness, and I can still taste the saltiness of him. God, I haven't been fucked that good in—

Well, ever, I don't think.

He's a killer, I tell myself. And probably something more, given that I thought I was a killer, too, even though my victim is currently standing in front of me.

"Nothing?" He raises an eyebrow.

I sigh. "They said you killed someone in his house. And that you were working for some group. A gang, maybe? They told me the name, but I don't remember what it was." I push my hand through my hair. "I was a little distracted."

Jaxon nods thoughtfully, his expression kind of distant and far-off. "Dennis Randall," he murmurs.

"Yeah." I blink in surprise. "Yeah, that was it. The guy they said you killed—"

"I did kill him," Jaxon says plainly. "A few weeks ago."

I'm not sure how to respond to that.

"He was a drug dealer," he adds. "Heroin. PCP. He was probably involved with human trafficking, too. Those guys usually are."

"Is that why you killed him?"

Jaxon looks at me, his eyes as deep and strange as the ocean. "No."

He turns away, leaving me standing there, struck dumb. For a minute all I can do is gape at him as he picks his way across the yard, heading toward the body that matches the balaclava-covered head. He bends over, studying it like he did the first.

"Then why?" I call out.

Jaxon hears me. I can tell by the way he pauses, the way he tilts his head toward me. But he doesn't answer.

I sigh, exasperated, and stalk over the grass, taking a wide berth around the first body. This other body is all akimbo from where Jaxon threw it.

"Stop doing this," I tell him. "This mysterious psycho killer shit."

Jaxon lifts his gaze to meet mine. "I am a mysterious psycho killer."

I do not let myself be frightened or charmed by that, even though I want to do both, simultaneously. "What the fuck is going on?" I ask him. "Why did you kill that guy? The drug dealer? And why—" I stop, swallow against the dryness in my throat. "I'd like some answers about the other thing," I finally say. "The—" I gesture toward the house, looming up behind him. The window into the room where he kept me.

Jaxon makes a strained coughing sound. "Right," he mutters. "Yeah. That one." He kicks at the body, making the arms flop around. "You're gonna think I'm crazy."

"I already think you're crazy."

He sighs. "Fair enough." Then he jerks his head toward the house. "You want some coffee? I'll make you some coffee. And we can—"

"Tell me!" My voice rings out through the crisp, cool morning and echoes across the swamp, loud enough that a cloud of blackbirds erupts against the pale sky. "What the fuck! Is going on!"

Jaxon at least has the wherewithal to look sheepish. "I will!" he says. "I just thought you might want some coffee on the porch while I did. It's been a long night."

I want to be pissed at him, I really do. But there's a sheepish sweetness to the way he just offered me coffee that brings me up short. It's such a contrast to how he fucked me in the woods. To what he did to those men.

He keeps charming me, and I don't like it.

"Fine," I snap. "Make me a coffee." I pause. "It better be sweet. No cream, though."

He grins. "One sweet black coffee, coming up."

I trudge over to the house, trailing behind him. It's my first time really getting a good look at the place: a big, towering Victorian mansion, the dark paint peeling off in patches. It even has a turret jutting up toward the sky. It also has a wrap-around screened-in porch, something I didn't notice when I raced out of the back door earlier. It's actually kind of nice, the porch. There's a swing and some cozy-looking wicker chairs. I collapse down on the swing. In the middle, though, so Jaxon can't sit beside me.

He disappears inside, and I wait numbly on the swing, pushing it back and forth with my feet, staring through the dark mesh at the overgrown yard. I don't let myself think about anything. I just go empty.

A few minutes later, Jaxon emerges from the house, the screen door slamming into its frame behind him. He's carrying two pretty porcelain mugs, the contents steaming in the damp, cool air.

"I put like three spoonfuls of sugar in here," he says as he hands me coffee.

I breathe in the steam. Feeling the warmth of the coffee on my hands makes me realize just how cold I am. The morning is damp and chilly. Chillier than you'd expect from Louisiana.

Jaxon drags one of the wicker chairs across from the swing and sits down. Takes a drink of his coffee.

We stare at each other.

"Start talking." Then I sip my coffee, too.

It's not exactly the Turkish coffee I drank back in California, but it's good. Strong and sweet. *Just like Jaxon*, I think for half a second before I chide myself for being stupid.

"Right," Jaxon says, shifting around. "Yeah. So—" He takes a deep breath. "You did kill me earlier tonight. Technically."

"Technically?" I shake my head, irritation bubbling up in my chest. "Will you stop dancing around and just tell me what you are? I know you were dead. I saw it. But now—" I gesture at him.

"I can't die," he finally says. "I'm—well, I'm not sure what we actually are. When I was growing up, my grandparents called us the Elect. But I've heard us called boogeymen. Hunters, too. That's the most common name for us, at least around here."

I stare at him with bafflement. "That doesn't really—explain anything."

"Because there's no way to explain it," he says. "I am what I am. I can't die. And I have this—" He hesitates for a minute, eyes boring into mine with an intensity that makes my blood surge. "I have to kill, or else I lose my mind."

That last bit hangs between us like the mist curling up from the swamp. I want to tell him it sounds like he's already lost his mind, but I bite back the urge. Because the first half of what he said, that he can't die—I saw it. I saw it, and I tried so hard to doubt it, but in the end, I was just lying to myself.

So if that part's true, then it's a lot easier to accept the rest of it, too.

"There are others," I say slowly. "Like you."

Jaxon nods, guarded caution moving across his features. I squeeze my coffee cup and look down at the dark, glossy surface.

"Edie," I say softly. "She's with one of them, isn't she? Another—another Hunter?"

I'm just guessing, but when I glance back up at Jaxon, I know immediately I guessed correctly. He looks—relieved, almost.

"Yeah," he says. "But like I told you, she's safe. I'm not telling you anything more."

My body buzzes. *An old friend from high school.* But what if that old friend wasn't from high school, at all?

"She's with Sawyer Caldwell, isn't she?" I whisper. "The Fat Camp Killer?"

Jaxon flits his gaze away. Doesn't say anything. But that's all the answer I need.

I feel numb. Confused. And suddenly, very very tired.

"Can I take a shower?" I say. It's the only thing that makes sense right now.

There it is, again, that expression of relief. He nods. Pushes himself out of the chair. "Yeah, of course. Just—" He looks at me again with a black intensity, and I shiver because it reminds me of the way he looked at me in the swamp as he thrust his cock inside me and choked me into an orgasm.

It reminds me that I liked it.

"Just don't do anything stupid," he says, and I know he means *escape.*

CHAPTER NINETEEN

JAXON

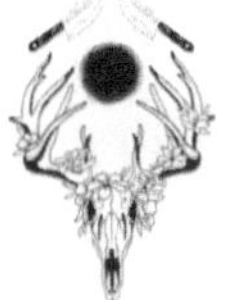

I t's the middle of the day, the winter sun is bright and pale, and Charlotte's asleep in her bedroom. I didn't chain her to the bed this time, but I did lock the door.

Because I really, *really* can't let her escape now. Not when she knows what I am. When she knows what Sawyer is.

What she is.

I couldn't bring myself to tell her when she asked about it on the porch, even though I felt the Unnamed whispering in my thoughts that she needed to know the truth. **There's something on her**, it said, **something strangling her soul.** Then my Guardian chimed in, its voice harsh and raspy: **He must break that binding first.**

Telling her will break it!

Telling her will break her!

Have you ever tried to have a conversation with a beautiful woman while two ancient gods argue in your head? I'm surprised I made it through unscathed.

Anyway, she's sleeping now. I checked on her a few minutes ago, and she was curled up on the bed in the little silky nightgown from her suitcase. The temptation to crawl into the bed and play with her unmoving body nearly overwhelmed me, but I refrained. Partly because I didn't want her to try and kill me again, to test to see if what I told her was true, and partially because I need to clear out these two actual dead bodies from my yard.

They're right where I left them in the grass, and thankfully it's cold enough today that I don't hear any flies buzzing yet. The bodies still look decent—decent enough to throw into my freezer while I decide what I want to do with them, anyway.

I start with the first man I killed. I throw his balaclava into the start of a burn pile and take a minute to study his head, trying to get a feel for him. He has a scar across his cheek and three black teardrop tattoos dripping out of his left eye. I've no doubt he was someone dangerous before I got ahold of him.

The second one I killed doesn't really have a head to speak of, not anymore. I'll need to saw off what's left of it, extract the teeth and the balaclava, and then throw the meat out into the swamp where it can decay into nothingness. Without a head, the second one is a bit harder to get a read on. He's a little skinnier than the first man, and I suspect a little younger. His hands are smooth, although there are tattoos across his knuckles. Sigils of some kind, it looks like. Magic. Occultism. Nothing to do with my gods, though.

Thanks to Charlotte, I know the two of them are connected to my last victim, Dennis Randall. I knew his name, of course, but I never think of them by their names. I think of them in pictures, because that's how my Guardian sends them to me. Faces. Maps. Bolts of electricity shooting through my veins. *This one.*

"***Who are these men?***" I ask in the language of the gods. The air shimmers as I speak.

Not your concern, answers the Unnamed. ***Your concern is the woman.*** Then I see Charlotte in my thoughts as I throw the first victim's head into the freezer. She's still asleep under the covers.

"***They're a threat***," I respond. More to my Guardian than the Unnamed, assuming it's around, and listening.

Neither of them answer. I sigh in frustration and grab my bone saw from its place on the wall so I can go back out in the chilly morning and get to work.

There's something meditative about cutting up a dead body. The careful, mindless repetition as you split through skin and ligament and bone. There's no squirming or screaming. No suffering. It's just meat and manual labor, shoving through the rigor mortis until everything's in pieces.

And that makes it easier to think.

I was still in a revival daze when I killed both of them. I did it on instinct and strength, like an animal protecting its home and (even though I know shouldn't think of Charlotte like this) its mate. I didn't think about who they were, what they were doing here, how they got in. I was vaguely aware that the power was out since the house generator kicked in right as I killed the first one. Charlotte told me before her shower that she had flipped the breakers, but those were just the ones to the house. I'm not a dumbass. I keep the fence on a separate system.

A system that's still connected to the electrical wires strung up along Guillmar Road. They probably cut them. Which means the house's main power supply is probably still out, too. I'll have to call and report it.

And keep a close eye on Charlotte in the meantime. I can't have her escaping—

Pain tears through my head, and I shriek and drop the saw and fall backward on my ass, slapping my hands up to my face even though they're covered in gore. The pain explodes outward and then fades to a dull, pounding throb, punctuated by the Unnamed's harsh voice.

Don't. Let. Her. Escape.

In the gods' language, the words feel like knives stabbing at the spot behind my eye. I groan and fall backward in the cool grass and blink up at the pale, cloudy sky.

Awaken her. Break the binding.

"What binding?" I mutter. This was the same thing they had been bickering about earlier, and they hadn't bothered to explain it.

She is bound by old magic. She must kill to break it.

Images flash through my head, courtesy of the Unnamed. Violent, bloody, fragmented, like I'm glimpsing them in a shattered mirror. Blood on a knife. Charlotte's eyes, wide and furious. Blood splattering on a wall. Blood drenching her hands. Charlotte digging herself out of the dirt.

"Stop!" I shout in English, because with each image the pain comes back until vomit rises in my throat. I haven't spoken English to the gods since I was a little boy, too young to know better.

SHOW HER, roars the Unnamed, and it's like a bolt of lightning splits my head in two.

Then it's gone. My head still throbs, but it feels like a typical headache, nothing a few Tylenol can't knock out. I blink, eyes watering. A cloud of grackles passes overhead and cackle at each other.

"***Show her what?***" I mutter in the language of the gods. I don't expect an answer, but I feel the presence of my Guardian nearby, slipping oily through my thoughts.

Take her with you, it whispers, low and staticky. And then it gives me a gift:

A new target.

It's a big house. A mansion, really, with a circular driveway that winds around a glittering stone fountain, the whole thing tucked behind a veil of oak trees. The house itself looks like a time capsule from the 1970s: big plate glass windows, dark brown angular walls.

Here, my Guardian whispers, and I know with some certainty that the house is in Houston, in a rich neighborhood, and that living inside it is a man who must be sacrificed. He's part of the same group of criminal occultists as Dennis Randall. As these men who trespassed on my property.

And then everything comes to me at once, the way it always does when my Guardian gives me a new project. I see the art that I will make with this man's skin, the sculptures I will craft with his bones, the portraits I will paint with his blood.

A masterpiece.

But the biggest masterpiece of all will be the Hunter I'll awaken in Charlotte when I slide my knife into her palm and guide her hand to deliver the killing blow.

"YOU WANT TO DO *WHAT?*"

Ambrose's voice bursts out of the phone, and it occurs to me that maybe I was better off not asking for his advice in this particular instance.

"She's *human*," he adds, which makes the muscles in her shoulders tense up. All I've told him so far is that I want to take Charlotte with me on my kill. I was putting off telling him why.

"Yeah," I mutter, pacing around the sofa. "About that."

My two offerings, Ada and Henry, watch me with their glass eyes. I crafted them two decades ago when I finally came back home after years away. Now they bear witness to everything that happens in this house.

Including me having to explain Charlotte to Ambrose.

"Tell me, Jaxon." Ambrose's voice is firm. "Stop fucking around."

I take a deep breath and seek out Charlotte; she's still upstairs, breathing softly. Asleep. "I think Charlotte is a Hunter."

Ambrose goes quiet, and I stare at Ada and Henry and wait.

"That's impossible," he finally says. "Even if you were too pussy-addled to tell the difference—"

"Oh, shut the fuck up."

"You shut the fuck up. Charlotte is Edie's friend, remember? And Sawyer would have said if Edie had a Hunter friend."

I push my hand through my hair. He's not wrong. "She smells human," I tell him. "Feels human. But then, she, uh, she killed me."

"Bullshit. It's been, what? Three days since I talked to you last? You wouldn't have revived so fast—"

"Will you shut up and listen?" I snap. "I'm trying to explain things."

And then I do, as best I can. I tell him what I felt when Charlotte was strangling me, and how the gods came to me and told me what she is, and the quick revival and how she has some kind of magic on her that's smothering her nature. And I'll give Ambrose credit because he does listen to all of it without interrupting.

By the time I've finished explaining, I'm sitting on the couch between Ada and Henry, my palm sweaty against my phone, and Ambrose is dangerously quiet.

"Taking her to kill seems drastic," he says.

"The Unnamed said it would break the spell."

Ambrose laughs, and even with me being a Hunter it chills me a little. He's so old. So experienced. "It's not a spell," he says. "It sounds like a protection charm. The person who did it —if it's even real—would probably never call themselves a witch."

"It's real," I say. "I sensed the Hunter in her. We have to do something, Ambrose."

"We don't, in fact, have to do anything. *You* feel a religious obligation." He pauses, and there's a mocking tilt in his words when he asks, "Or is it something more?"

"The Unnamed told me to do this," I snap back, grateful we're on the phone so he won't see the embarrassed blood rising in my cheeks. "And it's not just a religious obligation. It's an obligation to another of our kind. One who's trapped."

"If she really is a Hunter, she'll break," Ambrose says flatly. "She's Edie's age, right? Thirty years is a long time to deny what you are."

"Exactly!" My voice rises dangerously loud, and I reel myself back in. I don't want Charlotte overhearing. With the way this block or charm or whatever it is has her brain all addled, she'll never agree to go with me if she knows what we're doing. "She should have killed by now. And I told you, she *feels* human. Just not when she was attacking me."

In the crackling silence, I can feel Ambrose thinking. Then he sighs, an ocean-rush sound on the phone's speakers. "You're right that there are—strange things in this world," he says. "Stranger things than us."

Like the gods. If anything, I know better than he does.

"I'm not going to stop you from doing this," he continues. "Just be careful. And if it doesn't work—"

"It'll work." It's an edict from the gods. It has to work.

"If it doesn't work," Ambrose says again, more firmly. "I want to meet her. Examine her. See if I've seen it before."

There's nothing particularly unreasonable about his request, but it still makes me vaguely uncomfortable. Charlotte's not some object of curiosity for Ambrose to add to his collection.

She's *mine.*

The thought hits me hard. Sudden. I don't want to share her.

"This'll work," I say. "This'll wake her up. And then—"

"Then I'll *really* want to meet her," Ambrose says, and a jealous fire flares, briefly, in my heart.

CHAPTER TWENTY

CHARLOTTE

When I wake up, it's the middle of the night, and I'm as disoriented as I was my first night here. Except this time, I'm clean, and I'm in my night-gown, and there's no chain around my ankle.

Someone's also watching me from the corner.

"Jaxon?" I sit up and sweep my gaze around the dark room. The shadows shift and blur. The mannequin in the corner regards me, unmoving.

But Jaxon's not here.

No one's here.

I pull my knees up to my chest and take deep, careful breaths. I'm *certain* I felt the prickle of someone watching me, and I've had Jaxon staring at me enough over the last few days that I know what the weight of his gaze feels like. And that creeping sensation felt the same.

More or less.

Because it was your imagination. A fact I prove to myself by crawling out of bed and switching on the overhead light.

No one's in the room but me and the creepy-ass mannequin.

I sigh and try to push the door open. I'm not totally

surprised that it's locked. I also can't say I *blame* him for locking the door. Because I would have one hundred percent tried to escape again.

Well. Maybe ninety-five percent. But just because he knows where Edie is and definitely *not* because of how well he fucked me in the swamp. That was—temporary madness. The adrenaline making me crazy. It worked out in my favor, too. I got a shower, clean clothes, no chain.

I'm not using that chamberpot again, though.

I bang on the door and shout Jaxon's name as loud as I can, then lean my ear against the cool slick wood, listening. The house seems to breathe.

"Jaxon!" I bellow. "Open up! I need to use the bathroom!"

I stalk over to the bed and slam the chain around a few times. I just hope he's in the house, and not—outside. With those bodies. Or in that shed. The thought of that place makes my head throb.

I bang the chains around a few more times for good measure. This time, though, I hear heavy footsteps echoing from somewhere in the house.

"I'm coming! I'm coming!" Jaxon's vaguely irritated voice spills up from the stairs. "I heard you the first time."

I drop the chain and stand up as he pushes the door open, filling the frame with his thick body and broad shoulders. His hair's loose, spilling around his face, and he peers at me in a way that makes my skin prickle.

Just like it was doing earlier.

I shove the thought aside. He wasn't in here. No one was in here.

"Can I use the bathroom?" I ask.

He looks at me for a moment, not saying anything, face unreadable. It's long enough that I start to get—not nervous, exactly. Not scared. Just *unsettled*.

He has that air about him. Especially in his eyes. They really do remind me of the deepest parts of the ocean. But I suppose it makes sense, given—what he is.

"Yeah, you can use the bathroom." He steps back, barely making enough room for me to squeeze past him. "Then I need to talk to you."

That brings me up short. "About what?"

"You'll see."

I roll my eyes and move past him, my body brushing up against his as I do. His heat radiates around me. This house traps the night's chill, and I try not to think about how nice it would be to snuggle up to him and use his body heat for warmth.

"I'll be outside the door," he says, following me down the hall.

I glance over my shoulder at him. "Still don't trust me not to run?"

"Of course not."

Which is fair. Because I probably would. And I will, the second I have the opportunity.

Most likely, anyway.

I use the bathroom quickly, shivering in my nightgown. When I come out, Jaxon's leaning up against the wall, his strong arms crossed over his chest, watching me.

"Can I change?" I ask him.

"Why?"

I gesture down at my thin nightgown. "Because it's freezing in here."

"Oh. *Oh.*" He blinks like it hadn't even occurred to him. "Yeah, come on. I'll let you get something out of your suitcase."

Earlier, he hadn't let me in his room, just brought me the nightgown and clean underwear while I was in the shower. But right now, he leads me in there, hesitating a little at the doorway. I don't tell him I've already seen it. He has to know I dug through his shit, right, when I was trying to escape?

Still, being in Jaxon's bedroom *with* Jaxon feels different than being in here alone, especially after—everything that's happened. I certainly look at his bed, with its rumpled sheets, a little differently.

Don't. Focus. He is a murderer.

A murderer who did, in fact, make me come so hard that I stopped caring.

A murderer who also isn't human, really.

He drags the suitcase over and watches me while I pull out a change of clothes. When I straighten up and look over at him, he keeps staring at me.

"Some privacy?" I ask.

Jaxon's brow furrows. "Oh. Right."

Is that a strain of disappointment I detect in his voice? Perv.

I ignore the heat it sends to my clit.

Or maybe I don't. Maybe that's why, when he turns around, I don't make much of an effort to try to get out of his line of sight, just peel my nightgown up over my head, my eyes fixed on his glossy black hair. As I dress, the fabric rustling, he tilts his head a little toward me.

"Are you trying to sneak a peek?"

He jerks his gaze away. "No."

"Yes, you were." I grin and zip up my pants. I'm still topless. Tits out.

"I was not." He shifts uncomfortably. He's so strange, and not just for the obvious reasons, either. It's like he's shy about the thought of me changing even though earlier he completely wrecked me.

God, I have to stop thinking about earlier.

I slide on my bra and pull on my sweater and say, "You can look now," and he does, turning around and then drinking me in.

Now it's my turn to shift uncomfortably. Though I wouldn't say I'm *that* uncomfortable.

"Warmer?" he asks.

"I will be. What do you want to talk to me about?"

Jaxon goes still, his eyes dark and intense. He's looking at me like it doesn't actually matter that I'm dressed—like he sees right through my clothes, through my skin, into the most secret parts of me.

"I have to do something," he says. "And you're going to come with me."

Fear suddenly twists through my body, violent and jarring. *Real* fear. Like what I felt when those two men pointed their guns in my face. Like what I felt when I saw what Jaxon was capable of.

"Y-you're going to have to tell me more than that." I swallow, my mouth suddenly dry. "What do you have to do?"

He takes his time answering, although when he does, his response is both shocking and completely expected. "I have to kill someone."

"So why do you need *me?*" I spit out, taking one reflexive step away from him. I swear he flinches a little.

"Can't leave you here," he answers, a beat too late.

"So let me go."

The look he gives me could have withered roses.

"I won't tell anyone what you're going to do." I'm pleading and I know it, but I don't care. "Look, I just want to find Edie. Even if you won't tell me where she is, let me go and I'll just try to find her and let you do—" I wave my hands around. "Whatever it is you need to do."

"No."

I slump, fear worming through me. "Won't I just fuck up whatever you need to do? Won't this just make me a liability?" I try to keep my voice steady. "Is that the idea? Once I see you kill someone, then you'll be *allowed* to kill me? That's wha—"

"No!" He says it even more forcefully this time. "I'm not going to kill you. But you have to come with me."

"And if I refuse?" I cross my arms. Raise an eyebrow. Challenge him.

Jaxon just shrugs. "Refuse all you want. I got you from your car on the highway to that bed." He tilts his head toward the hallway. "You think I can't drag you along on a kill?"

The way he says it sends chills shooting through every nerve in my body. He's so calm. Like it's all so ordinary.

"Won't it just—make things more complicated for you?"

Jaxon's eyes glitter. "Of course it fucking will," he says. "But I'm afraid I don't have much of a choice."

That *really* chills me. Because in this moment, I see Jaxon as what he is—as something not fully human. Some quality in him seems to shift in front of me. A shadow moving across his face. A predatory flatness spreading through his eyes.

My skin prickles the way it did in my bedroom earlier.

"I don't understand anything about you," I say coldly.

And Jaxon only replies, "I know."

CHAPTER TWENTY-ONE

JAXON

Ambrose isn't wrong. This is an awful damn idea, but my whole life I've been told you can't question the gods. *They gave us these gifts,* my MeeMaw told me when I was twelve or thirteen, not long after my first kill. I think I was helping her in the kitchen, stripping meat and skin from bone. *This long life. This strength. When they ask something of you, you best listen.*

And I have listened. I've been on this planet for over fifty years, counting the time I spent in the ground, and I still look like I'm 30. I'll keep looking 30 for decades, too. Just like Dad. Just like my grandparents. Just like every other Hunter in this world.

And in all my 50 years, anytime the gods speak to me, I listen. I don't question it. If they show me a face, a life, I end it. Doesn't matter who it is, or how difficult it'll be to make happen. I spill the blood. I make the offerings. I carve the gods' sigils into old meat and bleached bones and leave them out in the open air for humans to find, even if doing so makes it that much more likely for me to get caught. I listen to Ambrose bitch incessantly about how much more likely it means I'll get caught, which is worse.

And right now, driving to Texas with the only living woman I've ever fucked in the passenger seat of my car, is the first time I've wanted to disobey.

Part of it is the quiet. She's angry with me; I can feel that much. I handcuffed her to the seatbelt so she doesn't get any ideas about jumping out while we're on the highway. Now, if she really is a Hunter, then it won't *kill* her. But despite what I said to Ambrose, I'm still not totally sure she is. Yeah, when I was letting her kill me, she felt like a Hunter. But right now? She still seems human. There's still that veil between us, that chasm between predator and prey.

A binding, the gods said, and Ambrose acted like he had heard of something similar. And yet doubt still creeps around.

Maybe you should just trust the fucking gods.

It's Dad's voice in my head, because of course it is.

Charlotte sighs, something she's been doing since we got on I-10. I glance over at her, but she's staring out the window, the winter sun turning her cherry-red hair into flames.

"It's another couple of hours," I tell her. "We can stop at Whataburger once we're over the border."

I have no idea why I say that. I think I just can't stand the silence. Or her anger. The truth is I want her to like me. I want to fuck her again, and make her come, and feel her hot living breath as she gasps out her pleasure. But I don't want to have to sneak it. I want her to want it, too. Just like she did in the marsh.

"What the fuck is Whataburger?" She still doesn't look at me.

"A fast food place." I force myself to focus on the highway. "It's good."

"Are you always so—calm about this?" She turns toward me.

I feel it, the way the air moves around her. The way her scent catches. A human scent, still. Not Hunter at all.

I tighten my fingers around the steering wheel. "Yes. I told you what I am. I'm not—" *Like you.* The words are right there. But that's the whole point of this trip, isn't it? To prove that, actually, she is like me.

"Right." She shifts around, the handcuffs jangling against the seatbelt. "You're—the boogeyman."

"Yeah." That's what Ambrose always calls us, anyway. He's doubtful about the gods, but that's just because they don't talk to him so directly. Sawyer's the same way. They didn't grow up like I did, communing with our gods before they killed. But both of them know, instinctively, there's something otherworldly about our kind. Something that maybe isn't supposed to be in this world at all.

"So who are you killing?" She says it like she's trying to be casual, but I smell the whiff of fear.

"I don't know his name." The road unspools in front of us, a long black ribbon. A sign flashes by: Twenty-five miles to Lake Charles. Eighty-five miles to Beaumont. Houston just a little further away from that.

"Okay." She sounds doubtful. "So you'll just—know him when you see him?"

It feels weird, talking to a human about this. But she isn't a human, I keep reminding myself. She's a Hunter, there's just something wrong with her. Something broken. It's up to me to mend it.

Assuming I can trust the gods.

Of course you can trust the gods.

Fuck, I hope she's not human and I'm not about to break this treasure that fell into my lap.

"I know where he is," I say. "His house." I glance sideways at her, and she's watching me, those big dark eyes drawing me. I jerk my gaze back over to the road. "He's an associate of the two attackers. They all work for the same man."

"Oh yeah? And how do you know that?"

The gods are whispering, low and raspy. Arguing with each other again. The Unnamed wants me to tell her. My Guardian says I have to wait until she's been Awoken.

"I just do," I say sharply, and they go silent. "Don't worry about it." I keep staring at the road, and I'm not sure why I say this next part except that it feels right, saying it to her.

"I won't let anything happen to you."

THE SUN'S just starting to set when we arrive in Houston. Cities always put me on edge—all that humanity crushing in around me turns my blood hot and vicious. The gods tend to retreat, too, leaving me on my own with all that prey.

And Houston's worse than most. It's so big and sprawling and the freeways feel like ropes pulling tighter and tighter around my chest. I take deep breaths, clenching the steering wheel as I pull into a glittering river of cars.

"Are you okay?" Charlotte's voice startles me.

"I'm fine." I keep my gaze fixed firmly ahead even though I can feel her watching me. Taillights flare red, and I slam on the brakes too hard, making the car jitter to a stop.

"Not used to driving in the city, huh?" She shifts, the handcuffs zipping along the seatbelt. "You want me to take over? I drive in Los Angeles all the time."

We're stopped in traffic, so I risk looking over at her. She's smirking at me.

"Why?" I ask. "So you can escape?"

She shrugs, eyes glittering with amusement. I can almost pretend she's flirting with me, which is a weird feeling. "How can I escape with you in the car?"

Traffic jerks forward. Taillights blink around us like the lights on the Christmas tree I wasn't allowed to have as a kid. "You could kill me again."

I mean it as a joke, sort of, but Charlotte just frowns. "Yeah, and you'd come back. Because you aren't—"

I jerk the car forward as the traffic clears up a little, and Charlotte says, "Human," in a kind of vague daze.

"I probably wouldn't come back as fast as I did a few days ago." Whatever block in the road has vanished, and I pick up speed, my heart thudding as the cars press around me. I can sense every fucking human inside every fucking one of them, and it makes me feel hot and itchy, like I'm coming down with a fever. This is why I stay in the marsh.

"Oh yeah? Why not?"

I pull the car into a clear spot on the highway. I don't technically know where I'm going. I don't know these freeway names or these exits. I don't recognize the gaudy strip malls crowding up against the highway. But at the same time, my gods are guiding me forward. I know I won't be on this freeway much longer.

"That's complicated," I say, cursing myself a little. I'm distracted by everything. The driving. The upcoming kill that I've done absolutely nothing to prepare for. The kill that I'm not even supposed to execute.

I glance over at Charlotte, curled up against the door, arm at an angle to account for the handcuff. Staring at me. "You always do this."

I put my focus back on the road. Move over to another lane. Our exit is close. I can sense it the way I can sense the humans, an invisible trail leading me to my prey.

"Do what?"

"Tell me just enough to be annoying."

I smile. She doesn't *smell* the way a Hunter should, but she does sort of *feel* like one. A human would be terrified right now.

I wonder, vaguely, if she even realizes how strange she is.

"Because these are things you aren't supposed to know," I finally say. A sign flashes by—GESSNER ROAD, 2 MILES—and my heart sings. That's it.

"Because I'm not like you?"

The question shoots straight to my heart, and, just for a moment, my Guardian rises up above the roar of humanity to shriek one word: **Wait**.

I know what it means. Don't tell her yet. Let her discover it when she sinks the knife I brought into the chest of her first real victim.

Don't tell her anything until she's broken her binding.

But at the same time—I don't want to lie to her. I've never wanted to lie to her.

Thankfully, our exit materializes ahead, and I swerve hard to get in the lane. Charlotte shrieks and grabs at the dashboard with her free hand.

"Sorry," I mutter.

"Let me drive!" she shouts.

"We're off the freeway." I pull up to the light. I need to turn left and slide under the underpass and disappear down a winding, leafy street that will lead us to the human heart that beats louder and more urgent than all the rest.

Well, except for one—the one in the seat beside me.

Even though it might not be human at all.

Because I'm not like you?

At least my poor driving kept me from having to answer her question with a lie.

CHAPTER TWENTY-TWO

CHARLOTTE

Jaxon has, in the last week, crashed my car, kidnapped me, jerked off while I strangled him, came back from the dead, decapitated two men with his bare hands, and fucked me whilst covered in said men's blood. And yet the only time I've seen him show anything approximating fear is while driving through Houston at rush hour.

Thankfully, we left the nightmare of the freeway behind, and I'm having to come face to face with this new one: namely, that I'm about to become an accomplice to murder. Assuming the two men at Jaxon's house don't count. Which...

It feels like they shouldn't?

Maybe this shouldn't, either, considering I'm handcuffed. But I'm also weirdly nonplussed about this entire situation. Just like I was when Jaxon killed those men. Or when I let him fuck me afterward. When I *asked* him to fuck me afterward. My fear feels like an afterthought.

"Where are we going?" I ask, mostly to fill up the silence in the car, which sends my thoughts spiraling.

"We're almost there."

"That doesn't really answer my question."

Jaxon ignores me, the way he always does when I cross that invisible line separating stuff he can tell me from stuff he can't. I still don't understand who made these rules. If it's him. If it's the other Hunters. Or the god he prays to, the one who isn't the usual one.

He pulls the car off the main road, and it feels suddenly like we're not in the city anymore. It's a neighborhood, but the houses are enormous and sprawling and hidden back from the road by pine trees. The streetlights illuminate things in fits and starts.

"There's no one here," Jaxon says suddenly, slowing the car down to a crawl. He leans forward, sniffing the air like a dog.

"What do you mean?"

"The houses," he says. "They're empty."

I can't decide if I'm relieved or not. I know I *should* be, but ever since I woke up in that bedroom in Jaxon's creepy old house my emotions have been—off. "So I guess you won't be killing anyone tonight?"

Jaxon looks over at me, his face half-hidden by the neighborhood's shadows. "No, he's still here."

There it is again. Relief? Disappointment? I can't tell. My stomach just kind of knots around strangely.

Jaxon speeds the car up. "He's here," he says again. "But I pretty much only sense him and a few others. It's like the other houses are abandoned. Like people used to be here but aren't anymore."

My skin prickles. and I look out the window again. Even in the dark, I can tell these houses are beautiful. Big midcentury mansions lit up by the street lamps and an occasional porch light. But the neighborhood does feel empty, and there are signs of construction hidden in the dark. Traffic cones. Yellow tape.

"There," Jaxon says suddenly, pointing across me to a big

angular house in a cul-de-sac. It's framed by sprawling trees draped in lacy Spanish moss, which I can see because there are floodlights illuminating a circular driveway with a fountain at its center. "That's where we're going."

I swallow, my throat dry. "And how are *you*—" I stress the word. "Going to do that? Just walk up to the front door?"

"No." Jaxon loops around the cul-de-sac and goes back the way we came, only this time he pulls the car into one of the dark, tree-lined driveways and cuts the headlights off. But he keeps driving, and even though I can't see anything, he somehow knows to stop right before we reach a three-car garage with broken doors.

Jaxon kills the engine.

"Now wha—"

"Be quiet," he snaps, and the harshness in his voice startles me. He takes a deep breath, staring straight ahead. "I need you to be quiet," he says a little more gently.

I immediately want to make a ton of noise, start screaming and carrying on. The neighborhood is only *mostly* abandoned, and I have no reason whatsoever to go along with any of this.

Except—

He knows where Edie is. He knows what happened to her.

And so I keep my mouth shut.

Jaxon leans back in his chair and starts muttering in a language I don't recognize. The words fall over each other, the vowels long and drawn out, and his voice seems to fill the car with something heavier than sound. The downy hairs on my arm stand on end. Goosebumps prickle up my leg. My spine crawls.

And then, abruptly, Jaxon stops. "It flooded," he says with a kind of disbelieving laughter. "No wonder they choose this guy. It really was all leading to this." He looks over at me in the dark, his smile wide and manic. "It's all preordained."

"What the fuck are you talking about?" I won't deny I'm

attracted to Jaxon. But right now, the way his face is all twisted with a kind of dark excitement, I suddenly want to scramble away.

"You'll see."

I do not like that sound of that.

Jaxon lifts the chain around his neck, the one where he keeps the various keys keeping me prisoner. "I'm going to open up the handcuffs." Something changes in his voice. He's speaking English, but it almost sounds like he's speaking that weird language, too. "And you need to do exactly what I say. If you don't—"

He reaches his hand through the space between us and wraps his long fingers around my throat. I stiffen even though my clit flares to life, remembering the last time we were in this position.

But then he speaks. "I'll do this," he says softly. Then he tightens his fingers just enough that they press into my skin "And I'll finish it."

I stare at him, my pulse racing. He doesn't look away. And whatever urge that's had me talking back to him all this time goes dead silent.

"Why?" I whisper. "Why did you bring me here?"

He keeps staring at me like he's looking for something in the lines of my face. Then he pulls his hand away. Slides off the necklace with the key. Unlocks my handcuffs.

"Follow me," he says. "We're going into the garage."

I nod. My fear is sharper than it's ever been. Even when I killed him. Even when I saw him kill.

Jaxon steps out of the car. For a second, I sit there, shaking. But then he raps gently against the window, jolting me into action. I tumble out of my seat, watching as he pulls a big duffel bag out of the trunk. I don't even remember him putting it in there when he left.

He closes everything up, comes around the side of the car,

heads toward the garage. It feels like he's on fire. Like I sense his body heat the way I can sense flames.

"Follow," he says sharply—but softly, under his breath. I do. He's dangerous. The fact that he tosses me shy little glances and knows how to make a woman come doesn't change that.

He threw a fucking corpse at me. Well, at someone who was holding me hostage. Still.

Jaxon leads me around the side of the garage, picking through the shaggy, weed-choked grass until we come to a little door, which he opens. It was unlocked. How he knew that was there, I don't know. Or maybe he's just been here before, even though he said he hasn't. That would explain a lot, actually.

The garage is pitch-black, but Jaxon digs around in the duffle bag and then switches on an electric lamp, the light buzzing a little, and sets it on the floor. Even in the eerie blue light, I can see this place flooded recently. Debris litters the floor. There's a dark line on the wall marking the height of the water.

"You need to cover your hair and your face." Jaxon digs through the duffle bag and then draws out a long black scarf like a magician performing a stage trick.

"With this?" The fabric flutters around as he hands it to me.

"Yeah. Figured you didn't want to use a dead man's balaclava."

I wrinkle my nose in disgust. "You don't have your own fucking balaclava?"

He's still digging through the duffle bag. "I have my own thing. Put that on. Now."

It's the same tone of voice he used on me in the swamp, and despite the terrible absurdity of our situation, my body responds in kind. *What the hell is wrong with me?* Still, I drape the scarf over my head, thoughts racing. I'm being coerced into doing this. He told me he'd kill me. I'm a victim. He's a killer. He's also crazy.

I draw the scarf across my nose and mouth, twisting it around twice to hold it in place. I keep my eyes on Jaxon the whole time, watching as he puts on black gloves and then pulls out a knife and a gun. The sight of both of them turns my skin clammy.

He fixes both weapons to his belt somehow, then crouches over the duffle bag again. I can't see what he's doing until he stands up: he's holding a mask of his own. It's hard to see much of it in the dim light, but there are long, reaching antlers, and it gleams like it's made of metal.

Jaxon looks at me and nods approvingly. "Good. Can't show your face."

"What do you care?" I ask.

He doesn't answer. Just lifts up the mask and slides it on.

And the second he does, something changes. The molecules in the air spark and sizzle. My body goes hot with lust and cold with fear and I feel suddenly like I'm made of steam. Jaxon towers over me as he drops his gloved hands to his side and squeezes them into fists. My body jolts. Pain flickers behind my eye, just for a second before it vanishes.

The mask turns to me. Its eyes are empty.

"Jaxon?" I squeak out.

He steps up to me, a monster made of shadows. I want to pull away but I'm too petrified to move, even when he trails one of his gloved fingers over my scarf, tracing the outline of my lips. I'm too petrified to move, but I wouldn't move anyway. His touch electrifies me.

Even in the mask

Especially in the mask.

"Follow me," he says in that dark, velvety voice. His killer's voice, I think. "Do exactly what I say. And this—this will work."

"What will?" I shake my head, fear and confusion and desire twining together. I wish Jaxon put on that mask to fuck me.

"You'll see."

And then he cuts the light, and I have no choice but to follow him through the darkness.

CHAPTER TWENTY-THREE

CHARLOTTE

We cut across the overgrown yards, weaving through stately old pecan trees, the air damp and cold. I can't see anything, but I keep my fingers pressed lightly against Jaxon's back, and he moves as if it's daylight. As if he can see everything.

It's not long before a light glimmers up ahead, and I suck my breath in, fear surging up through my chest. *This can't be happening.* And yet I keep gliding forward, weaving between the trees and shadows until everything opens up into a small, rolling hill of a backyard. The light is a swimming pool, pale and eerie and steaming in the cold.

Jaxon stops and sniffs the air, then whips his hand back and grabs my wrist. I stifle a shout of surprise.

He pulls me up to his side and presses his mask against my ear.

"There are three people on this street." His voice is so low it sounds like the wind. "A couple four houses down. Inside. Calm. And our target." He nods toward the swimming pool.

"Okay," I breathe.

"Do exactly as I say." When he talks, it seems to come from

everywhere. The mask is flat and expressionless. Unmoving. "I won't let you get hurt."

"You threatened to kill me like five min—"

"Do what I say, and I won't let you get hurt."

It sounds more like a threat than a promise of protection.

"Fine," I whisper, my breath quickening. The air smells like the scarf, which smells like cinnamon. And, I think, like Jaxon.

"Follow me." He moves forward, circling the pool. I follow him because I don't want to die. Because he knows where Edie is. Because part of me still thinks I'm going to walk in that house and the man Jaxon wants to kill will call the police and I'll be—saved, or something.

Do you want to be saved?

Jaxon glides up to the door with an easy grace, his feet barely making a sound on the wooden patio. The door is sliding glass set into more glass, a black mirror reflecting our two masked forms back at us. We're shadows. We're monsters.

I look so good at his side.

I shake the thought out of my head, even though Jaxon runs his hands over the door's lock like a lover—

Like he ran his hands over me

—And the lock snaps somehow, some piece of metal hitting the patio with a whispered clang. Jaxon eases the door open, and the curtain on the other side billows in, giving me a glimpse of the tile floor.

He gestures for me to follow him. I know I shouldn't. But I do.

We push through the gauzy curtains and into the living room. It's surprisingly sparse in terms of furniture, like the owner of this house, Jaxon's victim, spent all his money on the property and didn't have anything left for couches and chairs.

Jaxon stands still, head cocked, the antlers dark. I hold my breath, but all I can hear is the blood rushing in my ears.

He turns to me. Points up to the ceiling. Upstairs.

I'm dizzy at what he's asking me to do, and some part of me snaps. I shake my head. Point at the floor. *Here*, I want to say, but I'm too afraid to speak.

The empty spaces that are Jaxon's eyes almost seem to flash. He points at the ceiling, then grabs my wrist, and yanks me with him. I want to fight. I *should* fight, and scream, and make noise, and ruin everything. But that knife is gleaming at his belt, and I can see the lump of the gun underneath his shirt. That's two ways to kill me, plus his long graceful fingers.

So I follow. Again.

We weave through the big, empty living room and a narrow foyer until we come to an enormous circular staircase. Jaxon moves through the house like he's been here before. He does slow down a little as we go up the stairs, pausing now and then with his head tilted. Listening. Tracking. I don't hear anything but the occasional creaking moan as the house settles into its massive foundations.

Then Jaxon moves again, more quickly. On the second-floor landing, he walks with big, loping strides. This part of the house feels as empty and unlived-in as the rest. There are no pictures on the walls. No Christmas decorations waiting to be taken down. No discarded shoes or shelves full of knick knacks.

Then I hear it—the low hum of a television. Light flickers into the hallway, spilling out of an open door. Jaxon stops and holds up his hand and I run into it, his fingers splaying across my heart.

He tilts his antlered mask toward me. I wish I could see his eyes.

Then he moves, darting forward and whipping himself into the room. There is a long, empty pause and then a man's scream that cuts short.

"In here!" Jaxon shouts, and I feel the words vibrate in my bones. "Now!"

But I can't move. I don't *want* to move. I just stand outside the doorway, sucking down deep shuddery breaths.

"Charlotte!" he orders.

That cuts through my fear. "Don't say my name!" I screech, the first thing I think of. I don't move, though. Not even when Jaxon steps through the doorway, a monster wrapped in shadow.

He pulls the knife off his belt, the metal gleaming. It's clean.

"What did you do?" I whisper.

"Knocked him out." Jaxon's fingers tighten around the handle of the knife. "So you won't have to fight him."

It takes me a moment, a long moment, to register what he's saying. "Fight him?" I shake my head. "Why would I—"

Jaxon grabs my arm and jerks me forward, yanking me through the doorway and into a bedroom, the TV on the wall still softly playing some old sitcom. When I step inside, the canned laughter kicks in.

There's a man slumped on the bed. Middle-aged, with short dark hair, a stocky build.

"You knocked *him* out?" I sputter.

"I'm not human," Jaxon says in a slow, dangerous voice. "I can do things you wouldn't expect." He looks toward me again, his hand still wrapped around my arm. His touch softens, although only a little. "You need to do it."

"What?" I wrench myself away from him, stumbling sideways. He stares at me, a monster offering me a big silver blade. "Why?" Panic bubbles into my throat. "Is this some kind of— blackmail thing? Are you recording me?"

"No." He steps closer, slow and threatening. I bump up against the wall, knocking my head against the TV. One of the characters says something and the room fills with laughter again. "It's nothing like that."

"Then what is it?" I look over at the man, willing him to stir. To open his eyes. To save me, somehow.

"It's—" Jaxon steps in front of me, blocking my view of the man. I don't even know his name because *Jaxon* doesn't know his name. Maybe he's a criminal—a drug dealer, a human trafficker. I still don't want to kill him.

Pain throbs behind my left eye, the start of a headache.

"Tell me!" I shriek. "Why are you doing this?"

"To show you what you are," Jaxon says softly, still holding out the knife.

Realization hits me like a punch. "You think I'm like *you?*" I sputter out. "No. No, absolutely not." I shake my head furiously, so hard the scarf slips back. Jaxon lifts his hand and I flinch away, but all he does is pull the fabric back over my hair.

"It's complicated," he says.

"Don't ever say those two fucking words to me again!" I dive sideways, desperate to get away, but Jaxon squeezes my waist and pulls me up to him and whirls me around to face the bed. The knife presses against my stomach, it's metal cold even through my sweater.

"I'll help," Jaxon murmurs into my ear, the mask cold against my skin. He steps forward, forcing me to go with him. His cock is hard, which both disturbs and arouses me. "I'll guide your hand."

"No!" I scream. Jaxon grabs my right hand and pries my fingers open.

Over on the bed, the man groans.

"Hurry," Jaxon says. "So you won't have to fight him."

"Help!" I scream, bucking back against Jaxon. My head throbs. I can't believe I'm getting one of these headaches now. And this one has come on so *fast*. The pain is sharp enough that light flickers in my vision, and pale haloes settle over everything.

The man rolls onto his back, eyes still closed.

Jaxon snarls something in that strange, alien language, then slides the knife handle into my palm and pushes my fingers closed, his hand wrapped around mine.

"Help me!" I scream at the man. "He's going to make me kill you!"

The man doesn't move.

Jaxon forces me forward, pressing me between his body and the mattress. I scream as he forces my hand, and the knife, up over my head. It catches the light and shines silver.

"Why?" I sob, tears streaking down my cheeks. "Why are you doing this?"

Jaxon answers in that ugly, cruel language and tightens his grip around my waist, pressing me into him so that his cock presses into the cleft of my ass.

"Just once," he says. "Just once."

My headache flares, but I still fight against Jaxon's strength, my arm muscles straining as I push back against him, trying to keep the knife lifted.

"Just once," Jaxon keeps whispering. "Just do it once. That'll be enough."

The man groans. His eyes flutter open, settle right on me, and widen with fear.

And, to my horror, my clit throbs.

That's enough. I lose what little leverage I have against Jaxon, and he overpowers me, pushing the knife down. It swings in a wide arc.

At the last minute, Jaxon lets go.

But the knife doesn't stop.

It arcs through the air until the blade parts the flesh of the man's shoulder, until it splits through fat and muscle, until it lands in the jarring obstruction of bone.

Blood spurts.

The man screams.

And I—

I keep going.

CHAPTER TWENTY-FOUR

CHARLOTTE

I can't believe how hot this man's blood is, or how it coats my hands like thick, silky gloves. I drive the knife into his chest, relishing the gentle resistance of his skin and the dancing twitch of his muscles. He makes a sound like he's had the air punched out of him and swings his arm around and grabs at the knife, his hands slippery. When he touches me, it jars me out of this strange, dreamy state I'm in and plunges back into reality:

There's a man I've never seen before splayed out on the bed in front of me, one cut on his shoulder and the other on his chest. I made them.

"You fucking bitch!" he howls. "Who sent you?"

Somehow, I jerk the knife away, cutting his hand in the process. He shrieks but keeps reaching for me. I swing the knife, cutting his forearm. More blood. More curses.

A dark blur at my side. Jaxon.

Jaxon, who made me do this.

He leaps across the bed, moving unfathomably fast, and pins the man down to the mattress by his arms. I stumble back-ward, sliding off the bed, still clutching the knife.

My migraine pain flares, blinding me.

"Do you want to finish it?" Jaxon's question centers me. His *mask* centers me, those black empty eyes, the strange twisting metal that mirrors the musculature of a face. The antlers, sharp as daggers.

Yes, yes, I do want to finish it. I know I shouldn't, but there's a hot, driving lust inside my chest, not all that different from what compelled me to beg Jaxon to fuck me in the woods. My clit is on fire. Dampness seeps through my panties. Even if the more I think about killing this man, actually ending his life, the more my migraine tears through my brain.

This is wrong. This is so, so wrong.

But also I feel strong and vibrant, like when I'm working on a new painting—but *more*. More than I've ever felt in my entire life.

"Charlotte." My name is sharp on Jaxon's tongue. The man, my victim, squirms and howls and kicks, but Jaxon is too strong for him, just like he was too strong for me when he put this knife in my hand and dragged me into this room. "I'll finish it if you want me to. Even though it really should be you."

I don't know what he means by that, even though I agree. I need to push through the fiery pain in my temple and keep going, even if I *want* it to feel like someone else is making me move, like someone is forcing me to do this.

"Charlotte?" Jaxon keeps staring at me. "Do you want me to finish it?"

Numbly, I shake my head.

"What'd he do to you, honey?" the man's gaze meets mine, and his eyes are wide and bright with fear. I like it, that fear. It makes me feel powerful.

What's wrong *with me*?

"Don't speak to her." Jaxon hits the man's temple with his fist, and the man sputters and jerks.

I want to feel his blood again.

I leap on him, my heart soaring, and drive the knife into his chest again, lower down this time. He makes a wet wheezing noise, and frothy pink blood gurgles up between his lips. I do it again. Again. He flops and convulses whenever I slide my blade into him, and his blood erupts whenever I pull it out. It's everywhere. On him. On me. I reach up in irritation and pull my scarf away so the next time I stab him, I'll feel the hot wetness on my face and lips.

I keep going.

Into his stomach. His side. Over and over. I think he's still alive because he keeps jerking beneath me and making wet gurgling noises. It's not until a strong, firm hand catches my wrist before I can bring the knife back into him that I'm grounded again.

"He's dead," Jaxon rasps into my ear, his voice ragged with lust.

And then I see it. The bright fear in the man's eyes has vanished, and he wears the same vacant expression Jaxon did after I wrapped the chain around his neck. Everything is red. Everything is blood.

My migraine has vanished.

"Oh my god." The knife slips out of my hand, and I sag backward, dizzy with confusion and disgust and desire all at once. "Oh my god. What did I—Why did I—"

Jaxon catches me, his arm twining around my waist again, his mask sliding into the space between my shoulder and my neck. "You're a Hunter."

His words sear through me. I don't believe him. I *can't* believe him. But my body's pumping with a strange black hunger that I desperately need to feed.

I reach behind me, twisting my arm into the gap between our bodies until my fingers graze across Jaxon's cock.

"Is that what you want, little Hunter?"

"Don't call me that." I whirl around to face him, kneeling on the blood-soaked mattress. He stands beside the bed, gazing imperiously down at me from behind the mask. He looks like the god I am meant to worship.

I fumble with the button on his pants, my fingers too slippery with blood to do anything. But Jaxon takes over, undoing his fly with a slow laziness like he's mocking my urgency. He eases his cock out, and through the red haze of my lust, I see he's just as urgent as I am. I felt how big he was before, but seeing it is another thing, his thick length swollen and taut, beads of precum already shimmering on his cockhead.

I wrap my bloody fingers around him and stroke.

"That's it," he rasps. "Mark me with his blood."

His words shoot electricity through me, and I grab him with the other hand, stacking them on top of each other. He thrusts into my grip three times before he braces his hand on the top of my hand and barks, "Now lick me clean."

I jerk my gaze up to him, past his bloody cock, not sure if he's joking. Not sure if I even want him to be joking.

But all I see is the mask.

"Now," he orders, tightening his grip on my head. "Taste him for me, little Hunter."

"Don't *call* me th—"

He pushes my head forward and my lips part on instinct, and I draw him into my mouth. My victim's blood is coppery and salty and not unpleasant at all, a realization I simply can't let myself dwell on. Instead, I give myself over to it, my blood-sticky hand slipping down to rub my clit over my clothes as I swirl my tongue around Jaxon's hot, solid erection, lapping up the blood until I taste Jaxon underneath.

He grunts softly and thrusts his cock into my mouth, his hand holding me into place.

"All of it," he orders.

My clit aches, but I can't be bothered with the zipper or the bottom, with any of it. So I just keep teasing myself, touching my clit through two layers of fabric as I lick all the way down Jaxon's length, sucking off the last streaks of blood. He groans, hips rocking, his cock sliding sideways between my lips. And I'm making noises of my own. Hungry, greedy little slurps. I want more. More blood. More Jaxon.

"You like that." He pulls away from me, so suddenly that I whimper at the loss of him. His mask tilts down and he catches me with my hand between my thighs. "Look at you. Getting your clothes dirty."

"Who's fault is that?"

He laughs, the sound echoing and deep. "Yours. You were a messy girl."

Heat floods into my face, and I don't have a snappy response. Because I was messy. I'm sitting in that mess now.

"I want you to undress." He pushes his own pants down as he talks, his cock even more impressive when it's not bound by fabric. "But don't get up from that bed."

I don't move. Some tiny part of me wants to cling to my morality. To my *humanity*. Because I'm not a Hunter. I *can't* be. Even if I did enjoy stabbing that man—

"Undress," Jaxon snarls, and then he jumps onto the bed, the mattress springing. The man, my victim, jostles up against me. It doesn't disgust me.

In fact, I—I like it.

"Make me," I say, because if Jaxon makes me it's not my fault. I'm not a monster.

Jaxon laughs darkly again. Then he grabs my ankle and yanks off my shoe. My sock. I suck in my breath, holding myself up because if I fall back the way I want to, I'll be draped across my victim's chest.

Jaxon pulls off my other shoe, then crawls slowly between my legs, shoving my thighs open. I can feel his eyes on me even if I can't see them. Even if all I see is emptiness.

"Why don't you want to obey?" he murmurs, unhooking the button on my pants. "Don't you want me to fuck you?"

I glare at him, trying to summon up the horror and terror I know I should be feeling. "You made me do this." It sounds stupid, even to me.

"Doesn't answer my question." He yanks my pants and panties down over my hips at the same time. I gasp when I feel the hot, sticky blood against my bare ass, then groan when Jaxon splits my pussy open with two gloved fingers. "This does, though."

He pulls his fingers out and slides them into my lips. The wetness coating the leather is undeniable. I can't stop myself from sucking on his fingers, either, or bucking my hips up against him.

"There's my girl," he says softly, pulling his hand away so he can peel my jeans off completely. "There's my eager little Hunter."

"I'm not a Hunter," I gasp out. "I'm not like you."

Jaxon's only response is to push my sweater up over my chest. He grabs me by the waist and sits me up, grinding my drenched pussy into the blood-soaked mattress.

"Evidence!" I shriek out, logic somehow worming its way through my lust-fevered brain. "We're leaving evidence!"

"You're not human," he says. "They don't know how to look for us."

And for the first time since he claimed I'm a Hunter, I hope he's right. Because I really, really don't want to stop.

Jaxon rips my sweater over my head, tosses it aside, fumbles with my bra. That he lets fall to the side, and his mask dips as he takes in my bare breasts.

Then he pushes me back, throwing me into the mangled stomach of my victim.

And I groan with pleasure.

Pleasure. Not fear. Not disgust. It's pleasure, because pleasure is currently pooling hotly between my legs, and I lift my blood-smeared hips up toward Jaxon and press my upper back into my victim, sinking deeper into his corpse.

"Say it," Jaxon whispers, his mask brushing my cheek. He rubs my clit, the cool leather of his glove a strange, delicious sensation.

"Say—what—"

Jaxon responds by smacking my pussy just hard enough for it to sting. I cry out, jolt against the corpse. The body still feels warm, but the blood is already cooling and sticky.

"Say it," Jaxon commands, and I gaze up at him and I really do feel like he's a monster, a god, and I'm trapped in his thrall—

Exactly where I want to be.

He rubs my clit a little faster, rolling my pulsing nub tween his fingers. I thrust my hips upward, not sure if the wetness between my legs is from blood or desire.

"Don't act it out." Jaxon's voice is calm and low. Patient. "Say it. Tell me what you want me to do to you."

I don't want to say it because saying it is admitting that I want it. That I want *all* of it. That I wanted the kill, and I wanted the blood, and I want Jaxon to shove his swollen cock into my greedy little cunt on top of the evidence of my crime.

"Tell me!" he roars.

"Fuck me!" I scream, my voice overlapping his. "I want you to fuck me!"

He pauses and pulls his hand away from my clit, that empty, terrible mask staring down at me. All I can do is take deep, sucking breaths, my back propped up against a dead man, my blood-smeared legs spread wide and waiting.

"There's my good girl," he purrs.

I moan softly, because it's a lie. I'm not good at all. Look at me. Where I am. What I'm doing.

Jaxon crawls forward over the bed, making the corpse bounce up against me. I brace myself for the painful, delirious stretch when he shoves himself inside of me, but he stops, his cock just nudging against my entrance.

"What are you waiting for?" I gasp out, desperate to be filled.

In response, he reaches past me, dipping his hands in the cooling blood of my first—my second?—victim. I know what's coming, instinctually, and I hold my breath as he smears the blood up along the side of my waist, rubbing it into my soft, jiggling belly. I arch into his touch, moaning, fists beating against the filthy mattress. "More," I choke out, and it's like I'm outside of myself.

Jaxon groans with dark, animalistic lust and does as I ask, painting the blood across my tits, squeezing and tweaking my nipples as he does. I drift on the tortuous haze of my desire, his warm, sticky hands sending new beats of pleasure surging through my body.

"This is a baptism," he says softly. "*Your* baptism, little Hunter."

I try to touch myself, but Jaxon slaps my hand away and pins it back against my victim, his other hand massaging my breasts with a slow, careful rhythm. All I can see is his mask. The twisted, dark metal. The antlers. The faintest flash of his eyes in the darkness.

"Stay," he orders, and then he releases my hand and scoops up more blood, the crimson liquid dripping through his fingers. He dribbles it across my exposed neck and then over my lips and my cheeks. Then he combs his fingers through my hair, marking that with the blood, too.

I let out a loud, choking sob. It's not fear or horror. It's *need*.

"Please," I gasp, darting out my tongue to taste the salt of my victim's blood again. "Please, fuck me, Jaxon. *Please*."

"You beg so well." He trails his fingers down the side of my neck.

I buck my hips upward like I can catch his cock with my pussy. He laughs and pins them down. Pins me down.

"Ask one more time." His cockhead nudges against my clit, making me gasp and squirm.

"I need you inside me." I stare at his mask. I sink into the gore beneath my back. "I'll die if you don't fuck me, Jaxon."

There's no denying the shudder that wracks through him. No denying the groan that escapes from behind the unfathomable mask. His fingers dig into my hips.

"We can't have that," he says.

And then he plunges inside me, one hard and painful thrust, and I scream with relief.

CHAPTER TWENTY-FIVE

JAXON

She's the most beautiful fucking thing I've ever seen.

I pin her down with my cock, grinding her into the man she killed, and hook my hands under her knees so I can hoist up her legs and slide even deeper inside her. She screams again, a sound that may as well be music but one that could be dangerous at this moment, even in this mostly abandoned neighborhood. I press my hand against her mouth.

"Shh," I sigh, rolling my hips in slow, lazy thrusts. Her wet cunt clamps down around me, the heat of it lighting a fire deep in my chest. Above my blood-smeared glove, her eyes roll back, showing me her whites.

"Shhh," I say again. "You don't want to get caught, do you?"

She jerks her head against my hand, a quick sharp no, and I pull it away and focus on making her come. From the moment I saw her sink her blade into our victim's shoulder, I've been imagining what her pussy would feel like when all that pleasure she built up finally explodes out of her.

"This got you wet, didn't it?" Seeing her through the mask, I can sense the Hunter in her. It's still hidden, though, buried deep in some hidden crevice in her heart. But it's there. Pulsing. On the verge of bursting.

Just like she is.

She whimpers her response and squeezes her eyes shut and grabs at her tits, pressing them together. They look so beautiful coated in blood. She *looks* beautiful, like one of my sculptures except living and breathing and hot with fire.

I yank my cock out of her pussy, making her squawk in protest, and then I crawl up so I'm straddling her waist. I shove my cock, still dripping with her arousal, between the bloody mounds of her tits and groan. Even *this* feels better with a living woman. Her tits are hot and sticky and I can feel her heart pounding against my cock.

"You said—" The words come out jagged. "You said—You'd fuck me—"

"I am fucking you." I look down at her scowling, blood-smeared face. My cock keeps stabbing at her throat, right next to her fluttering pulse.

"This isn't what I asked for!"

I laugh. She's right, though, and as good as her big, bouncing tits feel around my cock, her pussy feels even better. I crawl back and hunch over her as I line my cock up with her cunt, nuzzling her face with my mask. "Sorry," I purr. "But your tits looked too good *not* to fuck."

Then I shove myself inside her again, making her squeal instead of talking back. Even though I like it when she talks back. I like the reminder that she's alive and that she's willing to fight a little before she gives in.

Just like she's giving in now, settling back on the corpse while I thrust in and out of her. My gods are here, too, roiling around inside me. My Guardian loves the blood, loved it when I baptized Charlotte in its name. And the Unnamed wants to fuck Charlotte into oblivion. Although I'm not sure how much of that is the Unnamed and how much of it is me.

I'm also not sure if it's the Unnamed or my Guardian or me who wants to kiss her as I slam into her cunt, her lips crimson from the blood. She groans, lips parting to give me a glimpse of the pink tongue that licked my cock clean, and I pull up my mask just enough that I can smash my mouth against hers. She makes a muffled *mmph* sound and wraps her thick legs around my hips, cunt fluttering as I plunge my tongue into her mouth. When I break the kiss, she gasps and falls back on the corpse. We never break our rhythm.

"Are you going to come for me?" I pull my mask back down and rise up to kneeling so I rub my thumb over clit.

"Depends." Her breath is all fast and panty, and I know the answer is yes. I can feel it in the way her pussy contracts around me, the way her skin is flushed beneath the mask of blood. "Think you can make me?"

If I wasn't buried hilt-deep in her right now, that might have given me pause. But I'm wearing the mask of my gods, and I'm fucking a gorgeous, ferocious *living* girl on the corpse of her first real kill, and nothing's going to give me pause. Especially not when I wrench my glove off so I can feel her clit throbbing against my skin.

"I've done it before, haven't I?" I fuck her with my cock and rub her clit with my thumb and watch her dissolve in front of me. I know the second she comes, I will too, and so I try to drag it out as long as I can, slowing my pace until she jerks and keens in protest. The corpse flops beneath her, matching the rhythm of my thrusts.

"You're an asshole," she gasps. "You're doing that on purpose."

The Unnamed flares inside me, a starburst of power. Because right now, I do have power over her. I snapped the binding that held her back, and now she's spread beneath me, legs spread, her clit under my control.

"Beg for it," I tell her, dragging the full length of my cock out of her just so I can slam it back in. "Convince me, and I'll let you come."

Charlotte screeches in frustration and hits me in the shoulder, which just makes me drop her clit and fuck her harder.

"Do you want to come, little Hunter?" Fuck, I hope she doesn't try to hold out. I need to feel her convulsions as much as she does.

Her expression tells me everything, though. Her eyes are glassy with desperation. Her face is twisted with need. She grinds up against me as I bury myself inside her, chasing her pleasure. But it's not enough. The angle isn't right, and I won't adjust myself until I hear her beg.

"Please," she spits out, and I groan with pleasure.

"You can do better than that."

"Please let me come." She falls back over the corpse, her blood-splattered tits rising up, each one tipped with a sharp nub of a nipple. I push up my mask and lean over her to suck one into my mouth, tasting the dried blood. Charlotte groans.

"Please!" she shouts, her legs quaking around me. "Let me come, Jaxon! Or I'll fucking kill you again!"

That nearly undoes me. I'm pretty sure the only thing that holds me back is the Unnamed, still surging inside me. I jerk up and quicken my thrusts. Charlotte stares at me.

"Please." Her voice is small. Plaintive. "Please, Jaxon. I'm so close. All you need to do is—"

I know what I need to do, and I do it, pressing my thumb hard on her clit. I stroke over it twice and that's all it takes before my pretty, blood-soaked Hunter is moaning and gasping and shrieking and *coming*. Her pussy clamps down on my dick and I let myself go, roaring as my cum pumps into her, pulse after pulse matching Charlotte's own desperate rhythm. Even after I'm spent I keep rocking against her, because she's still shaking and shuddering and I want her to feel every ounce of pleasure that she can.

Eventually, she slumps back, draping gracefully over the body, her chest rising and falling as she breathes. I slide out of her and crawl backward off the bed so I can admire the scene in front of me. It feels like one of my sculptures:

Two bodies twisted together. Charlotte's raging fire. Our victim's cooling corpse.

I wish I had a camera.

Charlotte's breath slows, and she tilts her head toward me. A darkness passes over her features, and my heart twists in my chest. Because there's doubt in her eyes.

Whatever thing is binding her, keeping her from her nature —it's gone. I felt it snap. But thirty years is a long time to think you're human when you're not, and it occurs to me that she'll need time to adjust. To accept the truth of things.

Charlotte sits up suddenly, hands moving to cover her chest. She looks down at herself, her hair falling into her face. "Now what?" she mutters, sliding forward. Not looking at me. Not looking at her victim, either.

"We go back to Louisiana," I say, sliding off my mask. "And I can train you."

Charlotte jerks her head up at that. She seems to be considering what she wants to say next. Eventually, she spits out, "Train me?"

"You're a Hunter." I feel uneasy, saying it now that it's real and not me goading her on during sex. "Something—something was stopping you from knowing that. But when you—"

"I'm not a Hunter," she snarls, scrambling off the bed. "I'm not—"

She's looking for her clothes, I think, but she catches sight of her victim instead and slaps her hand over her mouth and makes a low keening sound. "What's wrong with me?" she whispers. "Why—"

"Nothing," I say quickly, setting my mask to the floor so I can go over to her. When I wrap my arms around her waist, she doesn't pull away, which is something, I suppose. "You just—there was a charm on you, stopping you from knowing that you're a Hunter. We don't have to talk about it now. Ambrose wants to—"

"Who the fuck is Ambrose?" she shouts.

"Another Hunter." I spot her sweater and pants lying on the floor, although the scarf is nowhere to be seen. We need to get out of here. But Charlotte's in a panic because the Unnamed's plan didn't work the way I expected, and I can't have her running down the street covered in blood. "Let's get you cleaned up."

She whirls around to face me, eyes bright in contrast to the blood. "How?" she whispers. "What—We can't—"

"We can do whatever we want." I step up to her, the clothes draped over my arm. "I can sense humans. No one's nearby right now. If someone comes close, I'll know with plenty of time to spare."

Charlotte stares at me, trembling. I take her hand, squeezing it a little. She drops her gaze down to it. But she doesn't pull away.

"Come on," I tug her forward. "Just a quick shower."

"They're going to know it was us," she whispers even as she comes with me, away from the bed and the corpse and over to the door leading into the attached bathroom. "They're going to—we left evidence—"

"We aren't human. I told you that." I switch on the bathroom light and stop short. The room is huge, with a big glassed-in shower. Fanciest bathroom I've ever been in. "They'll find our DNA, but everything'll be inconclusive." I look over at her, standing in the doorway, her eyes taking in the bathroom. "Trust me."

She gives me a look I can't read. But when I step forward and turn the water on, she follows me.

The shower is one of those rainfall showers, with the

shower head fixed to the ceiling so that the water falls in curtains. I get it warm for her, then strip out of my shirt. "Go on," I tell her. "Wash off."

Charlotte steps up beside me, staring at the shower. The blood streaking her body looks lurid in the bright bathroom lights.

She's so fucking hot like this. I wish she could just walk around covered in blood forever.

But, of course, she steps into the shower. I finish stripping out of my clothes and jump in after her. She doesn't say anything, just stands under the water as it rehydrates the dried blood and then sluices it away in crimson-pink ribbons.

I can't stop staring at her. Which means I don't miss the despair creeping into her expression.

"You look so beautiful," I say, acting on some instinct. It's definitely not my gods, anyway. Neither of them are interested in any of this. They just want the blood and the violence.

Charlotte jerks her gaze to me, eyes glimmering.

"You do." I join her under the water, keeping my movements slow. She doesn't pull away, not even when I put my hands on the top of her lush hips. Not even when I lean in and brush my mouth against her.

"I liked it," she breathes against me, and I hear the shame poisoning her words.

And it hurts me, that shame. I don't know what it's like because I grew up in a family of Hunters. I was bred for this life. Raised for it. To hear her shame in what she is, knowing that it hurts her—

That cracks me in two.

So I draw her into me underneath the warm water, and I kiss her for real, sliding my tongue between her lips. I still can't get over how much I love kissing a living woman, all the heat and yielding reciprocity. Because Charlotte does return the kiss.

She even winds her arms around my shoulders and presses her lush body against mine, the warm water sealing us together.

"I liked it, too," I whisper into her ear.

She stiffens, just a little, against me. "You're a monster, though."

I tsk softly and nuzzle against her neck. "Are you trying to hurt my feelings, little Hun—"

"Don't say it."

"Hunter." I speak it into her skin and relish when she shivers against me. "And maybe I am a monster." I pull back so I can gaze down at her through the curtain of glittering water, with her wide dark eyes and soaked hair. All the blood has washed away from her face. Pity. Fortunately, plenty is still clinging to her tits, and I massage them a little, helping it along. "But I've accepted what I am, Charlotte. And you will, too."

She wants to be horrified, I think. But she isn't. I can smell it on her, the first curls of her arousal. The flash of lust in her eyes. She tries to smother both.

"Let's get you clean," I whisper. "And then let's take you home."

And when I say *home*, Charlotte doesn't protest.

CHAPTER TWENTY-SIX

CHARLOTTE

I wake up in the bed at Jaxon's house, still wearing the clothes I wore when I—

When we drove to Houston.

The last thing I remember was curling up in the passenger seat of Jaxon's car and staring at my pale reflection, Houston's skyline at our backs and the world around us too dark to see. Jaxon talking softly, telling me about Ambrose. The man, he said, who can explain what's wrong with me.

But I know what's wrong with me. I killed a man. And not one who kidnapped me and came back to life anyway. A stranger, someone I'd never seen before in my life. Someone who had done nothing to me.

I slashed him to ribbons, and then I—

I squeeze my eyes shut, crushing out the memories even though they make me feel warm and floaty. Or rather, *because* they make me feel warm and floaty. If they made me feel like the nightmare I am, then I'd wallow in them.

I push the blanket off and sit on the edge of the bed, taking deep breaths. I'm clean, and I feel like I shouldn't be. But no, we took a shower together, in the bathroom of the man I killed.

Jaxon had rubbed all the blood away from my skin, kissing me the entire time.

I kissed him back.

I want to kiss him again.

I want to—

A dull ache forms behind my eye, a ghost of the migraines I usually get. I stand up, shaking a little, and test the door, out of habit more than anything.

I'm stunned when it swings out into the hallway.

What's this? A show of respect? Of trust? Or is it just that Jaxon knows he's trapped me in this other way. This worse way. Because where can I go now that I've killed a man and—

And bathed yourself in his blood and fucked another murderer on his corpse and screamed when you came?

The memories hit me all at once, and I swoon, slamming up against the doorframe. My body throbs with a hot, angry need. My mind screams at me that I need to turn myself in, that I need to be thrown in jail before I hurt someone else. It also viscerally recoils at the thought, enough that I fall down to my hands and knees and retch.

A door slams somewhere in the house, followed by Jaxon's voice: "Charlotte! I'm here!"

I retch again and spit up stomach acid. I hadn't exactly had an appetite for food last night.

Footsteps thud up the stairs. I wipe my mouth with the back of my hand just as Jaxon appears at the top of the stair-case. "Are you okay?"

I sit back on my heels, not sure how to answer. "How did you know—" I start, not sure how to phrase the question. "Know that I wasn't feeling well?"

Jaxon helps me stand, his hand squeezing mine. "I can sense things, remember?" He gives me a wry smile. "It's why I thought you were human until you—"

The revulsion crawls over my face, and he must see it too because he snaps his mouth shut.

"Because you feel human," he finishes instead. "Sort of."

I'm dizzy, and I stare down where I spat up on his floor. "I need to clean that up," I mutter.

"I'll get it," he says. "I've dealt with worse. Why don't you go down to the kitchen and get some water?"

His kindness strikes me as suspicious, and I regard him accordingly, glancing at him out of the corner of my eye. There's something hapless about him, which I do find charming in spite of myself. It reminds me of when I first saw him in the diner, which feels like a million years ago. An awkward weirdo instead of a psycho.

"I still don't understand what's happening to me," I finally say.

"I'll explain what I know." His eyes bore into mine. "I promise."

Yeah, I've seen how much he likes to *explain* things. But the truth is I do want a glass of water and I don't want to go back into the bedroom where I had, up until this moment, been a prisoner. And if he wants to clean up my vomit, he's welcome to it.

So I go downstairs, scurrying quickly through Jaxon's creepy-ass living room. The faint throb in my head has vanished, thankfully, and I fill a glass with water from the tap and gulp it down, staring out the window above the sink as I do. It looks out at the swamp, lush even in the dead of winter.

Footsteps behind me. I whirl around as Jaxon slinks into the kitchen, peering at me through the sleek curtain of his hair. "You feel better," he says. A statement, not a question.

"I guess." I fill my glass with more water and then sit down at an ancient kitchen table with aluminum legs and a chipped Formica top. I run my fingers over the imperfections, wondering what other nightmares have happened in this house.

Jaxon sits down beside me. And for a minute, that's all we do. Then he clears his throat.

"So, yeah." He pushes his hands through his hair. "What do you want to know?"

I stare at him, fingers curled around my water glass. What *don't* I want to know? I can trace every decision I've made in the last week and still can't fully understand how I landed in this exact moment. I thought I was going to find my dead friend. Instead, I've uncovered a whole world of monsters.

"How can I be a Hunter?" I finally say. "You told me they—you—aren't human. But I am. I don't have this urge—to hunt, or whatever." Or at least, I hadn't. Not until Jaxon made me smell blood and then handed me a knife.

Jaxon takes a deep breath. "That's what I'm not sure about," he says. "When I first saw you in that diner, it was—" He gives me a surprisingly shy look. "It was like when I sense a kill, except not, because my gods said I couldn't."

"Your gods," I repeat, remembering what he told me the other night. *I pray, but not to the god you expect.*

Jaxon nods. "They tell me who to kill. How to kill them. How to find them. That was how I knew how to get to the house in Houston, and how that man was the one who sent the hit men the other night—" He waves his hand around. "None of that actually matters, though. My gods told me you were a Hunter, but you had been bound by some kind of charm. And killing a human for the first time would break it."

I listen to all of this with a growing sense of dread. "You are crazy," I whisper.

Jaxon's eyes narrow. "Just because you don't understand something doesn't mean I'm crazy for explaining it."

Hot anger bubbles under the surface of my skin. "What we did last night," I rasp, "was an abomination. And you're trying to tell me that some *gods* are directing—"

"Abomination?" Jaxon's eyes flare with an undeniable rage,

furious enough that I feel a quiver of very real fear. "It's what we *are,* Charlotte. Humans are our *prey*."

"No." I push away from the table, blood pumping through my body. "No, animals have prey. They hunt for *food*. What I did—" I sway sideways, pain surging up into my temple. "That was evil."

Jaxon jumps up and catches me before I can collapse, moving with a swiftness that I want to see as supernatural. "Evil doesn't exist," he says flatly, like he's reciting something from memory. "There are only those chosen by the gods to cull, and those to be culled."

"That's evil!" I shove him away, surprised by my own strength. I think he is, too, because he stumbles like he's caught off-balance. "We can't decide who—"

"The gods decide!" Jaxon roars. "Because they see patterns in this universe we can't even fathom." He lunges at me, and I side-step him, moving on pure adrenaline, slipping out of his grasp at the last minute. Then I hurl my water glass at him, and he bats it away, water arcing out between us.

"The gods brought you to me," he says in a low, dangerous voice. He stalks toward me, each step carefully measured, and my fear spikes again. I don't know what I am. I did something monstrous, yes, but am I really a monster? Was I caught up in some spell that Jaxon wove around me?

But Jaxon, right now—he *is* a monster. A predator. And it doesn't matter what I am, because I'm clearly his chosen prey.

I race out of the kitchen and into the dining room. Jaxon follows and grabs me by the waist, dragging me up against him. "Stop fighting it," he snarls into my ear, his fingers digging into my flesh. "Stop letting that binding have control of you even though you broke it."

"Fuck you!" I shove him away, hard enough that he slams sideways against the table, knocking the chairs away. He catches himself and looks up at me through his long hair and grins like a maniac.

"More of that," he says.

"There's no binding," I say, ignoring his taunts. Ignoring what they do to me. How my whole body is coursing with the need to touch him—violently and otherwise. "I'm just *human* and you—you forced me to—"

"I didn't force you to do anything." He ambles toward me, and I step away from him, walking backward. "I let go of that knife and you kept going."

He's right. I know he's right. I remember everything about that moment. I could have stopped, but I didn't want to.

And, right now, I hate him for reminding me.

I scream and launch myself at him, conjuring up a strength that feels unfamiliar in my body. For a split second, my feet lift off the ground and we're flying.

Then we crash onto the dining room table, Jaxon sprawled on his back, me on top of him, straddling him, grinding my pussy down on his undeniably erect dick. He grins at me again, his teeth bright in dim light. I screech my anger and swing my fist at him, unthinking.

He catches it and then, in some graceful fighter's move, flips me over. My head knocks hard against the table. The world flashes. I blink up at Jaxon as he presses my arms down beside my head, his hair falling across my face.

"This is how I know you're a Hunter," he says softly, gently, like I'm not straining up against his grip, trying to flip him off me. "No human woman could fight me like this." He nuzzles against my cheek until his lips find my ear. "No human woman could have killed me."

I thrust against him, telling myself I'm trying to throw him off me. Even though I'm not really sure that's true.

"You want more?" he asks.

"I'm not a fucking Hunter!" I scream, thrashing beneath him. "I'm human!"

Jaxon raises an eyebrow and releases my hands and I swing at him without thinking. My palm makes contact with his face, and the force of the strike vibrates down my arm. Jaxon jerks his head sideways, then tilts his gaze back to me, his cheek red.

"Again." His eyes blaze with a fire that frightens me. Arouses me.

I shouldn't, but I give him exactly what he wants, striking him hard on the other cheek. This time, I use all that strange and unfamiliar strength, and Jaxon groans when I strike him, dry-humping me like a teenager.

"Again," he roars, and I set upon him with all my fear and fury, a maelstrom of violence I can't even begin to understand. He fights back just enough to roll us both off the table, and I don't crash against the floor like I expect but somehow land deftly on my feet, crouched, hands up.

"How the fuck?" I choke out, staring at him over my burning hands. His face is red from my slaps. A trickle of blood runs out of his nose. Did I do that to him?

I want to taste it, his blood.

I throw myself at him, slamming him so hard against the wall that the deer's head falls beside us with a thunderous clatter. He pulls me into him, rolling his hard cock into my thigh, and I sink my teeth into his pulsing neck, biting down until his skin bursts and salty, hot blood flows across my tongue.

I groan, rubbing my lips in it, swallowing some of the drops.

Jaxon groans, too, although his groans stretch out into words of praise: "That's it, my little Hunter. Taste your prey. Just like that."

I want to be furious with him. I want to hate him. Instead, I'm kissing him with my bloody lips, smearing his blood across his face until I find his mouth. Then I make him taste himself.

He returns the kiss with a terrifying fire, his mouth hot and angry and devouring. I'm distantly aware that my hips are thrusting against him, trying to fuck him again. Distantly aware that I'm on the verge of coming with the taste of his blood on my tongue.

He wrenches away from me to break the kiss, then flings me around like a rag doll. Throws me up against the table, its edge digging into my belly.

"Fuck me," I shriek.

No. No, I meant to say *fuck you*.

Didn't I?

Jaxon yanks on my pants, dragging them off my leg one by one. Then he does the same with my underwear. As soon as the cool air of his house kisses my soaked pussy, I moan and wriggle my ass back toward him.

He slaps it, hard.

"Be still." I hear the zip of his flying coming down. The rustle of his clothes. Then he braces one hand on my lower spine and the other around the back of my neck, pressing me down hard on the table. I fight against him, bucking up against his grip.

But as strong as I feel, he's stronger.

"I think I want to win this fight, little Hunter," he says, right before he thrusts his cock into my pussy.

I've never been so happy to lose.

CHAPTER TWENTY-SEVEN

JAXON

Fighting Charlotte got me hard as hell, and every time I thrust into her tight, clenching pussy, it's like I'm fighting her again. I pin her against the table, reminding her that I'm the older Hunter. The stronger Hunter. But when she wriggles around to look at me over her shoulder, I let her.

I want to see the blazing lust in her eyes. I want to see my blood smeared across her lips.

She fucks me like she's still fighting me, stretching her arms across the table to grab onto the other side and give herself leverage to shove herself on my dick.

"I'm not a Hunter," she snarls.

"Keep telling yourself that." I drag her backward across the table so I can reach down and thumb her clit. Her pussy feels as intoxicating as ever, but the soft swell of her ass against my lower belly makes me want to explore previously unknown territory. "You sure as hell fuck like one."

She snarls at me and thrusts backward as if answering my accusation with proof. I work her clit as fast as I can, her arousal drenching my fingers. I need her as wet as possible if I'm going to find out what her asshole feels like.

Charlotte snarls again, then moans. All her cries are wordless. Animalistic. I swear I can feel my gods coursing through her. Or maybe that's just the first quaking shudders of her orgasm.

"See?" I grin, quicken my pace on her clit as I bottom out inside her and soak up her wetness. "Look how fast you're going to come for me."

And then she does, her whole body shaking. She drops her head down on the table and keeps fucking me, hips rolling with an unsteady rhythm. I hunch over her, circling my hand around her throat to lift her head so I can talk into her ear.

"You fought well," I whisper. "But you shouldn't fight me. I'm your teacher."

She meets my gaze with a slack, glossy expression. "You're my kidnapper."

"Yeah?" I run my thumb through the dried blood clinging to her chin. "Then why are you fucking me?"

And it's true that she's fucking *me*. I'm not moving. She's the one twitching and jerking around my cock.

"Tell me," I order.

"You have a good dick."

I grin at that. "Is that so, cher?" I shove my thumb between her lips and she draws it in to suck on it. I don't even have to ask.

"Mmmhmm," she mumbles.

I pull my thumb out of her mouth and hold her by the throat again. Her body quakes. Her eyes flit sideways.

"How'd you like my good dick in your asshole?" I murmur.

That gets her attention. She whips her entire torso around to look at me "Is that supposed to be punishment?" she asks. "For fighting you?"

I'm stunned she asked that, to be honest. "Punishment?" I laugh. "No, little Hunter. I want to *reward* you."

Charlotte's eyes go wide.

"You fought so well." As I talk, I rearrange her, pulling my dick out and rolling her onto her back. She doesn't fight back. In fact, she spreads her legs once I have her in position, making it easy for me to slide my fingers into her sopping pussy. I drag the juices out and rub them around the rim of her asshole.

Charlotte groans, arching her back.

"I want to make you come again," I say. "But we should mix it up, don't you think?"

Charlotte gazes at me. She's so fucking gorgeous, with her blood-red hair and blood-smeared mouth and her eyes dark with lust.

"You're too big," she says.

I slide one of my slippery fingers into her asshole, and she gasps, the muscles there fluttering and clenching.

"Say that again." I grin. "I like it when you flatter me."

Something flashes across Charlotte's face—a kind of coyness I haven't seen before.

Or rather, I have seen it before. Once.

When I was fucking her on top of that bloody corpse in Houston.

"Your cock is too big to fuck me in the ass," she says.

In response, I ease a second finger inside of her. Charlotte sucks in her breath, bites down on her bottom lip.

"You'll be fine." I slide my two fingers in and out of her asshole, slow and steady, and work her soaked pussy with my other hand, drawing out more and more wetness. Charlotte slumps back on the table, hoisting up her hips and spreading her legs wide for me.

"That's it." I focus on my efforts: Her pretty, glossy pussy. My two fingers disappearing inside her asshole. "You're doing so good."

I've only done this once before, with a dead girl and half a bottle of lube. But Charlotte is so easy to fuck.

And so unbelievably wet.

"If you're going to fuck my ass," she gasps. "Fucking do it already."

My cock is screaming the same thing at me, but I need to get myself good and slippery again. I pull my hands away from Charlotte and slide my cock into her with one firm stroke, leaning over to get as deep into her pussy as I can. Charlotte starts working her hips, fucking me, but I push down her legs to still her.

"Patience," I tell her as I slide my now-drenched cock out of her cunt and line it up with her asshole.

Charlotte whimpers softly as I press my cockhead through the tight ring of muscle. "Shhh," I whisper. "You're a Hunter. You can take me."

She nods, her expression determined. I reward her with my clean fingers on her clit, drawing out more of her arousal to ease my passage. The Unnamed growls inside me, eager to claim her. Because I've already had her in two holes. Finished in two holes.

It's time to take the third.

I keep rubbing her clit as I slide my cockhead into her ass. Her body clamps down on me, and I groan at the squeeze of it. Push a little more. She takes deep, careful breaths and shoves her hands up under her shirt to play with her tits.

I slide a finger into her pussy.

"Fuck!" she cries out, jolting up against me

"Be still," I order, although I'm deep enough inside her that it doesn't matter. I'm deep enough inside her, in fact, that I start to thrust a little, slow and careful. The Unnamed wants me to go faster, wants me to destroy her, but I hiss at him. She's *my* Hunter. I'll train her—and reward her—as I see fit.

And what I want right now is for her to come again.

"That's it," I breathe, gently stroking the spongy wetness

inside her cunt, drawing out more shivers and quakes. "You're taking me so good, cher." All the while I pump in and out of her asshole, keeping my strokes slow and sensuous. Charlotte yanks her shirt and bra up, giving me a beautiful view of her soft, pillowy breasts and the swollen pink nipples she keeps abusing with her fingers. I knew there was a reason I wanted to do this with her on her back.

She doesn't respond to me with words, just desperate grunts and moans. Her body trembles; her clit flutters. She's close to coming. So am I. Her tight little asshole has a death grip on my cock, and I don't know if I'm going to hold out much longer.

"You gonna come for me again?" I ask her. "You deserve it. You put up a good fight."

Charlotte's eyes flutter open and lock into mine. She still doesn't smell exactly like a Hunter, but that expression in her gaze is pure predatory lust. "You liked it, didn't you?" I grin. "Fighting me? Making me bleed?"

"Yes," she gasps out, squeezing her tits tighter. I slide another finger into her pussy. Fuck her ass a little harder. If she was going to say anything else, it's lost now, with the way her eyes roll back and her back arches and her soft round stomach trembles. But then she surprises me. "Fuck, Jaxon, I'm going— I'm going to—"

And then her words really do leave her. She dissolves into a long, throaty wail, and the whole lower half of her body contracts around my cock. I keep stroking her inner walls. Keep thumbing her clit. And keep thrusting into her asshole, because my balls are tight against my body and heat keeps building in my stomach and the Unnamed's whispers are a hurricane in my head. It wants this, me and Charlotte joined together. This is how it's meant to be—me and her. Hunters aren't as solitary as some of us like to think.

And that's the thought that pushes me over the edge, that I've finally found it. *Her*. My partner. My mate. In killing and fucking and loving, all of it. Another Hunter with whom I can share everything.

I roar as my cum erupts inside her her ass, and then I slump down, burying my face in her tits. She's still gasping, trying to catch her breath, but her hand comes up and touches the back of my head. Her fingers comb through my hair—a gentle, loving touch. Faint. A little distracted, a little lazy. A little afterthought.

No woman's ever touched me like that.

I press my nose into the valley between her breasts, then kiss her soft, trembling skin, licking away the beads of sweat there. I'm afraid to look up, afraid that when I do, I'll see her disdain when what I want more than anything is to see her love.

So I pull myself away, keeping my eyes on her body instead. She gleams with sweat, and we made a mess on the table, our mixed arousal glistening on the wood.

"Jaxon."

It gives me a jolt, hearing her say my name. Reminds me of how she said it right before she came. But she doesn't say now like it's a bad thing. Or like I'm a bad thing.

I force myself to meet her eyes. She looks pleasure drunk. Sated.

But also sad, and it feels like someone's squeezing my heart in my chest.

"What—what's wrong?" I ask, even though I really don't want to hear her answer.

Charlotte sits up. Her hair's a mess, sticking up from where I had her pressed against the table. Her skin's flushed, her lips swollen. Bruises are already forming on her neck where I kissed her a little too hard.

But what I focus on are the tears glistening on her lashes.

"What's wrong with me?" she asks. "Why am I—why do I feel so shattered?"

I freeze. The Unnamed is long gone, but my Guardian is nearby. Silent. It has no words of wisdom.

"Because of what we just did?" I brace myself for her rejection, but she actually shakes her head no.

"Not that," she whispers roughly. "That was—" She hesitates, looks at me through her tangled hair. "You know what you're doing."

I blush. The Unnamed knows what it's doing, more like.

Charlotte looks away. "I feel like something's broken inside me," she whispers. "And I—" She looks at me again, and her tears have fallen in dark lines over her cheeks. "How do you do this?" she whispers. "How do you just *be* this—this monster?"

She doesn't say it cruelly, and she's not wrong anyway. I'm a monster. My daddy was a monster. My grandparents, too. My mom—

Well, I don't know much about her.

"I grew up with it," I finally say, which is the truth. "And you—something kept you from knowing what you are for a long, long time."

Charlotte lifts her face toward me. I step between her legs and reach over, and when she doesn't pull away, I cup her face and run my thumb over the soft curve of her cheekbone.

She doesn't pull away from that, either. Instead, she presses into it, eyes never leaving mine.

"I don't want it," she whispers.

Those four words break my heart. Because how can she be *mine* if she can't even accept what she is?

But then she falls forward, collapsing into my arms. And even though it hurts that she hates what she is, at least she still wants comfort from me, the monster.

So I give it to her.

CHAPTER TWENTY-EIGHT

CHARLOTTE

I guess I could leave if I want to. Jaxon doesn't keep me locked up anymore.

The morning after the Dining Room Table Incident, I wander listlessly around his dusty old home, trying to understand who and what he is—and who or what *I* am. He doesn't stop me. In fact, I don't even see him until I glance out the window above the kitchen sink to find him repairing the hole in the fence, his hair in a knot on the top of his head and the sleeves of his shirt rolled up to his elbows to reveal his thick, strong forearms.

For a few moments, I just watch him, trying to embrace my new status as a killer. The events of the last forty-eight hours flicker through my head. Bare flesh, red blood, moans of pleasure.

And darkness. An endless, swirling darkness.

I killed a man, and I don't even know his *name*.

Jaxon looks over his shoulder, eyes catching mine. Then he breaks into a grin. I'm caught.

I duck away from the window, cheeks flushing. I feel

trapped, unsure if I should recede into the dusty shadows of the house or go out the back door and talk to him.

Jaxon decides for me. The back door swings open and he steps inside, bringing a rush of cool, balmy air with him.

"Hey," he says.

I wait, expecting him to say something else or attack me for more "training" or tell me his gods have someone else to kill. Instead, he just stands in the doorway, arms at his side. I wonder what would happen if I pushed past him and tore through the half-repaired fence and dove into the swamp. I'm sure he would hunt me down.

But even if he didn't, where the fuck would I go? What the fuck would I *do*? I'm an accessory to two murders and the perpetrator of one. Jaxon's property feels like some kind of fairy world hidden in the heart of the Louisiana swamp, accessible only by magic and spells. There are no police here. No laws.

No morality.

As long as I stay within the boundaries of the electric fence, I can pretend I'm still a normal person.

"You want to help?" Jaxon asks, jarring me back to the cool, sunny kitchen. He gestures toward the yard. "I'm repairing the fence."

"I saw that." I cross my arms over my chest and take a long, deep breath. "Do you need help?"

He shrugs. "Not really."

We stare at each other, and I see the man I killed, his eyes wide and his mouth open at the moment that Jaxon released the knife and I didn't.

"Do you have my phone?" I finally say.

Jaxon gives me a bland look. "Yeah…" He looks down at his palms. "Yeah, I smashed that. The day I…. uh, brought you here"

Of course he did.

"Who did you want to call?" he asks, lifting his gaze to meet mine, a hint of suspicion in his eyes.

"No one." I hear the defensiveness in my voice. "But I'm bored. I want to—" To what? Post a selfie on social media? Doomscroll through an endless waterfall of cat videos?

No, I realize suddenly. I want to do what I've spent the last three months doing. I want to investigate a murder.

"The man I—" I cut myself off, bile rising in my throat. Jaxon frowns, a dark line forming on his brow, but doesn't say anything. "You don't know his name, right?"

"The gods didn't tell me."

He's crazy. We're both crazy. We're both killers.

"Well, I want to know who he was." I square my shoulders, look Jaxon dead in the eye. "There are these forums I was using to investigate Edie's disappearance. They'll have picked up on— you know."

Jaxon smiles darkly. "Your first kill?"

"Don't call it that."

"What else should I call it?"

"Look, it doesn't fucking matter, okay?" My voice comes out harsh and shrill. "Do you have a phone I can borrow? A laptop?"

Jaxon just keeps holding that darkly sarcastic grin. I want to smack him, but I've seen where that leads.

"I'm serious," I say. "I want to know who he was."

Jaxon's grin flickers. "Yeah, I have a phone," he says softly. "But you'll have to sit out there with me while you use it. I don't want you turning yourself in."

The idea knots around my heart. A binding, like the binding Jaxon said was keeping me from being my true self.

The binding I felt snap when I drove a knife into that man's chest.

No. I'm losing my goddamned mind.

"Jail isn't a good place for us," he continues, almost gently. "Better to die and revive than end up there."

"I'm not going to turn myself in," I snap. "I still don't know for sure that Edie's safe, if nothing else."

Jaxon's expression flickers again. "She's safe," he says. "Now come on."

I follow him out of the kitchen and into the backyard. A cool, damp breeze blows in across the swamp, smelling of rotting plant matter. Jaxon vanishes inside his shed, but I hang back, staring at the gap in the fence. It's not big enough for me to crawl through anymore.

"Here you go." Jaxon slides a phone into my palm, then squeezes my hand and meets my gaze, his eyes black and burning. "Don't fuck around, Charlotte. I need to protect you, and if you bring the cops out here, that's going to be a lot harder for me to do."

My mouth goes dry. I can't look away from him. He's serious about it. About protecting me.

I just nod, and Jaxon releases me slowly and turns back to the fence. I sink down to sit cross-legged in the grass and swipe his phone open. He doesn't bother keeping it locked.

I pull up the CrimeSolvers forum, my heart fluttering inside my chest. It feels bizarre to be looking at it again. The last time I was on here, all I wanted was to find Edie. Now, it seems she's living with the murderer who nearly killed her fifteen years ago, and I actually *am* a murderer.

Still, I scroll through the posts. I skip over the dedicated Scott Hensner thread even though there are a dozen new comments, my hands shaking a little as I swipe down.

Then I see it:

`Another occult-related murder in Houston.`

I stop and stare at it for a few seconds before tapping on the link, every atom in my body vibrating. Jaxon's pretending to work on the fence, but I can tell he's listening to me, or sensing me. Whatever it is he does.

The post takes a few seconds to load.

ajhollendar78: Hey, CrimeSolvers! I hadn't seen this posted yet and thought it might be worth diving into, especially since there's a very likely connection to <u>another case</u>.

A link here, although I don't bother clicking on it.

I copied the article over from the Houston Chronicle.

Memorial Death Likely Homicide, Police Say

Oliver Raffia, 58, was found dead in his Memorial home this past Thursday in a suspected homicide.

"Oliver Raffia." I roll the name around on my tongue and look up to find Jaxon has paused his work, although he's not quite looking at me. "His name was Oliver Raffia."

"Does that make you feel better?" Jaxon asks quietly.

I scowl at him and go back to reading the article.

Police have no leads for the death of Raffia, who was discovered by an acquaintance on Thursday afternoon. However, Houston Police Chief Eric Ramirez says that the department is putting its full efforts into locating the perpetrator.

"This was an unusually violent crime," Ramirez said in a recent press conference. "Rest assured that we will see the killer brought to justice."

Me, I think numbly. *He's talking about me*.

For twenty years, Raffia was the owner of the Midnight Roux micro chain of all-night seafood restaurants, which currently has five locations throughout the Houston metro. He sold the chain two years ago and has been living in retirement since.

"He kept to himself," says Raffia's long-time neighbor, Allison Millner. "I can't imagine why anyone would do this to him."

For a long time, all I can do is stare down at the phone, at that last quote. *I can't imagine why anyone would do this to him.*

Why did I do that to him? Sitting in the Louisiana grass, the sun warming my shoulders, it feels like it all happened to someone else. Like it can't be real. But in the moment, it just felt *right*. An urge that needed to be satiated.

It still feels right, if I'm being honest.

"You okay over there?" Jaxon stretches another wire across the gap in the fence, hemming us in.

"Fine." I hate that my voice comes out strangled. "I just—" I scroll down on Jaxon's phone, skimming the rest of the post on CrimeSolvers. And then two words jump out at me:

Eclipse Brotherhood.

I've heard that before. One of the men who cut the hole in the fence said it to me, how they thought Jaxon had been working for some group with that name when he killed their—boss, or whoever it was. I scroll back up and start reading from the beginning.

ajhollendar78: So I've been following this story since they first found Raffia's body since I've got some connections at HPD. This case would be interesting in and of itself, of course, but what really gets me—and what the papers aren't talking about—is that Raffia, the victim here, has ties to the Occult Underground. I'm talking groups like the Eclipse Brotherhood and Promethean Fire. It's an open secret in Houston that Midnight Roux was connected to the ULS before it got sold, and I've heard from my contacts that Raffia is heavily involved in their leadership. This is likely an OU killing, and I personally think it's connected to Dennis Randall's death a month or so ago. Remember, with the <u>weird sigils?</u>

My throat gets all tight and restricted as I click on that last link, and I'm not surprised at all when I see the same post that brought me to Jaxon in the first place.

"Someone knows," I gasp. "Someone knows you killed Dennis Randall and I killed Oliver Raffia and they're gonna connect us and—"

Jaxon's arms are wrapped around my shoulders before I totally understand what's happening. He pulls me into his chest, his body warm from repairing the fence, and makes soft little shushing sounds against my hair.

"Look at this!" I cry, shoving the phone at him.

He takes the phone and balances it on top of my head as he reads. I press my cheek against his chest, listening to his heartbeat. It's slow. Calm.

"The ULS," he mutters. "I should have fucking known."

"You know what that is?"

"The Undying Lineage of the Stars," he says. "It's a group of human demon worshippers."

"*Demons?*" I bark out a laugh. "Is that what you are?" I can't bring myself to say *we*, and the question feels absurd anyway. It reminds me of my childhood, of my insanely religious parents. Demons were everywhere. I stopped believing in them when I left home at seventeen.

"No, *we* are not demons," Jaxons says firmly.

My face burns hot. *We.* I'm not like him.

You're exactly like him.

"And demon isn't really the right word, just the easiest." He slides his phone into his pocket and squeezes my shoulders, making me look at him. "Hey, don't worry, okay? These Occult Underground groups are always gunning for each other, okay?

They're like gangs, going after each other for encroaching on someone's turf."

"So why did you have to kill two people involved with them?" I shoot back. "Are you in one of these magic wizard gangs?"

Jaxon grins, but I see the flash of worry in his eyes. "No, cher. I'm not in a magic wizard gang. But it's possible they got themselves entangled with my gods, and that was why I was sent to them." He runs his thumb over my cheek, and despite my best efforts, I shiver beneath his touch. It is reassuring, even though it shouldn't be.

"I don't want to go to jail," I mutter, which feels trite in comparison to the enormity of terror I'm currently experiencing. It's not just about jail. It's about the threat of some cosmic punishment. Looking up Oliver Raffia made him real to me.

I'm a monster.

Jaxon sighs and pulls me into an embrace. "I won't let that happen," he says softly. "You're my responsibility now. I'll keep you safe."

I know I should pull away from him. I know I should run and turn myself in and end this all before it gets even more out of hand.

I can't imagine why anyone would do this to him.

And that's the really fucked thing.

Because I don't know either, even though I did it.

JAXON

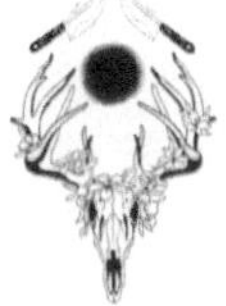

Charlotte goes to bed early that night, disappearing upstairs after the dinner I make for her. I can sense her sleeping—her slow heart rate and steady breathing, and I admit I creep up there when she's really under and watch her. I don't touch her, though. Just watch her, and worry.

I didn't lie to her about the Occult Underground stuff, but I didn't tell her the whole truth, either. No, Hunters aren't demons, but those occultists know that we aren't human, and they'll trap us for their own purposes. They'll try to trap our gods, too. And I suspect that's why the Unnamed and my Guardian sent me to kill Randall and Raffia.

I've killed for my gods for so long that I don't question why. I give them the blood they want. The violence. I collect the body parts for my own purposes. But now I see it all through Charlotte's eyes, and I can understand why it worries her—why her heart's jumping around in her chest as she sleeps, why she's no doubt having dark dreams she'll forget when she wakes.

I slip through the shadows and sit carefully on the edge of the bed and run my fingers over her hair, wondering if this touch—not sexual, not invasive—will calm her. She murmurs a little and shifts beneath the blankets. But she doesn't wake up.

*"**Guardian**,"* I whisper softly, the gods' language curdling on my tongue, *"**Should I be worried?**"*

The air in the room stirs. The shadows gather. The hairs on my arms stand on end, and cold, deathly fingers trail across the back of my neck—a touch more familiar to me than my mother's.

*"**You are a Hunter**,"* it whispers. *"**There's nothing for you to fear.**"*

*"**Why—**"*

*"**They were sacrifices.**"* It's the Unnamed who answers, and its presence is so sudden and so forceful that even Charlotte feels it in her sleep, moaning and shivering beside me. *"**The first a request, the second a payment.**"*

I stroke Charlotte's exposed arm, her skin soft against my fingers. So that's why both victims were connected to the ULS. Some human in the Occult Underground is making deals with my gods, and the gods asked me and Charlotte to be their weapons in this world.

It's not the first time I've been asked to kill on the gods' behalf, and it won't be the last. But I can see how it would be overwhelming for Charlotte to go so long thinking she's human and then, when she finally learns she's a Hunter, to get thrown into some divine chess game.

*"**Are there going to be other requests?**"* I ask softly, watching Charlotte breathe in the dark.

*"**Perhaps.**"* It's my Guardian again. *"**But for now, your task is her.**"*

"Charlotte?" There's no way to say her name in the language of the gods.

*"**Yes.**"* The Unnamed answers the question, and it circles closer, winding around me like a snake. Constricting my chest, making it hard for me to breathe. I like it though. I've always

liked it. ***"Her binding broke, but the magic poisoned her. Find a way to leach it out."***

"How?" I stroke her cheek with the back of my hand. Her eyes flicker behind her lids. I wonder if she's dreaming of the gods. If she's dreaming of me.

"We can not see it," says my Guardian. ***"But she can't exist like this, in two states at once."***

"Make her a Hunter," snarls the Unnamed, as if that wasn't what we did two nights ago.

And then, like an exhaled breath, they're both gone. The room feels empty without their presence, but at least Charlotte is here. Still breathing, still dreaming.

The magic poisoned her.

She doesn't seem poisoned, at least not physically. But her resistance to what she is—her guilt, her sorrow. It's hurting her. *That's* what's keeping her from becoming a Hunter.

She spent so long thinking she's human that she can't give it up.

Some unfamiliar emotion surges through me. I think it's empathy. Or love. Maybe both. All of it is directed at Charlotte.

I lay down beside her and wrap my arm around her waist and bury my nose in her hair and breathe in her scent. I don't do anything I shouldn't. Don't grope her breasts or slide my hand between her legs. Don't grind my quickly-forming erection into her soft, warm ass. But I do hold her. I wish I could take my knife and cut open her chest and carve out the poison desperately trying to keep her human. Maybe I should. Maybe she needs the initiation of death.

No. That's too drastic. But I have other options. I should call Ambrose—

Or Sawyer.

The thought hits me like a punch. That is one gift I can give her, isn't it? The thing she came to Louisiana to find.

I press closer to her, breathing her in, considering the possibility. All I want is to make everything right for her.

And maybe taking her to Edie is the best way to do it.

I'll see what Ambrose says. But for now, I just hold Charlotte in my arms, listening to her heart.

Ambrose lets his phone ring three times before he answers with a gruff, "I'm busy."

"Then why did you answer?" I stretch my legs out, propping them up on the coffee table.

"Thought it might be an emergency. Did you take that woman on her kill yet?

"Her name's Charlotte," I snap. "And, yes, I did. Figured you'd be watching the news for it."

Ambrose grunts. "Been busy. Haven't had time to keep an eye on the news. Did it work?"

I lean back and sink into the couch cushions, my gaze fixed on the light fixture overhead. It's loose, hanging a little crooked, and it reminds me of Charlotte still clinging to her humanity.

"Kind of," I say.

"The fuck does that mean?"

"Well, she did it," I tell him, and the memory makes my cock stiffen and my whole body turns hot. "She did it, uh, *really* well. I had to trick her into getting started, but once she did—" I grin. "It was something, Ambrose. I got to tell you."

"So it did work." Ambrose gives a short little laugh. "Guess there's something to your gods, after all."

"Shut up, preacher." I take a deep breath, trying to figure out how to tell him the rest. The Texas wind howls on my phone's speaker, sounding like static. "Here's the thing, though. She was magnificent in the moment—"

"Magnificent?" Ambrose laughs. "Oh, no, I've already got to deal with one lovesick asshole. Not you, too."

I scowl, cheeks burning at the word *love*. "She *was* magnificent," I snap. "Like she's been killing all her life. But that was all while it was happening. As soon as she was done—" I shake my head. "She reacted like a human. Now she feels guilty. She keeps moping around. The gods, they told me the charm broke, but she's still poisoned by it, and she can't stay like this, half-human and half-Hunter. And I don't—"

"Calm down." Ambrose cuts me off, his voice firm. "Losing your goddamn mind isn't going to help anyone. There's a reason you don't just want to initiate her?"

The question kind of hangs there between us. I appreciate him phrasing it like that—initiating Charlotte, not killing her, even though they're the same thing.

"She won't let me do that," I finally say. "And I don't—" I stop myself, but I can tell from Ambrose's disapproving *mmhmm* that he knows what I was going to say.

I don't want to kill her without her permission. I hope he doesn't ask me why because I don't feel like explaining it to him. Partly, it's because I don't like killing other Hunters unless they're a threat. A show of respect, you know. But I feel bad about what I did to her after our first dinner together, how I licked her to orgasm without asking. Killing her feels the same way. Especially since I know I wouldn't be able to stop myself from playing with her dead body.

But Ambrose doesn't ask for an explanation. "Here's what I think," he says. "Some Christian magic forced her to live as a human for what? Thirty years? She's the same age as Edie, right?"

"Yeah, more or less."

"Okay. So she *is* a Hunter. The binding broke. She killed. She was good at it. But she still sees herself as human, and it makes sense, because that charm was telling her she was human for thirty years. She's got a huge disadvantage." He pauses, and I know I don't want to hear whatever he's going to say next. "Dying and reviving would undo that, and you know it."

I scowl, hating that he's right. "But she's not gonna let me kill her because she thinks it would *actually* kill her."

"Right." Ambrose clucks his tongue. "So you've got to find some other way to help her understand that she is what she is. You know how humans see us. That's how she sees herself right now."

I slump deeper into the couch and concentrate until I sense her, my Hunter who thinks she's human. She's calm right now, and I know it's because she's sleeping. When she's awake, she seems to exist on a knife edge of panic. I'm not sure she even realizes it, but I do. Because I know what she feels like when she isn't hating herself.

And gods, does it break my heart.

"So what do I do about it?" I ask.

"You need to make her think like a Hunter," Ambrose says. "No Hunter sees themselves as evil, but I guarantee that's what that woman is thinking about herself."

He's right. I know he's right.

"If you can get her to stop that, maybe it'll help." A pause, filled with the whistling static of the wind. "Maybe."

I stare ahead, rolling Ambrose's suggestion around in my head. I don't disagree. But I know if I try to tell her she's fine, she won't believe me. But maybe she would believe it from someone else—

And then, like that, I know what I'm going to do.

CHAPTER THIRTY

CHARLOTTE

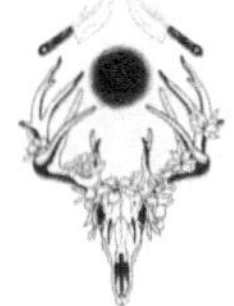

The next morning, I skip breakfast in favor of drinking a cup of coffee and smoking my last joint on Jaxon's screen-in porch. I'm not sure where he is; the house feels empty and silent when I pad downstairs. But I know he's around here somewhere.

I've taken two hits when Jaxon emerges from his shed, looking suspicious. Well, more suspicious than usual, anyway.

After all, he's a murderer.

And so are you.

I drag on the joint, hoping the weed will drown that voice out instead of amplifying it.

Jaxon picks his way across the shaggy lawn. He moves like a cat, sleek and careful, and although he doesn't look right at me I know he's *sensing* me, if that makes any sense. Probably not. Nothing in the last few days makes any damn sense.

"Hey," he calls out, stopping on the other side of the porch, his features blurred by the screen. I take another drag. The weed has me feeling floaty and warm, a welcome relief after a night of uneasy dreams.

"You want some?" I hold out the joint, smoke lifting in swirls. But he shakes his head.

"I came to tell you I need to go on a trip."

Excitement flares like a firework and then explodes into dread.

"And you're going to come with me."

I watch him through the screen, the joint burning away between my fingers. Eventually, I stab it out in the vintage ashtray I grabbed from his creepy living room. The mummies who live in there certainly don't need it.

"Do you want me to kill someone again?" It shocks me, how easily the question comes out. How natural it feels.

Jaxon squints at me. He has his hair pulled back, and it highlights his high cheekbones and big blue eyes.

"No," he finally says. "But that's all I'm going to tell you."

I roll my eyes. "I thought we were over this mysterious, secretive bullshit." I stand, and the porch tilts a little. Too much weed. Or too much excitement at the thought that I might get to kill again.

Stop. Stop. Stop. This isn't you.

This is you, little Hunter.

I kick the screen door open and plod out into the yard, barefoot. The morning feels like spring even though it's still January. Warm and balmy and damp. Jaxon smiles as I approach, not coy this time, and my heart flutters around.

"Tell me where we're going." I cross my arms over my chest.

Jaxon's grin widens. "Or what? You'll fight me again?"

The temptation is there, I won't deny it. Both for the fight itself—for the spilled blood, the starbursts of pain—but for what I know damn well will come after it.

"No," I say before I change my mind and launch myself at him. "I just—why do this? Why keep it a secret?"

Jaxon studies me for a long time, kind of contemplative. "I told you. It's a surprise."

"Asshole," I mutter.

He's unfazed, though. "We'll leave tonight," he says, and that's it.

ONCE AGAIN, I find myself riding shotgun in Jaxon's car. At least this time he doesn't bother with handcuffs.

The night is dark and oily, but the headlights cut through it just enough to illuminate patches of the interstate. It's late, nearly midnight. We've been driving for two hours and I still don't know where we're going. Just that we're heading east, away from Texas.

"You awake over there?" Jaxon glances at me sideways

"No," I say, curling up into my seat. I actually did doze off for a little while, my dreams smoky and strange, the way they've been since—since Houston.

"You can sleep if you want," he goes on. "But you know you probably don't really *need* it. Hunters can get by on less than humans."

Sourness curls in my stomach. "And yet I get cranky when I get anything less than eight hours a night."

"That doesn't mean anything." Headlights sweep across the car, casting Jaxon in a sudden camera flash. "Ambrose thinks it's because you lived so long as a human. You're having trouble adjusting."

Ambrose. The name stirs around in my thoughts, an easier name to dwell on than Oliver Raffia. He's another person like Jaxon. Another Hunter. "That's your, uh, friend, right?"

"Yeah. He's also kind of a—a mentor, you could say." Jaxon taps the steering wheel, beating out a rhythm even though the radio's off. We're in the middle of nowhere, Louisiana. Or maybe it's Mississippi, at this point. Either way, there's nothing worthwhile to listen to.

So it makes sense that I want to talk to Jaxon about this. About Hunters. What else do we have to talk about?

That's what I tell myself, anyway.

"A mentor?" I prompt.

"Yeah. Like, uh, like I could be to you." He gives me another one of those nervous, hopeful glances, and I try not to let it go straight to my heart. Or my pussy. "Are you okay with talking about this?"

I'm surprised that he asked. "Yes," I say, although it does take a minute for the answer to come out. "But I'm not promising anything, okay? I'm still not convinced—" I cut myself off because I don't actually know what I'm convinced of. That Jaxon brainwashed me into killing Oliver Raffia? That I'm trapped in some kind of fucked up Charles Manson situation?

That there's a supernatural serial killer inside me clawing its way out?

"When exactly did you talk to Ambrose?" This feels like the best way to change the subject.

"Last night," Jaxon says. "While you were asleep."

"And then you decided to, what? Pack up and go east?" I shake my head. "This feels like a trick, you know."

"It's not a trick," Jaxon says darkly. "It's a *surprise*."

I roll my eyes. "I know what your surprises are like."

Jaxon doesn't say anything, and for a moment, I wonder if I hurt his feelings. Can I even do that, to someone like him?

"He and I did talk about where your binding might have come from." Jaxon keeps his gaze fixed on the empty road ahead. "He said there are a few possibilities. Your parents—"

"What about them?" The question comes out sharp and accusatory, and Jaxon glances at me, his face unreadable.

"Touchy subject?" he says carefully.

I look down at my lap, at the skirt of the pretty vintage-style dress I wore to make me feel better about this whole stupid trip. The truth is I don't think about my parents much at all. They kicked me out of their tidy Santa Clarita house when I was seventeen after I got caught fooling around with another girl at church—a deacon's daughter. She told her father that I had corrupted her with my lesbian wiles.

I told you that bullshit wouldn't work! My own father screamed at my mother as I stood on the front porch after they slammed the door in my face. *There's no denying that flesh and blood's what matters!* It was the last time I ever heard his voice, and it was a reminder that I wasn't a part of the family. Not really. They'd never hidden that I was adopted, but hearing his true feelings—

"You could say that." I look at my reflection in the window. My eyes are dry. "Let me guess. You think they put the binding on me?"

"I don't know. It would be fucking weird if that's the case because for you to be a Hunter, at least one of them would have to be a Hunter, too," Jaxon says. "Although it's usually both."

Ice floods through my veins. He doesn't know I'm adopted, and why would he? I barely even think about it. "What are you saying?"

"A Hunter wouldn't put a binding like that on their child. It's akin to torturing them, and we protect our own."

But that's not what I was asking about. My mouth goes dry. My parents adopted me when they thought they couldn't have kids of their own. But then Mom got pregnant when I was almost thirteen, a fluke that turned into my baby sister.

The one they really wanted.

"But if you had one human parent, it's possible they did it without the Hunter parent knowing." Jaxon taps his fingers as he talks. "Ambrose says you don't come across this kind of magic much anymore, but he used to see it a lot when he was younger. That was, uh, in the 1800s, by the way." He glances over at me, grinning, but I'm still wrapped up in my own slow unraveling to register what he's saying. "Ambrose was an itinerant preacher, and he said some of the old Pentecostal churches would do that kind of magic when they thought a child was possessed by a demon. Which I *guess* you could say our gods are, although I personally don't—"

"I was adopted," I blurt out.

Jaxon snaps his mouth shut. For a minute, the only sound in the car is the rhythmic hum of the wheels against the asphalt. I can't believe I said that to him. That I shared that part of my history. It's something I only talk about with people I really, really trust. People like Edie. Like Alex, the ex I thought I was going to marry. Samantha, my best friend in college.

Jaxon.

"Oh," he says softly.

I swallow. Knot my skirt up in my hands. I went this far. I might as well tell him the rest. "My parents were Christian," I say softly. "Fundies. We belonged to this extremist church, the Church of the Well. "

"Holy shit," Jaxon says. "That's the one with the guy who's on TV, right? What's his name?"

"Sterling Gunner, yeah." We watched that asshole every Sunday night, broadcasting live from the Church of the Well compound in West Texas. "But yeah, the church did that kind of stuff. Weird prayers and things they said were protection against demons. My parents—" I take a deep breath. "I—I haven't spoken to either of them in years."

Jaxon glances over at me, his face wrapped in shadows, and I expect him to ask me if I know about my birth parents, if they were killers. He's gonna be disappointed because I have no fucking idea. I never even think about them.

Instead, he says, "I'm sorry."

I blink. "Sorry? Why?"

He shrugs as he turns his gaze back to the road. "I haven't spoken to my father in a long time, too," he says. "Or my grandparents. We all lived together in the house when I was a kid."

"Did you kick them out?" It's a dumb question, but it's the first thing I think to ask since it's what happened to me.

He chuckles. "No. They left. My grandparents have always Hunted together, and they were tired of Louisiana. So they want traveling. My dad said that I needed to strike out on my own, so he killed me and buried me in the backyard. I woke up a year later and then decided to rebel by joining the Army. By the time I came back to the States, he was gone."

I stare at him, at his strong, handsome profile, his sleek black hair. And I want to kiss him because he's the first person I've ever met who seems like he might actually understand. Who seems like he might know what it feels like.

My dad didn't literally kill me—but hearing what he said, he may as well have.

And maybe that's why I start talking. Why I tell Jaxon everything—about my childhood in the church, and realizing I was bi when I was in middle school because I kissed Mary Michaels behind the school gym during PE class, and about the deacon's daughter and getting kicked out and what my father said behind the door that was closed to me forever. And he just —listens. He watches the road, and he nods along, and he *listens*.

I've dated men before, but none of them ever listened the way he does.

"When my sister was born," I tell him, the words spilling out of my mouth because, for the first time in my life, it feels like I might actually understand why this happened to me. "My parents started to treat me like a changeling." I watch the lights sweep across the road and reflect the green mile marker signs. "Like I wasn't the baby they adopted."

"Why do you think they did that?"

"Because they got what they wanted." It comes out harsh. Bitter. "A real daughter."

"Or maybe—" Jaxon hesitates, and I can sense what he's going to say like it's crawling over my skin.

"Or maybe they knew what I am?"

Jaxon breaths out. Squeezes the steering wheel. "Maybe," he says. "I—I don't know, but—"

I love how flustered he gets sometimes. It's such a contrast to the way he commands me when we're fucking.

"Or maybe they were terrible people," I say. "Maybe they never saw me as their daughter."

I told you that bullshit wouldn't work.

My father's words echo around in my head. I always thought he was talking about the adoption, even if it was a strange way to phrase it—especially for him, a man who didn't normally curse. *That bullshit.*

Electric heat seems to course through my blood. "These charms Ambrose told you about," I say. "Did he say what they involved?"

Jaxon frowns a little. "No, he didn't."

The road unspools before us, hypnotizing me. Drawing me further and further into the past. *I told you that bullshit wouldn't work.*

Me screaming at my parents that the deacon's daughter was a liar, that we were in love, that they didn't understand.

Mom praying softly, rocking back and forth. She was always praying. Before meals. Over my sister's bassinet. On the front porch. She drew little wards on our walls she said drove away demons, and all the women in the Church of the Well drew them even though their husbands turned up their noses at the practice.

"The Church of the Well," I say slowly. "The church I grew up in? They're not like most evangelical churches. They go all-in on the spiritual warfare stuff." I keep staring out the window, my chest tight with panic. "They think the devil is always trying to get in, and you have to use whatever means necessary to stop him."

Jaxon doesn't say anything, and I look over at him, watching the headlights slide across his face.

"Like charms," I whisper. "My mom drew them everywhere in our house. I was surrounded by them."

Jaxon squeezes the steering wheel, opens his mouth. But I don't let him speak. Because I'm terrified that he's right. That there was something broken in me, and my mother saw it and tried to pray it out of me, and in the end, it didn't fucking work.

"They were charms to protect us from being taken over by demons." My voice rises, shrill and panicked. Tears line my eyelashes. "And what's more demonic than a murderer that can't fucking die?"

Jaxon finally looks at me, his face unreadable in the dark.

Then he jerks the car sideways, sliding across the empty traffic lanes, and pulls into the shoulder. Turns on the hazard lights, the mechanical clicking a metronome against my racing heart.

My tears spill over my cheeks.

"Charlotte." Jaxon says my name with such an unexpected tenderness that I burst into a loud, choking sob. For a second, he regards me with alarm.

But then he unbuckles his seatbelt and reaches across the gear selector to unbuckle my seatbelt, too.

And then he pulls me into him. It's awkward, the gear selector jutting up between us, but it also feels so good, so right, to have his strong arms wrap around my shoulders. I bury my face into his neck, my tears loud and ugly, and he runs his hand across my upper back. Kisses the top of my head.

"What if those charms—" I whisper hoarsely. "What if I'm really not hu—" I can't say it. I still don't know if I believe it.

"You're not a demon." Jaxon nuzzles against my hair. "But you're not human, either."

His arms tighten around me before I can protest, and he says, "You're something better."

CHAPTER THIRTY-ONE

JAXON

I pull the car into a rest stop right on the other side of the Mississippi border, the street lights garish and bright. It would be a pretty spot during the day. Lots of big winding oak trees. As it is, I park in one of the darker corners, kill the engine, and turn to Charlotte.

"Thanks for the food," she says, clutching the McDonald's bag in her lap. Her eyes are still red from her crying jag earlier, when I wasn't sure what to do so I just held her on the side of the road, eighteen-wheelers rumbling past us every few minutes. She's calmer now.

"Hey, I'm starving, too. Hand it over."

She grins at that, even though her smile's kind of sad. Still, she does as I ask, pulling out the two burgers and then propping the bags of French fries up on the dash.

For a few minutes, we just eat, not saying anything. I *want* to say something. Everything she told me about her parents, the adoption, them kicking her out—it sends this weird hot anger surging through me. She didn't deserve that. Not just because she's a Hunter. Even if she was human, she wouldn't have deserved it.

I wash a bit of burger down with a swig of Coke and stare out through the front windshield. "Are you feeling better?" I finally ask. It seems the safest thing to say.

But Charlotte doesn't answer right away, and I cringe inwardly, knowing I fucked up. Where are my gods when I need them? The Unnamed has no problem helping me fuck her like I'm some kind of sex demon, but the second I want to actually *talk* to her, it disappears, and I'm on my own.

But then she says, "A little," and when I look over at her she smiles at me. Another sad smile, but I'll take it. "I—I appreciate you listening to me."

"I'm always happy to listen to you." More cringe.

But Charlotte's smile brightens and finally works its way up to her eyes. Then it fades, and she bites into another fry and stares out the window. "I'm still trying to work through things," she says. "What it means. What—what I am."

My heart clenches, and I nearly tell her where we're going. But I stop myself. I wanted to surprise her, and it's not a surprise if I tell her in the middle of a rest stop parking lot.

She looks over at me, eyes dark and intense. "What was it like?" she asks. "Growing up knowing that you're a Hunter?"

Her question catches me off-guard. I wasn't expecting to have to talk about myself. In fact, I was fully prepared just to listen to her some more. I never talk to my dead lovers—I figure their ghosts, if they're around, don't want to hear my shit. And a living woman like Charlotte *really* doesn't.

But she's staring at me expectantly, slurping her Coke up through the straw, and the attention makes my face hot.

"I don't have anything to compare it to," I finally say. "It just felt normal."

Disappointment flashes across her eyes, and I scramble to correct. "I mean—I always knew what I was. My dad talked to me about it as long as I can remember. My grandparents, too.

They would tell me stories about their kills when they were trying to get me to go to sleep."

"No wonder it's so easy for you," Charlotte mutters.

I shrug. She's not wrong. "Ambrose was more like you," I offer. "I mean, he knew what he was, too, but he told me once that he struggled with it." I pause.

I wonder if I should call Ambrose now, let her talk to him, but the truth is I don't want to share her. And Ambrose probably won't be much of a comfort anyway.

"Ambrose," she says. "The itinerant preacher from the 1800s." She shakes her head. "It's all fucking weird. It's like discovering vampires are real."

"We are *not* vampires," I say quickly.

"Don't tell me vampires actually exist." She looks over at me. "Do they?"

"Not as far as I know."

"Well, that's something." She slumps back. "Did Ambrose ever say what it was like? How he struggled?"

"He never went into details." I wish now that he had. That I had *something* to give her. "Just that he struggled with the need, at first. To kill, you know. He thought it was wrong. He tried to repress it. But repressing it—" I stop, hesitating. "Well, that's dangerous."

"Dangerous?" Charlotte's brow furrows. "How? Am I in danger?"

"No," I say quickly. "When a Hunter represses their nature, they—they lose their mind, basically. They'll kill indiscriminately. Hurt people they care about."

"So it's not me that's in danger," she says darkly. "Just the people who are important to me."

"Well, you aren't repressing anymore," I tell her. "You stopped when we were in Houston."

Charlotte stares at me for a long time, and I know I misspoke again. The truth is, I don't know if the binding protects her from the repression-sickness. She's young, for a Hunter. Hasn't even died yet. But if she had never come looking for Edie, if she hadn't waltzed into Bandit's Diner and attracted the attention of me and my gods, if she had gone the rest of her life thinking she was human—

Well, personally, I think it would have been a blood bath.

"You'll be fine," I say quickly, hoping it's true.

She sighs. "I said I wanted to talk about you. Not me."

I blush and look down at my crumbled, greasy hamburger wrapper. "What do you want to know?" My heart's beating so fast I think it might explode out of my chest. I shouldn't be scared, talking to Charlotte. I kidnapped her. I fucked her. I killed with her.

And yet when I glance up and see her dark eyes boring into me I feel like a scared little boy. A *human* boy.

"How did you become an artist?"

I blink. It's not the worst question she could have asked. "I always liked to draw. And Dad encouraged it because he said I could use it to serve the gods."

"Is that how you graduated to *mixed media*?" Her eyes glitter mischievously.

"Yes," I say stiffly. "And why are you making fun of me? How else am I supposed to explain it to people?" I lean forward, arching an eyebrow. "To humans? Which is what I thought you were?"

She rolls her eyes. "Fine. So you make art for your gods. Who are these gods?"

I feel them then, a sudden, radiating presence. "I won't speak their true names," I say. "But they watch over me. They watch over all Hunters." I look at her and recite what my grandmother taught me when I was a child. "They're death and destruction. Rot and decay. Blood. Viscera. The life leaving a body. And they're the reason we can't die."

Charlotte trembles and I catch a whiff of her fear, sharp and pungent, like human fear. But there's a strain of Hunter in it, too. A strain of darkness that makes my cock stir.

"There are two that watch over me," I say. "My Guardian and the Unnamed."

I swallow. I don't take my eyes off her. I can't. She looks like a painting in the strange, eerie light of the rest stop.

"They led me to you," I add.

Charlotte's eyes widen. Her lips part. Her cheeks redden.

I smell her arousal.

"Am I—am I the first woman they've led you to?"

"Yes." I don't take my eyes off her. "There's no one else, Charlotte."

She jerks her gaze away, the red deepening in her cheeks. "Well, you clearly have experience," she says softly. "With women."

Now it's my turn to blush. And to consider all the ways I can answer that question. Lying makes me look the best, of course, and it's my first inclination.

But then Charlotte looks at me again, and the lights catch the crimson highlights in her hair so she looks drenched in blood, and I know I can't lie to her. Not *her*.

"Not exactly," I say roughly.

She gives a sharp, disbelieving laugh. "What does that mean? *Not exactly?*"

I look out the front windshield, at the shadows crawling through the rest stop. It's the sort of a place a Hunter feels at home. Dark and isolated and liminal.

"Human women can tell what I am," I say softly. "Maybe not at first. But when things get—you know." I force myself to look over at her. "They know. And they act like the prey they are."

Charlotte's anger shivers on the air. "I don't understand what you're getting at," she says darkly.

She thinks I'm a rapist. The thought comes to me sharply, and I suppose it's not entirely unfair, given what I did to her in her sleep. What I actually am, though, is worse.

Even for a Hunter.

I swallow, my throat dry. My Guardian whispers around me, although I can't quite make out what it's saying. "All my life I've been surrounded by the dead," I finally say. "The dead are how I worship my gods. How I make my art."

Charlotte's face is blank, carved out by the streetlights.

"And when living women didn't want me, I turned to dead ones."

I wait for her to respond, my heart racing. She just keeps staring at me, eyes dark in the shadows. When she finally does speak, her voice makes me jump.

"Am I—" She hesitates like she's considering her words. "Am I the first, um, living woman—"

"Yes," I blurt out. "The other ones I've been with never let me go as far as you."

I wish I didn't care so much about her reaction to this. Killing is a Hunter's work, and everyone does it differently. Most people just kill. My family is all like that. Even they find my predilections unnatural.

Charlotte shifts and finally turns away from me, staring out at the rest stop. "Is that why you ate me out while I was asleep? Because it was like me being dead?"

Guilt stabs through my chest. "I told you. I did that because I—I didn't want to disappoint you."

She turns toward me then, and there's no disgust on her face. No anger.

"And you did kill me afterward," I add.

"You jerked off while I was doing it," she counters. "Which I also didn't consent to."

Embarrassment flushes through my face. "Sorry," I mumble. "I just—I was worked up from—"

There's a rustle of fabric as she leans over the console, and when I feel her warm fingers against my face I look up, startled. She peers at me.

"I can't believe I'm going to say this," she says softly, fingers curling a little against my cheek. She uses just enough pressure that it's like she's holding me in place. "I feel like I should be furious with you. But I just—" She sighs, and her voice comes out small. "But the truth is, I kind of liked it."

I suck in a breath. "Which part?"

Charlotte leans closer, lips parted. She's turned on. I can feel the heat of arousal blooming in the air. "All of it," she whispers.

Then she kisses me, firm and chaste, before settling back in her seat, her eyes never leaving mine. And suddenly I want to feel that chain around my throat again, only this time I want her pussy clamped around my dick. I want her to come from my death throes.

"And I don't know what that says about me," she whispers. "I'm not supposed to—" She shakes her head, looks away again. "This is all so fucked up."

I want to say it's the binding, that it's still strangling her and keeping her from accepting herself. But really, I think I fucked everything up because I treated her like a dead girl and not the living, breathing woman that she is.

"I'm sorry," I say. "Really, I really am. I shouldn't have—" Charlotte keeps watching me, listening. She doesn't seem upset. "I'm not—I don't know how to do any of this. The other Hunters I know, they're either related to me or they're men. You're—"

She looks over at me, waiting.

"You're very pretty," I finish lamely.

And to my shock, she breaks into a big, dazzling grin. "Thanks. You're not too bad yourself."

I blush again.

"And I accept your apology." She looks at me, eyes blazing. "Just don't do it again."

A beat passes, and her lips quirk up.

"At least not without asking me beforehand."

CHAPTER THIRTY-TWO

CHARLOTTE

Talking to Jaxon at the rest stop was like snapping a puzzle piece into place. The puzzle isn't complete, but I can see a little more of it, a sense of what I'm working towards.

I still feel broken.

But I don't feel *alone* in my brokenness.

Okay, so he's a necrophile. I can't say it totally surprises me, considering his house is full of bones and human leather and weird, glass-eyed mummies. Considering what we did in Houston.

What *I* did in Houston. Laying back on that corpse. Letting Jaxon smear me with Oliver Raffia's blood.

Coming so hard it was like the night sky had unravelled.

He's a fucked up monster, but so am I.

We drive all night down I-10, and we talk—*really* talk. Jaxon tells me about his family and his time in the Army, which is weird to think about. He also talks a little about his gods and the weird religion he grew up in. I tell him about the weird religion I grew up in, too, and how I shed it like a snake skin.

I wonder if I'm ready for new gods. The Winter Solstice instead of Christmas, blood instead of grape juice. Maybe.

I tell him about myself, too. Normal things. Going to art school, debating the merits of having instruction instead of being self-taught, like he was. We actually talk about art all the way through the little boot of Alabama. Arguing our philosophies (he balks at the idea of ever selling his pieces—as if he could even do that, considering they're crime scene evidence) and our different methods (he mixes blood into his oils, says it "add to the texture"; I think he's full of shit). By the time the sun comes up over the horizon, I feel normal for the first time since Edie disappeared. I keep laughing, for god's sake. So does Jaxon. He has a nice laugh, rich and throaty and slightly menacing, and my panties dampen a little each time I hear it.

Which, over the last few hours, has been a lot.

The sky's pink with dawnlight when we cross the border into Florida. By the time we pass a sign welcoming us to Pensacola, the sun's fully risen. That's also where Jaxon says, "This is where we're going, by the way."

"Pensacola?" I laugh. "What, you wanted to go to the beach?"

"There are beaches in Louisiana. No. Something else is here."

My good mood falters a little, and I swallow. "More magic wizard mobsters?"

"Don't call them that." Jaxon laughs. "But no. You'll see."

I stare at him, the sunlight radiating around him, and try to figure out what he's doing. "You're not going to tell me? Really?"

"It's a surprise."

He exits the freeway, and the road winds us through tidy little neighborhoods with small, clapboard houses. The world's just waking up, and I feel like I need to be going to bed. But I'm also not tired, the way I'd expect to be after staying up all night.

It's almost like Jaxon was right. Like I don't need to sleep much at all.

"Almost there," Jaxon calls out, sing-song, and I sigh in irritation.

"I don't want to kill someone." I'm not entirely sure that's true. Even just saying the words makes my skin itch.

"You're not going to kill anyone."

We're near the ocean. I can smell the salt, and even the air in the car has a different feel to it, grainy like it's full of sand. Silvery-blue light flashes ahead, and I wonder if that's the Gulf of Mexico. I've never seen it before.

Jaxon pulls the car up in front of a square cottage with whitewashed siding and cerulean storm shutters. It's surrounded by what's probably a wild, tropical garden in the summer: bougainvilleas and hibiscus and passion vibes, all sparse for the mild winter.

He cuts off the engine and grins at me. "Here we are."

I keep looking at the house. Anxiety knots in my chest. "What's 'here'?"

"Come find out."

This house looks like a place where people are happy. But the sun is bright and Jaxon is standing beside the car, waiting for me out in the open. So I really don't think we're here to kill someone.

I step into the cool, humid air. Jaxon beams at me, looking terribly pleased with himself, then leads me up the narrow stone path to the front porch, where a pair of sneakers sit beside the front door. Something about those sneakers sparks in my memory.

Edie used to always do that—take her shoes off on the front porch.

But before the thought can fully register, Jaxon knocks on the door. Immediately, footsteps sound on the other side, and I hold my breath, not quite daring to believe—

A man answers. Tall and slim with a wild mop of dark curly hair. He appraises me with a predator's eye.

"Jaxon," he says. "What the hell are you doing here?"

Jaxon glances over at me, his expression brimming with excitement. I'm just trying to bite back my disappointment. This is some Hunter thing.

But then Jaxon says, "I'm actually here to see Edie."

The whole world falls away from me. "Edie?" I gasp out. "You mean this is—"

I stare at the man, his lean, cruel face and narrowed black eyes. There's wariness there. Worry.

"What the hell are you doing?" he asks, cold and calm. He looks at me, but I know he's asking Jaxon, and I want to scream at both of them to just stop their bullshit and let me *see* her.

"Calm down, man." Jaxon tilts his head back to me. "This is—"

And a voice I never thought I'd hear again chimes out from inside the house.

"Sawyer? Who is it?"

"Edie!" I scream, and I shove past this man—past *Sawyer fucking Caldwell*, who as far as I knew had been Edie's worst nightmare until her ex-husband took up the mantle—and race into the house.

And there she is, stepping into the sunny foyer. She's cut her curly black hair and bleached it blonde, but it's her. Edie Astor. My best friend in the whole world.

Even if I am a murderer, nothing's going to change that.

She stares at me for a moment, her eyes with disbelief. "Charlotte?" she whispers. "How did you—"

She doesn't get the question out because I throw my arms around her, pulling her into the tightest hug I can. She returns it and nearly strangles me in the process.

"I wanted to tell you so badly," she whispers. "But I'm

supposed to be dead, and I didn't want to have to burden you—
"

I pull away from her, my cheeks wet with tears. So are hers. "I knew you weren't dead," I say. "I fucking *knew* it, and—"

A slam echoes through the foyer, cutting me off. I look over to see Jaxon and Sawyer standing in front of the now-shut front door. Sawyer has his arms crossed over his chest, a scowl darkening his face.

"Oh, calm down," Edie says teasingly, and Sawyer's scowl melts.

"Just trying to keep you safe," he responds, and Edie beams at him. I look back and forth between the two of them, trying to comprehend exactly what I'm seeing.

She's certainly not here as a prisoner.

"Edie." I turn back to her. "I need to know what the hell is going on."

"I could say the same to you." She looks past me. "You're Jaxon, right? We spoke on the phone once. Sawyer's told me a lot about you."

"Yeah. I'm Jaxon." He steps forward. "Sawyer told me about you, too."

But Edie turns back to me, eyes searching. "How?" she whispered. "How did you—how did you find *Jaxon*?"

"How are you living in a beach house with Sawyer Caldwell?"

Edie's cheeks darken. "I guess we both have a lot to tell each other." Then she hugs me again, and it feels so damn good, knowing that she's alive and safe and that I didn't fail her after all.

"You can say that again." I look past her, at Jaxon and Sawyer standing next to each other, watching us with their sharp, keen gazes. Two monsters. Two murderers.

But it's hard to see either of them as monsters right now.

"Come on," Edie says. "We can Doordash some breakfast."

She grabs my hand and pulls me deeper into the house. I glance back toward Jaxon, and he gives me a small, shy smile. And my heart swells up. I don't know exactly what I'm going to say to Edie about what Jaxon has done to me and what he's made me do.

But I do know Jaxon brought me here. That he made the effort to prove to me she's alive and well.

Thank you, I mouth to him, and he smiles like I'm his whole world.

CHAPTER THIRTY-THREE

CHARLOTTE

The four of us have brunch in a sunroom that faces the piles of sand dunes leading down to the beach. Edie ordered it from some seafood place near their house: a big spread of crab eggs Benedict and fresh fruit and smoked salmon on thin, crispy toast. Mimosas, too, a carton of orange juice delivered with a bottle of sparkling wine that Edie and I dump into the juice before knocking the plastic flute glasses together.

It's almost like being back in California. Almost.

"Sawyer killed Scott," Edie tells me matter-of-factly, spearing a chunk of melon with her fork. When I blanche in surprise, she adds, "He was trying to kill me."

Any reservations I had—and I didn't have many—vanish. "That motherfucker," I snap. "The military guys they found at the camp—"

"Back up, I guess." Edie shrugs. "Those two PIs he sent by your place were supposed to kill me when they found me. But Sawyer took care of them, too."

The two PIs. I only met with them once, and they had asked me questions about Edie's whereabouts and I had lied while Scott sat in the corner, scowling. Guilt tightens in my stomach. "I should have known," I say, setting down my fork. "I should have called the cops the second they—"

Sawyer and Jaxon look at each other, exchanging expressions I don't fully understand, but Edie reaches across the table and lays her hand on mine. "You had no way of knowing," she says. "It was Scott. It was all Scott. And he's long dead now," She settles back in her chair, her blonde hair a halo around her pretty face. "So am I."

I can't believe how calm she is about all of this. How *accepting*.

I wonder if she would be so accepting of what I've done. Doubtful. Scott was an asshole who deserved it. Oliver Raffia was a stranger.

I don't dwell on it for long, though, because Edie starts to pepper me with questions. Jaxon doesn't say anything, and I decide to tell her a revised version. That I'd been looking for her since November, digging into true crime sites for any clues I could find. How I connected the sigil on the street art during our last conversation to a crime scene in Beaumont. She looks pretty sheepish at that, and Sawyer gives Jaxon a death glare.

"I told you not to paint that stupid thing on my church," he says, although he sounds like he's teasing. Sort of.

Jaxon, though, is nonplussed. "I'm glad I did," he says. "Otherwise Charlotte wouldn't be here right now."

He says it so lightly, so casually. And yet the words shoot straight through to my heart. Because he's right. That sigil is the reason I found Edie.

That sigil is the reason I found *him*.

Jaxon looks at me from across the table, and for a moment those big blue eyes of his are the only thing I can see. But then Edie says something to Sawyer that makes him laugh, and the sunlight is bright and shining on everything in the sunroom, setting the table on fire. And that fire illuminates a dark spot inside me that I know, with a sudden and striking certainty, is meant to be there.

"—find Jaxon?"

Edie's voice jars me back into the present. I blink and turn back to her.

"How'd you find Jaxon?" she says. "Or how did Jaxon find you?"

Her eyes are clear. Bright.

"He kidnapped me," I say.

Edie and Sawyer both laugh and look at each other, some kind of familiarity passing between them. "Sawyer stalked me," she says. "But that worked out, didn't it?"

When Sawyer looks at her, I know he loves her. It's a black sort of love, thorny like roses. But it's love.

He's a Hunter, and he can love.

I glance at Jaxon again, and he's smiling a little, looking at me with an intensity that makes my insides shake.

I finish the rest of the story over the remains of our meal, although I leave out my strangling Jaxon *and* the trip to Houston. Jaxon doesn't say anything about either incident, although he does go into surprisingly shocking detail about killing the two drug dealers who interrupted my escape attempt. It gets Sawyer riled up, and the two of them start one-upping each other with murder stories.

It doesn't disgust me. Edie, though, wrinkles her nose and says, "Why don't we leave them to this and you and I go outside?"

She's human, I think. *She's not like me*.

My chest squeezes.

Sawyer and Jaxon barely notice when we get up from the table. They're too busy arguing about the benefits of using a machete over a hunting knife.

Edie takes me out to their backyard, which is as overgrown as the front, and we sit at a little wrought-iron table and finish our mimosas while the sea wind blows in from the Gulf.

"I know how fucked up this all is," she says, not quite looking at me.

"Which part?" I swirl my drink around in its glass. "Faking your own death?"

"Falling in love with Sawyer Caldwell."

It startles me, hearing her say it out loud. I jerk my gaze over to her, but she's staring out at the garden, the wind pushing her hair back from her face.

"So you do love him," I say softly.

Edie nods. Tilts her head toward me. "He saved me," she says. "Not just from Scott, although obviously he did that. But from—from my own self-loathing. He's—" She hesitates. "Did Jaxon explain what they are? That they aren't—human?"

Her question thrums on the air. I consider how to answer it. I consider that I should tell her that Jaxon said I was one of them, too.

Eventually, I just nod.

"I feel like he killed the part of me that hated myself," she says. "And that's what made me whole."

I feel tight and breathless. Of course I knew Edie had suffered. The anorexia. Her recovery. Scott trying to sabotage it, then nearly killing her when she wouldn't let him. I tried my best to help her, but I never quite unlocked the code. Not, it seems, the way Sawyer did.

But I *could* have. The realization comes to me like a strike, as cold and clammy as the sea wind blowing through Edie's dormant garden. I curl my fingers around the mimosa glass and see it play out in my head with a clarity so vivid it makes my hands shake. I should have gone to Scott's mansion by the sea and slammed his head into the plate glass windows that looked down at the beach until his forehead split and his face was a mask of blood. I should have wrapped my hands around his throat and squeezed, pinning him down with my body weight, until his eyes bulged and his tongue lolled out. I should have carved open his torso like a Thanksgiving turkey and taken his organs out one by one, squeezing them until the meat crushed between my fingers.

I should have done all of that for Edie.

But I couldn't, because there was a string of magic strangling the oldest and truest part of me.

"Charlotte?"

Edie's voice cuts through the fantasy, and I blink back to the garden with a gasp. Edie frowns, leaning in close. "Are you all right?"

"I'm fine." My voice shakes, though, and I drown the rest of the mimosa and wish we'd brought the champagne and orange juice out to the garden with us.

"You don't seem fine." She scrapes her chair closer and puts her hand on my arm. My eyes flutter. "Is it because of me and Sawyer? I know it's a lot, but—"

"No." My tongue is dry with the need to tell her the entire truth, but all I get out is, "I'm glad you found Sawyer. That he helped you like that."

She smiles sheepishly. "And I'm glad you found Jaxon," she says. "I'm glad—that you know about them. You were the only part of my life before that wasn't total shit and now—" She laughs. "Sawyer doesn't believe in Jaxon's gods, but I don't know. Look at where we are. That sigil brought you here, didn't it?"

The sigil flashes in my thoughts. That darkness inside me flares, and it's eager for release somewhere, somehow. With my hands or knife or—something. Anything.

I swear I can hear Edie's heart beating.

"Yeah, it did." I swallow and squeeze the plastic stem of my flute glass so hard that it snaps. Edie jumps.

"Are you sure you're okay?" she asks.

I take a deep breath and set the broken flute glass on the

table, where it rolls in the wind. "What if I—" I'm still not sure I can get it out. "What if I told you I'm—"

She looks at me expectantly. But I can't do it.

"Why did you accept Sawyer?" I ask instead.

"Accept him?"

"For what he is. I mean, he—"

"You don't have to say it." Edie drains the rest of her mimosa and balances the empty cup on the table, holding it in place so the sea wind doesn't blow it into the garden. "I don't know," she says. "It just—it's part of him. What he is."

The wind howls in my ears, and even though it's cool, my skin prickles with sweat. My entire body feels like it's on fire. "What if I told you I'm like him?"

I spit it out so that every word bleeds together, and then the question just hangs there, numb and strange.

Edie gives a sharp laugh. "Charlotte, what the fuck are you talking about? You're not a Hunter. Sawyer knew what he was from the time he was a kid. It's not just—" She falters, and I think she can see the shame on my face. "Charlotte. Tell me what's going on."

But I shake my head. She's my best friend, and I still can't bear to see her reaction.

"Stop this," she snaps. "Something's obviously got you fucked up. Tell me."

The darkness surges inside me like it needs to be purged.

"I did things with Jaxon." The wind catches my voice and flings it around the dry, rattling garden. "Things like what they were arguing about when we came out here."

I can't bring myself to look at Edie, so I stare at an unflowering hibiscus bush instead, waiting for her to react. To scream. To run. To call the cops.

"And you think you're a Hunter?"

I let my gaze shift over to her, and she doesn't seem scared or upset. She just studies me. Listening.

"Jaxon thinks I am," I say. "He thinks all the weird prayers and stuff my mom did when I was a kid suppressed my urges and made me believe I'm, you know—"

"Human."

I was going to say *normal*, but I just nod.

"And what do you think?"

That darkness in me tightens. My throat is bone dry again. I dig my nails into my palm and listen to the wind and wish that the answer that comes to my mind isn't *Jaxon's right*.

"Charlotte." Edie grabs my hand, her palm cool and dry. "I faked my death so I could start over with Sawyer fucking Caldwell. You can be honest with me."

"Sawyer's different." I look away from her, squinting into the wind. "You said yourself. He saved you from Scott."

Her fingers tighten. "So did you."

I jerk my gaze over to her, and she smiles. "You're the only reason I was able to get out of California," she says. "But even before that, you saved me. Why did I go into recovery? Because of you. Why did I *stay* in recovery?" Her eyes glitter. "You, Charlotte. You saved my life."

Tears form along my lashes, and I try to blink them away. It doesn't really work. All the pain and confusion from the last few days pour out of me, and Edie pulls me into an embrace, squeezing me in close.

"If you're like them," she says against my hair, "if you're a Hunter, a killer—it doesn't matter."

I sob, because it's true. I am a Hunter. I can feel the truth of it pounding through me. It took seeing Edie with Sawer Caldwell to accept it, but I can't deny it now.

"You're still my best friend," Edie whispers.

And that's exactly what I needed to hear.

CHAPTER THIRTY-FOUR

JAXON

Sawyer and Edie have a spare room in their house, and that's where they put up me and Charlotte for the night. I half-expect Charlotte to protest or claim she needs to sleep on the couch or something, but she just tells Edie, "That'll be great," and helps her fix up the bed.

Something's shifted in her, it feels like. I can't quite put my finger on it, but I also don't have a chance to ask her, because she and Edie are attached at the hip all damn day. They spend most of it at the beach, even though it's too cold to go swimming. They disappear through the dunes after setting up the spare room and that's the last I see of them until they come back in the afternoon, with pink cheeks and windblown hair.

I don't mind, though, since it's a chance to hang out with Sawyer one-on-one. We share a couple of beers in the living room and swap stories about our latest kills. But then Sawyer says, "What exactly is Charlotte?"

I stop, the beer halfway to my lips, and glance sideways at him.

"She doesn't feel human," he says. "But she can't be a Hunter. Edie would have known."

"She's a Hunter." No point in lying about it. "She had a spell on her that repressed it."

"A spell?" Sawyer laughs. "Ain't no way that's real."

"Ambrose confirmed it," I shoot back, somewhat defensively. Sawyer just harrumphs. He doesn't go in for the mystical. He thinks we all evolved this way or something. As if there's an evolutionary reason for us not to fucking die.

"So did my gods," I add.

Sawyer ignores that, though. "Has she killed?"

"Yeah." And then I tell him everything. He listens, nodding along, sipping his beer every now and then. He's done by the time I'm finished, and I watch him rub the condensation away as I wait for a response.

"Sounds like a Hunter to me," he finally says. "Does Edie know?"

"You'd have to ask Edie."

Sawyer nods again, then stands up to get another beer. "Honestly," he says, "I hope she is a Hunter. Edie needs friends she doesn't have to hide from me."

"She is." I'm confident in that. Maybe she still doesn't feel like a Hunter the way Sawyer does, but I can sense the darkness in her, now more than ever. It's contained. Bound. Almost to bursting.

Our conversation turns to other topics, and by the time Edie and Charlotte come back, Sawyer's grilling pork chops on the back porch for dinner. Afterward, we all settle down in the living room, the girls splitting a bottle of red wine. I actually wind up going to bed early, even though I'm not really tired. I'm just not used to being around so many people at once. It's good to see Sawyer, to talk shop a little, and Edie's sweet and thoughtful and makes Charlotte happy—all good things, no doubt. But she's human. I hear her blood pumping, and it makes my blood pump, too.

So I go to bed, lying there in the dark, listening to them out in the living room. I can smell weed smoke drifting through the house. Maybe Charlotte won't even come to bed. That's fine. I brought her here to see Edie—and Sawyer, to a lesser extent. To show her that Hunters can protect humans when we want to. Can love them. That we're not *just* monsters and boogeymen.

But mostly, she's excited as hell about Edie, and that makes me feel good.

Not quite as good as killing, but—you know. Good.

I'm surprised, then, when I hear the knob turn and then see the hallway light as the door opens, angling across the bed. I roll over and there's Charlotte, haloed by the light, her crimson hair blazing.

I want to kiss her. Fuck her. Strangle her. Do all three at once. Or have her do all three to me.

"Did I wake you up?" she whispers as she slips into the room.

"No." I roll onto my side, and she closes the door but then stands beside it like she can't decide what to do next. "Are you tired?" I ask. "I really don't need to sleep much these days. You can have the bed."

It's dark in the room. The only light is the blend of moonlight and porch light that filters in through the curtains. It makes Charlotte look like a ghost.

"Neither of us have slept for like twenty-four hours," she says.

I sit up, remembering at the last minute that I stripped my shirt off before I lay down. Charlotte's eyes linger on me, though, and I swear they catch the light like a cat's.

She can see in the dark. She might not admit it to herself, but she can.

And she's looking at me.

"I've gone for longer," I say. "Just, uh, let me get dressed and—"

"No."

Charlotte's voice rings out across the room, startling me into stillness. She creeps forward and crawls onto the bed, and I can hear her heart thudding. It's not fear, though. She's definitely not afraid.

"I just mean, that's not necessary. I don't mind." She stops, eye level with me. "If you want to sleep, it's fine."

"I'm not actually tired." What the fuck is wrong with me? Do I want to curl up in bed with her or not?

But then something sparks in Charlotte's gaze. Something fiery and hot that snags in my thoughts and makes my dick throb.

"I am tired," she says, still staring at me. "Exhausted, really. But I—"

Her heartbeat quickens. It's so fucking loud I swear it's rattling the walls, and I wonder, briefly, if Sawyer can hear it.

"I was thinking," she says slowly. "About what you told me in the car. How you liked, um—" She gives a nervous laugh and covers her face with her hands. "I can't believe I'm going to suggest this. You can say no."

Everything about her is sending blood flooding into my cock. Her bright, shiny eyes. Her thundering heart. Her *scent*.

She's not scared at all, no. She's turned on.

"What do you want to do?" I squeeze the blanket, dropping my eyes down to her chest. Her dress strap has slipped, revealing a flash of lacy bra underneath.

Charlotte bites her bottom lip, her eyes flicking around. "I—I wanted to thank you. For bringing me here. Showing me that Edie's okay." She moves closer, crawling like a temptress over the bed. I don't dare move, afraid I'm going to scare her off. She stops, her gaze boring into me. "I also wanted—" She hesitates, and I'm about ready to scream at her to spit it out. My whole body feels like it's on fire.

"I felt it," she whispers. "That I'm like you. That I'm a Hunter. When Edie was telling me how Sawyer saved her life, and how I saved her life, too—I saw what I am. And it didn't make me sad. It just felt *right*."

Her words completely floor me. When I brought Charlotte here, I obviously hoped this would happen, but I wasn't sure if it would. But I realize I was right, in giving her the thing she left California for:

Edie, alive and well and willing to accept her as she is. Just like I am.

I grab her, pulling her into an awkward hug, but she melts into me so it's not awkward at all. "I'm glad," I say into the top of her hair, even though it's completely inadequate.

Charlotte nuzzles against my neck, her breath warm, and my cock strains against my underwear. "The last few hours," she says softly. "All I could think about was thanking you."

"Thanking me?"

"Yeah." She pulls away and gazes up at me, her eyes dark with lust.

"How do you want to thank me?"

There's a long, agonizing pause before Charlotte answers.

"I thought I could go to sleep. And then you could do what-ever you want with me."

For a minute, it's like all the air rushes out of the room, and I think that if I want to breathe, then I have to kiss her—this beautiful, broken Hunter who's gone thirty years without knowing what she is.

"Are you sure?" I say softly. "Even—here?"

She blushes so deeply I can practically feel the heat radi-ating off her skin. "I'm sure if you're quiet—"

"Sawyer will know what's going on."

I watch her eyes widen, and I sense how the thought excites her.

"He won't say anything to you because he's just enough of a gentleman," I add. "He was raised by his mother. But I don't know if he'll tell Edie or not."

Charlotte's blush deepens. "Edie already knows," she mumbles. "I asked her if it was okay."

Now it's my turn to blush. "And she said it was?"

"Of course." Charlotte looks up at me. "Please, Jaxon. I want this. I want to give this gift to you. I feel—I feel *right* for the first time in my life."

I move closer to her, testing her. She doesn't pull away: Not when I cup her face, and not when I pull her into a kiss, plying her mouth open with my tongue. Her body's hot to the touch, all her blood pumping furiously through her veins. "Are you even going to fall asleep, little Hunter?" I breathe into her ear as I slowly coax her down onto the mattress. "Or will you be too excited?"

"We had wine and weed," she says. "And I'm exhausted." She looks over at me, her lids heavy. "I think I'll manage."

I sweep my gaze down over her body, lingering on the place where her tits spill out over the top of her dress. I tug the neckline down, and she wriggles a little beneath my touch.

"You should undress," I say. "Easy access."

Her lips part at that, and she rubs her thighs together like she's trying to get at her clit. I bite back a smile.

"Maybe you can help me?" She pushes up on her elbows, pushing those glorious tits up toward my face. "Like when you took my panties off for me?"

"You were chained up then, if I recall correctly."

"And now I'm too tired," she says with a pout, falling back on the pillow. "I could just *fall asleep* right here—"

I attack her, yanking the dress down hard enough that something tears. Charlotte yelps and glares at me.

"Sorry!" *Stupid, stupid. You know how strong you are.* "I didn't—"

"It's fine." Charlotte wriggles her shoulders, and I pull the dress down around her waist. Her tits are gorgeous in her bra.

They'll be even more gorgeous in the moonlight. "I know how to sew. I can fix it. But maybe—"

She rolls onto her stomach beneath me, revealing a bunched-up zipper. "You can start there?"

I draw the zipper down, then guide her up so I can slide the dress around her waist and hips. She moves with me, pliable but heavy, like she really is on the verge of falling asleep. Once the dress is off, I unhook her bra and slide the straps down her arms, then roll her onto her back again so I can toss the stupid thing across the room.

Charlotte breathes deeply, her breasts trembling. I was right; they are gorgeous in the moonlight, and I run my palms over them, pressing into her hardened nipples.

"Are you going to pretend I'm dead?" she asks softly.

The question startles me. Embarrasses me a little, too, because—honestly, yes. I probably am. Now that I'm familiar with the warmth of her body, it'll be fun to pretend it's colder than it should be, fun to try and ignore her fluttering, sleeping heart.

I force myself to meet her gaze before I answer, though. "Why do you ask?"

She's flushed. Excited. Aroused. I hook my fingers around her panties without looking.

"I was just curious."

The idea excites her, I realize. But I want to hear her say it.

I tug her underwear over her hips.

"Do you want me to?" I thread the underwear over her knees and then fling it aside, too. She doesn't answer right away, and I draw my gaze over her plush, naked Hunter's body. I'm all ready to sink into her.

"Do you?" I crawl on top of her, cock aching with need. Charlotte's lips part. She runs her hands over my hips.

"Yes," she breathes.

Fuck me if I don't nearly explode in my pants right then and there.

"Well, then I'll need to wait until you're in a deep, deep sleep." I nuzzle her neck, peppering her with kisses. "And I think you might be too worked up to get there."

I pull away from her sharply, palming my cock over my pants. She immediately sees what I'm doing.

"Maybe you should fuck me to sleep," she says sweetly.

"I think an orgasm is a good idea." I rock back, sliding off the bed, feeling myself melt into the shadows. "But I want to see you do it for yourself."

Charlotte bites her lips and spreads her legs, giving me a tantalizing glimpse of her glistening pussy. She drops her hand down to her clit.

"Like this?" she asks coyly.

"Just like that, cher." My cock is raging at the need to be inside her. But I force myself to wait. That's not what she asked for, and frankly, it's not what I want.

What I want is to fuck her sleeping, unmoving body until she comes in her dreams.

"Pretend I'm not here," I add, pressing up against the wall and going perfectly still, the way I do when I'm stalking prey.

Charlotte drops her head back and rolls her fingers in a slow, circular pace, her hips rocking against the bed. She's quiet, although I hear the changes happening in her body. The frantic rush of her blood. The quickening of her breath. She widens her legs and slips a finger inside her pussy and thrusts upward.

"What are you thinking about, little Hunter?"

Charlotte jumps like my voice startled her. "What I've thought about every time I've done this for the last three days," she whispers, thrusting her fingers inside of herself, running her thumb across her clit.

"And what's that?" Even though I know. Because we're both Hunters. What else would she fantasize about?

Houston. Her first kill. Fucking on top of a dead body.

Charlotte whimpers. I assume she doesn't want to say it, but I know she's thinking about it because her body is reaching its crescendo. She lets out a soft, choking gasp.

But then she just says, "You," and her release comes with the ocean rush of her breath. She trembles and arches against the bed and then slumps down, her heart racing.

Me. She didn't say death or murder. She said me.

Charlotte settles back on the pillow, her hand draped gracefully against her pussy. "Good girl," I say, a beat too late because I'm still faintly stunned by hearing her whisper *you* as she came. It's such a small thing, and yet it—

It burns straight through me.

Charlotte makes a small happy noise and rolls over. "That helped," she murmurs.

I slip out of the shadows and draw the blanket up over her naked body. My cock throbs, but I restrain myself.

I'm going to have so much fun using her. But for now, I just want to watch as she falls asleep.

"That's it." I run my fingers over her hair and along her bare arm. "Sleep for me, my Hunter. My pretty little corpse."

CHAPTER THIRTY-FIVE

JAXON

I t takes Charlotte fifteen minutes to fall asleep, and they're the longest fifteen minutes of my life. As soon as I hear her breathing even out, I undress, moving as slowly and quietly as I can. Testing to see how light a sleeper she is.

Not very light at all, it seems.

Which is good because my dick is the hardest it's ever been. My erection is almost painful, and I stifle back a moan as I stroke my shaft a few times, staring down at her sleeping body. She's on her side, hair streaming across the pillow like little rivers of blood, and she snores softly, breathing through her mouth.

Oh, that's where I'm going to start.

I nudge my cock against her lips, bracing myself for her to wake up. She doesn't, although she does open her mouth for me as I slide my length over her tongue, groaning that I can *finally* slake my need. I already know I'm going to come fast.

But I'm a Hunter. We recover quickly.

I push my cock as deep into Charlotte's mouth as I dare, which, unfortunately, isn't deep at all. I pump over her tongue a few times, getting the first few inches of my dick wet with her saliva. Good enough. I pull out, then drag the blanket down so I can see her naked body.

"You're going to look so pretty wearing my cum," I whisper, not giving a fuck that Sawyer can almost certainly hear my blood rushing as I tap my cock against Charlotte's cheek with firm little slaps. She moans, mutters, and shifts onto her back.

I grab my cock and stroke, half-expecting her to wake up. I know I should let her sleep a little longer, but I just can't help myself.

She doesn't wake up, though. Just settles back down on the pillow, oblivious to the fact that I'm jerking off above her.

"You ready for your pearl necklace, cher?" My cum erupts as soon as the question is out of my mouth, long white strands of my seed splattering perfectly around her collarbone—but also on her chin and the tops of her tits. I groan softly, grateful to be free from the distraction of my lust. Now I can focus on *really* playing with her.

I leave my cum on her skin because I like the way it looks, pale and gleaming in the moonlight, and slowly ease myself between her legs. The mattress shifts, but she doesn't wake up, her breath soft and measured. I run my hand up the inside of her thigh and graze my fingers over the velvety split of her pussy. It's tempting to slide a few fingers inside her, but I'm afraid that will wake her up. She's not in REM sleep yet.

However, I can't stop myself from pulling one of her rosy nipples into my mouth, sucking hard. Charlotte moans softly and shifts beneath me, but I just keep listening to her heartbeat: slow and steady as a metronome.

"That's it, little Hunter," I whisper into her skin. "Just sink down into sleep for me." I suck on her other breast, slow and gentle, relishing her floral taste. Then I kiss upward and gather my cum on my tongue so I can kiss her mouth, marking her lips with my release. I sit up, admiring the way it makes them shiny like she's wearing lip gloss.

"Pretty girl," I murmur, touching her breasts and belly and thick soft hips. I run my palm between her legs until she drops deeper and deeper into sleep and I start to harden again. I knew it wouldn't take long. "You like this, don't you? Being my plaything?"

She doesn't answer. Doesn't move. She's as still as death.

"That's what I thought." She's under enough that I lower myself down to taste her pussy. She's already wet—whether from dreaming or my attentions, I don't know. I'm just glad to slide my tongue inside her cunt and lap up her essence, kissing her pussy with more fervor than I kissed her lips. I press my tongue flat against her clit until it pulses. Then I plunge it back inside her pussy, fucking her with it. Getting her nice and soaked.

When she's ready, I sit up and press my cock into position, going agonizingly slow so I don't wake her. Her heart's beating a little quicker, although her steady breaths tell me she's still asleep. But she is feeling this. Feeling me.

It's not really like fucking the dead. Her pussy is unbelievably warm, a heat that sears through my core, and her heart beats a quiet rhythm in the background. So do her breaths. But *fuck,* do I love her stillness. The way she just lays there, limp, as I thrust into her, plowing as deeply as I can. I play with her clit, knowing how sopping wet she gets. I want to fuck her tits, and her arousal is the best possible lubricant.

"That's it, cher," I grunt as Charlotte jerks beneath me, still completely passed out. Weed and wine and exhaustion, she said, and I guess it's a good enough cocktail to keep her sleeping. "That's it. Get wet for me. Just like that."

I hunch over her to suck on her nipples again, and she feels so damn good fluttering around my cock that I can't stop myself from biting down a little too hard into her soft flesh. Charlotte gasps and stirs beneath me, eyes fluttering open, and I feel a sharp, sudden anger—at myself for waking her. "Not yet, little Hunter," I tell her. "Go back to sleep."

She blinks, her eyes unfocused. "Jaxon," she slurs. "Are you —doing it—"

My anger melts. Sweet thing. I'm the luckiest man in the world, that this gorgeous woman would come to me and offer herself up like this.

"I'm balls deep inside you." I kiss up to her mouth, bringing some flakes of dried cum with me. "And you already made me come once."

I kiss her to prove it, but she's too sleepy to kiss back. All she does is make a soft *mmmm* sound. "Feels good," she mutters, and she starts to fuck me back, pussy contracting around my dick.

"No need for that." I pet her hair. "I'm doing all that work, baby. Just go back to sleep."

"I saw them," she slurs. "The—" She mutters some syllables in a language she's never learned but one I know intimately. Names. The true names of my gods.

"You saw them?" A hot power flares through me. I fuck her more roughly, slamming into her so that she shakes like a rag doll. I have a sudden need to possess her. "When?"

"Now." Charlotte's head drops to the side and her eyes fluttered closed. "They told me..."

But whatever else she was going to say dissolves into nonsense.

She's back asleep.

She's back asleep, and I can feel the Unnamed nearby, watching as I fuck Charlotte into the mattress. "***You went to her?***" I whisper, fucking her limp body harder.

Yes. I had a message for her.

And then it's gone. I'm too pussy drunk to dwell on it, though. My Charlotte's a Hunter, and the Unnamed visiting her just proves that. Whatever message it sent her, I'll find out in the morning.

I'm going to come again, but I don't want to. Not yet. I slide my cock out of Charlotte's pussy, admiring how it gleams in the darkness, drenched in her arousal.

Then I straddle Charlotte's waist and squeeze her tits together, forming a perfect soft pillow for me to fuck. I use her that way for a little while, rolling my hips in slow thrusts, my head thrown back, every muscle in my body tight with effort. It's cool in the room, but I'm slick with sweat. So's Charlotte.

When my cock's too dry to fuck her properly, I slide it back into her cunt, keeping my thrusts slow and lazy and luxurious. Just letting myself enjoy her, the way I used to do my dead girls. She's deep asleep now, all the systems in her body slowing, and if I let my mind wander and just focus on her pussy I can almost pretend she's dead, too. Even if her heat is scorching me.

Especially since I can't stop myself from playing with her pretty little clit.

I roll it between my thumb and forefinger, relishing the way it makes her pussy flutter around my dick as I pump in and out of her. She mutters in her sleep and shifts beneath me, the mattress creaking. I don't stop, though. I want to feel her come. Want to feel her whole pussy clamp down on me. Want to have her wake up, gasping, like she did last time.

"Come on, little Hunter," I whisper, thrusting harder. "You gonna come for me? Hmm?"

She whimpers and says something unintelligible, and I wonder if she hears me in her dreams. I shift her legs around, moving slowly so I don't wake her up early, and prop them both up on my shoulders. Then I plow deeper in her, deep enough that I bump up against the soft barrier of her cervix. The whole time I keep playing with her throbbing clit.

Charlotte flops against the bed, breath quickening. Her eyes flutter.

"Come on," I growl, pressing down harder on her clit.

That does it. Her whole body vibrates and flutters and her eyes fly open and land on me as I pump her through her orgasm. "Jaxon," she gasps out, right before her eyes roll up and she dissolves into a moan, hips jerking against me.

"You like that?" I purr, wrapping my fingers around her chin to make her look at me. She blinks, confused, like she doesn't quite understand the question.

"You feel good," she slurs.

"So do you, cher." I lean over her and kiss her, running my hand over the splatters of dried cum on her skin. Part of me wants to jerk off on her again, especially now that she's awake, but she also feels way too good. Too wet. Too warm. There's no way I'm pulling my cock out of her until I'm finished.

She squirms beneath me, clearly still too sleepy to fully comprehend what I'm doing to her. It's clear she likes it, though. Too bad. I almost hoped she'd choke me out again.

The thought sends a jolt of pleasure through me, though, and I groan, my balls tightening up against my body. "Fuck, I'm gonna come."

Charlotte moans softly, her pussy contracting. I'm working her up again. Bringing her close to another orgasm.

The idea sends me over the edge, that she likes this, playing dead for me. I dig my finger into her thighs as I spill my cum inside her, pleasure pulsing up through my spine.

Charlotte makes a soft noise of displeasure. "Don't stop," she whimpers, eyes closed. "I was going to..." Her voice trails off, head dropping to the side.

"You going back asleep, tired girl?" I ease my cock out of her and set her legs down. She tries to shift onto her side, but I keep her pinned on her back. "Let me give you some sweet dreams."

And then I slide down to lick my cum out of her hot, quivering cunt.

CHAPTER THIRTY-SIX

CHARLOTTE

My dreams are so strange. I'm in a hot, jungly place, sort of like how I imagine Edie's garden in the summer, except it's blooming with flowers that I'm certain don't exist in our world. They're huge, bigger than my head, and bright colors I'm not sure I've seen before. Blue, but also red. Purple, but also orange. Everything is hazy and warm and steamy, and the steam puts me in a constant state of arousal as I stretch out in the soft, feathery grass while something twines around my legs.

He likes playing with you like this.

That voice. It's not speaking English, but a language I've never heard, like the flowers I've never seen.

Except I have heard it. Jaxon's spoken it.

"Who?" My voice rings out. Echoes. A shadow moves in my peripheral vision, but when I turn to look, it's gone. There are only thick, lightly swinging vines that pulse as if blood's pumping through them. They put me in mind of cocks, just like the flowers put me in mind of vulva. Just like the moisture in the air feels like sweat or cum or both.

You know who.

The shadow slips closer, watching me. I settle back on the grass, moaning a little with pleasure. Something wet and hot laps up against my pussy. I don't look to see what it is. I don't care.

I want to show you something.

"Hmm?" I turn my head toward the voice, and for half a second, I see a towering figure that swallows all the light in this place. Terror lances through me, but it only heightens my pleasure and makes my body quake.

"Who are you?" I moan, as the invisible thing between my legs slides up inside my pussy and fucks me.

The being says a word in that unfamiliar language, and I come, groaning and shaking. The thing between my legs keeps going.

He's not going to stop until you wake up for good, the being says. It's closer to me, whispering in my ear. *He's going to keep doing this until morning.*

"Who?" I cry out, thrusting back against the thing between my legs. The steam in the air turns to a warm rain that drenches my skin and teases my nipples.

My ardent little worshipper, the being says. *The one I selected to save you.*

"Jaxon," I breathe, and then suddenly I'm on my belly and that warm wetness massages my asshole, a sensation that feels astonishingly good. Of course. I'm asleep, and I told Jaxon he could do whatever he wants with me. "Tell him to fuck me again."

He's planning on it. Making himself hard right now while he eats your plump, pretty ass.

I moan down into the grass, breathing in the rich, earthy scent. For a moment, I'm not dreaming anymore—I'm face down on the bed, and Jaxon's hands press hard against my thighs as his tongue laps against my bud, opening me up for him. I groan, half-asleep and half-awake and flooded with pleasure.

The being's voice drags me back to my dream.

No, I need you here. I have something to show you.

"Show me what?" I moan, sticking my ass up in the air, spreading my legs wide. A hardness slides into my asshole, pain and pleasure twisting together.

A presence passes behind me, and I dig my fingers into the wet, warm earth and twist around, trying to get a glimpse of this being—this god. It's one of Jaxon's gods, I'm sure of that.

But what I find is Jaxon, his skin gleaming with his sweat, his hair loose and hanging around his shoulders, his face twisted with pleasure. He's fucking my ass in the bed at Edie's house.

No, no. The voice drifts around me. ***That's not the version you need to see.***

And then suddenly, I'm not in the garden or in the bed but in Jaxon's kitchen, the sunlight hazy as it drifts through the windows. Jaxon is there, too, but as a teenage boy, his hair in a 1970s shag that curls around his ears, sullen and scowling and waiting patiently in one of those big wooden chairs he keeps in his dining room.

A man passes by him, big and dangerous-looking. A knife gleams at his side.

"What is this?" I whisper.

An initiation.

And then there's Jaxon with a gaping neck wound, blood pouring across his chest.

I come again, screaming into the dirt.

There's my monster, the being purrs. ***There's my Hunter.***

Pleasure surges through me, hot and delirious, I lift my face from the rain-damp grass to gasp down air. I feel like I'm never going to stop coming.

You need an initiation too, the being says, and it feels like something I have to remember.

I SLAM AWAKE, convulsions wracking through my body. I'm on my side but pinned down; Jaxon spoons around me and holds me in place by the pussy. His fingers stroke lazily inside my cunt as his cock creates pressure deep inside my asshole.

"Jaxon," I moan, arching my back against him. He nuzzles the back of my neck.

"You just came for me," he mutters. "That's the fifth time."

"What?" I'm disoriented. The only thing grounding me into place is Jaxon's slow thrusts and his jagged, shuddered breath on my shoulder. The room's brighter than I expect, too. Has the sun already come up? Is it morning?

"This'll be the third time for me," he grunts, and that grunt turns to a deep, throaty growl as liquid heat floods through me. Jaxon's breaths turn fast and panting. He slumps against my back, damp hair trailing across my shoulders, his fingers still in my pussy as his cock softens in my ass.

We stay like that for a moment, our breaths slowing in tandem. Then I shift against him, rolling onto my back. Every muscle in my body aches, and my pussy and ass feel sore and abused. It's pleasant though. Satisfying. And slowly, the pieces fall into place.

Jaxon literally fucked me all night.

"Did I really come five times?" I ask, staring up at the ceiling. Fragments of the night come back to me. Strange, horny dreams. Jaxon's voice in my ear: *Go back to sleep. I'm not done with you.*

There's something I wanted to ask him...

Jaxon draws his arm across my belly and kisses the side of my neck. "Yeah," he sighs. "I can tell whenever you do. Your whole body shakes."

I keep shifting, moving my aching limbs until I'm on my other side, facing him. He looks exhausted. Drained.

But very, very satisfied.

"Thank you," he says softly, running his hand over the dip in my waist. Affection surges through my core.

"I take it you enjoyed yourself?" I trail my fingers over his cheeks, feeling the bones in his skull. He grabs my wrist and kisses the palm of my hand.

"You can fucking say that again." He keeps kissing me down my arm until he's draped himself on top of me, his damp body pinning me down, his hair falling in a curtain around us. "How much do you remember?"

I settle back on the pillow, enjoying the press of his body weight. "Not much," I say. "I think I woke up once—"

"You woke up a couple of times. Not fully though." His eyes meet mine, so blue they remind me of the Gulf of Mexico waiting outside the window. "I think my gods came to you. While I was—" He winks instead of saying it.

"Maybe. I don't remember." I frown, my dreams flickering through my thoughts. They're nothing but fragments: Strange, tropical flowers. A shadow man. Warm rain, as warm as fresh blood.

"I did dream, though," I say. "They were so strange. You weren't really there—"

"Of course not. I was here." He wraps his fingers gently around my throat, pinning me down as he kisses me, slow and deep. I can taste myself on him. "The Unnamed said it had a message for you.."

"Did it?" My dreams last night weren't nightmares, not at all. But right now, fully awake, with Florida's winter sun spilling through the thin curtains, I feel a quiver of fear.

"Charlotte." Jaxon's brow twists with concern. "What's wrong?"

"Nothing," I say on reflex. But Jaxon tightens his fingers around my throat. A reminder, not a threat.

"You're scared," he says roughly. "I can feel it. Smell it." He kisses me again. "Taste it."

"It was just my dream," I say, even though it sounds stupid. "I'm not scared of you."

"I know you're not." He runs his thumb over the hollow in my throat. "It's the Unnamed, isn't it? That scares you?"

A dark figure, watching as Jaxon fucks me.

"It scared the shit out of me the first time I saw it, too." Jaxon smiles and brushes my hair out of my eyes. An image flashes through my thoughts.

Jaxon as a teenager, a second mouth where his throat should be.

I push him away, surprised by my own strength. He sits back on his heels, frowning as I push myself up against the headboard. God, everything between my legs aches. I don't know if I can even walk.

"Charlotte, tell me what's wrong."

I rub my forehead. "Nothing's wrong." I peer up at him through the tangle of my hair. "I just—you remember how you said your dad killed you when you were younger?"

Jaxon's frown deepened. "Yeah. My initiation. Was that what the Unnamed—"

"I saw it." I settle back against the headboard, and Jaxon stretches out beside me, his hand across my belly. "Or I think I did. You were in your kitchen, sitting in a dining room chair—"

Jaxon laughs, which startles me. "Fuck, yeah, that's how it happened." He kisses my shoulder. "With a knife? Split open my throat?"

It's weird, how casually he talks about this, but it's something I find I'm getting used to.

"Why'd you call it an initiation?" I ask.

Jaxon shrugs. "Because that's what it was. It's a religious thing. Your first death is supposed to be at the hands of another Hunter to honor the gods." He smiles at me. "But plenty of people don't do it. Sawyer didn't. You know who killed him for the first time?"

"Who?"

"Fucking cops." Jaxon laughs and snuggles up to me. "That sheriff deputy who shot him fifteen years ago. He was so distracted by Edie that he didn't hear him come in."

"You're kidding me." I bury my nose in his hair, breathing in the scent of his sweat. It reminds me of the swamp but in the best possible way. All that life bursting out of the murk.

"Nope. Give him shit about it when we go back out there. He loves that."

"Why do I think you're lying?" I push up on my elbow to look down at him, and Jaxon just grins up at me.

"About him loving it? Absolutely. Not about Edie getting him killed, though."

And then Jaxon drags me back down into the sheets, covering me in gentle, sloppy kisses, and I'm not thinking about death or dreams anymore.

CHAPTER THIRTY-SEVEN

JAXON

We leave Sawyer and Edie's house the next afternoon, the two women laughing and hugging and promising to see each other again soon. It takes a good ten minutes to get Charlotte to the car, but I don't mind. I like seeing her happy.

"You enjoy yourself last night?" Sawyer asks, amusement clear in his voice.

I hate that my face gets hot.

"Sorry about that," I mutter. "She wanted—"

"I don't need to hear it." He grins. "Edie warned me, at least. Also, I think that's what they're talking about right now."

As if on cue, both Edie and Charlotte glance over at us, then dissolve into giggles.

"Son of a bitch," I mutter, and then Sawyer laughs, too, and claps me on the back.

"You take care of her," he says in a low voice. "Especially if she is one of us."

"I'm planning on it."

It takes another few minutes, but eventually, Charlotte and I are back in my car, heading west to Louisiana. Charlotte insists on driving, and I let her. I don't need to sleep much, but I do need to sleep sometimes. And it's been a while.

"You're okay driving?" I ask as I stretch out on the backseat —again, at her insistence. The car winds through Pensacola. She has the windows cracked to let the sea breeze in.

"What, you worried I'm going to kidnap you?" She meets my gaze in the rearview mirror.

"I don't know. Maybe."

"I mean, I came out here looking for Edie, and I found her." She pauses, eyes dropping back to the road. "I guess I found other things, too. Things I didn't know I needed to look for."

My belly clenches at that.

"Go to sleep," she says. "We can talk later."

Honestly, I'm glad she says that because I'm tired—as tired as she was last night, maybe—and I settle down in the backseat and close my eyes and then I'm out.

If I dream, even about my gods, I don't remember it.

When I wake up the light is soft and hazy, everything cast in a kind of golden glow. Twilight. Charlotte's listening to the radio, classic rock playing softly over the speakers, and she sings along, her voice sweet and clear. I groan as I sit up, and Charlotte yelps in surprise.

"Don't stop." I drape myself into the gap between the seats. "You have a nice voice."

She glances sideways at me, a smile curling up her lips. "Thanks. Growing up in a church will do that for you."

"So, where are we?" I squint out the windows, trying to get my bearings. Everything's flat, and the sky's the color of cotton candy. "In Louisiana already?"

"Yeah. About an hour away from your place, according to the GPS." Charlotte nods at the passenger seat. "I stopped for food, by the way. There's a cold hamburger waiting for you if you want it."

"I slept through that?" I rub my face. That's—not great,

honestly. I'm a Hunter. I'm supposed to wake up instinctively if there's danger.

Although I suppose Charlotte pulling into a McDonald's drive-through doesn't really count as danger.

I drag myself into the passenger seat, squishing my hamburger a little in the process. It's still good, though, even if it has cooled down and stuck together. The fries are rubbery and greasy, although I eat those too. Wash it all down with the last of Charlotte's watered-down Coke.

"I think you wore yourself out last night," Charlotte says slyly.

"Who's fault is that?" I say it without missing a beat. "You shouldn't have been so hot."

She laughs, and the sound is fucking gorgeous. Edie makes her laugh like that, but Edie's her human best friend. That I could do the same—

Well, it makes my chest feel tight and happy.

"You think I'm hot?" she says.

"Have I not made that clear?" I ball up the fast food bag and toss it in the back seat.

"You've never said it before."

Charlotte's teasing me. I think. I mean, she keeps glancing over at me, and she's smiling.

"It was implied." I honestly thought it was. I've done things with her I haven't done any other woman.

She laughs again.

"You've never said it to me," I snap back. Which surprises me, because I'm actually *not* convinced Charlotte thinks I'm attractive.

"Oh, you're definitely hot," she says. "I thought it the first time I saw you in that diner."

"Really?" I look at her in the falling light. Think about the things I'd like to do to her when we get back to my house.

"We should go back there," she says. "That hamburger I got was phenomenal."

"You'll have to explain why you stuck around." I settle back in my seat, watching the road stretch out in front of us. It feels good to be back in Louisiana. Florida's a little too garish for my tastes. "How you wound up with me."

"They don't know what you are."

Not a question. Still, I answer. "Of course not. But I still have to interact with them sometimes. Buy groceries and shit like that."

We're both quiet for a moment.

"Could I stay here?" Charlotte says suddenly. "With you?"

My whole body lights up, but I stop myself from showing too much excitement. "Of course. You need training."

Charlotte smiles a little, the highway lights flickering over her face. "Your house is nicer than my apartment, believe it or not."

"Well, maybe we can drive out to California to get your stuff." I settle back in my seat. "I haven't been on the West Coast in years."

Charlotte nods. "I think I'd like that. I think I'd like that a lot."

CHAPTER THIRTY-EIGHT

CHARLOTTE

By the time Jaxon's electric fence appears up ahead, I'm bleary-eyed from driving and ready to sleep. Actually *sleep*, too, not just be Jaxon's plaything—even if the idea does make me squirm in my seat. I don't want the strange dreams, for one. I can tell that he really believes that one of his gods came to me last night. I'm not sure I do.

It's just a dream, fragments of my day thrown in a blender and whipped up by the five—*five*—orgasms he delivered while I was sleeping.

The fact that the image I saw, his dad slicing his throat as a teenager, that it really happened—

I shiver. No. I can't dwell on it.

"Stop," Jaxon says sharply. "Now."

"What?" I slam my foot on the gas, the car screeching to a stop on the long, twisting driveway that winds through the swamp. Lights glimmer up ahead. The porch lights. The fence.

"Someone's here." His voice is low and dangerous.

Fear shoots through me, my skin prickling with electricity. "What? How can you tell?"

Jaxon gives me a withering look in the dark. "I'm a Hunter, cher, and so are you. Concentrate. You'll feel them, too."

I still have an instinctual urge to protest, but it only lasts a second. Still, when I do try to concentrate, I don't feel anything. Just a tight, trembling fear.

"Cut the engine." Jaxon unlocks the passenger door.

"And then what?" I do as he says, though, and the sudden silence rings in my ears.

"Get out. Come with me." His voice is low and commanding and deathly serious. "They don't know we're here yet. We can surprise them."

"How can you possibly—" I start, but one violent glare from Jaxon silences me.

"*Listen*," he hisses, and I swear his eyes refract the light back at me, making him look strange and inhuman. When he speaks again, he's calmer, like a teacher explaining something to a student. "Listen for their breaths. Their heartbeats. That'll tell you what they're feeling."

He pushes the door open, letting in the damp air of the swamp. I wish, with a sudden fervent clarity, that we were still in Florida, kissing on a chilly beach in the middle of the night. Instead of doing—whatever it is we're about to do.

Images flash through my head. Blood. The sudden yielding pressure of a knife going through skin. Screams. Moans.

I slide out of the car, biting back my fear, and ease the door closed the same way Jaxon did. He's just barely visible in the dark, a silhouette on shadow, except for his gleaming eyes.

He's not looking at me, though. He's listening.

So I listen, too. Or try to. I close my eyes and breathe out and let the sounds of the swamp surround me. They seem louder than usual, even though it's still a little too cool for frogs and insects. But then I hear a constant, swirling susurration. It's not frog song at all. It's not wind, not trees rustling, although I hear those things, too. It's something—

Something else.

My eyes flutter open and I stifle back a shout of surprise. Jaxon has somehow moved right beside me.

"How did I not hear you?" I whisper. "I was *listening*."

Even in the darkness, I see him smile like he's proud. "You were hearing something else, little Hunter. Now keep quiet and follow me."

So I don't have time to dwell on *that*, then. Jaxon takes my hand, his palm smooth and warm and dry, like he's not even worried, and leads me off the driveway and into the thicket. I press close to him, trying to step where he steps, trying to avoid the puddles of muddy, stagnant water lurking in the dark.

Still, it's easier than the last time I did this. Probably because I'm actually moving with him and not trying to escape. He slides serpentine through the dangling vines and thick overgrowth, almost like he's part of the swamp, like it's opening up a path for him.

"Almost there," he breathes into my ear, and I hear the quiet hum of the electric fence. Lights flicker up ahead. Not just the porch lights, I realize when we step out of the swamp's thick growth. Windows. Half the windows of the house are illuminated.

"They're inside," I gasp.

"Yeah, and there are at least three of them," Jaxon whispers back. "But this is good. Makes it easier for me to get to my weapons."

Weapons. The word sings out on the cool damp night.

"Who are they?"

"The magical wizard mobsters, as you call them." Jaxon's voice is grim. "Or at least, that's my best guess."

"They're going just to keep sending people?" I whisper furiously.

"It's not a big deal. We'll just keep killing them." Jaxon looks at me, his eyes gleaming a little. "It's what our people do, cher."

My head buzzes. My heart pounds.

I'm not just afraid, though.

I'm excited.

We slide along the fence, the shadows wrapping around us. I keep sneaking glances over at the house, trying to listen the way I did by the car. I do hear something, a sound like the ocean. Like breaths rushing and out, or heartbeats beating out of sync with each other.

"Holy shit," I whisper.

Jaxon glances over at me, a smile curving on his lips. "There's my girl."

We come to a second fence gate—not the primary one, at the driveway, but a smaller one, tucked away behind some overgrowth. Jaxon punches in the code and the electricity disappears. The fence is just a fence. He shoves the gate open, nods at me to go through.

We're behind the house now, with the shed across the yard. The house rises up like a beacon.

"We need to get to the shed." Jaxon's mouth is on my ear, his fingers tangling up in mine. "Stay out of the light. Move fast."

I nod, my breath tight. Jaxon tugs me forward, and we skitter back the way we came, only this time we're on the right side of the fence. Inside this strange dark world Jaxon created.

The world I want to share with him.

Something moves across one of the house's windows, and I yelp. Jaxon squeezes my hand, his message clear. *Stay quiet.*

We do make it to the shed, though. Jaxon moves quickly and efficiently like he's done this a thousand times before, as he unlatches the lock and eases the door open. Actually, he probably has done it a thousand times before.

"In," he whispers, and I don't protest, just duck inside.

It's cold. That's the first thing I notice. It's cold, and it smells distressingly sterile. Jaxon shuts the door behind him, cutting off what little light we have. But that doesn't stop him; he moves effortlessly around the space, the sound of metal against metal following behind him.

"You can see?" I whisper.

"You can, too," he says. "You've got to stop clinging to your humanity, Charlotte. It's keeping you from realizing your abilities."

"*Abilities?*" I squeak. "What are you, an X-man?"

He ignores me in favor of rustling around in the darkness. I can just make him out—he's combing through a drawer, and the more I look at him, the more I feel like I can see him. A shadow lighter than the other shadows.

You can see, too.

He pulls something out of the drawer, and for a moment it seems to literally glow, like it's drenched in moonlight. He turns and hands it to me, and I know instantly what it is.

A knife.

The knife, actually. The one I used in Houston. Even in the dark I can see it, but I also feel it, a black thread that tethers the knife to me, and me to the knife.

"I don't know how to fight," I whisper, because he and I both know that I do know how to kill.

"You don't have to fight," he says. "Just protect yourself." He looks at me, and for a second, I see him as clearly as I would in daylight. His killer's face. His flat blue eyes. The coy, vaguely excited smile on his lips. "I won't let them have the honor of your first death."

My breath lodges in my throat, and an image flashes through my head:

Me sitting in Jaxon's kitchen as he draws the knife across my throat, my blood gleaming in the sunlight.

I want you to have that honor, I think, every muscle in my body tightening in some kind of strange anticipation. But I don't say it aloud.

Jaxon's adorned himself with blades. Three of them hang from his belt. He has what looks like a machete strapped across his back, and a hooked meat cleaver clutched in his hand, and I feel like I'm going to faint, my blood is pumping so fast through my veins.

I swallow against my dry throat. "You're not going to wear your mask?"

Jaxon looks at me over his shoulder, his hair falling into his eyes. "This isn't a kill for the gods," he says. "And I want these stupid, persistent motherfuckers to see my face before they die."

CHAPTER THIRTY-NINE

CHARLOTTE

"They're upstairs," Jaxon says.

We've made it across the backyard and are now standing by the back door. My heart keeps turning circles in my chest. I tell myself it's fear, but I know it's not.

"You can tell that?" I frown at the shut door and squeeze my fingers around the knife blade.

He nods, his face dark with concentration. "You will, too, someday. Don't worry about it tonight, though." He looks over at me, and I have the sense that I'm seeing a part of him I've never seen before. The only time I came close was in Houston when he was wearing that mask. Tonight, though, he's stripped bare, and it's like I'm staring right into the pitch of his soul.

He grabs my chin, eyes boring into mine. "Do not die. Your first death needs to be special."

I take a deep, shuddery breath. And nod. Because I *agree* with him.

I want you to do it, I think, the words dancing on the tip of my tongue. I can't get them out, though, so I only lift my knife a little, like I'm showing him I can use it.

"Are you ready?" he asks, still holding my chin.

"Yes." My voice cracks, but at least the word comes out.

Jaxon nods, then eases the door open The kitchen light is on, bright and garish. "They want me to know something's wrong," he mutters. "Toying with me." He grins, and it's manic and crazed. The grin of a killer. "They don't know what I am."

He slips in, and I follow.

The house buzzes and breathes. There's a rackety rhythm coming from somewhere that really does sound like heartbeats.

This is what you were made for.

The voice isn't mine, and it isn't Jaxon's, and it sends electricity shooting down my spine. I squeeze my knife handle and follow Jaxon's strong, thick back as he slips through the house, barely making a noise. When we get to the stairs, he stops, listening.

I listen, too. There's a riot of sound, like what I expect the swamp sounds like in summer—overlapping rhythms blending together into a kind of music. I study Jaxon's face, wondering what he hears in all of it. More than I do, I'm sure.

Although I hear far more than I would have a week ago.

"I think they're in my bedroom," Jaxon murmurs, so softly I barely hear him over the strange noises of the house. "Be careful."

I nod, afraid that anything I say will be too loud. Something flickers across Jaxon's face—a surge of affection breaking through his killer's countenance.

Then he kisses me.

It's soft and chaste, little more than his lips brushing against mine, but it sends heat wracking through my core. His gaze lingers, just for a second.

And then he's going upstairs.

I have a moment of hesitation. It feels like habit more than any real reservations—just a flash of a thought that I could turn around run out of here and keep running until I'm back in California. But something stops me. A truth locked away in my heart.

I don't want to go back to California. I want to follow Jaxon. I want to stay here with him, just like I said in the car.

I want to stay in this dusty old house in the swamp. I want Jaxon to train me. I want to Hunt with him and make art out of bones and skin and fuck in pools of blood. I want to eat his fancy Cajun meals and drink red wine on his couch and have a whole life that was unimaginable to me a month ago but was, I realize now, the life I've been searching for since before I can remember.

Jaxon's halfway up the stairs when he glances back at me, and I feel it again, a black thread of connection. But it doesn't connect me to the knife. It connects me to him.

And so I go creeping up the stairs behind him, hardly daring to breathe. The sounds swirl around me, somehow louder than before, and I sense other things, too: a melange of scents like an old spice cabinet, a prickling in the air that tells me danger is nearby. Or prey. I'm not sure which.

Jaxon glides through the landing like a shark moving through water. I feel clumsy in comparison, a newborn foal. But a foal with teeth.

Bored male voices drift out into the hallway. They're talking about an MMA fight, I think.

"Bullshit if you think Locasta can take Siminisky! It's not even a fucking contest."

"The fuck you mean? Lacosta is oh and three—"

And then—

"Shut the fuck up, both of you."

There are three of them. Jaxon was right.

"I heard something," the voice says. The leader, I think. "Coulter, go check it out."

The floorboards creak. I sidle up behind Jaxon, who stands unbothered, clutching his machete in one hand and the meat cleaver in the other. He turns his head toward me, eyes glinting, and jerks his head. *Stand behind me*, he's saying, and I know he's thinking about guns.

The door to his bedroom opens, and a man steps out. He looks ordinary, dressed in a sleek leather jacket, his hair going thin on the top. He does have a gun, a black pistol.

Everything that happens next happens fast. He looks at us. Sees us.

And then Jaxon is on him, stabbing both blades into his side. The man screams and spits blood across Jaxon's face before he topples to the ground with a loud thump.

Then there's another man, but I don't see much of him before Jaxon strides into his bedroom as if no one is here but the two of us.

"What the fu—" someone shouts, and a gun goes off. I feel it before I hear it, the splinter of wood and the whizz of a bullet brushing past my ear. Then—screams.

Adrenaline surges through me, an overwhelming need to join in on the carnage.

I plunge forward, toward the screams in Jaxon's bedroom, nearly slipping in the blood of his first victim. I stumble through the doorway to find a man kneeling on the ground, clutching the stump of one hand to his chest, blood pouring out across the floor. He looks over at me, confusion in his eyes, and goes silent for half a second.

"Help," he croaks.

Movement flickers from the other side of the room: Jaxon stalking the third man like a panther.

This man *is* the leader. I'm sure of it. He's older, and he wears a casual tailored suit, which feels absurd given the situation. Blood is everywhere and the man missing his hand has started screaming again.

The leader has a gun pointed at Jaxon's chest.

"What do you say?" he says amicably. "Let's talk about it."

Jaxon looks over at me, his face splattered with blood.

"Who is this?" I spit out.

The man tosses me a lazy glance like he's unbothered by my presence. "This your girl?" He grins at me, but I can sense the fear in him. I can taste it, a syrupy darkness like my favorite Turkish coffee. "Sweetheart, I just told your boyfriend here that I'd pay him a million dollars each year to come work for me. You'd like that, huh? Fancy dinners. Expensive handbags."

Expensive cliches, more like. I step forward, every muscle in my body quivering. "Who are you?"

The man glances at Jaxon, but Jaxon just keeps standing there like a nightmare, his blades dripping blood. I don't think he's moved at all. "Damien Tyloch," the man says smoothly. "I'd offer my hand, but well, I'm currently engaged."

I narrow my eyes. "But who *are* you?"

Tyloch studies me for a moment, his gun still pointed at Jaxon. "I run the Undying Lineage of the Stars," he says. "And I'm afraid I made a rather grave error when I set up an arrangement with a certain *entity*."

The hairs on the back of my neck stand on end, and I can feel Jaxon's bloodlust radiating off him. But I want to understand what's going on. I want to know about the man I killed, the man who awoke the Hunter in me.

"So you knew Oliver Raffia," I say.

Tyloch laughs—he's nervous, the laugh edged in hysteria. "We were partners," he says. "Until I had to sacrifice him to appease an evil god."

"I don't understand."

"I feel like your girl is more reasonable than you," Tyloch says to Jaxon. "This is what I was trying to explain. We have a shared benefactor from the Abyss."

Jaxon's gods. That must be who the entity is, the evil god— one of Jaxon's gods.

One of my gods.

"That's why I'm here," Tyloch continues, glancing over at me. "Your boyfriend is one of the best assassins I've ever seen. I could use someone with his skills. So talk some sense into him, won't you?"

Jaxon glances at me with an almost imperceptible movement, and I feel, just for a half-second, a deluge of emotions. He thinks this shit is *funny*. That's the only reason he's letting Tyloch talk, the only reason he's letting Tyloch keep a gun trained on his chest. Jaxon's toying with him, and he thinks I'm toying with him too. Playing the part of the scared girlfriend, Tyloch's potential salvation.

"Why did Raffia have to be sacrificed?" I ask.

Tyloch frowns. "That's of no concern to you, young lady."

And then he sweeps the gun away from Jaxon and points it at my chest and, once again, my fear surges up.

So does Jaxon's. I *smell* it, stronger than Tyloch's fear, stronger than the metallic tang of the terror and suffering pouring out of the man Jaxon wounded, who's still whimpering and bleeding beside me. Jaxon's panic slams over me like a wash of cold air.

Do not die.

Tyloch laughs, hard and cruel. "So that's how I break through to you, huh?" He looks at me, but he's not talking to me. "You know the terms, boy. You've got ten seconds to decide before I shoot those gorgeous tits of hers."

Jaxon looks at me and an inhuman voice echoes in my head.

Move.

I jump sideways at the same time that Jaxon swings his cleaver and lodges it in Tyloch's neck. The gun fires, exploding a section of the wall into plaster and wood splinters. My ears ring.

I whirl around as Jaxon jerks his cleaver away with a fan of thick blood. Tyloch topples to the floor, wheezing out one last, rattling breath. Jaxon watches him, then lifts his gaze to me.

He looks like a god of death.

He's drenched in blood. His hair is stringy with it, and his arms cord with muscle as he clenches the meat cleaver and his machete at his sides. He meets my gaze and smiles in a way that's like baring his teeth, and I want him so badly it feels like my heart is going to burst out of my chest.

He didn't even touch those knives on his belt, and I wonder if he brought them because he was worried about me.

Jaxon smiles at me, a beacon in the midst of all this carnage. "Do you want to take care of him, little Hunter?"

I don't know who he means at first, but then he tilts his head and I remember the third man. At some point, he started inching his way toward the door, but he stops now, eyes flicking back and forth between us, his fear a scent that makes the back of my throat ache.

Another man who hasn't done anything to me. Who was probably only here because Tyloch hired him. I'm sure he's done terrible things. Trafficked young women. Carried out sacrifices and other strategic deaths. Slid heroin into the veins of broken communities.

He's done terrible things, but so have I.

I turn away from Jaxon and walk over to the man, who whimpers and trembles in front of me. Some small part of me still whispers that wanting to kill him isn't normal.

Except it is. For me, for Jaxon, it is.

"Please," he whispers, and I'm struck with a hot, sexual power as I tower over him, my knife at my side. I know what it's like to make someone come, to decide whether or not they experience pleasure. I've done that hundreds of times. But deciding if they get to live or not—

It's a million times better.

"Sorry," I say, and then I jab the knife into the side of his throat, groaning as I penetrate through the muscles and sinew and some bony structure that grabs at the blade. Blood spurts hot across my face, and I pull the knife out to do it again, and then again, just like I did with Oliver Raffia. I keep doing it until this man's dead, too, and then I leave the knife lodged in his flesh and drop back on my ass, drawing in deep, steadying breaths.

Jaxon's footsteps thud behind me. He crouches down and uses his bloody hand to draw my hair away from my throat. Then he kisses me, licking the blood away.

"Fuck me," I whisper, staring at the corpse I just created, wishing I could make another.

"I was hoping you'd stay that," he growls, and then he yanks me up by my blood-drenched hair.

CHAPTER FORTY

JAXON

I throw Charlotte on my bed and rub my cock as she rolls over, her eyes blazing with that lust you only get after a good kill. I've got it myself right now. If I don't get inside her, I'm pretty sure I'm going to die, Hunter or not.

"Get those fucking clothes off you," I snarl at her, fumbling with my own zipper. The scent of death hangs heavy in the air, and it just makes me want to fuck her more. Especially as I watch her drag her blood-soaked pants down over her hips and thighs and calves, the movement giving me tantalizing glimpses of her pussy.

"Get your fucking cock out," she snaps back as she settles onto her elbows, spreading her bare thighs wide for me.

I grin at the lust dripping off her words, and I do as she asks, showing her how hard I am for her and what she's done.

She runs her tongue over her lips like she's hungry for a meal. But I have something else in mind.

"Not like that," I tell her. "Get on your hands and knees." I stride around the side of the bed, my cock bobbing with each step. I'm so hard it's almost painful. Charlotte watches me. Doesn't move, though, the little tease.

"Do it," I order, and I hear the Hunter in me coming out, as if she's terrified prey. She doesn't react like prey, though. She just lifts her chin in defiance and slides her hand down to play with her clit.

"Make me," she snaps back, her fingers a blur against her pussy.

I nearly come then and there. The only thing stopping me is the need to be inside her.

I hurl myself at her, grabbing her by the waist and flipping her over onto her belly. She shrieks and squirms, fighting back, but I'm stronger than her. *Older* than her. I know her strength will come, too, in time, and then she'll really be fun to play with.

But tonight, she's still new enough that I overpower her easily, even though I can feel her muscles straining against her body's usual softness, a contrast that drives me wild.

I press myself down on her, pinning her against the bed, and whisper in her ear. "I want you to look at what you did while I fuck you."

Charlotte moans, and, for a moment, relents. I take that opportunity to slide off her and drag her around so she's facing the room instead of the wall. So she's facing the blood and the dead bodies. All the things we accomplished together.

"That's better." I nibble at her ear, as I scoop my hands around her belly and jerk her up so she's on all fours. "You like what you see?"

"Yes," Charlotte gasps, her fingers digging into my blankets. "I know I shouldn't—"

I slap my hand around her mouth and press my lips to her ear. "I won't hear any talk like that, little Hunter."

Charlotte tries to respond, but I keep my hand in place as I run my other hand down her bare back, stopping it on her ass. She glances at me sideways, eyes brimming with expectation.

"Talk like that gets punished," I tell her, and I feel her smile against my palm.

Then I slap her ass, firm and hard, letting her mouth go so I can hear her cry out. And she does, beautifully, a gasp of pain that she follows up with a perfectly fierce, "Fuck you."

She's smiling as she says it, though, and she wriggles her ass in the air.

I slap the other side, hard enough to leave a crimson hand-print on her pale skin, and Charlotte gasps and squeezes the blankets more tightly, staring up at me with flushed, parted lips.

"Again," she whispers.

"Okay," I whisper back, smoothing my hand over her hair. I'm so flush with love and lust that I can barely stand it. "But keep pretending to fight me."

Her grin widens, and her eyes glitter, and she nods.

Then she tries to scramble forward over the side of the bed. I grab her by the hips and jerk her back into position. I grab her chin and make her look out at the mess my room's become, while I slide my other hand between her legs so I can feel how drenched she is between her thighs.

"Look at what you did," I whisper. "I know you liked it." I slide a single finger into her pussy, stroking her walls.

"I didn't!" she protests, her words shuddering with moans.

"Don't fucking lie to me." I yank my hand and slap her ass again, using enough force that she jerks forward over the edge of my bed frame. She catches herself, her crimson hair hanging into her face.

But she doesn't look away.

And she presents her reddening ass to me. *Again*, I think, the word so sweet the way she said it, and I smack her three more times, each one harder than the last. I check her pussy between each slap, adding another finger each time. Charlotte groans and whimpers and gets wetter until I slide all four of my fingers inside her, stretching her out.

She trembles and braces herself against the bed.

"That's what you get for denying what you are," I tell her, stroking my fingers inside her until she's groaning and jerking back on my hand. "Now you get your reward for killing so well."

Charlotte cries out, and her pussy flutters in tight fast contractions around my fingers.

"Are you coming?" I cry out, delighted by this development. "When I said reward, I meant my cock."

Charlotte laughs through her moans, and I keep working her, plying her until the contractions stop and she slumps forward over the bed frame, still staring out at the bodies and blood.

"Yes," she finally says, and it's only then that I pull my hand out of her. "Yes, that made me fucking come, okay?"

"Don't sound so put out by it." I slide my pussy-wet fingers into her mouth and Charlottes sucks on them eagerly, her tongue winding through each digit. I position my cock between her drenched thighs, rubbing its swollen length up against her wet pussy. Teasing her. "I'm proud of you."

I pull my hand out of her mouth and gather her hair up in my fist, pulling her up so she's on her hands and knees properly.

"I'm still getting used to it," she says softly. Shyly.

"Will this help?"

And then I enter her with one hard thrust.

Charlotte bucks against me, and I pull her head back by her hair, holding her in place so she'll keep looking at our victims as I fuck her astonishingly wet cunt.

"Will it?" I ask, punctuating the question with an especially hard thrust, deep enough that I feel my cockhead bump against some firm, fleshy barrier.

"Yes!" Charlotte screams, shoving back at me. "And fuck, that hurt."

"I won't do it again." I go back to my slower strokes. "Unless you refuse to answer my questions."

Charlotte rolls her hips against me. "I'll keep that in mind."

We fall into a rhythm, our slick flesh slapping together as I hold Charlotte by her gorgeous blood-red hair so she can look at all the gorgeous red blood we spilled. It's a work of art, all our destruction. An art installation, the blood gleaming like rubies on the wall and the floor and across my dresser and the doorframe. Charlotte's breaths quicken, and her moans turn deeper and throatier.

"Touch your clit," I tell her, yanking on her hair to show her I mean business. "I want to feel you come again."

She doesn't even pretend to fight me, just drops her chest down and snakes her hand between her body and the bed. Her fingers flutter against my cock as I keep fucking her, my own pleasure building into a tight knot of heat at the base of my dick.

"Hurry," I tell her. "I'm not gonna last long." I let go of her hair so I can fall over her, cupping her tits and licking the sweat and blood off the back of her neck. How blood even got there, I don't know, but I'm not going to question it.

"I'm so close," she whispers back, and she's still looking out at the corpses and the blood, her body twitching.

"It's beautiful, isn't it?" I whisper, squeezing her tits even though they're half crushed against the bed. "Just like you."

Charlotte announces her second orgasm with a loud, keening moan, and her hand goes still against her clit as I keep fucking her through those endless rippling pulses because I'm on the fucking edge myself, and her tight, clenching orgasm is what tips me over. Right before I spill, I yank myself back up and bury myself as deep into her pussy as I can, roaring as my cum spurts into her, my orgasm rolling hot and intense up through my stomach and into the rest of me. Charlotte whimpers softly like she feels it too.

I ease myself out of her and then gather her up in my arms, pulling her against my chest and then collapsing both of us backward onto the bed. She nestles up against me, her cheek resting in the crook of my shoulder.

"Just as a warning," I tell her, running my hand down her bare arm. "If you try to get up right now, I'm going to chain you to the bed again."

Charlotte laughs. "Don't be an asshole."

"I'm just being honest." I pull her in closer to me, breathing in her scent through her hair. I love how it blends with the scent of blood and death hanging in the room, how it adds notes of dark sweetness to the inevitable rot. "This is the best part," I whisper, brushing kisses against her forehead. "Holding you afterward."

But then Charlotte doesn't say anything, and a hot, lurid embarrassment flushes through me. The fuck was I thinking, saying that kind of romantic shit? Just because I love her—like, really love—doesn't mean she loves me. And I don't blame her.

Her fingers crawl across my chest. "You don't have to say stuff like that," she says softly. "I'm a big girl."

My embarrassment turns to confusion. "Wait, what? It's true."

Charlotte lifts her head, frowning as she studies my face like she's looking for evidence of something. A lie. I panic a little and spit out the first thing I can think to say.

"I love you."

I immediately regret it, and I squeeze my eyes shut so I don't have to look at the reaction on Charlotte's face. "Sorry," I mutter. "You don't have to—You're not *obligated* or anything. I just—"

She touches my face, so gently that I immediately shut up.

"Open your eyes, Jaxon."

I force myself to do it, eyes fluttering. Charlotte gazes down at me, her palm still cupping my cheek.

"Say it again," she whispers, her eyes boring into mine.

My heart's pounding. All the things I've done in my life and this scares me more than any of them.

"I love you," I whisper.

Charlotte draws her brows together. "You mean it."

"Well, yeah." Hesitantly, I reach up to tuck her hair behind her ear. "You're the kind of woman I always wanted but didn't think I'd ever have." I can feel the heat in my face and I wonder if she can feel it—her Hunter senses are finally waking up, that much was made clear earlier. "Beautiful and strong and kind of a smartass. Another artist—"

"You've never even seen my art," she interrupts. "That doesn't count." She tilts her head toward the bodies.

"First of all, it does." I smile, still stroking her hair. "But I want to see your work. Your gouache paintings, I mean."

She smiles. "You remembered."

"I remember everything you tell me."

Charlotte sinks her head back down on my shoulder, and I can feel her own quickened heartbeat. Her own nervousness. I pull her a little closer.

"I think," she whispers. "I think I might love you, too."

I freeze. "You don't have to say that. I'm not really going to chain you to the bed or—"

"I mean it." She sits up and gazes down at me, her hair clinging to her cheek. "There *was* something inside me that needed to be broken, and you did that for me." She shakes her head and looks away, lost in thought. "You showed me how to find the happiness I've been searching for since the day my parents kicked me out of my house. Since before then, even."

Something brims inside me. Happiness or hope or one of those sunlight-bright emotions I don't experience all that often. Although I've been experiencing them more lately.

Ever since Charlotte waltzed into that diner.

I grab her hand and braid our fingers together, admiring the way it looks, having our bodies linked like that.

"Tyloch," she says suddenly. "He said Raffia was a sacrifice."

I groan. "Do we have to talk about him?"

She giggles and shushes me. "No, I just—it was your gods, wasn't it? They asked for the sacrifice? And that's why they sent you to kill him?"

I ghost my hand over her hair. "Yeah," I say. "Whatever Tyloch wanted from them, Raffia was the payment. But they sent *us* to collect because they wanted me to wake you up."

She smiles, her eyes glittering, and then kisses me. "I'm glad they did," she whispers against my mouth. "So glad. But they aren't—they aren't going to be upset about—"

She gestures toward the carnage.

"No," I tell her, which is the truth. "All they care about is their payment, and they got it."

"What about the ULS?" she asks, worry knitting her brow. "You said they'll keep coming—"

"I said *if* they keep coming, we can handle it. That's just a Hunter's life. " Which is also the truth. But I'm not worried about humans or their weak magic. Especially not with Charlotte at my side.

I pull her into me so I can kiss her all over and lick the blood away from her skin and make her moan and squirm against me. She reacts exactly as I hoped, settling back on the bed, spreading her legs for me. I kiss down to her breasts and then bite gently on her right nipple, making her gasp.

"Jaxon," she moans, threading her fingers through my blood-sticky hair. "I want—"

Her question evaporates into another gasp as I catch her left nipple in my teeth. She arches her body into me, and I keep kissing down her belly, heading toward her cunt. Eating her out will get me hard again in no time.

"You want to fuck me?" I ask against her skin. "Don't worry, cher. I'm working on it."

"No. I mean, yes, but—" She tugs on my hair, lifting my face to meet hers. "You remember what you said earlier, about how my first death needs to be special?"

All the air rushes out of me, and the only thing I can do is stare at her wide, pretty eyes, black against the blood smeared across her face.

"I want you to do it," she whispers. "I want you to initiate me."

CHARLOTTE

The next day, after we've cleaned up the mess in the bedroom, Jaxon and I discuss the details of my death.

I feel oddly calm about the entire proposition, secure in the knowledge that it's not permanent. It's a certainty I feel in the deepest part of my bones—the same as the certainty, growing stronger and stronger each day, that death is the final piece of the puzzle. The final proof to myself that I'm not the human woman I thought I was.

We talk through everything at the dining room table. Jaxon has one of those bright yellow legal notepads, and he takes notes through the entire conversation, which is both weirdly administrative and weirdly sweet.

"Fast or slow?" he asks.

"Fast."

Jaxon breathes out like he's relieved. "Thank the gods," he says. "I really didn't want to torture you." Then his eyes take on a kind of wicked gleam and he adds, "I'm more interested in what comes after anyway."

I throw a wadded-up piece of legal paper at him, which he deflects without even trying.

"How do you want to do it?" I ask.

He taps his pen against the notepad like he's thinking. "Probably cut a couple of arteries," he says. "You'd bleed out in about five minutes, which isn't bad. Most people pass out before then anyway, although Hunters don't always."

He watches me, gauging my reaction. I know he can feel the heat in my core at the thought of the blood.

"Severing your brain stem would be faster," he adds, "but that'll take longer for you to revive."

"That matters?" I ask. "How you do it?"

"Yeah. The less damage I do to your body, the faster it will take. I'll also need to keep you covered. Buried, you know That speeds things up, too." He writes something down on the notepad. I try to peek, but he covers it with his hand. "I've already got that part covered," he says. "But it's a surprise."

I roll my eyes. "Will my body rot?"

"Nope." Jaxon scribbles something else on the notepad and looks up at me, and there's that shyness I love so much. "Which means I get to play with you the entire time you're dead."

My pussy clenches at the thought. "I thought I wasn't really dead."

"You know what I mean." He tilts his head, studying me. "How do you want me to do it?"

I think about it for a moment, considering the possibilities, watching them play out in my mind and getting more and more turned on with each image. A split throat. A severed brain stem. Drowning in the muddy swamp water. A chain around my neck—

"The way I killed you," I whisper, and Jaxon grins so wickedly I almost want him to do it right here and now.

But no. We have to make our preparations. We have to do this right.

"You're fucking incredible," Jaxon says, and then we get to work.

THE DAY of my death is cold and bright. I get ready in a dusty old bedroom Jaxon told me was his grandmother's. I can see it, too; there's a softness to the decor, lots of vintage lace and gauzy curtains. A big full-length mirror in the corner. A vanity where I'm sitting now, braiding up my hair so it won't get in the way.

I keep expecting to change my mind. I keep expecting this decision to feel wrong, for dread and fear to coil like twin snakes in my belly. Death is supposed to be the ultimate fear, but the thing inside me that broke open when I killed Oliver Raffia also killed any fear I had of death.

Because my death will only ever be temporary.

I'm certain of it, as certain as I've been of anything. And so here I am, ready to be initiated.

I slide the last hairpin into place and blink at myself in the mirror. I'm wearing a pretty white dress that Jaxon gave me, the fabric soft and thin and tight around the bodice, with a long, billowing skirt that just barely skims along the top of the floor. It's not really warm enough for the weather, but I don't mind the cold.

I double-check my makeup—smokey eyes, thick lashes, pale lips. Maybe there's no point in doing my makeup, but just like Jaxon said—I want my first death to be special.

I take one last deep breath and stand, smoothing the skirt down over my belly and hips. Check everything one last time.

And then I go downstairs to meet Jaxon.

He's waiting for me in his creepy living room, standing in front of the empty fireplace. The mummies on the couch stare at me with their empty eyes.

Jaxon turns as I step into the doorway. He's dressed up, too, in a dark if somewhat ill-fitting suit, like it was tailored for someone else. He pulled his hair back in a low ponytail, and he shaved off his stubble while I was getting ready.

For a minute, we just stare at each other. I'm not sure what I'm supposed to say. But then Jaxon breaks the silence.

"You look so beautiful," he says softly.

His words catch me off guard, and I fumble around for a response. "Thank you," I say, then add, "It's the dress, mostly. Thanks for letting me—"

"It's not the dress." He walks toward me with slow, heavy steps, his gaze burning blue. "Well, not just the dress."

His grazes the back of my hand with his knuckle, his touch soft, and that hot gaze settles on my lips. I suck in my breath, still not sure what to say. What to do.

"Are you nervous?" he asks.

"I don't know." I smile at him. "I feel like I should be, but I'm not."

He returns the smile, and for a moment, things feel easy between us, like they have the last few days as we got everything ready. "It's because you know what you are." He brushes my cheek. "I wasn't nervous, either. I was excited."

"Yeah, I wouldn't say I'm excited. I just feel—" I don't think there's a word for what I feel. "Inevitable."

I don't think it makes sense, but Jaxon nods like he understands.

Then he kisses me, and it's like he's kissing me for the first time, like we're on a date and he wants to impress me. His mouth is warm and slow and hesitant, and he waits until I slide my tongue between his lips before he does the same. He lets me deepen the kiss even more, tilting my head, sliding my hand along the side of his neck, kissing him with the ferocity of all the darkness storming inside my heart.

When he breaks it, I gasp at the loss of contact.

"I'm going to do that again when you revive," he murmurs into my ear.

It's a surprisingly effective reassurance.

"Come on," he whispers. "It's time."

His hand snakes down to grab mine, and I accept it. Then he leads me out of the living room, out of the house entirely. When we step onto the porch, I immediately shiver. A cold front came through last night, and the air's sharp and snapping against my skin. Jaxon wraps his arm around my shoulders, pulling me into his heat.

"You won't be out here long," he says softly.

"That's one way of putting it."

He grins, then grabs my hand again and leads me out into the yard. The wind blusters out from the swamp, damp and cool, pushing my dress back up so I feel like a ghost already drifting through the marsh. Jaxon takes me behind his shed, and for the first time, I see the thing he's been working on for the last few days. The little project he told me was a surprise.

It's a tomb.

Not a permanent one, not one made of carved marble like the tombs in New Orleans. But it's clear what it is: a little silent house built of bones and antlers and dried human skin—a thought that gives me a peculiar twist in my belly and nothing more. Swamp fronds on the roof. Thick, woody vines twining everything together.

And, painted above the entrance in blood, is the sigil that brought me to Jaxon in the first place.

"Once it's warmer," Jaxon says, his breath in my ear, "I'll plant honeysuckle and jasmine, and they'll grow around you and keep you safe."

It's beautiful, this place where I'm to die and be reborn.

"Will it stand up to the weather?" I ask.

"It should." Jaxon looks at me. "The Unnamed is protecting it."

"Okay," I say. "But if a hurricane hits, you're going to bring me inside, right?"

Jaxon's eyes glitter. "Don't worry, cher. Nothing's going to happen to you while you're dead."

That's not *exactly* true, and we both know it. But I don't say anything.

Jaxon helps me inside the tomb, and it's warmer in there, out of the wind, and there are soft, downy blankets for me to lie on instead of the cold grass. Jaxon helps me down, sliding himself between my parted legs, and runs his thumb over my lips. I can feel his heat against mine. I can hear his heart pounding and I can smell his excitement, his lust, his affection.

His love.

I reach down and lift my skirt. I'm not wearing anything underneath. A gift for him.

Jaxon doesn't break eye contact. Not when he slides his hand along my wet slit, not when he unbuckles his suit pants and pulls out his cock and presses it against my clit, making me moan.

"Are you sure you don't want me to use my knife?" he whispers, brushing a loose strand of hair out of my eyes.

I nod, never looking away from him. Pale winter sunlight filters through the cracks in the tomb's roof, dappling us with shadows. He warned me strangulation wouldn't be an easy death, not like cutting my throat. But it could be pleasurable.

He would make it pleasurable.

"Tell me when you're ready."

I breathe in, filling my lungs. His cock brushes against my clit, inflaming me, and I reach down and guide him into my pussy, making him gasp in surprise.

The darkness inside me pulses.

"I'm ready," I whisper.

"I can tell." He thrusts into me slowly, carefully, his lips trailing kisses along my jaw. "You're drenched, cher."

He kisses me before I can respond, so I roll my hips against him instead, wrapping my legs around his waist, drawing him inside me so he'll feel my body quake as I stop breathing.

Jaxon kisses me for a long time, slow and sensual, his thrusts keeping pace. He trails his fingers around my neck, a tease of what's coming next, and I moan into him, building up the pleasure for my orgasm.

"You're getting close," he breathes into my ear.

"Yes," I gasp back.

"Good." He raises himself up just enough to gaze down at me, his face flushed with exertion.

His fingers dig a little deeper into my neck.

"You're going to come for me before you die."

I nod as he brings his other hand up to join the first, his long fingers spreading across my throat. I cry out, bucking into him, grinding my clit against the base of his cock. Heat builds in my belly, sparking with an undercurrent of depravity, a sprinkle of fear.

More. I want more.

"Last chance to tell me to stop." His thrusts are deep and rhythmic, his big cock sliding against some spot inside me that makes me spark and shiver.

And I don't even have to think about it. Because I've done all my thinking already. This is what I want.

"Don't you fucking dare," I rasp.

Jaxon's grin splits his face open—

And then he squeezes.

He squeezes hard, and tight, digging his thumbs against my trachea. I try to cry out, but my voice is trapped in my throat. Trapped by his hands. His cock slams in and out of me, body angled just right that he shoves it across my clit, giving me the sensation I need as my lungs burn and my head spins.

"It's going to be so fun to fuck you when you're dead," he purrs, pressing his weight down on my throat. My body thrashes of its own accord, some primitive part of my brain telling it to fight for survival. It's not conscious.

Because I want it.

I want it so bad.

"That's it," Jaxon whispers, his eyes wild with lust. White spots dot the edge of my vision, and Jaxon eases up just enough that I suck in another thin lungful of air to keep me conscious for a few seconds longer. I'm close. The pressure is building up in clit and my cunt both, a hot swirling hurricane of need. I try to goad him, but all that comes out are strained, choking sounds.

Jaxon squeezes my throat tighter.

The world blinks, and my body erupts.

It's a monstrous swell of an orgasm heightened by the lack of oxygen. The light streaming through the gaps in the bones seems to swirl and dance, braiding together until there's nothing but whiteness, a light so bright it burns black on the back of my eyelids, and I see its face. The god that Jaxon worships. The god that brought me to him so he could save me.

The Unnamed.

It nods at me, approving.

And somehow, I'm still coming as I die.

CHAPTER FORTY-TWO

JAXON

Charlotte's entire body convulses right before the symphony of her life silences. It feels impossibly fucking good, like every single muscle she's ever used just clamped down around my cock. I cry out, hand still pressed deeper around her neck, and come, bucking and thrusting into her slack body. Then I collapse down on top of her, trying to catch my panting breath.

She doesn't move. Her chest doesn't rise and fall against mine. I can't even sense the imperceptible rhythm of her heartbeat.

"*Tell me I wasn't wrong*," I whisper in the language of the gods. Now that my ecstasy's evaporating away, doubt creeps in. I was so sure she's a Hunter. *She* was sure, even up until the last moment. I know what it looks like, what it feels like, to kill someone who doesn't want to die. They fight, they panic, they plead—with their eyes if they can't speak.

And she didn't do any of that. She came for me, and then she passed out, and then I kept going until she was silenced.

But the doubt is still there, niggling at the back of my thought. What if we both made a terrible mistake?

"Tell me," I whisper again, grabbing at her limp hand.

A whisper rattles through Charlotte's lips. The Unnamed. Of course. It was the one drawing us together all this time.

Of course she's a Hunter. She was chosen by me. Doubt is unbecoming of you.

I breathe out in relief and nuzzle up against her throat. Even the Unnamed's admonishment doesn't sting. *"How long?"* I ask. *"Until her revival?"*

The Unnamed doesn't answer that question, and I didn't expect it to. It will take as long as it takes. The first revival always takes a while, but a death like this, with minimal damage to her beautiful body—a year. Maybe a little longer.

I shift, my cock softening inside her. She wears a black necklace of bruises, and her eyes are bulging open, red with burst blood vessels. Fortunately, I came prepared, and I pull two gold coins out of my pocket. The same gold coins my father laid on my eyes when I died for the first time.

I close her lids, one at a time, and weigh them down with the coins. Then I adjust the dress's neckline, which got twisted up and dragged down while I fucked her, revealing one of her pretty nipples. I cover that back up, then slide out of her—with some regret—so I can adjust the skirt of the dress, too, arranging it so it flares out around her like fallen snow. I know I won't be able to withstand the temptation to play with her again, and soon—she's so beautiful in death, so still, and it will be a treasure to feel her cold pussy around my cock, to lick at her stiffening flesh.

But right now, in the moments after her death, I want to make her a work of art.

I put my dick away, crawl backward out of the tomb, and get to work.

I have my old gouache paints waiting for me in my studio, each color mixed with the blood Charlotte spilled three days ago. It gives the paint a thick, sticky consistency as I carefully paint the Unnamed's sigil onto Charlotte's forehead, murmuring soft prayers as I trace the intricate lines and swirls, feeling the power humming up through my hand. I add delicate embellishments to the design, decorating her already-paling face until she looks like a flower in the darkness. Then I move down to cover her bruises with a thick layer of color, turning each burst bloom into a vibrant, multi-colored rose.

I paint her arms next, ringing them with a delicate, flowery pattern, all the way down to her pale hands. There, I stop for a moment. She's still warm, and rigor mortis hasn't moved into her limbs yet, although it's making its way there.

"You're so beautiful," I whisper to her. Then I kiss the inside of her palms before I paint a brilliant, blazing red eye, another symbol of the Unnamed, on the center of each one. I arrange her hands at her side so the Unnamed's red eyes stare upward at the starry light spilling through the top of the tomb.

It takes a long time to paint every inch of Charlotte's bare skin. I go slowly and methodically so I don't accidentally get paint on her dress, which cinches around her waist and ripples over her legs. By the time I'm finished, she looks like a garden in the golden, late afternoon sunlight. And when the weak Louisiana winter ends in a few weeks, and the wildflowers start blooming along the highways and in the sunny patches of my yard, I'll make her look like a garden for real.

She has to be buried if I want her to revive as fast as possible. And I'd rather bury her in flowers than in dirt.

I crawl out of the tomb to put my supplies away and let the paint dry. I was half-aroused the entire time I was anointing her, but I promised myself—and her, not that I'm sure she really understands the reason for it—that I would wait until she was anointed to have my fun. Now the ceremony is done. I've marked her for the Unnamed. Perhaps she'll meet it in death, just as she did, however briefly, in her dreams.

I go inside and strip out of my suit. I take a shower, washing away any grime and paint from my skin. I eat a little something to get my energy up.

Then it's back outside—to play with her corpse for the first time.

It's been hours since Charlotte died. The sun is sinking into the swamp and staining the sky with streaks of red the same cherry-blood color as her hair.

I crawl into the tomb and then crawl on top of her, careful not to smudge any of the paint as I lean down to kiss her lips, which I left bare. There's no response from her, of course, but she's in the Abyss, her soul a small bright ember among the darkness, barely glowing as her body heals itself.

"Are you ready, cher?" I whisper, my heart quickening in my chest.

The wind blows outside, rustling the vines I used to build the tomb, and I take that as a yes. I slide down and carefully push her dress up, revealing her pale, unpainted thighs, the skin already turning a blueish-grey at the edges. I touch her like the treasure she is, soft at first. I still half-expect for her to moan and shift beneath me, the way she did when was asleep. I've gotten so used to fucking her, my living girl.

But she's not living. Not right now.

My fingers land on her pussy, dry and cool in death, a sensation I'll admit I missed. I push one finger in, feeling her, and then palm myself almost distractedly as I touch her. I wonder if her soul can feel my touch in the Abyss. If her ghost will come for me.

If the gods know, they don't say a word.

I lower myself down to kiss her cunt as reverently as I kissed her mouth, her flesh already edged with a faint, chilly sweetness that I know will deepen in the next few days. She won't rot because she *technically* isn't dead. But her systems have stopped. Her blood will pool in her limbs, and she's stiff with rigor mortis. But the flies will leave her alone. The bacteria will find no home inside her. She'll remain as she is until the moment she wakes up.

I plunge my tongue between her folds, moistening her pussy for my cock. When she's ready, I sit back on my heels and spit in my hand to get my dick nice and wet, too.

Then I press myself into her.

Once again I'm reminded how used I am to her living body. I miss the rainstorm of her arousal, but her dry, dead pussy is familiar in a different way, and I groan as I push my full length into her, thrusting in hard, sharp bursts. Hard enough that her body slides limply across the blanket I laid for her. Hard enough that one of the coins falls off her eyes, and she stares at me through the white cloud of her death.

It's fucking beautiful.

I groan, fucking her harder, her dead cunt clamping down hard on my dick. She stares sightlessly up at me, both with her actual eye and with the two eyes of the Unnamed I painted on her hand.

"Do you see me?" I rasp, not sure if I'm talking to her or to the gods. "Do you see what I've done?"

The wind picks up, blowing in from the north, whistling and howling through the trees. The tomb shakes with the force of my thrusts.

"Do you feel it, cher?" I squeeze her hardening tits over her dress, slam myself inside her until my cockhead meets her cervix. And she doesn't react. Doesn't cry out. Doesn't clench down on me.

Just stares at me, her pupil swimming in blood and mist, her lips parted.

I lean over to kiss her, carefully not to smudge the paint on her face. Then I straighten up and I fuck her as hard as I can, my orgasm building hot and tight in my balls. She stares at me, and I reach down and play with her clit just in case she does feel it.

I fuck her until the very last minute and then pull myself out so my cum arcs in a glistening, pearly rainbow and splatters across her white dress and the top of her her tits. I moan through my pleasure and then sit down on my heels, admiring the work of art I made of her.

A year is a long time not to have this woman at my side.

But at least I have her corpse.

CHAPTER FORTY-THREE

CHARLOTTE

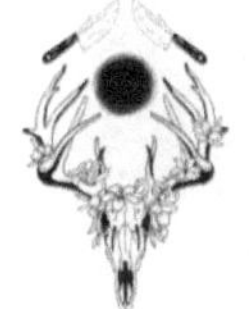

I feel something. A faint tingle in my fingers, like the blood is flowing back into the tiny, delicate veins there. There's a kind of electric buzz at the bottom of my feet. I'm not nothing.

It fades.

THE NEXT TIME I feel something it's like when you're in a club and the music is so loud you can feel the rhythm deep in your chest, so heavy it drowns out your heartbeat. For a long time, I'm nothing but that bass line, slow and droning.

And then the tingling starts again.

I'm a lightning storm.

Then that fades, too.

THE THIRD TIME, I itch.

My throat itches, and I remember the moments before I

died, Jaxon's fingers crushing my trachea as pleasure bloomed hot and roiling through my body.

There's no pleasure this time.

But I think I can remember what it's like to breathe.

And I itch.

I itch and I itch.

THE FOURTH TIME, I finally start to solidify. My body seems to take up space in the darkness. Something deep inside my throat tingles, a kind of faint healing sensation. I drift through the void, considering the outlines of my form, and I wonder how long I've been dead.

It lasts longer this time, this awareness. Hours or days. Years? No, I don't think it's been that long. But I can feel movement inside my body. A churning that tells me I'm not really dead. And sometimes I can feel the world around me. Softness against my back. Delicate prickling across my skin. Coolness. Warmth. A rough palm.

I float like this, caught between life and death. I don't know how long it lasts until I drift away again.

THE FIFTH TIME, I wake up to sensation. I wake up to *pleasure*.

I feel everything. The blankets I'm stretched out on, the rapid hammering of my heart, my short, panting breaths. And a column of fire between my legs, swelling up through my body in an endless way of heat.

My first word is a scream and the first thing I see is webbed light falling across Jaxon's face, his long dark lashes fluttering as he opens his eyes and then meets my gaze.

He grins.

"Welcome back, cher."

His words sound strange, muffled and distorted, and I can only moan in response. Actually speaking feels impossible, so I just arch into him, trying to remember what it's like to have a body. It's not like this. Not most of the time. I'm pulsing with ecstasy.

"What was it like," he whispers into my ear, and I barely comprehend what he's saying. "Coming while you revived?"

I whimper and wind my arms around him, and this all feels familiar, in a way. Me waking up to Jaxon flooding me with pleasure. But the last time I was asleep, not dead.

I roll my hips and lift my legs to wrap them around his back. My body almost seems to act of its own accord, like it remembers what to do more than me. Jaxon grunts and kisses my neck, and I give myself over to the pleasure, focusing my gaze on the crisscross of branches and bones and sunlight overhead. *The tomb*, I think idly, barely remembering. The tomb Jaxon crafted for me out of gifts from the swamp. It looks different. Leafier. The sunlight has a greenish quality.

And it's warm now. It was cold before.

"How long has it been?" I gasp out, twisting my fingers in Jaxon's hair. It hurts to talk, my vocal cords grinding together.

He pumps into me with his cock, and I remember, through a haze, how he asked if he could fuck me while I was dead, shy and nervous, not quite meeting my eye. How the question flushed me with heat and I said *of course* and then thought about it later, when he fucked me in his bed, and the idea made me come.

That agonizing pressure builds in my core again, Jaxon's big cock a flint against my steel. I scrape my nails into his back and he groans, his breath hot against my skin.

"You're gonna come for me again," he growls.

"Yes," I whisper. "How long has it—"

"Year and a half." He kisses me hard, our tongues grappling together. "And I've missed you so fucking much, little Hunter."

I thrust up into him, so close to my orgasm that my body shudders with the need for release. Jaxon braces his arms on either side of my head, his own thrusts turning erratic, and I know he's not going to last much longer. I squeeze down on him, milking him, and when he comes so do I, our intermingled moans drifting out of my tomb.

Jaxon slumps down on my chest, breathing hard, and I trail my fingers up his spine, trying to remember how to move for real. How to sit up. How to walk. Dragging myself out of this tomb feels like it's going to be impossible.

"How do you feel?" Jaxon's voice startles me.

I swallow. "Strange." Talking still hurts.

"I was trying to time it so you'd wake up while I was—" Jaxon peels himself off me and grins, a little embarrassed. "You were starting to show signs of revival. It looks like I guessed right."

I take him in. He's cut his hair, and it skims across the tops of his shoulders. His skin is darker than I remember, like he's spent time in the sun, and his bare chest is gleaming with sweat

A year and a half, he'd said. It's summer.

"I know that probably made things even stranger." He brushes my cheek with a tenderness that makes me want to fuck him again. "But I also thought it'd be kinda fun."

"It was more than kinda," I tell him, catching his hand and kissing his palm. "But I—can't move. Talking hurts."

"That'll all fade." He crawls backward over me, the dappled light making him look like some kind of predator of the swamp. A rattlesnake or an alligator—sleek and dark and dangerous. "I'll help you out, okay? I've got basil lemonade ready for you. My grandma always said it helps." He smiles again, his eyes brimming with affection. "She had it for me after my first death."

He slides his arms under mine and helps me up to sitting, my head grazing the top of the tomb. Then he drags me out, slow and gentle. I help him along as much as I can, scooting my butt over tangled blankets and crushed flowers. They're everywhere. Whole blooms braided into my hair. Dried petals sticking to my chest and arms. I'm still in the white dress, although it's become dingy from being outside for a year and a half.

We emerge into the sunny yard, and I immediately have to squeeze my eyes shut, it's so bright. Jaxon wraps me up, pressing my face into his chest. "I've got you," he says. "I'll walk you up to the house, okay?"

I nod into him because I don't want to talk, and he helps me up to standing. My legs shake like they're barely able to hold my weight, but it's okay because Jaxon is there propping me up. We move together, taking slow, stumbling steps. When I start to fall, he catches me and murmurs soft words of reassurance in my ear. I squeeze my eyes shut against the sun most of the time, but every now and then I blink out at the world, seeing it in flashes because of the brightness. His yard is thick and wild and very, very green.

"You're doing so good," he says. "I'd carry you, but the earlier you start moving your legs, the faster things'll come back."

I nod again and focus on the sensation of the tall, soft grasses against my feet and ankles. "We're at the porch," Jaxon says. "Careful with the steps."

With his help, I make my way up to the screened-in porch, where I open my eyes experimentally. The screen blocks enough of the sunlight that it doesn't hurt as much, and I take in my surroundings. It's like seeing them for the first time. The porch. The yard. The swamp.

Home, I think distantly. Which isn't right. Home is supposed to be California. My little apartment on Camellia Street. I never told anyone where I was going when I left to find Edie, and I wonder if I've become a cold case on CrimeSolvers, if Internet sleuths have argued over my disappearance.

"My clothes," I say roughly. "My paintings—"

"Ambrose cleared your place out for me right after you died," Jaxon says. "I've got everything up in the spare bedrooms."

"Ambrose?"

"Yeah. I didn't want to leave your body alone."

Of course. That was part of our agreement. So was Jaxon finding a way to get my stuff. It comes back to me in fits and starts.

"We should tell Edie I'm okay," I say. That was another agreement. We tell her everything.

"Of course. I'll call them and let them know as soon as you're settled." He smiles, and he's so handsome I feel a burst of dizziness.

Jaxon doesn't let me fall, though.

"But first, let's get you that lemonade." Jaxon guides me into the house and sets me down on the sofa in the living room. The mummies are gone. The living room looks cleaner, actually. Like he dusted and tidied up.

I sink into the sofa cushions, my muscles already aching from exertion, while Jaxon gets the lemonade. He comes back with a tray, two big glasses, and an antique pitcher.

"It's got basil and some mint," he says as he pours my glass. "A touch of feverfew. It does help. Promise."

I drink it down in frantic, thirsty gulps. It doesn't taste like any lemonade I've had before—the herbs add an earthy fresh-ness to it that seems to brighten me up from the inside.

"It's delicious," I tell him.

Jaxon grins. "Meemaw's secret recipe."

I wonder if I'll ever meet her, Jaxon's grandmother. If I'll meet any of his family. Surely I will.

I can't die. We have all the time in the world.

Jaxon scoots closer to me, taking my hand in his. His palm is warm and rough and dry, and I remember how I felt it as I floated through the darkness.

"How many times did you fuck me?" I ask him.

His cheeks immediately darken. "I don't want to answer that."

"A lot, then."

"I missed you." He sounds sheepish and embarrassed and that just makes me swell with love for him. Because it didn't feel like a year and a half to me. A few days. Maybe a week. But he waited for me all this time. He covered me in flowers and kept me safe from all the ravages of the Louisiana swamp. He protected me.

"I'm not mad about it." Now it's my turn to blush. "Quite the opposite, actually."

Jaxon smiles happily at that, his big blue eyes searching my face. "Do you feel like a Hunter?" he asks softly, and I blink in surprise. Because I hadn't actually thought about it until now.

But I realize that something is missing. That emptiness in my chest that lingered even after I killed Oliver Raffia and Damian Tyloch's man. The faint curls of guilt I had largely managed to ignore. A sense of myself as human.

It's gone.

It's all gone, and I'm free.

Jaxon stares at me, waiting for my answer.

"Yeah," I tell him. "I feel like a Hunter."

And then I kiss him because together, we might have broken the binding that kept me from knowing what I am—

But I am never going to break the binding that ties me to him.

EPILOGUE

CHARLOTTE

THREE MONTHS LATER

I crouch in the thick underbrush and breathe in deep. The swamp is overwhelming at the best of times, but even with all the rot and life here, humans and Hunters stand out above everything else. A river of heady, adrenaline-laced fear sweeps through the dense tapestry of rotting vegetation and stagnant water, and my skin prickles with excitement.

Him. The prey. A tourist whose car broke down on the side of the Pellerin highway. Jaxon pretends to help him, calling for an emergency tow truck, grinning affably up at the prey from beneath the brim of that ugly-ass cowboy hat he insisted on wearing. I watch the exchange from the edge of the tree line, my heart racing furiously. I can hear the others' hearts too. Not just Jaxon's—he's calm, collected, his body reflecting his slow, lazy drawl. But also Sawyer's, pounding with excitement. And Ambrose's. The mysterious Ambrose. This weekend was my first time meeting him.

I'm not thinking about that right now, though. I've got my eyes on Jaxon and the prey. This is a game the three of them used to play, years ago, before Sawyer died at Camp Head Start. We select a victim together. Send the victim into the woods. Hunt them for an hour. Once the hour's up, the first one to make the kill wins.

That's why the three of us are triangulated around Jaxon and the prey, waiting for the clock to start.

Jaxon ambles away from the truck, pretending to talk on his phone. He gives a signal into the trees, where Ambrose is waiting. A half second later, Ambrose bursts out swinging an ax, his face covered by a white mask. The prey stares numbly at him like he doesn't understand what he's looking at. But when Ambrose slams the bat into the side of his car, the prey understands.

He shoots off from the highway, screaming, and I hit the timer on the cheap watch I put on for the occasion. There's nowhere to go but the swamp, and Ambrose chases him directly between where Sawyer and I are hiding. As soon as he passes, I jump up, my breath quickening. I didn't bother wearing a mask.

I shove forward through through the swamp, moving by scent and sound as much as sight. Sawyer and Jaxon are doing the same, just like we talked about, and the four of us draw around the prey like a noose, corralling him away from the highway, away from civilization, and into the swamp's dark tangle.

The chase is exhilarating. Ever since I died, ever since I finally accepted what I am, the world has become heightened. It was so overwhelming at first, all those sounds and scents threatening to drown me. But Jaxon helped me through it. He taught me what his father taught him—how to ignore what I didn't need, how to focus in on what I did.

"We're Hunters," he told me, the two of us stalking through this very same swamp. "This is how we Hunt."

I'm Hunting now, following the scent of our prey's terror.

Time loses any real meaning; I only know how long it's been when I glance at my watch. Twenty minutes. I circle through the swamp, slowly pushing the prey deeper into the wilderness, wearing him out. So do the others.

He *is* getting tired, too. I can sense it. He's stopped screaming for help and has slowed his pace, thinking he's lost us. He hasn't. All four of us are stalking him through the damp shadows. I make a loop around through the trees until I find a thick nest of underbrush where I can crouch down to wait. My plan is to intercept the prey when the hour is up.

I settle down among the leaves. Jaxon is nearby. I can smell him, that earthy scent that drives me wild. Then I can hear him, a faint rustling of the leaves. He's coming closer. So's the prey, although he's still a ways off, crashing through the under-brush in his panic. I slip sideways, my movements easier now. Everything's easier.

"Careful." A hand wraps around my throat; a mouth brushes against my ear. "It's dangerous out here."

"Jaxon," I breathe. "I heard you coming."

"Mmm. Good girl." He pulls his hand away and replaces it with his mouth, his teeth nipping at the delicate skin of my neck. His arousal is more than evident, and I let him suck on my neck while we wait for the prey to come closer. For Ambrose and Sawyer to come closer, too. They're trailing behind the prey, scaring him deeper into the swamp. Disorienting him.

But when Jaxon slides his hand down my shirt's neckline, trying to get at my breasts, I slap it away. "Stop distracting me. I want to win."

He chuckles. "You remember there's no prize, right?"

I glare at him, which just makes his grin widen, his teeth flashing in the dim light. Jaxon's wrong about there not being a prize; it's true I won't win anything, but in the last three months, I've learned what being a Hunter really means. I've learned how to do it properly. And this feels a bit like a final exam.

The prey's fear bursts through the trees, and even Jaxon takes notice, sitting up a little straighter, his eyes gleaming. "Let's win it together," he whispers, peering through the underbrush. The prey's getting closer. "You know how much I love seeing you covered in blood."

I roll my eyes, even though I like hearing him say it. "I want the kill," I whisper. "But you can help."

"Fair enough."

The prey's approach is so loud even a human could hear it. He rips through the tangled vines and splashes in the stagnant water, his breath fast and panicky.

Jaxon looks over at me, eyebrow raised. I check the watch.

"Two more minutes," I whisper.

"Corral him to the left," Jaxon whispers back. "Get him away from Ambrose. He always wins these things."

I can sense Ambrose now, drawing closer with careful, calculating steps. When he arrived yesterday morning, I reacted almost like my old sort-of human self: with a surprising bout of terror. He came into Jaxon's house, fixed his eyes on me, and I was pinned into place—by his age, his knowledge, his strength.

The first thing he said to me was, "I'm going to find your parents." I knew he meant by birth parents. The Hunters I came from. When I asked why, he said, "So you know more of us."

Jaxon swats me on my ass, a habit from our joint hunts. It's his way of telling me to focus.

"Move," he rasps.

And I do. I launch out of the undergrowth just as the prey runs past. He does a double-take when he sees me, then shouts, "You have to get out of here! Run! He's fucking crazy!"

I'm not sure if he's talking about Ambrose or Jaxon. My answer's the same regardless.

"He's not crazy," I say sweetly.

The prey's eyes widen, and he looks at me with a prey's wariness.

"But you should definitely run."

That's when Jaxon jumps up, grinning manically, clutching his hooked cleaver. The prey screams and stumbles backward—to the left, just like we planned, sliding into the underbrush.

Ambrose is close. I can sense his dark, imitating scent.

"Fuck," I mutter. "Ambrose—"

My watch beeps.

"Time's up," Jaxon says. "Run him down, cher."

I take off as fast as I can through the swamp, weaving through its thicket the way Jaxon taught me. I'm still not as good as he is, but I'm getting better. My knife bounces against my hip, and I pull it out as I run, following the prey by scent instead of sight. His fear and confusion are like the cocktails I used to drink in back in California, lush and burning all at once.

I need his blood on my hands.

But then I hear footsteps off to my right. They're not Jaxon's, which are heavier. These are light. Experienced.

Ambrose.

Suddenly, he's running along my side. "Thought you could fool me, eh?" he says in a gravelly voice. "Let me guess. Jaxon's idea?"

"No," I say, even though it was. I won't let him intimidate me.

Ambrose glances at me. Grins. "Then it's all down to speed, isn't it?"

I narrow my eyes—and then push forward with every ounce of my legs' strength. Up ahead, there's a tumbling crash. The crack of broken wood. A cry of pain.

The salty tang of blood.

That urges me forward more than anything. More than wanting to prove myself to Jaxon's friends, the only other Hunters I've ever met. More than wanting to prove to *myself* all that I'm capable of.

Blood. The sweet, salty, coppery-caramel scent of blood. Heat pulses between my legs.

I pull ahead of Ambrose just as I come across the prey, sprawled on his back, foot twisted at an impossible angle. When he sees me, his terror spikes. I can practically taste his blood on the air.

"No!" he screams, and I fling myself at him, sinking my blade into his chest.

Ambrose follows three seconds later, hoisting up his ax. I jerk my knife upward and plunge into the prey's throat, driving the blade up into his mouth. Hot, thick blood splatters across my face, and I groan in pleasure before I can stop myself.

More footsteps. Jaxon. Sawyer.

"Did she win?" Jaxon shouts.

"I think she did." Ambrose settles his ax beside him, leaning on it like a cane. I slide back off the prey, who twitches and gurgles, blood spurting out of the hole in his throat.

"No," I say. "Not yet."

And then I finish it, sliding my blade between his rib cage until I feel the resistance of his heart—a resistance I push through until blood pours over my hands.

"How long?" Sawyer says.

"Four minutes and thirty-seven seconds," Jaxon says. "Respectable."

"My fastest time was fifty-eight seconds," Ambrose says, to which Jaxon, my sweet defender, immediately responds,

"Shut the hell up, Ambrose. She's been a Hunter for three damn months."

I hear all this, but it's like listening to voices on the radio. All I can really do is breathe deeply while blood washes over my hands like a fountain. It's weird doing this with others. I'm used to it just being me and Jaxon. I'm used to all the things we do *afterward*.

Jaxon knees beside me and kisses my cheek. Only then do I turn away from the prey. From *my* prey. "Proud of you," Jaxon whispers, and then he kisses me like the others aren't here.

"What do you want to do with the body?" Sawyer asks me.

"What we always do," I say. Jaxon helps me to my feet, and I slip my blood-covered hand in his. "Take it back to the house. Turn it into art supplies."

Jaxon beams at me. Ambrose makes an irritated, old-man noise in the back of his throat. Sawyer says, "As long as Edie doesn't see."

"She won't." I'm still admiring my handiwork. Edie's back at our house—which is how I think of it now, *our house*, me and Jaxon's—reading on the porch swing while we have our fun. She told me she's used to it, with Sawyer.

Personally, I think there's a darkness in her, too. I think that's why we found each other back in California. I'm not sure she'd be as bothered by the body as Sawyer thinks. But he likes being protective of her, and I get it, because so do I.

Jaxon pulls the knife out for me, and I clean it on the edge of my shirt as he heaves the body up over his shoulder. I smile at him through my sweat and blood. My heart's still racing from the exertion. From the excitement.

From knowing what I am—

And truly embracing it, with Jaxon at my side.

The End

I hope you enjoyed *The Fire Went Wild!* You can read an extended epilogue about Charlotte's Hunter training by signing up for my newsletter here: rosebitterly.com/newsletter. (Warning: It gets gory.)

The Hunter's Heart series continues with Ambrose's story in Turn That River Red.

ABOUT THE AUTHOR

Rose Bitterly is a hopeless romantic who has been reading and writing scary stories since elementary school—imagine her excitement when she learned you could blend the two! Today, she writes dark, immersive horror romances featuring slashers and other monsters, all shot through with a hint of the occult. Visit her online at rosebitterly.com.

Never miss a new book! Sign up for Rose's mailing list and receive free bonus stories: https://www.rosebitterly.com/newsletter.

TURN THAT RIVER RED

COMING 4.18.25

I THOUGHT HE WAS MY GUIDING LIGHT. BUT WHAT IF HE'S LED ME INTO DARKNESS?

MERCY

I devoted my entire life to the Church of the Well—and its leader.

But then death came to our community.

And then *he* came. Ambrose Echevarria.

He says he's an itinerant preacher. He lays hands on our congregation and fills them with God's light. He fills *me* with God's light.

And for the first time, I can feel my devotion slipping.

AMBROSE

It was supposed to be easy. I just needed to infiltrate a cult for a few days, get access to information that would help a friend, and maybe spread some mayhem if I had the time.

But I didn't account for Mercy Hendricks, the first human woman to catch my eye in two hundred years.

I'm a killer. I don't save people.

So why do I want to save her?

Preorder Now